JASON ANSPACH

NICK COLE

IMPERATOR

GALAXY'S EDGE

Edited by David Gatewood
Published by Galaxy's Edge Press

Cover Art: Tommaso Renieri
Cover Design: Ryan Bubion
Formatting: Kevin G. Summers

Website: InTheLegion.com
Facebook: facebook.com/atgalaxysedge
Newsletter (get a free short story): InTheLegion.com

FREE SHORT STORY

TIN MAN

WHEN YOU SIGN UP FOR OUR VIP MAILING LIST

A long, long time from now,
at the edge of the galaxy...

Whenever one reads a history of the Galactic Republic, one always starts well before the Republic was formed. Long before the rise of that thing that would become known as the Empire. Before the once-proud Republic crumbled and rotted from within. Before the Savages. Before the discovery of the hyperdrive. Before all those things...

... was the Big Uplift.

It began when Earth started to finally die for what looked like the last time. Poisoned, war-torn, and ruined. It was then that the massive generational ships, the lighthuggers, filled with humanity's best and brightest, began their decades-long, sometimes centuries-long, sublight treks toward new worlds they could shape as their own. This was the Exodus, and it came at the very beginning.

Then came the Great Leap. Just fifteen years after the last generational ships had cleared orbit, and while they were still hauling themselves up to just this side of the speed of light, the people who'd been left behind on that dying Earth—which some now believe is just a myth told and retold a thousand times—discovered a fantastic new device called the hyperdrive. True faster-than-light travel. Beyond anything the generational ships could achieve. And suddenly these abandoned souls, left behind by their so-called betters, were set free from the ruined skies and poisoned lands of Earth. Fleeing en masse, they raced ahead of those crawling lighthuggers, reaching new and alien worlds decades ahead of those who had left them behind. And soon a loose confederation of hyper-drive-connected worlds was formed. And in time, a new galactic civilization was cobbled together, connected by strands of gossamer light speed. This was the Great Leap, and it was the second, and final, part of the Big Uplift. It was the end of Earth, and the start of something new.

The Savages defined the next great period in history. Trapped in their slow lighthuggers, creeping along, isolated and alone for hundreds of years, they went mad out there in the voids between the stars, trying to form their perfect technology-driven utopias. And when they emerged, they brought with them a war that would last close to fifteen hundred years. This was the era known as the Savage Wars. It was this era, this conflict, that birthed the Legion, which would fight the wars, and the Galactic Republic, which would rule the galaxy, for better or worse. And often worse it was.

Then came the Empire, and with it, the Emperor. A man known only through whispers. A man barely seen in the darkest of shadows.

A man some named *Goth Sullus*.

This is his story. And it is a history of the past and where it all began, and the present, and how it all ended.

PROLOGUE

The Present

Even now his forces were in motion. Gathering like hungry ravens around a corpse-laden battlefield, while other battles were breaking out all across his New Imperial Frontier. That was what his admirals now called it on all their constantly updating maps. The Imperial Frontier. The Frontier of an Empire. The growing circle of influence on the stellar map that centered on Tarrago.

Only a few scant weeks prior, what had been a rogue fleet of three state-of-the-art battleships, built in total secrecy out beyond galaxy's edge, had jumped in to take a major sector capital. The mighty and well-defended Tarrago.

And now he ruled a planet. And that rogue fleet was now an imperial fleet. Belonging to... an empire. The fleet would watch over that empire. Would *expand* that empire.

Goth Sullus acknowledged that it was, for now, an empire with only one world—but it was a beginning. And he was its emperor, by unanimous assent. His army had knelt on the hangar deck in obeisance, led by Fleet Admiral Rommal, and declared such in the aftermath of the Battle of Tarrago.

"All hail the emperor!" they sounded as one. They shouted the words again and again, as if each repetition made it just a little more true.

And it was, undoubtedly, true. Even as they knelt, the Republic's defeated Seventh Fleet burned and broke up in the wake of their passing battleships. His battle-scarred shock troopers raised the Imperial flag over the ruined sector capital of Tarrago. The last of the formidable Legion's defenses were swept aside out on Tarrago Moon. Tarrago Prime was taken, and the orbital defense gun captured.

He had been victorious in his first battle against the legendary Legion.

And now there was very little the dithering Republic could do against his fleet. Goth Sullus knew this, because he knew their darkest and best-kept secret.

There were no other active combat fleets to oppose him now.

The vaunted "fifteen fleets of the Republic" were a mere myth. A clever bit of propaganda designed to assure the sleeping citizens of the crumbling Republic. There had only ever been one fully capable combat fleet—the Seventh Fleet—and even that fleet had trained for little beyond the occasional planetary assault against some local demagogue, minor warlord, or Pirate King of Clans. Pretenders seeking to become major players in the galactic scheme of things.

The Seventh had been no match for Goth Sullus's Black Fleet. *He* was no pretender; he was a conqueror. *Revenge*, *Terror*, and *Imperator* had taken the battle straight to the heart of their enemy, launching full fighter wing strikes against the Seventh's carrier and engaging in furious ship-to-ship turret broadsides against the Seventh's super-destroyer and her escorts. Both sides had taken significant damage; only one side emerged victorious.

And since then, he'd sent *Revenge* to lash out at Bantaar Reef, in what had proved to be a devastating raid. Bantaar was a major commercial shipping nexus between the core and mid-core worlds, where a third of the Republic's market traffic did trade and exchange—and that meant it was also a huge revenue base for the Republic, who watched over it from their naval operations center located in the planet-surrounding asteroid belt. Heavy customs taxes were an essential component of the cash-strapped government's constant demands from its citizens, and thus it was the most important military base to the Republic.

No doubt the elites of the Senate and House of Reason were feeling the economic sting already, Sullus thought. Their flow of graft and corruption would now be thinning from a raging river to a trickling stream.

Yes, Goth Sullus intended to hurt his enemy financially as well as militarily. This was Total War, after all. And Total War converted everything into a battlefield. There would be no rules. No compromises. No boundaries. Nothing off-limits. There were precisely two conditions that would cause him to end his war against the House of Reason: total annihilation of the Republic... or its unconditional surrender and acceptance of his rule. All other outcomes were unacceptable.

He would save the galaxy from itself even if that required destroying most of it to do so. Knowing what he knew, there was no other way forward. Seeing what he'd seen...

Soon he would send the *Terror*, commanded by the clever Captain Vampa and accompanied by six squadrons of tri-fighters, against the Legion outpost at Daetroon. Daetroon was only a Legion division training center specializing in jungle warfare, but it was the central Legion presence in its sector. Knocking it out now, along with Bantaar Reef, would secure control of the Tarrago sector, and give the...

He hesitated.

Even he, the new emperor, Goth Sullus, was unused to the title. He found himself momentarily unable to think it. Dwelled on the implications that came with it. All the meaning such an incredible rank conveyed. The word carried a weight beyond measure—a weight few had ever known, or would ever know. It was something he'd never anticipated in all the years that had passed since the moment he'd chosen this path.

He remembered an old phrase from long ago—from back when real books could still be found in the ruined playgrounds of his youth.

Heavy is the head that wears the crown.

Though his admirals and generals gave him no laurel wreath or archaic crown, the meaning of the phrase was clear. Now more than ever.

And something else bothered him, too. Something coming into focus within the palace of his mind. He could *sense* it coming more than see it.

He had been badly wounded in the assault on Tarrago Moon. His injuries had caused an extreme amount of pain, and they affected his ability to focus. He was far more hurt than his admirals suspected. And of course, they could not be allowed to know. They were just as greedy for power as those within the House of Reason. Different motivations, same end.

Sullus could not go into stasis and request skinpacks and other healing remedies. They would then know. Nor could he consume the powerful tranquilizers or sedatives that would assist his healing. They would affect him. Affect his powers.

He closed his eyes, freeing his mind from the anchors of pain, life, the galaxy, and all its problems. All about him, even now, he could feel their thirst for his power. Even if they themselves did not know it yet. He saw dark forces gathering against him, gathering in the shadows of his own fleet. Gathering against him to take what he had built. What he had conceived. What was *his*.

This was where the next battle would be fought. Not at Daetroon. Not at the Republic's capital at Utopion, or wherever he decided to fight the Republic's ad hoc reserve fleet they were no doubt scrambling to assemble.

Then next battle would be fought here. The next fight would be within his own fleet.

He concentrated on revealing the hidden faces of those who plotted his demise. Surrounding him like predators in a pack, because they sensed his weakness. They felt the victory of the kill, and they wanted it all for their own.

Oh, what good I could do with that unlimited power, each man told himself. And so they decided to come for him. At this moment. When he was wounded. When he was at his weakest.

As he had so many times before, he swept away the darkness and gazed into the hearts of the conspirators. In the past he'd found the ones with fractures inside. Those who would eventually turn against him someday, even if they didn't think they were capable of it. He'd found them before they'd even known what they truly were.

And he would find them now. While there was still time.

"Gah!"

Sullus's wounds tore him away from that quiet ominous place of power deep within him. Nerve endings screamed with searing pain as his body tried to heal itself but instead opened some fresh hell of suffering. His eyes remained closed in the guise of meditation, but his mind had been pulled back to rejoin his physical body on the battleship *Imperator.*

He felt the reality of the throne on which he sat. He heard the distant, low thrum of the *Imperator*'s massive engines. He sensed only what was physical. As though he were blind. Because once he had tasted the power that coursed within him—once he had used it, wielded it—anything else was *much* less. Blindness. Deafness. A half-life, stillborn.

Poverty, where there had once been luxury.

Empire.

There it was—the word he'd hesitated to take up in the moments before he'd reached out to find his soon-to-be betrayers. It came back to him now, like a comfort that whispered promises.

Empire.

He would have an empire now.

Today, Tarrago sector. Tomorrow, the span of the galaxy.

There was a battle coming. A major battle. A battle to end all battles. A battle to end all the foolishness of the Galactic Republic and the House of Reason and its Senate Council lap dogs. The Seventh had gone down in flames, escaping with only her one lone carrier, but the Republic would cobble together a new fleet. This wasn't over yet.

And the Legion. They, too, were gathering. And unlike the Republic's navy, the Legion represented a significant foe. A true test.

Goth Sullus stood. He would walk. Because it was beginning. The inner battle before what was to come. Even now, in the corridors beyond his private sanctum, he could feel them coming for him. He could feel the wolves gathering for the kill.

His left side was in agony. He let go of the pain and walked through the darkness of his inner refuge within the *Imperator*'s private decks. In time, if he survived, he would heal. His body had been doing that for almost two thousand years. Since his time as a slave on the *Obsidia*.

His mind tried to un-focus as he gathered himself for what was coming. An image of a long-lost friend appeared. Tyrus Rex. He, too, had been a slave. And a friend. And a savior.

The last friend of all friends.

There can be no more friends now.

Emperor.

An emperor has no friends. Only enemies, ever gathering against him.

Even though they are loyal? he asked himself. *All of them?*

He thought about the crews of the ships surrounding him. He thought of their captains, their grunts, their fighter pilots. Like the woman they'd awarded the medal to that morning. Lieutenant Haladis, a deadly interceptor pilot. She was still recovering from wounds she'd acquired in the last moments of the battle for Tarrago, when victory was already so clearly won, but she'd looked at him with a fierce pride as he stood over her in the medical bay.

Sullus had sensed the drive for revenge within her—a revenge she thought would now be sated. He knew it wouldn't be. He sensed it growing again. She had believed that her revenge could be sated by the dreams of another. She had confused her revenge with his dreams.

The dreams of an emperor.

Yes, those dreams.

They'd also given a medal to a shock trooper, a black giant who'd captured one of the Republic's corvettes, single-handedly, during the height of the battle. Sullus confessed to himself that he liked that giant man. *Bombassa* was his name. Sergeant Okindo Bombassa.

Why do you like him? he asked himself. He waited for the darkness to provide the answer—the distraction he needed to escape the pain of his wounds. He flexed and opened his badly scarred left hand over and over. It was a miracle he still had it.

You like him because he reminds you of Rex, the darkness whispered.

It had been Rex's armor he'd worn when he was wounded. The old Mark I armor he'd had refitted after... after he'd last seen his friend. Armor forged by the mad aboard a ghost ship called the *Moirai*. Lost in a place the galactic survey charts called the Dead Zone.

Okindo Bombassa.

Rex.

The Mark I armor.

The dreams of empire.

All things were colliding now.

Goth Sullus stood for a long time in that same spot, thinking of his old friend Tyrus Rex. A friend he'd killed on a forgotten planet, all because of a promise that needed to be broken in order to save the galaxy from itself. All those old memories came and stood about him, pushing their way past his meditation, seeking a way into his mind just as they had so long ago.

Within the darkness of his private decks, he found himself standing before something Sergeant Bombassa had given him when they'd awarded the shock trooper his medal.

A cutting torch.

A simple tool the NCO had used to take the Republic corvette alone.

He studied the tool on the pedestal in front of him. It was utterly ordinary, formed of flimsy metal. A cheap tool.

For an entire year during the Savage Wars, Rex had used one of these as his only weapon. When they were stranded on a violent world being overrun by those monsters, fighting for a beached whale of a ship, deck by deck, day by day. Those were the most desperate of times. Modern warfare had devolved down into hand weapons wielded with savagery like some ancient fantasy novel of never was. Swords and magic.

The torch was utilitarian. It was fashioned like an oversized ancient flashlight. Heavy duty. A piece of equipment some sanitation worker might carry on his belt when going down into the dirty dark for the most practical of reasons. There was nothing elegant, or even beautiful, about it. It was not some weapon from a lost age of nobility and honor.

But its flame had always mesmerized him.

Reminded him of a past forgotten by most, when men fought and won empires with swords forged of steel.

Empires.

The black giant had won Goth Sullus an empire with this torch. And he had then given the torch to his emperor, as a gift.

"It is the way of my people," he'd told Goth Sullus in his deep basso rumble. "Every gift must be answered with a gift."

Sullus had accepted, and he had placed it here, most likely to be forgotten, on this pedestal in his inner sanctum. But now he could sense the violent destructive power within the tool. It was like a kind of salve to him at this moment—as though that pure potential for destruction was a sort of peace. A symbol. Perhaps even a symbol of himself. Within the chaos forming all about him.

Because he'd come to destroy the Republic. He would destroy it so that it could be made ready for what was coming.

If it must be an empire that rises from the ashes, then let it be one taken with a sword. Like it always and ever has been.

He closed his eyes and understood the entire meditation his mind had been caressing now. Understood what must be done next. He'd considered the past, the present, the future, and the possibilities that might be.

They were coming for him. Right now, at this very moment. Three teams formed from the best of the best of the shock troopers. Former members of the Legion. Men who obeyed orders. Men who would not have signed on for an emperor or an empire.

But it was still a group of desperate men. A group like the raiders who had killed his old life, the one he'd first started out with, long ago when he was a child. He'd been afraid of such men back then. Afraid until one day... he wasn't anymore.

Those coming for him now were half of his personal guard. Two full companies of heavily armed shock troopers massing in the shadows of his private hangar deck, supported by two HK-SW mechs beyond the massive impervisteel portal that sent silver starlight down into his shadowy blue chambers. It was possible they might even use tri-fighter interceptors to make an attack run, venting the entire deck to open vacuum. A sure death for all. Even him. The vacuum of space cared little for arcane and ancient powers. Space was, as it had ever been, mercilessly unforgiving.

Goth Sullus pushed the cowl of his hooded robe back, revealing a large bald head, coal-dark eyes, and a lantern jaw. The years had changed him. In more ways than his fear-driven subjects could ever imagine.

The times were dangerous indeed.

A storm was gathering.

A storm that would ruin the galaxy.

He had become what the galaxy needed, long ago, in many places, bringing him now to this critical moment. But of course, none of his would-be assassins had any idea what they were truly dealing with. How could they? Even he did not understand it when he first began his long quest for power. When he looked upon a ruined Earth, two thousand years ago, with his child's eyes. When he crashed on a planet, no more than fifty years ago.

When he was someone else.

PART ONE

JUNGLES OF MADNESS

01

The Past

He pushed away all thoughts of death as he fought to get the speeding light freighter under control. If he didn't concentrate, he was going to crash into the massive mountain before him—the mountain carved into the likeness of some alien warlord from a long-gone age. The gravity of the lost world had embraced the falling starship, pulling it into a deadly caress. Below him, past the metal-latticed cockpit windows, burning red wastes gave way to a high desert plateau of wind-carved rock and forbidding cliffs swallowed by a sea of shifting sand dunes.

At first, as he'd dropped through an upper atmosphere shrouded in smoky haze and sulfur-colored clouds, he hadn't even seen the edifice. And then, below ten thousand feet, with every warning light indicator flashing across the controls, he'd been too busy getting a glide slope set up. But now the massive carved rock rose out of the alien landscape like an inevitability, as though his long leap out through the darkness between galaxies was fated to end there. A monument that been waiting eons to receive his violent impact.

The engine power loss horn chanted its automated litany of doom—an impending stall warning. He would be dead in the next few seconds if he didn't do something fast.

"I believe we are about to be disintegrated should we strike the obstacle in our flight path, master," warned the bot sitting in the co-pilot's chair.

This sounded like less of a warning and more of a judgment, as though the bot somehow relished their impending demise. The bot had a superior tone that made it come across as sinister and condescending regardless of its words.

"Lock in the ventral repulsors," the pilot shouted back, raising his voice to be heard over the screaming wind beyond the hull and the turbulence-driven rattling of almost everything inside the ship. Their speed was well beyond standard re-entry guidelines. "We're gonna try a dead stick approach."

The VN-708 series freighters were equipped with two ancient Tratt and Kleider ionic engine thrusters for maneuvering—and currently, the engine panels inside the cockpit were indicating bad starts in *both* engines. They'd lain cold and dormant during the five-year jump through hyperspace it had taken to reach this forgotten planet, and now, when they were desperately needed, they failed to come online.

The pilot frowned at his own neglect. He should have done a maintenance check.

"Seven thousand and falling," chanted the bot.

Yes, it definitely sounded enthusiastic. As though a wager had been placed, and the bot would collect only in the case of an epic fail with terminal results.

The pilot was well aware of the altitude. They were running out of it quickly. He needed those thrusters to kick in and shift the falling starship away from the massive mountain that raced toward them.

For a brief second, staring out through the cockpit window, he caught a glimpse of some giant lizard-like creature down below on a high desert plateau. It had a bull neck and walked on two legs. It must've been ten stories tall.

There was no time for a second look.

"Take the controls," he ordered the bot. "I'm gonna try to windmill the turbines."

"Whatever you're going to do, I suggest you do it quickly, master, if you wish to continue," the bot answered. It paused and inclined its head, as if considering. "Though I am not severely attached to runtime, I had always envisioned an end much more worthy of my service capacity. Perhaps a company of dead legionnaires at my feet, vanquished by my considerable termination skills."

The pilot lunged for the engine panels at the rear of the cockpit. He found the master bus for the ion thrusters and switched them both to the off position. Then he threw the claw-switch master into the start position and waited.

Nothing.

As he turned to re-check the altimeter, he saw through the window the rising carved rock on the horizon. It was an epic statue the likes of which he'd never seen on any world back in the Galactic Republic. A massive alien warrior every bit the size of the mountain, shaped like a humanoid crocodile, was carved right into the natural stone. The warrior had one clawed hand raised toward the red dwarf giant high in the burning sky. As though it had been clutching at that dying star all through its eons-long existence.

It reminded the pilot vaguely of something from Egypt, before the Uplift. He tried to remember Egypt. A place of dead pharaohs and lost tombs was all he could bring to mind—and barely, at that. Some days, he had to concentrate to remember Earth at all.

Don't waste your time thinking about that now, he yelled at himself as the ship refused to come to life.

It's not a waste of time, because this is the end, he replied. *The end of your foolish quest.*

He set both turbines in the ion thrusters to windmill, hoping that would bump the startup sequence and cause the engines to fire the next time he threw the master start.

"Sir..." intoned the bot. The condescension was gone this time, replaced by caution, warning, and maybe the realization that runtime was a more coveted thing than previously calculated.

The bot wants to go on living, the pilot thought in some distant part of his mind that was always speaking. Always watching. Always weighing.

He flicked the master off, closed his eyes, and set the sequence to cold start. The entire ship felt like it was on the verge of rattling itself apart at any moment, and even if the engines started, they were rapidly running out of time to evade the mountain-sized lizard man.

He brought the master bus back online.

A loud *baaang* echoed from the portside thruster, and a damage indicator began to whoop repeatedly. The portside engine instruments all went red.

The pilot looked out the side cockpit window, craning his neck to check for the massive rectangle of the thruster that protruded from the wing. It had exploded, and now they were trailing thick black smoke across the sulfur-laden sky behind them.

But the number two engine, on the starboard side, had caught. They had power. Some.

Barely.

The bot was already yanking the control yoke over to starboard, narrowly dodging the massive statue that had once been a mountain. They came within a hundred meters, close enough to see the chipped and missing chunks in the weathered ochre stone, beaten by untold millennia beneath a burning sun on a world untagged by any Republic stellar chart the pilot had ever seen. Through the upper cockpit glass the ancient stone monster seemed to glare down at them, grinning malevolently.

On the far side of the monument the freighter leaped the jagged ridgeline and soared above a vast valley of dark jungle and steaming yellow swamp. The pilot searched frantically for any place to land. This was the end of the flight, no matter what. They were going down.

"Strap in!" he cried as he threw himself back into the pilot's seat and grabbed the control yoke. "Flaps to full. Bringing in the reversers now!" He could hear himself hyperventilating as he gave the commands that would determine the ship's final seconds. Very few people ever survived a starship crash.

"I will remind you, sir, that I can maintain my position regardless of the fragile safety devices you biologics require to maintain your delicate existence."

The pilot ignored the bot. He made sure the ventral repulsors beneath the ship were set to full, then snapped on the deflectors—for all the good they would do once they hit the jungle canopy.

He took it all in during the brief, but somehow incredibly long seconds before impact. Bizarre flocks of bats swooped and circled above the jungle's haze. In the distance, vine-covered ruins rose from the treetops.

And then the ship plunged into the dark twilight depths of the tangle.

There was a loud and terrific *CRRAAACK*, as though some giant stick had been snapped. An explosion followed as the starboard engine, under the strain of the repulsors set to full, went off like a firecracker. Rending metal cried from the disintegrating hull.

And then all was silent.

In the instants after the crash, above the dense jungle foliage, it looked as though there had never been some starship speeding in from the outer dark. It was as if the steaming yellow jungle had swallowed it and forgotten it in the same instant.

And then the ancient forest of that lost world resumed its normal pace. Unseen monsters cried out forlornly across the sweltering distances. Some strange bird gave a haunting, ululating wail.

The pilot was vaguely aware of these sounds. Barely aware of the need to get up. To make sure he was all right. He wanted his bot to talk to him, to wake him from the hovering feeling of living between consciousness and unconsciousness.

In time, the lost world surrendered daylight to its night. Swollen and corpulent moons rose above its jagged mountains, dark jungles, and the gray ruins of a civilization lost before the Galactic Republic ever rose.

A Republic that now ruled everything with an unseen iron fist. Back in the rest of the galaxy. Back home.

But not here, beyond the edge, out in the long dark distance between the Milky Way and the Lesser Magellanic

Cloud. Out here beyond the edges of galaxies is a place where distances are almost inconceivable to the rational mind.

Out here there is no such thing as a Galactic Republic. Out here there are only monsters.

Out here... we are perfectly lost.

02

It was raining.

He felt the thick drops hit his face. With his eyes closed he became aware of the sound of wet slaps. Heavy rain on leaves. Sudden sharp *thwaps*. He could hear it against the hull, too, like a constant, hollow hailstorm.

The hull of my ship, he thought.

He was still in the ship. And there had been a crash. He was still strapped in. Every muscle ached. His head felt like it... like... it was dull. Like it had been split open. His ears were ringing, but distantly. A background noise to the driving rain.

He screamed. Or at least, he thought he did. In the dreamlike state between wakefulness and unconsciousness, he was screaming—but as he began to come to, he realized the noise was more of a groan. He was groaning. Or croaking, because his throat was so dry.

He opened his eyes and saw nothing. Was he blind? Were his eyes still closed? He fluttered them, could sense his eyes being open, searching, but he saw only darkness all around him.

Then he saw crystals.

No, not crystals. Rain. On the smashed cockpit windshield. Running down along the fractured and spider-webbed glass. He could see nothing beyond its watery starbursts.

Where am I?

That was more important than almost anything else.

And the next thought... the next thought scared him a little bit. It would have scared him more had he not been suffering from some kind of... concussion. Yes. He was definitely suffering a concussion.

And how do you know that?

Which brought him to...

Who are you?

That was the question that had scared him. Because he wasn't sure he could answer it. He wasn't sure who he *really* was. He'd been many people, over many years. But... who was he *right now*?

One shoulder was dislocated. Perhaps a wrist was broken. He felt around in the darkness, with his good hand, for the harness release. He pulled, heard a thick metallic click, and felt himself slump free of the heavy straps that had held him tight. He took a deep breath. It hurt to breathe deeply. He coughed.

Rain streamed in from above, through a rent in the cockpit. He wiped the water from his face. His hand came away bloody.

He'd taken a good hard crack to the head.

That was all. He hoped.

Because there probably wasn't a doctor in... well, there wasn't a doctor in a very long way from here. And he'd come all the way out here to save the galaxy. And that wasn't going to happen if he died before he made it back.

Except you seem to have some medical training.

But... *Who am I?*

He stumbled through the darkness of the ruined flight deck, crawling hand over hand back through the fallen-in panels and smashed flight computers. The ship was full dark. No power. Not even emergency power.

He checked for smoke, sniffing at the cool air. Every astronaut knew, was trained thoroughly, to check for smoke first. Always. Constantly, in fact.

Astronaut?

Now *there* was an ancient word.

Are you an astronaut? he asked himself. *Were you an astronaut? Once... long ago?*

He couldn't answer.

He continued crawling toward the rear of the ship, feeling his way through something that was familiar to him. Known to him. And yet now everything was different because of its ruined state. Ruined.

You spent five straight years in this ship.

That seemed impossible. With hyperspace, who would ever need to spend that long in a ship?

He made it to the upper hatch along the portside, the one that let out just before the wing. *The wing.* It truly was an ancient freighter. Built back when freighters needed aerodynamic capabilities to work hand-in-hand with the new repulsor technology.

That was a long time ago...

He tapped at the lock controls. Dead.

Lowering himself to the deck with a groan, he opened a panel and took out a lock bar. He fitted it into the manual cycle mechanism that opened the hatch and began to crank it.

That was even before we met...

The sudden memory was gone, now meaningless. Or at least incomplete. All he could see in his mind, when he thought of that memory, was shadows above him. Things that had once been men and fancied themselves gods. The Pantheon, they called themselves. Back when he was a slave on a ship called the *Obsidia*. Even now that memory caused him to shudder.

He continued to crank the cycling mechanism, ignoring the screaming sharp jolts in his dislocated shoulder. He should set it. Fix it. But first, he wanted out.

The rain continued to strike the hull of the ship. Steady, but softer and slower now. As if the storm in the unknown skies above had lost its furious rage and was content to merely drift off into an oblivion of comforting white noise.

The hatch popped open, and the smells of the night rushed in. The sharp iron scent of rainwater falling from the sky. The sweet decay of a self-consuming jungle. Grow or die. Move or die.

He could see nothing beyond the ship. No distant fires, no hints of help. Nothing but blackness. He had told himself he was alone, and now he'd proven it to himself. But he could hear. He could hear the soft rain hitting the puddles and the leaves. They sounded like big, fat leaves. Palm leaves of some type.

There was no sense in leaving the ship until daylight came, whenever that would be. Wandering out there in the dark was a good way to hurt himself. There would be debris from the crash. Dangerous terrain. Predators.

The crash.

He knew there had been a crash. That much was obvious.

He had crashed on a planet. A planet he had searched for... searched for for a very long time. And that was an amazing thing to recall, because he still didn't know who he was, exactly, at this moment. It was as if his identity wasn't as important as remembering how long he'd searched for this lost planet. As though his brain had long ago made some filing decision that placed one bit of information above the other in order of importance. And now, in the kingdom of fractured skulls, that hierarchy reigned.

Or maybe you made that decision? The choice to make one more important than the other.

Maybe.

This planet was called *Morghul.* An ancient world found recorded in a place of madness, by madmen who'd been worshipped as gods and lived like devils.

And perhaps Morghul wasn't even the planet's name. Maybe that had merely been a direction in some symbology—or a warning in some forgotten tongue. Because who would ever trust the ravings of the insane? Who would put themselves in the confidences of devils?

He remembered more...

Morghul lay a quarter of the way out into the yawning emptiness that existed between the great galaxies. In the gulfs of nothingness, out in the darkness. Between the massive super-clusters of stars where the living and the dead worlds gathered and circled, between those gathering points lay the lost places, cast off into the interstellar nothingness like unwanted children flung into chasms of the forgotten void. That was where Morgul traveled endlessly around its ancient star.

It was theorized—by a mumbling blind scout from the old survey service, who'd wildly claimed to have visited this place during an infrequent moment of lucidity—that the planet's star, a dying red dwarf giant, had once been part of the Milky Way.

Which is your galaxy, thought the man who couldn't remember who he was.

And like many such worlds beholden to their stars, this lost planet was long ago cast off into the outer dark. Cast off to wander unclaimed, unrecognized, and unknown by the frightened races who claimed the hot swirls as their own and turned the unknown in-between into ghost stories and superstition. That very old scout—the seemingly crazy scout—claimed as much. He said the planet had been cast out of the galaxy.

And when the man who couldn't remember who he was thought about those words—*cast out*—it felt like some kind of punishment. Some kind of judgment reserved for fallen angels become demons. *Cast out of paradise.*

But really, it was most likely due to the cosmic game of marbles played by physics inside every galaxy. This lost world and her dying star had simply been knocked from the galactic circle, a stellar loser in a cosmic game. Some unvalued tiger's eye with a fracture in its surface that could be traded for a better marble.

Stellar marbles. That's all it probably was.

But if the rumors and legends were true... then it was something much, much more. If the legends were true, it was worth investigating. Because, despite all the things he could not remember, he remembered that the galaxy was in trouble. The Galactic Republic especially. From within and without. And he'd come here to find a power that might make the difference to its survival. Not to mention the uncounted populations of many, many worlds. Every other option had already been tried, like some desperate family member trying to stop an addict from using. Nothing had worked. And in the end... there was only this last desperate effort. Even though it had been forbidden by the most serious of oaths.

The castaway pilot leaned back against the bulkhead and sank down in front of the open hatch and the rainy night beyond. At least some of it was coming back to him.

At least the how.

But not the who.

And not the why.

He could remember being a slave on the *Obsidia*. Yes. And remembering just that, that horrible time, caused him to find other pieces to the puzzle of himself. The *Obsidia* had come after the Martian War. That seemed right. And the Martian War had come after the Big Leap brought on by the discovery of the hyperdrive. That also seemed right. And that had come just a few years before you were born in the ruins of Los Angeles, he told himself. And before that...

His mind wandered off, and he forced it to come back to the problem of his personal history.

And before that had been the Exodus, when ships like the *Obsidia*, and the *Moirai*, had fled Earth, taking the rich and powerful away from a ruined world.

And what makes the *Obsidia* and the Pantheon so important? Right now at this can't-remember-because-I-have-a-concussion moment? Why is that ship the starting point?

He thought about that for a long moment.

It isn't. It came before. But it's important that it did.

The *Obsidia* had been a lighthugger. A generational lighthugger plowing away through the dark at sublight speeds—even while the Terran Navy, and all the other hyperspace-connected worlds the *Obisidia* was headed toward, already possessed the ability to leap between planets in days, sometimes hours. Almost forty years of hyperspace travel passed before some functionary thought it might be nice to track down the old generational ships and fold them into the slowly growing galactic community. And so the Terran Navy dispatched the *Challenger* to make contact with the slow-crawling *Obsidia*.

He thought about that. He remembered being an officer aboard the UNS *Challenger*. He and the rest of the crew had boarded a ship full of maniacal megalomaniacs who'd spent their forty years and more of monastic isolation perfecting some wild technological advances, in addition to building a civilization that was half madhouse.

And they, the crew of the *Challenger*, had become slaves on board that ship. Slaves who served the twisted pleasures of the Pantheon. Rex. Reina. And you. Crewmembers of the *Challenger*. Others, too. But you were the only ones who made it off that ship... fifteen years later. Fifteen years after the Terran Navy had officially declared you lost in the stellar dark. Fifteen years of being experimented on, altered by scientific advances the Galactic Republic wouldn't match over the next nearly two thousand years.

How do you know that? he asked himself. And then he remembered why the *Obsidia* was important. It wasn't the reason he was here, on this lost planet beyond galaxy's edge, searching for something that might save the Republic from itself. But it was the answer to why he *could* be here. How he could live long enough to find all the clues that led here.

Because the experiments, the ones performed on Rex, Reina, and... himself... had given them longevity beyond imagining. The Pantheon had wanted to keep them alive and serving their dark desires for decades unending.

You are nearly two thousand years old, and you were just in your fifties when the Challenger *docked with that nightmare.*

There were some longevity techniques in use back then. But nothing matched the discoveries of the *Obsidia*.

You were in your fifties and looked twenty-eight when the Challenger *docked. Fifteen years later you looked even younger than twenty-eight. And nearly two millennia after that, lying in the ruins of a wrecked freighter, you could pass for barely forty-two.*

The only reason the *Obsidia* is important is because it allowed him to live far longer than other people.

A little over a hundred years after the escape from the *Obsidia*, when he was the captain of his own ship, the *Lexington*, he docked with another lighthugger. The *Moirai*. He'd been sent there. And it, too, was a nightmare.

And that ship was the beginning of the trail that led here to this planet lost beyond the known of the galaxy.

03

When there is nothing to do in the night but listen to the rain falling on a strange and alien world, one has time to think. The night is long. Its hours pass slowly. Sleep... or think. And in the thinking, one remembers the things that have been forgotten.

Like why. Why did he come here?

Why had he come so far out into the big empty spaces within the universe? Past the edges. Beyond the knowing of what was known. Out into the unknown.

Slavery.

It had started with slavery, of all things. A slavery he'd endured aboard the lighthugger *Obsidia* for years. A slavery that had given him the ability to live a very long life. It was a parting gift of sorts, its givers grinning at its presentation, knowing it to be a curse.

The event that brought him out here came later, when he found the Quantum Palace... and the lighthugger *Moirai*... and an insane crew's quest to discover what they'd called the Quantum—a thing far bigger than they understood at the time. It was in those years that he found the trailhead that provided an answer to all the questions that had ever plagued him.

That was a hundred years after the time of slavery aboard the *Obsidia*. The Galactic Republic wasn't even a thing back then. Fewer than thirty inhabitable worlds had been reached by the hyperdrive, and those thirty growing worlds were just a loose alliance, trying to work together to solve the problems that confronted them. And occasionally, they started shooting at each other.

But before all that, back in that long-ago time, when the man who could not remember was on his way to Houston to attend the academy at NASA, he read an article in some surviving magazine. It was a museum piece about the Exodus, when the elites fled the dying Earth. Away they went in massive sublight ships—*lighthuggers*, some wag named them, bitterly—to other stars, other planets theorized to be amenable to life. These ships were arks. *Mayflowers* and explorers' vessels. Colonization ships. But they were also massive pleasure palaces, with state-of-the-art technology, advanced research and design. Technological wonders. Just like the *Obsidia* had been. Just like the *Moirai* was.

These weren't the first sublight ships. Those left Earth during what came to be called the Pilgrimage. These early versions, the experimental versions, were utilitarian, stripped clean of comfort or luxury. They'd set off into the deep dark nearly a century earlier, carrying the pilgrims and religious zealots. All of whom were probably dead.

But the elites—the celebrity betters and the oligarchs from all the bankrupted nations of Earth's past—they traveled in style. They left together, humanity's "best hope," when the poisoned seas finally *did* rise after centuries of warnings. By that time the environment had been ruined by their perpetual wars for some elusive peace they were always promising. Just one more campaign.

When the ancient power grids couldn't handle the strain and finally went down, and the plagues came like whirlwinds out of the ever-spreading slums of the have-nots, "humanity's best hope" just up and left on their big ships, taking their coveted gene pool and accumulated wealth and knowledge base with them.

Earth was done. And they were done with it.

Those not in the circle could have what was left of it now.

For those left behind, it was the best thing that ever happened. Because fifteen years later, the people found their own way off planet—and their way was far better than crawling along at unimaginably slow sublight speeds.

Hyperdrive.

A wonderful technology that let man leap between stars in the blink of an eye.

The new ships put the lighthuggers to shame.

And now here you are. Five years of hyperspeed, and here you finally are. Two thousand years later and beyond the edge of the galaxy.

For just a moment, sitting there in the smashed hatch of the ruined freighter, marooned and watching the jungle dark, the soft rain beginning to let up some, the wind causing broad palm leaves to toss and bustle like dancing shadows... for just a moment he almost remembered his real name.

His lost name.

The name he'd stopped using so long ago.

He'd had to use a lot of names. Most people couldn't deal with someone who lived so much longer than they did. And so, every fifty years or so, he and Rex and, yes, Reina, started anew with different names. Not aliases. Because in a way they all began to *become* that new name. Letting the old name die. Like some star cast off into the dark between galaxies.

Cas—?

It was Cas...

The name escaped him. Not all the others he'd gone by—those crowded into his mind, along with all their memories. But that first name... it had been his nearly two thousand years ago.

That was a long time.

No one was as old as him and the two others.

One of the others was his best friend. A great gift in a life where you tended to make fewer and fewer friends. In a life where any friend you made would die long before you ever would. The burden of that...

The other was the love of his life. She had been since the day she first awakened him aboard the *Obsidia*. And that love had only grown stronger, despite the years and truths that came along with so much time.

They were the only three to survive the journey into the Quantum Palace a hundred years after the *Obsidia*... to survive and return. Rex and Reina were there when he found the trail of secrets that led to this lost planet. It was just a secret back then, really. A thing to discover, a way to pass the time, for a man with centuries to pass. But the secret that had brought him to this lonely little planet, lost out in the grand darkness beyond the edge of the galaxy, was more than just a secret. Like some secrets, the best secrets... it guarded something great.

The secret of true power. A power that could fix a galaxy feeding on itself to the point of death. A galaxy where the weak ruled the brave and the bold. A galaxy that wouldn't stand up to the troubles coming its way if someone didn't take the reins with a firm hand.

Inside the Quantum Palace, he'd found the trail. That trail had led him here. And though he'd never known it, it had been leading him here all along. Calling him. Summoning him. As if to find out if he was worthy.

Those were the musings that waited out the rainy night with him. He turned the mysteries over and over, watching, waiting for them to slip into their places and form a pattern that could be recognized.

The secret he'd come looking for waited in the darkness out there, in the rainy jungle night. He'd come here to find it. To make it his. To take it back... and save the Republic from itself. From everything.

He would make things right, if they ever could be made right. His reasons had always been noble. Those who questioned his methods could go to hell.

An image came to mind then, unbidden. An image of a proud young man. Eager. Hopeful. Naive. Ready to leave Earth and set forth into the unknown.

I was twenty then, he remembered. *Just twenty years old*.

Born the year of the Exodus. Turned fifteen the year of our freedom. The year of the hyperdrive.

Fifteen years after the Exodus, after the elitist betters had fled the ruined Earth, the geeks unlocked the secrets of the hyperdrive, and the people who'd been left behind—the ones deemed unworthy of the salvation the lighthuggers promised—were no longer prisoners of a ruined world. They were now, in fact, inheritors of the galaxy, ready to pioneer it as fast as they could reach it. It was manifest destiny.

The incredible hyperdrive.

The first test ship was cobbled together in the junkyard at Houston. The geeks did it all on their own. No funding. No government. No bureaucracy.

Just the impossible made suddenly real. Right now.

He laughed at that now, sitting in the hatch of the ruined freighter he'd picked up on some world turned into a salvage bazaar. But the sound that came from him was only slight. Dry. A soft once-chuckle. They were geeks, and they saved us all.

Geeks. An ancient word. He was an ancient man who knew all the ancient words. And in time, he and these old words would become like the ruins of the enigmatic Ancients. Ruins they'd found on almost every planet the hyperdrive had taken them to.

He laughed because the Galactic Republic, the most monstrously bloated government ever known, had been made possible by the geeks, on their own, without the slightest bit of help from any politician. Because you couldn't have a galaxy-spanning Republic without the hyperdrive. It just wasn't possible.

The geeks made one orbit around a habitable planet over in Alpha Centauri, recorded it all, and then jumped back to Earth. In less than a day they'd gone farther than anyone had ever been. Later that night they uploaded the plans for the fantastic new hyperdrive onto the New World Wide Web's open source servers. Now everyone could have freedom.

They just had to build it for themselves.

Everyone—*everyone*—could go wherever they wanted. Wherever light speed took them. And of course, there would be consequences, but that too, was also their responsibility.

Many were never heard from again. And all throughout the nearly two-thousand-year history of hyperdrive travel, scouts, explorers, and colonists would occasionally find the ending of some of those lost to history during the Pilgrimage or the Exodus. Some survey ship would find a tribal group gone almost full savage, like lost children who'd never known where they came from other than badly related myths. But more often than not, they would uncover the remains of old ships and bad landings on worlds that were unforgiving and harsh. Not everyone was lucky enough to survive reentry aboard an ancient freighter that would never fly again. Not everyone could handle the challenge of surviving a jungle where every plant and predator might be deadly.

And who knew how many just plowed into stars and were consumed. Lost forever.

Lost... forever.

As he sat there listening to the rain and watching the night, he wasn't ready to deal with that.

He pushed those thoughts away and opened his mouth to the rain. Eventually he'd have to find out if it was poisonous, so why not now? Why prolong the agony?

He drank. It tasted like water. Sharp. Iron. Wet.

All those elites... the celebrities, the politicians, the one percent, the mega-capitalists and the demagogues of the people... they'd all gone sailing on glittering private cities out into the stellar dark. Some asleep, some wallowing in all the pleasures their advanced longevity techniques could buy them. As the Exodus unfolded, they were just forgotten by hyperspace travelers who could reach other worlds in hours.

At twenty I joined the Terran Navy.

He had been trained by NASA to work in space aboard the first capital ships. He was assigned to the *Challenger.*

Right then he remembered.

Casper.

His name had been Casper.

Ensign Sullivan. That had been the whole of it. Ensign Casper Sullivan.

In the era in which he'd been born, before the hyperdrive, in the shadowy, nuclear ash of the New American Dark Age, the old names had been in fashion. *As though,* he thought, *our mothers giving birth in the ruins of some mall had looked around and known we'd need something better than what we'd arrived at.*

That life would be hard.

That the galaxy would be cruel.

So here's a bit of nobility, child. Sorry we almost nuked ourselves into a second Stone Age. Here's a name I found in a book before we burned it for heat... something from way back when humanity was really something. Sorry we blew ourselves up and the best of us were so disgusted they just up and left the losers behind. Like some ditching prank nine tenths of the planet wasn't in on.

Sorry.

Casper. It was a name from way back. Back when the world was new. When there were heroes who fought monsters and did brave things.

He stared out into the darkness, out there beyond the wreckage of the ship. By the light of one of the planet's two moons, he could see something out there, a shape moving around in the dark. Crossing the jungle night back and forth.

It turned suddenly toward him. The thing had red, glowing eyes. Inhuman eyes, both familiar and terrible.

But it did not come closer.

Casper continued his watch.

In time the bot appeared in the darkness just below him. He could barely make it out, but its shape was unmistakable.

It was a THK model. Tactical Hunter-Killer. Reaper Variant. And it was his.

"Ah... master!" it exclaimed. The bot was holding one of the heavy automatic blasters from the ship's well-stocked arsenal. He'd spent a month on Ankalor, in the Night Market, collecting all the specialized gear he'd need for this expedition. But THK-133 had been with him long before that. They didn't even make THKs anymore. The machines were banned, categorized as weapons capable of war crimes. Too good at what they did. The Sayed Massacre and all. And they'd never been *entirely* trustworthy, even according to those who designed them.

"You are alive," it said with a droll little fanfare in its malevolent English butler voice. "I had assumed you were dead, or dying slowly. And since I possess no lifesaving programming, nor desire to perform such menial tasks, as they would be inconsistent with my main purpose of taking life, I opted for a *wait and see* outcome."

Casper said nothing.

I am Casper, he thought. *And I've been other people. And maybe those other people have even been different than me. Maybe each one was a role I had to play to get a little farther down the trail that led all the way to here. A chance to do things differently and make the galaxy into what it needed to be. But I am Casper. That's who I started out as. That's who I was at the first. And who I've come here as.*

But who will I be when I leave?

Who says you're leaving? whispered some other voice.

Casper. I am Casper.

"How long have I been out?" he asked the bot.

THK-133 stood amid the debris of the ruined ship, a ship torn apart by its furious descent into the dense jungle, and scanned the darkness slowly. The wind and the rain were dying down, and one of the moons, a fat bone-white orb, rode high above the tall skeletal limbs of the silhouetted treetops.

"Three days, master. I planned to bury you tomorrow. I am glad that I will not have to add that to my task list for the day."

There was a long pause.

Then the bot's deep burning red optical assemblies pivoted and landed on him. Casper wondered if it would activate its laser-assist targeting system. Landing a red dot right in the center of his skull.

"We are not alone here, master," stated the bot matter-of-factly. "There is something out there."

04

Dim, almost wan light filtered down through the dense alien foliage. As the skies lightened in the east, Casper pulled himself out of the wreckage and climbed down to the ground.

The ruin of his ship, a ship he'd never bothered to name, a ship he'd bought in a salvage bazaar on Tongath, lay before him, at the end of a blackened wake of debris. Burnt bushes and torn trees trailed off into the distant pink morning haze. It had once been a medium-sized light freighter. Now it was almost cracked in half, both wing sections had broken away from the central keel, and the engines were sinking into a moss-laden waterway that wandered off into the depths of the jungle. How much worse might it have been if the repulsors and deflectors hadn't absorbed some of the damage?

It would never fly again. It would never leave this planet.

Casper thought of just how far out he was in the chasm between galaxies. The thought threatened to replace his strategies with hopelessness.

No one would come here looking for him.

No one would find him.

How could they? No one back in the galaxy even knew he was still alive. He'd "died" at the Battle of Telos. Gone down on the battleship *Unity* inside the atmosphere of

Telos IV, surrounded by Savage cruisers blasting the Republic's latest behemoth to pieces.

Officially, that was what had happened.

"But obviously it didn't," he chuckled to himself.

During the night, he'd popped his shoulder back into place and made a sling to give his arm a rest. Maybe the wrist wasn't fractured. Maybe, maybe not. It hurt, but not nearly as bad as it had.

He walked along the hull, thinking how best to salvage what could be salvaged. How to fortify himself, for however long it took for him to get ready for what came next. And what came next was to search for a place he'd only found rumors of. A place called the Temple of Morghul.

When he'd asked THK-133 what he meant by "We are not alone," all he'd gotten was an enigmatic, "That's all I can reliably report at this time... master."

Casper had thought the bot referred to the predator with the unsettling eyes. But THK-133 had seemed even more sinister than usual. Like he was withholding information of some sort. Like he knew exactly what was out there, but he didn't want to say.

More fun that way.

To be honest, the bot had been weird for a long time. Most people would have had its memory wiped by now. That, or cashed it in for scrap bounty. Casper had done neither. He'd kept it hidden after the Massacre at Sayed, in the caves below his estate on Bahaca.

THKs had strange programming to begin with. They were used for terminations in missions where no one on a kill team was expected to survive. So unlike most bots, they had little sympathy or emotive pathing.

But in theory, Casper reminded himself, as he often had, *its programming was set to protect me.*

And now, it was the only thing he had to talk to—and he knew how important that was, to have someone, or something, to talk to in survival situations. Once he'd gone two years, he remembered, a very long time ago, without talking to anyone. He'd felt himself going mad during those long and lonely months. And it was a horrible thing to lose your mind. So, for however long he was here—and with the longevity he'd had forced upon him, he might be out here a very long time—he would talk to the strange bot. If only to keep himself sane.

"Let's clear away some debris for a campsite," he told the bot as though he were once again a Terran Navy junior officer organizing a naval work detail. "Just outside this cargo hold. We'll use that for stores."

The bot scanned the debris field. "I require very little in the way of stores, master. My current battery shall last another one hundred and twenty-six years. Besides, I doubt we shall survive that long on such a hostile world as this."

Casper stopped. "What do you mean, 'hostile'?"

But the bot merely went off to place its weapon down against the hull. It picked up a piece of the ship's armor that had sheared away and tossed it into the jungle. It was clear the bot wasn't interested in saying anything more.

Let it go, Casper, he told himself.

My name is Casper. That's right.

He was still having trouble remembering everything. It was coming back, but it all had a sense of not-quite.

For the rest of the day they worked on setting up a campsite. By evening they'd collected some firewood that burned well—bright and hot—and salvaged what they could of the food stores. Casper had armed himself with a small but powerful holdout blaster from the ship's armory. He strapped on the weapon's belt and holster, and practiced a few draws.

The night would be spent in his quarters, the same as every other night for the past five years, save the last one. THK-133 would provide close perimeter patrol.

The day had been almost insect-free, which was an unusual thing for a jungle swamp. But now, as thick darkness came quickly, tearing the light away from world, and as the swamp grew eerily quiet in the gloaming, large insects appeared and dove at the fire. Fortunately, none seemed interested in him.

For hours he sat, staring at the fire, thinking about why he'd come here. It came back to him in waves.

THK-133 stared at him across the fire. "You're remembering, master."

The vocalization from the bot had caught him by surprise. Bots, at least to him, had seldom seemed interested in the inner lives of living beings, unless they were asked to be.

He wanted to ignore the observation. When he was a fleet admiral, people had accepted his long, brooding silences. They had never required him to respond when he'd been teasing out some difficult tactical decision. But out here, beyond the edge of the galaxy, he could not afford to be moody or internalized. That way lay madness. He needed to force himself to respond, if only for his own sanity.

And yet, how had the bot known he was remembering?

"I was," Casper replied, as though the bot were a living being, a long-time acquaintance. It was better to humanize the bot than to totally disconnect and treat it as a tool or a servant. He could deal with the anthropomorphizing issues once he made it out of here.

If he made it out of here.

"About the Quantum Palace," said the bot.

It wasn't a question.

It was a statement.

Casper looked up from the fire and stared at THK-133. The bot was staring dispassionately back at him. Returning his gaze. He could feel the red lights in its optical assemblies on him. They weren't just taking him in and cataloging all the observable data they could capture, so that the bot's processors could crunch it and make their thousands of millions per minute decisions. No, those cameras were searching him for something beyond data. Something intangible.

You've reached a ridiculous level of anthropomorphizing in an insanely fast amount of time, Casper told himself.

Casper realized his mouth was hanging slightly open. He wondered if maybe his bell was still rung from the crash. If maybe the long work throughout the day had exhausted him more than it should have. If maybe he was finally getting old.

Almost two thousand years old, but you don't look a day over forty-two.

"I was remembering," Casper said.

He waited to see what would happen next. Watching the automated killing machine that wanted to talk. As if it would somehow non-verbally react to any stimuli he gave it. A thing it had never been programmed to do.

Except... it shrugged. Right in front of him. Just barely. For a brief moment, its shoulder chassis rose up toward its insectile MicroFrame processor head.

Or maybe that was just a trick of the light?

Maybe.

"How do you know about the Quantum Palace?" Casper asked. Because only three people knew about it, and they'd made a pact.

The machine pivoted its head slowly, turning to scan some noise off in the jungle deeps. When night fell, strange unseen birds—at least Casper suspected they were birds—had begun to cry forlornly to the consuming darkness. The noise periodically drove away the rising insect chorus of sub-aural clicking. The plaintive wails of the unseen birds would erupt out across the night, and the sounds of the crickets, as Casper had taken to thinking of them, would cease at once.

And sometimes, the cry of another bird would come. Some answer, off in the night, from another creature like the first. Which seemed almost... wonderful, amazing, even beautiful in a haunting way.

Unless one knew about xenozoological predator theory. Then the strange cries took on a whole different meaning.

They *could* be predators. Communicating. Hunting.

The bot slowly panned its head back toward Casper across the fire. Its unblinking red optical assemblies watched him in the flickering light.

"Because you told me everything," it said.

"Why?" asked Casper without pause. "Why would I tell you everything?"

Because he wouldn't have.

"Because the fate of the Republic depends on what we do here, master. That was the 'Importance of Orders' setting you engaged in my mission protocol database. Secondary reason provided for information-sharing was that you have been having memory problems. A side effect of your advanced age—although you have been tested for dementia and a host of other genetic diseases, and none have appeared in the results. You are in excellent health, other than your current injuries. Perhaps your memory problems are because you are human, and therefore fragile in ways I am not."

Casper listened to the low snap and pop of the fire between them. The smoke smelled floral and weird. In time he would get used to it.

"Perhaps humans are not meant to live as long as you have," stated THK-133 in the long silence that followed. "I speculate that you are losing your capacity to remember. Reasoning should become impaired next, according to my analysis of the neurological data files on human cognition I was given in order to effect more efficient terminations."

"Why am I here?" Casper asked the bot.

The bot didn't immediately answer. A few uncomfortable seconds passed.

"You believe this planet contains the key to a power that will allow you to bring order to the disintegrating Republic. What you have not been able to accomplish with subterfuge, assassination, war, diplomacy, economic theory, and a host of other options, you believe will be possible once you unlock the secrets of this place. To be specific: you seek the Temple of Low Men. The Morghul Gate."

And it all came back to him.

The *Lexington*.

The Quantum Palace.

And of course the Dark Wanderer.

All the clues that had led from the battle inside the palace, inside that other nether reality, that blank space in the universe... to here.

He had come here to save a galaxy that didn't want to be saved. A galaxy that wouldn't save itself. He'd come to find a power source unlike anything ever known, a power source encountered only once—by him, in a place that didn't exist as far as existence seemed concerned.

Casper stood. "I'm tired. I'll turn in now. Stay close to the ship tonight, 133."

He left the bot there, watching the firelight and sensing the night all around it.

Later, he lay in his bunk within the wreckage, thinking about the lighthugger *Moirai* and the Martian light infantry. About all the dead they'd left in that lifeless place. About his friend Tyrus Rex. And about how all of this had begun. Soon he was asleep and dreaming, though he didn't know it. The dreams were like watching a memory.

05

Casper wanders in his dream past all the dead left behind after the *Lexington* landed, under heavy fire, to secure the hangar of the massive ark ship known as the *Moirai*. This was early in the Savage Wars. So early it wasn't even really a part of the major conflicts that would follow as the Savages came in from the dark voids in their sublight ships and started raiding planets, connecting with other lost lighthuggers, and then spreading like some out-of-control virus of closed loop insanity. Before everyone understood just how savage those wars would become.

This is one hundred years after the *Obsidia*. Casper, commander of the assault frigate *Lexington*, has been sent by the Confederation of Worlds to board the lighthugger *Moirai* and rescue a scientist the savages captured in a recent raid. Fate has brought Tyrus Rex into this because he leads the boarding party, which consists of a force of Martian light infantry, formerly enemies of Earth, now members of the loose Confederation of Worlds that will one day form the Galactic Republic.

They have come to rescue Reina. That too is fate. She is the captured scientist the Savages hold somewhere deep within their lighthugger ship.

Casper finds himself watching some of the deceased, thinking they are not truly dead, but merely playing a part. As though this is some entertainment, or exercise, in which the "dead" must pretend to be such for the purpose of the show. Or the lesson. But in his memory it was not so. In his memory they were really dead.

Asleep in the wrecked ship two thousand years in the future, Casper somehow knows this is just a dream.

He steps over the corpses of the Martian light infantrymen who formed part of the combined arms task force. He leaves the Terran Navy assault frigate *Lexington*, the *Lex*, its boarding ramps extended and gears down, and makes his way across the ancient hangar deck of the *Moirai*.

Most of the dead are the men of Delta Company, Third Battalion, Forty-Seventh Martian Light Infantry. They were assigned as the first wave to secure the landing zone within the *Moirai* hangar. They went down hard under the defenses of the Savages. Cut to pieces by the strange half humans that came rushing out from across all decks. Half-man, half-machine lunatics ululating electronic eight-bit war cries and brandishing ancient slug throwers. These are sometimes the descendants of those long-ago best and brightest of ancient Earth who fled during the Exodus, and sometimes those best and brightest themselves. But they are strange and post-human now. Made almost animal and backwards by their cloistered sublight societies that have gone philosophically strange in their long crawl out through the darkness between worlds.

Casper passes by their energy bolt–riddled corpses, their eyes fluttering behind closed lids in his memories, as though the dead are dreaming too. Occasionally, one of them opens their eyes and smiles as if to say, "It's all right, I didn't really die here in what the old calendar used to call 2122. We're just acting."

But then, thinks Casper, who hears the low thump of automatic gunfire ahead, *you would have lived and made it to see the Republic. And even if you'd lived a very long time, you'd* still *be long dead by the time I'm having this dream. You were never a slave on the* Obsidia. *You were never experimented on like I was. Like Rex was. Like Reina was.*

The staccato rattle of gunfire echoes in rapid hollow booms across the hangar deck of the *Moirai*, a forty-kilometer-wide spinning cylinder that's over fifty thousand meters long. The tiny *Lex* looks like a mere shuttle in comparison.

I'm very old, thinks Casper as he surveys the cyclopean innards of the great lighthugger, *but never older than what came before me.*

The Martian Light Infantry uses Krieg Systems forty-watt magnetically accelerated ultrahigh directed energy rifles. KS-99s. Blasters won't come into use for another hundred years. The KS-99s fire small bolts of disrupted energy that can do brutal damage to flesh and unarmored systems. They were manufactured in the armaments districts of Saffron City back on Mars. Most likely before the last Terran War, when Mars was still a planet and not a crescent-shaped chunk of debris trailing red dust in its degrading wake around the sun.

Casper wears a Terran Navy tactical environment uniform. He stayed in the navy after the escape from the *Obsidia*, while Rex went off to Mars to join their new army. And when there was war, they fought on opposite sides, even though they were friends—and survivors of the same horrible nightmare. Eventually peace followed war, if only because by that time there wasn't much left of Mars to fight for. By then the Martian Infantry was serving as a sort of foreign legion for the Terran forces. And now they are part of the combined arms task force that has come to assault the *Moirai* along with the crew of the *Lexington*.

Casper goes forward over the eviscerated soldiers of Delta Company. He is alone, seeking to link up with Rex—but the *Lexington*'s comms aren't working inside the lighthugger for some strange reason. Yet there is another, more pressing reason for the captain of the *Lexington* to leave his assault frigate and go forward to link up with the boarding party fighting its way into the interior of the *Moirai*. The lighthugger is rapidly approaching an area of no-go space known as the Dead Zone.

Casper reaches the infantrymen. They're pinned down by enemy fire. Major Rex leads the attack. They are attempting to penetrate the Savage defenses that prevent access to the interior of the ship.

"I see three entrances into the main hab systems," Rex shouts to his soldiers. "Team One, with me. We'll assault forward. Teams Two and Three, flank those Savages while they try and stop us."

Rex leads Team One forward under heavy fire.

The flanking teams draw the attention of the Savages while Rex's squad tries to breach the maze of tunnels down to the hab. Casper remembers that he has gone forward to re-establish comm. To tell Rex that their window to safely disengage with the lighthugger is closing.

The *Moirai* is approaching the Dead Zone. Ships don't return from there.

He joins Rex as the Martian commandos endure furious fusillades of automatic return gunfire coming from the passages beyond. Subsonic rounds zip past their buckets and ricochet off the bulkheads all around them. The Savages still use combustion-based firearms. Ancient automatic weaponry.

"Rex, we're almost out of time," Casper warns. "Push through now, or pull out and let the ship enter the Dead Zone."

A giant hatch, two stories high, like some ancient and gleaming bank vault door, is blown from its hinges. More bullets rip from the maw left behind.

One of the Martian soldiers pulls away from the wall and lets loose with a furious blast from his KS-249—the heavier version of the KS-99. A burst of ethereal electrical snaps signifies the charge chamber being converted into pulsed rounds of energy. They are sent at the enemy in blistering sprays of flashing light.

But the awe-inspiring display doesn't drive the Savages into cover; they merely concentrate their automatic weapons fire on the Martian soldier, who dies knowing his cover fire helped Rex and the team move into a dark passage farther down the way.

Casper feels a chill as the corridor is illuminated by flashes of eerie green light from the Martian light infantry's forty-watt weapons. The infantry wear graphene space suits with hardened ceramic alloy chest plates, shoulder and arm guards, shin and knee protectors, and heavy combat boots. Their helmets are Kevlar that can seal with the graphene armor for limited operations in poisonous environments and environments with no oxygen.

A soldier takes a shot right in the faceplate. He falls to the deck. The Terran Navy corpsmen, attached in support, are too busy with those who can be saved.

"Ten minutes and we'll pass into the Dead Zone, Rex."

What Casper means is clear. No scout ships have ever returned from that navigational dead space within the universe. It's an almost completely starless zone where instruments and readings turn weird when even close proximity is attempted. Most astrogation charts list the area as off-limits.

And yet the *Moirai* was headed straight into it after its raid on Al-Baquar Seven. And now together, both *Moirai* and *Lex* are flying straight into a zone of space no captain in their right mind would ever venture into.

"Clear!" says one of the soldiers pinned to the wall beyond the massive hatch.

Rex pumps his fist twice and makes a quick knife-edge gesture with his hand. The infantrymen move into the darkness ahead.

Casper's oldest friend turns back to him and says across the static-filled comm provided by a line-of-sight connection, "We're not leaving her here."

The "her" is Dr. Reina Benedetti.

Casper is glad, in the dream, that they will not leave her this time. He has had other dreams where they *did* leave her. And those dreams aren't dreams... they're nightmares.

At this moment, he cannot remember what really happened in the record of the past. As though, in this dream, all things are possible. The future doesn't have to be what it will become.

To Casper, there are two horrors to fear. There is the horror of being left on the *Moirai*. And then there is the horror of leaving someone *else* there. Especially Reina. In the Dead Zone. In the Quantum Palace. Forever with the Dark Wanderer.

The horror.

The horror of... being abandoned in Hell forever.

Casper bolted upright, awake and breathing heavily. Sucking in humid jungle air as though he had been drowning in the dream.

He was awake, but he remembered where his dream left off. He remembered the truth of what happened next. They'd hacked and cycled an airlock to get to the outer hab decks where the air smelled and tasted of death, and Casper followed Rex and his teams deeper into the *Moirai*'s shadowy interior.

He remembered much more than that.

He remembered the Dark Wanderer in the Quantum Palace on the other side of the Dead Zone.

He remembered the nightmares that flayed his mind.

What had they called them?

Casper took a pull from a canteen he'd left by his bunk inside the ruined freighter. He struggled to remember what they'd called them...

Prophetesses.

And in the jungle night of this lost and lonely planet beyond the galaxy's edge, he heard footsteps crunching slowly through the undergrowth. THK-133 was walking past the hull, trampling the foliage that had already begun to clutch at the ruined vessel. The bot was like some devil in the night, passing by the place where Casper slept.

06

The strange dream stayed with him the next day. In the milky light that filtered down through the strange and alien jungle, fragmented bits of it returned over and over again. Casper tried to work out what had been real, and what had been false.

He spent the day fortifying the wreck of the freighter and organizing salvageable supplies. He wasn't staying. Getting to the planet had been only the beginning. Now would come the real journey—a search across the length and breadth of an unknown world. A search for the Temple of Morghul. It might take years to find.

It might be the last hope of the galaxy.

The armory was organized first. He checked the condition of each blaster, oiled it, and sealed it in a clamshell case, hoping the jungle's oppressive humidity didn't find a way inside. He selected a hunting blaster rifle with a powerful scope and set that to one side. The holdout blaster pistol was still strapped to his thigh. After all the organizing, his wrist felt swollen and tight, but it would work. It wasn't broken.

When he got outside, THK-133 informed him there was a spring with drinkable water two clicks to the south. "I have left a marked trail for you, master," it intoned dispassionately. "Once I discovered the spring, I thought of you. I know water is important to your feeble species if you are to sustain operations. And therefore I decided to let you know of its existence. No doubt you would have discovered it on your own... given time."

Casper's mind moved slowly, working out the next step. Now that they'd found water, he would need food. The ship was stocked, given the length of the journey, but not all the supplies in the hold could come with him. Besides, Casper would prefer to eat those rations as a last resort. Those supplies had a long shelf life, and would be needed in the event of a famine or drought.

Some other part of the bot's statement niggled at his mind. The bot's choice of words...

"Therefore I decided to let you know of its existence."

As though it had considered other options. Thought of something else *besides* helping him survive.

Did you want to watch me die of thirst? Casper wondered to himself. *Watch me die while knowing the water I needed was just within reach?*

In the end, it didn't matter. The bot was his only companion on this forsaken planet.

And maybe it was just a quirk of the machine's programming. The THK series had been used in some of the Republic's nastier conflicts. Wars that hadn't made the news feeds. Wars with no heroes. Wars where brutality had been an essential part of the tactics, alongside chemical warfare and orbital bombardments.

Wars with no winners.

Or... maybe there was nothing odd about the bot's programming at all. Maybe this was all in his head. His mind was sound enough—it wasn't shattered from the long flight—but it still felt... strange. He'd been alone for five years in cryosleep, hurtling through hyperspace. What did that do to a man's mind?

There was a surprising lack of research on the effects of long-term cryosleep—probably because there was no need for it. You could go from one edge of the galaxy to the other in a few standard months. Cryosleep was tech from a pre-hyperspace age, and it was no longer necessary, unless you were making jumps that took years. And no one did that.

Except you, Casper thought to himself. *Because where this planet is, lies years beyond the known of the galaxy.*

There was a theory that it was decades of cryosleep that had made some of those Savages so outright insane. Not all of the lighthuggers had chosen to begin forming their personal utopias while in flight; some had opted for cryosleep, postponing their elaborately designed Edens until they arrived at their own Promised Land, or whatever distant rock they had targeted as their destination. For them, those extended flights through the void were like floating along like some lost soap bubble in a dark bath, until finally the bubble popped to reveal howling beasts of death and terror. Beasts that had once been the best of humanity, but which were now savage post-humans, their minds almost alien.

Like the prophetesses, said some whispering shade inside his head. Said that constant observer brought on by the concussion—or awakened by the five years hurtling through hyperspace.

Or had it been THK-133, who was back to organizing the wreckage into neat piles? Had the bot said something, and he'd mistaken it as a voice in his head?

That voice, whatever its source, whispered again. *What would happen if you died out here? What would the bot do? What would he build left all alone out here and by himself?*

Nothing good, thought Casper. And he knew this to be truer than he actually understood. As though he'd received some terrible dark vision of possible futures. The thought sent a cold shiver up his spine. He decided to think of something else.

Like the prophetesses?

They, the prophetesses, had been the first clue to the hidden power that waited beneath the universe. They had found the first secrets. Their steps had marked the trail into the mists of the unknown. And even though—he told himself now as he sat down on a log they'd hauled over to their campsite—even though you'd never known what you were looking for, he told himself... you'd been searching for it all along. A way to do all the things when mankind and the galaxy itself couldn't accomplish what needed to be done.

It was that rescue mission aboard the *Moirai* that began the...

The...

The...

This search?

Yes.

That mission was like some ancient scroll being unrolled, revealing a fable of mythic heroes and magic powers. The beginning and a journey, both things at once. A quest that led from the past to here. This planet. This unfound planet, forgotten and cast beyond the embrace of the galactic spiral like some unwanted child.

And it was the prophetesses who had shown Casper the way. That was how it all had begun, though he hadn't known it at first.

His first glimpse of a prophetess was of a strange, almost poverty-stricken figure behind a cohort of uplifted half-human Savages. "Uplifted" was what they, like many Savage societies, had called the interface of tech and man. As though they had evolved themselves on their own, rejecting evolution's poor performance record and humanity's lack of commitment to survival of the fittest.

Casper absently chewed his rations, and his mind went back to the dream.

Intense energy fire erupted from Rex's light infantry. But the Uplifted Savages' cybernetic parts formed an armor system that protected them. And around each Savage, a swarm of tiny drones flitted about like vampire butterflies, deflecting damage and doing who knew what else. It was rare to get a Savage with a single shot in those early days. They absorbed large doses of firepower.

But they were slaves too, just as you and Rex had been, on a different ship, Casper remembered. *They just didn't know it.*

The Martian Light Infantry was the toughest fighting force operating in the pre-Republic stellar frontier back then. They fired and advanced into the face of the Savages, spending their lives to gain precious corridors in order to complete the mission. To find a hackable terminal and get a location on the scientist they'd come for.

No, not just a scientist.

Reina.

The girl Casper loved though he'd never told her so, apart from that one time... a time best left forgotten.

He remembered kissing her. Just once. And thinking that if the shape of the galaxy were such as it was at that moment, he could take things as they were. He could put aside his continual quest to right some wrong he'd forgotten the origin of so long ago. As long as he had her, the galaxy could have the rest. It could crumble all around them if that was what it wanted to do.

She had offered him that road. To be the opposite of himself.

In the corridors, a soldier went down, and Rex covered Casper with a blistering barrage of electric fire in short suppressive bursts. Casper ran for all he was worth and dragged the wounded man out of harm's way. The squad medic was busy with another downed soldier.

By the luminescent green electrical flashes of the infantrymen's assault rifles, Casper surveyed the scene. The Savages were faceless, almost blurry. Their strange tech swarmed about them, looking now more like miniature crows than butterflies—dark and swirling, an extension of themselves. And on the walls all around the advancing force, madness was written. The graffiti of minds that had snapped out there in the interstellar darkness.

The Heart of Man is one of the Darkest Places in the Galaxy

The Conquest of the Stars won't be a pretty thing... so don't look too closely

When we're finished they'll see who they really are

You don't talk with the brutes. You teach them. And if they cannot learn... exterminate them.

Death has Become Me.

All that and much more was written on those walls. Walls that had once been cold-room perfect and a movie set designer's dream of a future of polished chrome and mad science. Some high-tech store selling the latest gadgets like cheap miracles to the richest of the rich.

Once, as a child, Casper had wandered the ruins of a mall. His father had pointed out something called the Apple Store. The glass was shattered and the tables had long since been broken up for fuel. Smartphones lay smashed in the grit and dust, their useful parts taken, their original purpose thwarted. And while his father stripped copper wiring from the walls, Casper found pictures of what the store had once looked like in its heyday.

A very different place.

A beautiful place.

The ship from the dream of the past, the *Moirai*, had once looked like that. But it, too, had faded into disuse and darkness.

The dead Savage marines on the floor wore mirrored masks. No eyes, no obvious sensors... nothing. Just a blank mirror. And there was something extremely disconcerting about this in those last horrible few minutes as the *Moirai* dove into the Dead Zone, engines at full. Leaving the known for the unknown.

Casper remembered thinking that no one really knew what happened in there. In the Dead Zone. That instantaneous annihilation was just as possible as any other outcome that had been theorized and never tested. That the Dead Zone was like something beyond the Black Hole of Legend. That it would take the massive lighthugger and crunch it down into the smallest possible thing.

He would begin to think this after the first prophetess they encountered said what she said. Dying with the word "Quantum" on her lips. Because that was what the word meant: the smallest known unit of information. That was how the Savages had dealt with what they'd been up to out there on their own. Doing the things that shouldn't be done.

Casper had faced aliens before—horrible, multi-eyed, many-tentacled monsters, humanoid variations of Earth-based life forms. Races like the Tennar, who were to squids what the wobanki were to cats. The known galaxy, at that time, was full of some pretty scary stuff. It would only get scarier as the Republic reached for the dark edges. And beyond the edges seemed to be something no one was brave enough to risk. Beyond the edges was a place of monsters and superstition.

But out here in the shadowy parts of the galaxy, aboard the *Moirai* with a ticking clock running out to an unknown event horizon that most likely ended in some kind of oblivion in which everything got crushed down to nothingness, here in the dark corridors with insanity written large on the walls, it was the prophetesses who were the most bizarre and disturbing thing he'd ever experienced. They violated the known laws of the universe. And that had changed the course of his life.

Casper dragged the downed soldier into some kind of dark maintenance alcove. Heavy fire burned and streaked through the air all around him. The passage was rounded, like a tube, some great artery within the belly of a leviathan. An artery tattooed with the mad ramblings of a crazy man lost in the wastes.

There weren't many soldiers left now. Rex was still on his feet, surrounded by men getting cut down by the unforgiving bullets of the Savages. Somehow those speeding slugs, thrown by a weapon so ancient as to have once been normal to mankind, were worse than the hyper-charged destabilized energy return fire. The wet slaps and shattering armor. The screams as muscle and bone were torn to shreds. The bright sudden cry of ricochet fire close and personal. All of this made those slugs somehow a worse thing than being burned through by white-hot loose energy.

It was only natural to think about falling back to the *Lexington*. But there was Rex. A man Casper had known for lifetimes. A friend. His only friend. Blasting away at the surging Savages trying to overrun them inside the crazy warren of the outer hull above the inner hab of the giant *Moirai*. Rex was unable to advance, and refusing to retreat.

That was when the Savages pushed hard with their secret weapons, and the prophetess came forward out of their ranks. It was the first time he would meet one, yet it would seem as though the memories of their terrible power had always been with him. She walked straight into the thick of the battle with the dead and the dying lying all about the deck and all the way back to the hangar.

A powerful *bang* sounded, like a lightning strike. But it had come from out beyond the hull. Or at least that's the way it felt. The strange purple lighting the Savages had crafted inside the ship flickered on and off. And in that moment Casper remembered that this lighting had once been the standard soft white ambient of the high-end super luxury stores that catered to the haves in a world filled with have-nots. He'd seen pictures of these ships in long-dead celebrity and gossip websites that had been recovered by preservationists. Long ago, when everyone had been sane, things had looked much better. Idyllic.

The reality he witnessed now was like a funhouse nightmare mirror.

Somehow Rex managed to push the Savages back another ten feet. Some of the Savages were falling back, loping away like something less than men. Like jackals, or monkeys suddenly frightened by the onslaught of technology. Half human, half machine... they seemed to be nothing more than electronically gibbering beasts. Violent, snarling creatures armed with ancient and terrible firearms. It was like looking at what you once were, and what you would become in the ages far from now when everything had not gone according to plan. It was like looking at a deranged grandparent and a savage child in the same moment.

And because of my time on the Obsidia, thought Casper later when he considered all these memories, *I've lived to see those horrors made real in the millennium of war that was to follow.*

The prophetess came through the press of fleeing Savages. Walking as though she were oblivious to return fire from Rex and the soldiers around him. She held up one hand, her left. It was bony and pale. Almost bloodless. She seemed like a normal, if alien, woman. Like some ideal representation in a museum to be viewed and wondered at. Though she was oddly slender. Periods of extended weightlessness had made some humans turn into living scarecrows. Long life in the big lighthuggers had often done that same thing to Savages.

Rex and his fire team had no reservations about putting her down. They switched from engaging the running Savages, disappearing into the dark warren of passages, to targeting her. The first shots lanced out almost in slow motion. Hot green energy sizzled from the weapons' barrels, illuminating the graffiti-mad walls. It felt to Casper as though the camera of time inside his mind was under-cranking into slow motion to show him all the anticipated horror that was about to be done to her body.

Casper remembered that. Remembered watching those first shots of charged electricity speed toward her in slow motion. Knowing they'd punch burning holes in her slender form and continue off into the dark tunnels past her. Illuminating the tiny tube of death as they went off into the darkness, eventually exploding across some arcane piece of equipment in a shower of festive sparks.

Except the shots did not do that.

Instead the concentrated fire was deflected away from her, as though she had some kind of personal deflector shield. Which was impossible at that time. Deflector shields, back in those days, took up huge sections of any given ship. One deflected shot smashed into the ceiling just above her head, sending a shower of bright sparks down around her, announcing her presence with pyrotechnic fanfare. Other shots simply curved away, the tight discs of destabilized energy seemingly controlled by something beyond their own force and momentum.

The soldiers continued firing, for all the good it was doing.

Casper crouched over the dying soldier's body, drew his sidearm, and fired at her as well, his shots joining the fusillade of bright electrical fury that did nothing but destroy everything around her.

In his mind she loomed over them all, and she was death incarnate.

Death has become Me.

And then she held one hand up to her temple. The other hand. The hand that had been hanging limply at her side. Her right hand. She held it as though she were suddenly experiencing a sharp headache, or having some serious thought that needed concentration—a deep thought that needed the real world to be blocked out, if only just for a moment.

And then one of the soldiers' heads, a man near Rex, exploded inside his Kevlar helmet.

The infantrymen beside Rex stopped firing. Casper, still kneeling, ceased fire as well. His mouth hung open. None of them had ever seen anything like that. And as they would've told you, they'd seen a lot of strange things in their many crossings and deployments throughout the known galaxy. Or at least what was known of the galaxy at that time. Which, in hindsight, wasn't all that much.

It was clear that this slender woman had used her mind to pop the soldier's head like it was some blemish that needed getting.

But that was hocus-pocus stuff.

Voodoo. Superstition.

The opposite of the science they'd worshipped back then.

And still do, Casper mused, here in the present. *As if they know there's a supernatural and so refuse to allow it to jam a foot in the door of their imaginations, lest something uncomfortable wedge its whole body in after that.*

Science now was more like superstition, a religion, some wanton idol carved to fit the times by the House of Reason. But back then they thought they were living in the new enlightenment that had come with hyperspace travel. There was no room for witchcraft and prayer.

There was only science.

Same as it ever was, someone had once said to him.

But what he was seeing right now was *power*. A power that defied explanation, that verged on the uncomfortable realms of sorcery and the supernatural. Because if she was not a witch... then what was she? What was the explanation for someone who could destroy another through the will of her mind?

Her hand fell away from her skull. Her breathing was heavy. They could see she was drained by the effort required to hold their shots at bay, not to mention exploding a man's head. Everything was deadly silent.

Rex tossed his rifle to the deck and surged toward her. This was always his way. Where others ran from the fire, Rex ran toward it. He dragged the plate cutter from off his harness. Martian infantrymen all kept the circular saw breaching tool on their back, handlebar above their right shoulder blade, attached to their rucks. He pulled the tool, pressed auto-start, and swung it at her in a furious arc of savagery.

Its spinning blade hissed to life just an instant before he started slicing her from shoulder to hip. She screamed as he drove its industrial diamond circular saw into her frail body.

She collapsed to the ground in a gauzy and gory heap.

In the half-light of the mad tunnel, standing over the body of the dead girl, Rex looked like some primordial warrior who'd just clubbed the other tribe's high priestess to death with a bone-handled axe or a rock. Never mind the tech, weapons and armor. This was an ancient image, and he was like some ancient warrior. He always would be. And now he stood staring down at his vanquished foe.

Casper came up alongside him, pistol out. Still pointing down at her as though she might suddenly reassemble and levitate off the deck to feast on their souls.

She was murmuring something.

Her wan, almost ethereal face was blood-spattered. Stained from her own blood. But it was still the face of a young woman. Still alive. Almost.

Casper wondered if she was as old then as he was now, a victim of the Savages' thirst for eternal life. Or had she been born out in the darkness on the long flight through the cosmos? Looking for the Savages' promised land no one had ever promised them but themselves.

Her lips moved. Repeating something as she wound down and let go of this life and all that the galaxy ever was.

Casper bent down to listen. Rex did not. He'd never been curious. To him, life—and death—was black and white. There were no great mysteries. There was only remaining on your feet. That's how you went forward.

"I embrace the Quantum... and it embraces me," she whispered. Over and over as she left this mortal coil.

As Casper comes back fully to himself, hearing that long-dead girl speaking those words in his memory, he is sitting by the cold ashes of the fire near the wreck of his ship. The sky has turned red. The dying giant red dwarf is fading into the west, and night is coming on. The trees look like bony fingers clutching at the fading firelight in the sky. As though they are pleading. Or taking something from the sky.

THK-133 is sitting across from him.

Casper blinks twice.

"You are back, master. Shall I build a fire?" And then, rather ominously, the machine adds, "Someone is coming."

07

They heard it from a long way off. Like artillery on a hot day, rolling across the land and falling suddenly in great concussive *whumps*. The first strike was a dull yet resonant *whump*, as though something had fallen from a great height.

Casper cast a quick glance at the bot. It was full dark now. The moons hung fat and bloated over the jungle forest.

He wondered, in the half-moment before the next strike, what, on such a deserted and forlorn planet, could have caused that sound to issue out over the jungle. And whether it would happen again.

He was half expecting it wouldn't, remaining forever a mystery on this strange planet... when it did. The next strike was also distant. It was followed by another. And another. As though some four-legged giant were walking over the tops of the jungle, its massive tree-trunk legs striking the ground beneath the canopy with explosive, rhythmic *boom*s.

The strikes came closer. A burning log in the fire shifted and rolled out onto the swampy ground of their camp. Casper jumped as hot sparks shot up into the night.

The slow, ponderous explosions continued, growing ever so slightly from one to the next. Bizarre birds circled off into the dark like unwanted guests who'd been offended at a party and decided to leave, shrieking and calling to one another to the protest of no one.

Casper felt extremely vulnerable and exposed. He grabbed the hunting rifle blaster and held it across his knees. He could now *feel* the ground shaking beneath him. But when the nearby wreckage of the ruined ship shifted and groaned in response to the steady, regular seismic tremors, it was clear that whatever it was, it was big enough to ignore a high-powered blaster rifle.

There was a feeling in Casper's stomach that told him it was coming this way. It had to be. It was as if there were no other option than this.

The next sound he heard was the shrieking cracks of distant trees. In the still lifelessness of the heat-swollen night, their ancient trunks were thrust aside.

Casper's mind struggled to put the pieces together. Any pieces. And in the end he found there were none that fit. Was this some kind of subterranean gas explosion opening a new chasm in the land by natural means? Was the landscape collapsing in increments, coming his way? Had he come so far only to be swallowed into some kind of jungle sinkhole, with the wreckage of his ship coming down upon him?

Or was this a machine?

Or a monster?

In those terrible moments of not knowing, anything terrible was possible. Which is the worst thing about those kinds of moments.

The ground shook as though it had been hit by an entire wing of Republican bombers. He'd been close to that once. Dangerously close. But that's what happened when you were overrun and out of options. You called everything in, and dropped it on yourself.

And this thing, whatever it was, out there in the jungle dark... it roared. Prehistorically. And the roar became a screech—and then a howl. It was the very definition of titanic.

Casper dashed for the bugout bag he'd prepped that afternoon out of salvaged supplies from the ruined ship.

"C'mon!" he yelled at the bot. "Get your blaster rifle and follow me."

Whatever it was, it was *definitely* headed this way. Maybe it was the alpha predator of this castaway planet. Maybe it had seen the ship fall from the sky and was coming to see if it was some kind of food. Maybe it had been headed here all along. Who knew. Casper knew only that he had to get away from the crash site. Quickly.

He remembered the monstrous lizard that had walked on two legs out on the red desert plain, before the giant statue he'd almost crashed the ship into. Beyond the mountains and out in the burning wastes. That two-legged lizard had been the size of a building. Maybe even taller.

"Where, exactly," began THK-133 as they ran through the jungle, "does one hide from something my sensors are indicating to be at least twenty meters tall, master? And by the way... it is moving at an average speed of forty kilometers per hour. I highly doubt we will be able to outrun it. You should prepare for your end by making sure your weapon is fully loaded. I have always found this to be a comfort in that I might just acquire an opportunity to kill one or more of my enemies in their moment of victory."

Casper threaded his way down a tight jungle trail leading away from the wreck. Hard, sharp leaves pulled and cut at him, and slimy vines felt like pythons intent on coiling about him. He shook them off and thought only of putting as much distance between himself and the wreck of the ship as possible.

They came to a sandy beach beside a moonlit river, its curving quicksilver trail wandering off into the jungle night. Above the distant tops of the fetid jungle behind them, they now saw a dark shape in front of the lone visible moon hanging low in the sky. The shape was moving toward the ship.

It was like a lizard. A giant lizard. Its head smooth. Its ridged brow heavy. Its scaly snout filled with sharp teeth. It opened its mouth and howled, and the jungle shook all about them. Trees swayed, and some collapsed from jungle rot eons old.

"Down!" hissed Casper as the monster panned its head across the dark blue night sky.

The bot took a knee and scanned the jungle. "Now that we have encountered the locals, I predict our odds of surviving the first week of our stay here are considerably less than my initial projections, master. Have you any last wishes, or requests, that I may pass on to the search and rescue teams should I survive your demise? Although I doubt we will ever be found."

Casper heard the rending of metal. Impervisteel to be specific. The ship to be exact. Casper knew that sound. He'd heard hulls surrender under the strain of combat. He knew what a collapsing bulkhead sounded like. The strain of screaming spars as they snapped in heavy gravitation wells. The terrific crash of a ship colliding with a force bigger than its own.

"It's going after the ship, master," THK-133 intoned. "We may yet live to die in some much more horrible fashion on this forsaken planet. Alone in a place no one knows exists. When you calculate the odds, the possibilities for our demise are nearly endless."

Casper listened as the creature tore the ship to pieces. At one point a section of the hull, of the cockpit, was tossed above the treetops as though it were not a multi-ton piece of an interstellar starship, but rather a simple toy. A toy that no longer amused the petulant child that played with it. The massive piece of impervisteel arched through the night above them, moonlight gleaming off of it, bits of loose equipment raining down beneath it.

It crashed onto the beach behind them.

Casper overcharged the blaster rifle, dumping all its energy into the next shot. A soft, high-pitched note disappeared into nothingness, signaling the shot was ready to be fired.

"Really?" asked the bot. Its droll tone was made even drier by its electronic voice. "I highly doubt your blaster will do anything beyond attract the beast to our exact position—and possibly enrage it enough to go on a stomping spree with us underneath... master."

Casper ignored this and waited. Much of his life had been down to last shots, last chances, last stands. Why not now?

Same as it ever was.

Hadn't all of it, his whole life crossing the stars, hadn't it always headed toward this kind of conclusion?

Casper waited for the monster's next move. Ignoring the only answer he could provide. He tried to make sure defeat was never an option... until it was.

The violence at the crash site was dying down now. The monster howled, as though robbed of some prize. As though claiming enigmatic victory over manufactured inanimate objects. As though promising them that they were now good and well marooned.

As if that had not been abundantly clear already.

And then... the monster began to head off into the night, in another direction, away from the river. Away from Casper. Its massive footfalls shook the ground, causing the sand to shift beneath his feet. The destruction of its going was heard for some time as it wandered off into the nether reaches of the strange jungle. But finally, whatever it was, monster, demon, predator, animal, dream... it was gone.

They stood.

All was quiet now.

Casper watched the night. Waiting. Feeling himself begin to shake. There was something so primordial about that. Some ancient fear hard-wired into him. Running from a monster the size of a building. And there was nothing he could do about it.

It reminded him that despite his longevity, he was still fragile. It could've crushed him, and there was nothing in what the Pantheon on the *Obsidia* had done that could've fixed that. Bullets, blasts, knives—or being crushed to death by a monster in a jungle... anything that could end his life, would end it.

In that, he was just like everyone else.

Like his ancient cave-dwelling ancestors, when mankind was not the uber predator of his planet, he was painfully aware of his mortality.

He checked the blaster rifle and redistributed the charge. Then he walked over to the portion of the cockpit that had landed on the beach.

Its windows stared out at the lazy water. In the area below the main cockpit where the avionics processors had once been, there was enough space for him to shelter. It reminded him of a cave. One like those ancestors might have hidden in, to avoid being trampled by *their* monsters. Or like mice in the walls of an old and haunted house.

Five years ago, he'd been the highest-ranking admiral in the Republic. Commander of a fleet that consisted of two battleships, three carriers, fourteen cruisers, and numerous destroyers and corvettes. The crew of the battleship was over fifteen thousand alone.

Now...

He looked at the accidental cave formed by his ruined ship. "We'll camp here... next to the river," he announced in a whisper.

The bot clicked and adjusted itself. "Shall I gather dead wood and build a fire, master? I know how much fire comforts your kind in such dire, and most likely fatal, situations as this."

08

The night wore on into the still hours where time didn't seem to move in the least. And for that matter, what was time now? The ship was smashed. The ship's clock was gone. Given long enough, any personal devices that kept standard Galactic would wear down and run out. Become unreliable. For all intents and purposes, time was meaningless.

Casper sat in front of the fire, trying to develop a list of what he'd need to look for in the morning, while trying to ignore that he'd most likely killed himself by coming to this planet. Yes, he was *capable* of a long life, but he wasn't invulnerable to pain, injury, disease, or starvation. Or exposure.

He was probably going to die out here. And soon. So he focused on the priorities.

Food.

Shelter.

Medicine.

Weapons.

And while his initial plan had been to get some scouting missions going to find the Temple of Morghul, always with the ability to return back to his ship for more supplies, now there was nothing to return to. No ship, and the supplies... well, with as exposed as everything was in this jungle environment, rot and degradation would soon set in. Nothing could be counted on past a few days. Anything that had been relied upon before, now could not be.

It was time to make a choice.

During the crash, he'd had no time to get a reading on the planet's topography. Just vague images he barely remembered now. They'd come in too hot. Too fast. Too close to the planet. He'd been too busy trying to keep the ship from crashing to get all the scans he'd intended to get. Scans that would have made the search a lot easier.

The only reference points he had were the jungle, the mountains, and the desert. And the enigmatic statue of the giant lizard. That statue was the only evidence of any kind of civilization. So—he would make for the statue. And then, perhaps, to the desert beyond? There had been a sea at the end of it, hadn't there? He thought he could remember that much. He would—

"Master," the bot began.

But Casper had also seen what the bot was about to alert him to, and he held up a hand for silence.

A small creature was coming up the beach, along the dark river. The visible moon had dropped down now, behind the distant mountains where the lonely statue waited, watching an ancient wasteland that was home only to birds, insects, and wandering monsters.

Casper flicked off the safety on the hunting rifle. THK picked up the heavy blaster and did the same. Which all seemed rather ridiculous once the thing came into the firelight. Whatever it was, it wasn't more than half a meter tall.

It came down the beach in an almost haphazard fashion, as though it was investigating every rock, pebble, and stray stick, but its destination was clear. It was headed straight for their fire.

"Shall I kill it, master? So that you might sate your hunger with its roasted flesh? Because you are weak that way in your constant need for sustenance. And I do enjoy killing."

Casper shook his head.

It was carrying a walking stick. So it wasn't just an animal. It was an intelligent life form. Probably tribal or nomadic. Possibly territorial. Maybe it knew where the Temple of Morghul was. Or maybe their tribe had songs and stories that could point him toward the ancient ruins he sought.

And then this small dark figure, its humanoid shape masked by the night, passed into the firelight.

It had two arms, two legs, and it was shaggy. Not in the way human hair is shaggy, but in the way some floor coverings are shaggy. Its entire body was covered in short, curling, crimson hair. It had a large bulb of a nose, and its two coal-dark soulful eyes were even larger than the nose. Within those eyes the light of the fire danced and twirled.

Without fanfare or introduction it sat down on a log across the fire. It settled itself with no small amount of guttural grumbling and difficulty. As if this were all perfectly normal. As if this was the way things were done.

Looking at them, it spoke.

"Urmo."

There was a long silence, during which the only sound was of the fire gently crackling. The creature just watched and waited for a response. Its dark eyes wandered back and forth between the bot and the man.

Casper had been through first-contact scenarios before. Long ago, when much of the galaxy was unknown, he'd been the first to meet the Tennar. He tried to remember the protocols, but in the end he came up with nothing more than repeating the word that had been spoken.

"Urmo," he said.

The small thing nodded emphatically and began to bounce up and down on the log.

"Urmo!"

"Urmo!"

"URMO!" it exclaimed.

Possibly, thought Casper, "Urmo" was its name?

Remembering the blaster rifle across his knees, he set it aside. "Are you... Urmo?" he asked.

"URMO! URMO! URMO!" it exclaimed.

But this didn't clarify whether the little thing acknowledged itself as "Urmo." It only seemed excited to repeat the enigmatic word.

Casper turned toward the bot. "Does Urmo mean anything to you, 133?"

"Hmmm..." intoned the bot. It emitted a whirring and clicking as it went from perfect stillness to sudden activity. It panned its head across the night as though sensing something. "Nothing rings a bell, as they say, master. But I recall a rather violent encounter at the Battle of Zanzabaad in which a Hool I had just garroted made a similar sound. Whether it was a word, a curse, or some sort of ineloquent final statement as death came, I do not know. I suspect it was merely strangling in its own poisonous blood. Hence the sound."

Pause.

"Is that helpful, master?"

Casper shook his head.

Looking at the little creature, he tried once more. He circled his hand to take in the forest, the river, and the night.

"Urmo?"

Again the little beast erupted. "URMO! URMO!"

This was repeated as the night wore on. Anything Casper tried was met with the same one-word exultation. And then the little creature would wait for the next time Casper spoke. It waited expectantly. It waited hopefully. And it was never disappointed.

And then it would repeat, "URMO, URMO, URMO!" over and over.

In time, Casper, frustrated, abruptly rose and walked to the dark river. The cool of the night felt good against his face after too long in front of a fire, trying desperately to communicate with what apparently amounted to an alien moron. He closed his eyes and listened to the sound of water running over the stones. Its gentle burble relaxed his mind. He just faded into that and tried not to think about...

Being stranded on a planet no one knew existed.

Imminent death.

And the Republic, and all its problems.

His thoughts were always about the Republic. He had been instrumental in its creation, though no one—or rather very few—had ever known the extent of his involvement. And even those few were dead now. The history books listed him as Cyrus Caine, original signer of the first draft of the Constitutional Charter that created the Galactic Republic. Back when that had been something to be proud of. Back before the courts had cored it out and made a plaything of it. Subtracting Founding Rights and adding new rights merely to secure power with special interest galactic minority groups. The Charter had really been something once—but that was long ago, before the rot set in.

Back then, people had a lot of grand ideas. When the Republic was much loved and everyone had a sense of patriotism about it. When it was an enterprise. A grand experiment. Something noble.

They even made movies about it.

Actors had played him. Had played Cyrus Caine. Several times over.

Actors who were now long dead.

Then the revisionist history had come along and made something else of the man he'd been for a time.

The music of the water over stones in the river reminded him of all those lost things he was here for. All the right things that needed to be brought back, never mind how.

And then, for a moment, he realized he was hearing voices having a conversation. An interchange. An exchange of words. Something other than...

"URMO! URMO! URMO!"

He spun about, and it seemed, though just for a moment, that the THK was nodding emphatically at the little creature. As if an actual dialogue was being exchanged between the creature and the bot.

As if the two of them were talking.

But when he got back to the fire, they were merely staring at each other.

"Did he say... anything else?" Casper asked 133.

The bot panned its head until its gaze—or what Casper chose not to think of as its targeting system—focused on him. "No, master. We haven't said a word. We've just been sitting here, staring at each other."

From across the jungle a bird called out suddenly, shrieking like it was being violently murdered. The fire snapped, and only the mournful cry of that animal's echo remained. As though it would forever wander all the night paths of this strange and forgotten place beyond the ken of the known galaxy. Constantly crying out its grievance for no one to hear.

THE LESSON OF OTHER WAYS

The Master has led the student deeper and deeper into the darkness, to a place of deep silences within the temple.

But the temple is so many places, and to say that one is within the temple is to not be specific. We have passed beyond such vagaries.

Yet to say that one is with the Master... now this, of course, is very specific. And there is only one statement beyond this that can convey all things.

But of course, that is the first lesson. Learned at the beginning. Known before it was known. Waiting all along for it to be merely accepted.

It is within you, and you are within it.

Meditation.

This place of deep silences where the student finds himself is like a plain with no horizon. It is a gray and featureless place. Its existence screams nothingness. Which is ironic. But the student has found that when there is irony to be detected, a lesson is close at hand. Forces must collide, in order for clarity to reveal itself. In order for wisdom to be gained.

And so he wonders what is the lesson of this place.

The Master comes close.

"Confronted by obstacles you will always be. Along the way... always." The master pauses, as is his way. His every word carries weight, meaning, a conclusion in and of itself. The student must be allowed sufficient time to absorb these truths.

And then he resumes. "Choices are never easy. Clarity you will lack. See not just the right choice and the wrong... obvious both always are... but all the possibilities one might choose. Choose from these... and then powerful you will become."

In the temple, time has no meaning.

Unless that is part of the lesson.

The Taurax appears in the mist of nothingness. But not the Taurax as the galaxy knows it to be now. Not the four-armed raptor gone savage, little more than a beast. A plaything to be captured and caged, an amusement for fights gladiatorial. No. Once, long ago, before there was what is, and will one day be no more, before that thing called the Galactic Republic his mind has had to let go of in order that he may know it better, in order that he may destroy it better... before all that, the Taurax were the guardians of the Ancients.

This is known to no one save those within the temple.

As are so many other things about the galaxy.

And there is only the Master and the student, here in the temple.

Once, the Taurax were an elite warrior class. The wars they fought were savage beyond comprehending, and they, the Taurax, were considered a sort of doomsday weapon. A terrible whirlwind unleashed upon species that no longer existed. Imagine once-fertile worlds turned to desolate, airless, ruined moonscapes. The debris rings of gas giants were once stately worldlets.

And these were not just mindless monsters, some primordial saurians roaming the land for blood and meat. The Taurax were cruel. Because the minds that worked within them delighted in the pleasures of cruelty. Masters of weapons. Masters of pain. Masters of suffering.

Forward came the Taurax, a terrible thing to behold.

Nothingness shakes, trembling at the approach of a nightmare.

As the Taurax runs forward, its massive hindquarters pump hard.

It bears down on the student.

There is no time to do anything but dodge.

The dodge the student chooses is somehow wrong. The Taurax runs down its prey, crushing most of the bones in the student's body beneath its two-ton frame.

Impossibly, its dead-sprint run stops in an instant atop the student's body. It reaches down with one of its four long arms, and its claws rip the student to pieces while its weight pins the student to the nothingness.

The student feels all of this. Every breaking bone. Every ripping muscle. Every pulped organ. Every nerve ending shrieking madness.

And then the student is back in the nothingness—but within sight of that other self who has been torn to pieces. Brutally.

Forward comes the Taurax again, a terrible thing to behold.

This time, the student assumes a fighting stance. Though his frame and ability to defend himself will do little good against such an impressive weapon as the Taurax... it is a different choice.

A new choice.

The Taurax draws four ancient swords. Each is shaped like a butcher's gleaming cleaver. Each whirls as the clawed hands at the ends of four bulging arms handle the blades with a sublime deftness.

The student's right hand is removed at the wrist. The left arm comes away at the elbow. The third cleaver plants itself in the student's breast, breaking bone and cartilage. Crunching through, by sheer force, to the life-giving organs quivering beneath.

The student has time to register each swift attack. Each terrible cut.

The fourth cleaver sweeps in and removes the student's head.

He feels all of this, and he senses the impossibility of standing before such an opponent.

And then the student finds himself just a short distance from the other sites of slaughter within the gray nothingness. Seeing where each decision has met its end.

Forward comes the Taurax, a terrible thing to behold.

See all the possibilities one might take, whispers the Master across the ether of the nothingness. *Choose... and powerful you will become.*

Again the Taurax wins, tearing the student in two. The student had begun to reach out with his mind, to direct a wave of energy that has knocked lesser foes back—but he sees the hopelessness of this before it happens. And so he runs.

Because he does not want to die horribly again.

Which he does.

Forward comes the Taurax, a terrible thing to behold.

The student draws a long, single-bladed weapon of ancient origin. In those onrushing moments he considers each cut he might try. The forward slash. The overhand cleave. The final thrust. The whirlwind of blows. The death of a thousand cuts.

All of these appear about him as choices. All fail.

And the student feels all the failures in the terrible tableau that appears about him.

Feels all the deaths.

All the pain.

All the failure.

A hundred different deaths turn to two hundred. It is not until he has passed beyond a thousand gruesome and violent deaths that the student begins to let them all go. His mind instead plays a game of possibilities. If this won't work, will that? And if that won't, what about the five permutations that evolve?

And what if there are other forces?

He tries the most powerful weapons he knows.

The N-50.

The Taurax, bloody and shredded, still rips his head from his shoulders.

The student sees this and feels it, and it doesn't matter. Because just a few feet away in the nothingness, he has hurled a fragger.

The Taurax bats that away and closes with extreme brutality.

But that's not important, because that other student who he is now unloads with a full charge pack from a heavy assault blaster, giving ground and burning through charges, until the beast is shot through and through. Then the student leaps forward, letting go of the weapon and calling the power within himself to strike at the beast's throat.

Except the Taurax sweeps one blade up and cuts the student in half.

And so a few feet away he does not leap but instead uses the fragger, and the Taurax grabs it and runs close enough to blow them both to shreds.

And on and on.

He even uses the fabled hand cannon of his friend Rex, blazing away as he chokes the creature with the power his mind can forge, feeling himself drained of all his reserves down to the last iota. The Taurax responds by surging forward and punching straight through the student's heart and out his back.

And finally the student is not the student. He is the uncountable field of deaths represented in a thousand bloody tableaus of a single combat. A combat that repeats itself exponentially, expanding, branching, evolving with each nuance generated by each new encounter.

He sees them all.

He is them all.

He reaches out to find the one that will work. His mind lets go of all the savagery and pain that surrounds him, the pain he feels each time the Taurax wins. He lets go, and he sees one possible reality...

... where the Taurax does *not* win.

Forward comes the Taurax, a terrible thing to behold.

The student shifts to the right, causing the beast to check its rush. To reorient. To sweep with one claw instead of the other. Because all of this has happened before. Several times.

The student thrusts with the ancient sword at the place where the claw will be, driving the scalene, razor-sharp tip straight through the meat of the claw.

The beast howls and brings its three other weapons to bear on where the student should be... but the student is not there. Because this move, the beast's move, has been witnessed so many other times, and the student has stepped away.

The beast howls in rage, expelling all of its breath in an inhuman roar. And with the shaping of power, a shaping born of a thousand thousand deaths, the student cuts off the monster's air supply.

Nothing is as important to the beast as its next breath.

It manages only two steps before it topples in its unconsciousness, surrendering to the black hole that has consumed its vision.

It is powerless, unable to resist, as the student snaps its neck. This final note punctuates who, exactly, is the victor.

The master weaves through the carnage of a million dead students and one dead Taurax. The student falls to his knees. Drained. Empty. And yet he feels new power surge through him. As though his weakness has only made him stronger.

In the temple, such are the lessons of the Master.

"Obvious is the way to failure. Beyond these you choose. Then powerful you will become."

Thus ends this lesson.

09

Casper drifted off to the sound of rain. It thrummed lightly on the hull of the smashed cockpit. He'd crawled up onto the remains of the flight deck and spread out a jacket to sleep on. At least he was up off the ground. There were always snakes on every planet he'd ever been to.

He dreamt of those lost times of the *Moirai* and its journey into the Quantum Palace, or what the stellar maps had erroneously called the Dead Zone. Those long-gone hours, maybe days, where time had no meaning. That place where he'd first found the clues that had led him here, across all the years ever since.

"I embrace the Quantum... and the Quantum embraces me."

That's what she murmured as she died. The prophetess. A seemingly normal human with almost magical powers.

By that time, what remained of Rex's Martian light infantry combat team had come from the other passages along the outer hull in order to link up for the final assault into the *Moirai*'s main hab. As the soldiers planned their next move, they formed a perimeter, a patrol circle, or at least as much of one as they could in the tight corridors.

"What did she say?" Rex asked Casper as the platoon sergeant redistributed charge packs, and gear was either shed or adjusted.

That was when you first lied to him, thought Casper. *You didn't even know why at the time... but you did.*

Why? asked the questioning voice inside his head. *At that moment... "Quantum" meant nothing to you. So why did you lie to your best friend?*

Quantum. The smallest divisible unit of energy. A metric for counting.

Even then—he reminded himself now, on the other side of all the years—he had known she'd told him a secret. A powerful secret. After all, he'd just witnessed a power unlike anything in the known galaxy. And from that first moment, that secret had become like an electric fire all over his skin and buzzing deep inside his skull. Like Gollum of old, he hadn't wanted to share it. He'd known it was something... precious. Something special. Something important.

Something just for him.

Was that it? he asked himself, feeling that familiar discomfort with this old line of questioning.

Casper lay on the floor of a twice-wrecked ship deep in a dark jungle where terrible giant monsters roamed the night. Here, he could hear that other more honest part of his mind asking him, questioning him, and yes... *indicting* him for all the wrongs he'd committed along the way.

In his defense, he did have a security directive. From UNS Command. Even in the dream, that name—*United Nations Space Command*—felt ancient. It had nothing to do with the stellar governing body called the Galactic Republic, which stretched across all the spiral arms of the Milky Way.

United Nations Space Command was as old as that forgotten place called Rome. Or the Hittites. Or Nimrod the Mighty Hunter of Ur.

But back then, back when the hyperdrive was just a hundred years old, back then the UNS Command was law. And they'd told him to find out what secrets the lighthuggers they'd been tracking contained. Because they knew those old ships contained new secrets. Incredible secrets. And Earth wanted them. Needed them. Or so they thought.

Why?

Two reasons.

Reason One was the hyperdrive. Or rather, what the hyperdrive had done. See, once everyone had the formulas, schematics, and everything one needed to know about faster-than-light travel, well, all over the planet people built themselves ships and just headed out off-world. Because at this point, Earth was a constantly unfolding disaster, day by day. Humanity had spread wide and thin, separated by vast interstellar distances—and the species as a whole wasn't getting much R and D done.

And that led to Reason Two. The lighthuggers had become grand science experiments in social engineering, among other things. That had been their intent from the very beginning. The elites had been crazy about utopianism, and aboard the lighthuggers, they saw their opportunity. They controlled an environment in totality, with a nearly unlimited amount of time to tinker as they wandered out into the dark at sublight speeds. With no outside influence, they could hyper-focus on social engineering. On genetics.

They could experiment.

And experiment they did.

What the vast spreading mass of humanity didn't have the time or commitment to do—because they were too busy rushing about with their fantastic new hyperdrive—the slow-crawling elites invested in. Their bubble civilizations, wandering at sublight speeds, devoted themselves entirely to R and D.

One lighthugger had tried to develop the powers of the mind by living in total darkness and going long periods without sleep. When the UNS found the ship and cracked the hull, the people they found within referred to themselves as demons. They said the humans who had once occupied their bodies were all gone now. They said they, the demons, had come in from the outer dark. Their minds were shattered. They were stark raving mad.

Or is that just what we wanted to believe? Casper asked himself.

Another ship had tried to implement a completely communal society—which had quickly devolved into tribal warfare. They fought a civil war and destroyed their life support systems. One of their leaders formed a death cult and was "uploading" the survivors into a cloud he'd called Valhalla. Even in the Republic's most advanced state, no one had ever figured out how to digitize a human personality. So really he'd just been murdering them and butchering their corpses for food. The UNS found the ship about five years after they'd run out of "food."

But although many of the lighthuggers revealed living nightmares full of crazies—often armed to the teeth with terrible new weapons based on formerly state-of-the-art weapon systems—they also contained valuable research into longevity, energy, communication, and tech. That was the real reason the UN wanted those old lighthuggers cracked and looted. For the tech that seemed, at times, like miracles.

That was the problem with hyperspace. Everybody was too busy heading for the frontier to carve out their little slice of the galaxy. No one was sitting around and actually *developing* stuff like the lighthugger micro-civilizations had the time to do. After so much of Earth's population just fled the planet, scattered, society fragmented overnight, and it took a long time to get everybody back in relative coordination with one another. Not only was not a lot of research getting done, but a lot of people were getting killed out there in a very dangerous universe.

Also, just because you could jump into hyperspace didn't mean you knew where you were going. To be honest, by modern astrogation standards, it was a miracle everybody who engaged a hyperdrive wasn't killed. At one point, at the rate the population kept fragmenting, and its members dying, as they raced outward and away from Earth, it was statistically possible for humanity to reach zero viability within five years.

And thus the UNS had two prime directives. One was public, the other very secret. The public one was to keep humanity united in some form or fashion by providing a governing body. To keep the hundred new political experiments that had sprouted up across a dozen worlds somehow tethered to a single cohesive sense of humanity. Even as new alien species and their governments were starting to become players, folding themselves into the gossamer hyperdrive-connected worlds.

Hence the UNS Navy.

Hence the *Lexington*.

Directive Number Two, the secret directive, was to recover the tech and research from those lighthuggers the elites had run off in. The primary reason for secrecy was, of course, that if the UN could maintain a proprietary and controlling interest in anything new—anything discovered, developed, or stolen—then they'd have something with which to draw all the separate entities back to the table of galactic coherence. Away from the edge of zero viability.

And so it was that the dying prophetess whispered... that secret.

You knew it from the start, Casper accused himself. *You recognized something valuable. But the question is... did you know* how *valuable?*

"I embrace the Quantum... and the Quantum embraces me."

And so you look up at a man you've known as a friend since the time you were enslaved on the Obsidia... *and you just lie to him. Is that about right?*

"Nothing. Just babble. She's insane," Casper said to Rex as the soldiers all about them readied themselves to move deeper into the *Moirai.*

I had some idea, Casper admits to himself in the dream. In his observation of the dream. *To be honest, yes, I knew it was something big even then. I could... sense it.*

He was guilty of that. As he was of many far worse crimes.

"Was," said Rex. "She *was* insane. Now she's dead." He slapped in a new charge pack for his rifle. "We're going forward. Inner hab should be a few more decks in. You don't have to go with us, Cas. You can head back to the *Lex.* If we're not back in two hours, or you don't hear from us, lift off and get clear. Then hit the ship with a full spread of SSMs."

"I think we're in this for the long haul. We'll rescue her," Casper replied, and he didn't need to explain who "her" was. They both knew.

So you left the mangled body, the voice told Casper as he continued to watch that dream of events long done.

The prophetess, though at that moment no one in his little company, no one who had boarded this lost ship, this tragic wandering nightmare of a ghost ship, no one yet knew that those who could do the magic tricks were called prophetesses. Emissaries of something greater. Something powerful. Something found out there in the long dark.

Casper went forward with Rex and what remained of the company. The light infantry, moving in teams, checking corners and clearing abandoned rooms, headed deeper into the ship.

The clock was now meaningless. The soldiers' chronometers weren't working here inside the Dead Zone.

You know, Casper tells himself in the dream, *because for all the things you are, you were first an astronaut. A sailor of the stars. And you know that the* Moirai, *and thus the docked* Lexington, *has already entered the Dead Zone. A kind of Stellar Horse Latitudes no other ship has emerged from.*

A place of nightmares.

A place of lost ships.

And lost souls.

When Casper awoke, he remembered everything that had happened in the night before. A shadow passed across the wan morning light coming in through the cracked cockpit glass, filtered by the dense jungle that surrounded the beach and the river. And in that shadow was the desire to lie back down and give up.

Because...

Let's just add this up, Casper thought to himself in the silence.

The crash.

The monster that had destroyed what he'd tried to gather in order to survive the crash.

And the quest itself.

The quest of finding the Temple of Morghul. The temple the prophetesses had pointed the way toward.

Were they really called prophetesses? Or were they just that to you and you alone?

Why? Why come all this way to die alone on a planet beyond the love of the galaxies' embrace?

To save the Republic from itself.

To save the galaxy from itself.

He'd slept with his blaster rifle next to him. At this point in the expedition he was down to this one piece of working equipment. Nothing else could be counted on. Nothing else was known for sure. This and the jacket he was lying on were all that he truly had.

Why aren't you counting the bot? that other voice asked him.

He didn't bother to answer himself because he'd been thinking so much his thoughts were starting to babble. And that seemed too crazy for this early in the morning. He would save the talking to himself for the night, when he doubted his quest and needed to be reassured.

"I either get up," he whispered tiredly to the shattered glass of the cockpit, "or I never move from this spot."

He climbed down the ladder that led from the flight deck to the beach.

The bot had been dragging salvaged wreckage out onto the sand, and the little red-haired creature was going through it all, taking twisted pieces of once-useful items and beating them into a further uselessness.

"Urmo. Urmo. Urmo."

Give up now, whispered that other voice under the weight of everything that needed to be done. *Give up now... while you still can.*

Not yet, he replied.

And he went to see what else of value he could salvage from the jungle, and from the wreck, wherever it was.

10

There wasn't much to find. The ship had been trampled and tossed all about the jungle, its pieces lost to river and mud and bogs. But he had his bugout bag. His rifle. A blaster. The jacket. And some food.

The ennui of self-annihilation tried for him once more. The hopelessness of his situation washed over him as he cast his tired eyes over the wanton destruction of the vessel that had brought him here.

What had been the purpose of it? It was as if the giant thing...

Don't say monster, he told himself.

... had purposely followed him, followed the crash out to this lost spot in the jungle, to do nothing but trash and smash. To lower his chances of survival. To lower his chances of success.

As though it had been *sent*.

Or summoned?

As though the destruction had been personal.

He pushed all that away, because to personalize the attack, to attribute it to some dark sinister force, after he'd searched the galaxy for as long as he had for the clues that led to this place, to think now that monsters were being sent against him to prevent him from finding what he'd come for... it was just too much to even consider.

He turned and walked back to his new camp by the river.

He would run from monsters.

He would deal with the problems.

He would make his way forward and complete this epic quest begun so long ago within the Quantum Palace aboard the *Moirai*. He would find the temple the prophetesses had pointed toward, even though she hadn't known she was doing so.

As he headed back, he smelled smoke. And when he made the clearing, he saw the little creature sitting near the fire. Two huge, flat-mouthed, and large-fanged nightmare fish had been spitted and were roasting slowly over lazy smoke.

So there was food, at least. Though it had been made from monsters that lived in the river. Apparently.

And there was water.

Stay here and live out your days. Water and food. A camp. Sleeping in the wreckage of the ship. You'll make some kind of life.

And... just let the galaxy handle itself.

Did you ever think, that other part of his mind asked, that the galaxy didn't *ask* you to save it from itself? That it never had? And that it would, most likely, find a way to go on without you?

The little red-haired creature was muttering "Urmo" over and over as it fussed about the fire, testing the tenderness of the fish with one of its tiny, almost delicate paws. Fat dripped, and a flame leapt up to sizzle the hair on the little creature's arm. It yanked back its singed paw and shook a tiny fist at the fire comically.

And why, Casper wondered, why was that dream of what had happened so long ago running inside his mind like some linear entertainment for him to watch? He knew the end. He knew the tragedies, the losses, the horrors...

and yes, the *hope* of the trail that had led here. But why replay it? Why was it running at a pace he could not control? As though his memories were being viewed by someone else. As though he were providing them something.

Enjoyment?

Validation?

Confession?

They'd all died inside the *Moirai*.

Everyone... almost.

Or was it some kind of judgment? And if he passed could he move forward?

What was found on the *Moirai* was... something that could be wonderful. Something that, in the right hands, could save the galaxy from itself. And no one knew it but him. No one had seen the signs, followed the clues, taken the literal one-way leap of faith into the universal nothingness.

Isn't that how the mad think? that other voice asked. *That they're the only ones who see the things that cannot be seen. That they're the ones who can save everyone from themselves. That they have special powers.*

Who is watching the dream of all my memories? Who is judging me?

The little beast—he had decided to call the little creature "Urmo"—seemed to feel the meal was done. Urmo snatched one of the fish from the fire, blew on it, chanted "Urmo" over it with his eyes closed in some sort of beatific satisfaction, then fell on its flesh with tiny fangs and gusty relish. There was snorting. The creature's delight in eating the fish transformed it from a cute, almost puppet-like creature to a monster revealed.

It paused, looking up at Casper warily.

Casper reached a hand forward for the other spitted toothy nightmare fish. Urmo watched, waiting. Would it suddenly attack out of some territorial desire to protect its food, or would it share based on some kind of intelligence? The line was indistinguishable and unknowable until the deed was done. Until the line was crossed and teeth were bared. Or not.

Casper removed the fish. Urmo merely watched. So the little creature wasn't going to kill him.

But the fish might.

He took a bite. It was rather bland, but it was edible. It was sustenance. And it didn't kill him—yet.

He took a walk down to the lazy river's edge, drank cool water, and listened to the quiet of the jungle forest all around.

He put off deciding what to do next until the next morning. The hopelessness that had come over him had left him in no position to make a tactical decision of any kind, and he reasoned that in the morning he might feel better—and thus, be in a better state of mind to decide what to do next.

That night, after sitting by the fire and listening to nothing but the ever-silent forest and the occasional "Urmo," he fished around in the medical pouches of his bugout bag and found some tranquilizers. He knew they would cut down on the dreams. Maybe he just needed a good night's sleep. He popped two and rolled up in one of the surplus legionnaire mummy bags he'd brought in the cargo hold. He'd found it in a tree far from the wreckage.

And before he knew it he'd shifted from trying to think of nothing to thinking about the outer hull of the *Moirai*, the Martian infantrymen who would die there in its shadowy nightmare corridors, and his old friend Rex.

11

"Somethin' don't make sense," said Private LeRoy, who wouldn't make it. *Yes, that was the soldier's name,* thought Casper in the dream. *LeRoy.* And he would not survive the *Moirai.*

Casper moved with the Martian light infantry through the dark corridors of the outer hull. The marines were using lighting systems mounted on the barrels of their KSs to scan and pan the dark spaces that littered the derelict ship.

"Somethin' that don't make sense is these old colony ships..." the soldier said.

"Cut it, LeRoy," hissed Sergeant Trask. "First thing you need to learn, kid, nothin' 'bout Savages ever makes any sense."

Casper was right behind Sergeant Trask. There were two squads of Martian light infantry, plus Rex, the platoon sergeant, and Casper. Twenty-three of them went down into that massive ship. Only two would make it out. Casper did not count himself in this sum. Nor one other person.

"Captain," said Trask over the comm. He'd switched channels to the command team.

Casper realized after a second that the platoon sergeant was talking to him. Rex was technically a major in the Martian Light Infantry. He, Casper, was the captain of the *Lexington.*

Was.

Was the captain.

He *is* the captain. In the dream he is still the captain of the assault frigate *Lexington*.

"Yes, Sergeant," Casper replied.

"We in the Dead Zone yet?" the NCO asked.

Casper checked his watch—an old Omega Seamaster from Earth. A gift from his father when he graduated from the NASA academy.

"For about ten minutes, Sergeant," Casper replied, knowing the timepieces had started to work a little bit funny.

"So... we ain't dead yet, then?"

"Doesn't feel like it."

Ahead, past a deserted intersection where decimated piping hung from the ceiling like the tendrils of a witch's hair, stood the massive main door that should, according to the old schematics they'd downloaded off the archives, lead into the main hab.

"No one ever returns from here, do they?" the NCO asked. Still talking privately over the command channel. Still desperate to find out anything about the Dead Zone other than the ghost stories they all knew. As if Casper had been holding something back. Something that would save their lives despite the historical record.

Rex, in the lead, signaled to his men to cover the intersection. After the initial attack, the Savages had withdrawn deeper into the hull, but occasionally they'd all heard insane cackles off in the darkness, or abrupt gibbering laughter coming from long curving cross passages that disappeared into distant shadows.

"No. But we'll make it out, Sergeant," Casper replied as he watched Rex's killers go about their work.

They stacked around the big hatch that led into the inner hab. Expecting a big firefight. Ready to give someone on the other side of that hundreds-of-years-old lock the surprise of their very long life out here in the dark.

"You can't make that promise, sir," whispered Trask over the comm. Then he cut the link and hustled forward to adjust his men before the breach.

Rex signaled Casper to stay back with the fire support team and the big heavy they carried. The wicked-looking gun was aimed straight at the door. Anybody on the other side would be torn to pieces by its incredible volume of rapid-fire hyper-static charged shots. The gun heated up fast, and it didn't leave much standing once it had done its killing work.

This place brings back too many memories of the Obsidia, he thought in the seconds before breach. Many of the lighthuggers had been built by the same corporation, and the similarities were pronounced. But he blocked out the fifteen years he'd spent as a mindless slave on one of those ships. Blocked out the horrors his mind was trained to forget so that he could go on living.

Half the reason he'd stayed in the navy was to blast to shreds any Savage hulks they encountered without ever having to board one again. But then he'd found out the UN didn't want to destroy those ships. They wanted them investigated, searched, and looted.

Looted was what they really wanted.

Looted tech.

The dreams of the mad made real, for the profit of others.

Same as it ever was.

12

Beyond the central lock that led into the old ship's main hab was nothing but a vast open darkness. And this, Casper sensed, unnerved the grunts. All of them were killers. All of them had seen action in the Martian War and on more than a dozen planets and countless ships. They'd been around enough of the cosmos, back in the early hyperspace days, to have seen some pretty weird stuff. But there was something about this spooky old ship. Everything about it screamed "ghost ship."

The legendary Rama-class vessels were forty kilometers wide. Within the inner hab they should be looking at a living, breathing world with its own gravity, its own skies and clouds. Cities should be crawling across the inside of the cylinder, above, below and to the sides. A world inverted in upon itself. But instead of any of those things, the grunts and Casper were looking at nothing but darkness.

"We got air," murmured Sergeant Trask over the comm.

Casper knew Rex was studying every ounce of information he could glean before he made his next move. That had always been his way. He was slow most of the time, but when he needed to be, he was the quickest man alive. He'd left enough dead in his wake to make that abundantly clear to anyone who cared to search the public record.

"Patrol formation. Watch your sectors. First Squad, move out. Sergeant Trask, you take second. Don't bunch up," ordered Rex.

Without hesitation, the foremost grunts moved out onto the loading ramp that rose up to the surface, the ground as it were, of that man-made world that gazed in upon itself. When they reached the lip and saw there was some bare illumination coming from far away down-cylinder, creating some sort of constant twilight, Casper knelt and felt the ground.

It was dirt. Real dirt.

Just like on the *Obsidia*.

They stood on a vast spreading plain that curved up into the sky and then hung there, marking the ghostly outlines of ruined cities above. The wan light that came from down-cylinder made the buildings that stood between them and the light source look like tombstones in a graveyard at midnight. Or scarecrows in an abandoned field deep in late winter.

"We got a city two clicks at... uh... cardinal directions ain't working in here, sir. My HUD's fritzing. Let's call it two-eighty on the compass."

That had come from one of the grunts on point. Corporal Davis. The Martian infantrymen were wearing combat helmets that looked like modern versions of the old Spartan war helmet. They had internal HUDs displaying all the comm and tactical information in real time. Casper wore a thin SmartEye over his cornea that gave him similar HUD access. The Terran Navy didn't issue armor.

"Shoulda brought drones," one of the grunts said over comm. "Coulda got this place hatched in seconds."

"Shoulda, coulda, woulda," someone else chided.

"Cut it," Trask ordered.

Trask seemed much more worried than any of his troops. Like he'd been in enough bad situations to smell one coming on. Maybe, thought Casper, the young feel too invulnerable to be worried when confronted with the evidence that they are most likely already dead.

Or maybe they just don't care.

Or, some voice reminded him, *maybe that's how they're dealing with the unknown.*

"Move out... toward that city," Rex said. "Contact and we break into teams. Bounding over watch. Assault through any resistance. Find a prisoner if you can." Worry didn't affect Rex. There was only the mission, and he was always on it. And of all the things Casper held on to, right now at this not-wanting-to-be-here moment, he held on to that. Rex had gotten him through the *Obsidia*. Maybe they'd survive this one too.

Crossing an open field, an actual open field where a farm had once been and now dying tall grass grew, they passed a scarecrow.

As though there had once been crows here.

One of the grunts had just reached out an armored glove to touch the hanging shrouds that were the scarecrow's rags when a bullet took his head off in a clean spray that misted everyone near him.

"Contact!" someone screamed redundantly, and Martian infantrymen were hitting the dirt, dirt probably harvested off some asteroid in the long trek away from Earth.

And now bullets, actual bullets were streaking over their heads. They were tearing through the tall dead grass that didn't move in the permanent twilight. As the subsonic rounds passed through the dead brown stalks they made a sound like corn husks being rubbed together.

"First Squad returning fire!" one of the team leaders shouted over comm. But Casper couldn't see anything. He can only hear the spooling whines of their energy weapons hurling hot disks of destabilized energy out into the shadows.

"It's coming from that berm!" screamed another infantryman over the comm. "Tagging it."

Casper could see the visualized battlefield in his HUD now. The farm crossed a series of dry levees and berms, and the enemy, according to the tag, was using one of these levees to fire at the column.

"Trask! Provide a base of fire on their position," said Rex over the comm.

"Roger that, sir! Second Squad firing!"

Everyone near Casper, including the heavy weapon team, opened up on the levee.

"First Squad moving!" shouted Rex over the frenetic energy fire. "Follow me, First Squad!"

Casper watched as Rex's unit, depicted on the overlay map inside his HUD, attempted to flank the levee. Men were being cut down in both squads. Near Casper, one of the heavy gunners went down. Casper low-crawled over to the man, who was gasping, clutching at a sucking chest wound where a bullet had smashed through his ablative armor. Pink frothy bubbles appeared around the edges of the wound.

Rex's SmartEye assessed the wound and told him how to treat it, but he didn't need the instruction. He'd done this before. He pulled a thermal adhesive patch from his gear and slapped it over the man's wound.

The SmartEye told him that blood pressure and pulse were both bottoming out. The man was dying despite Casper's efforts.

"Start chest compressions," the HUD ordered him. Except there was no chest. It was all a bloody mess.

The man was whispering something, and Casper leaned over to hear. That action saved his life; even as he leaned down, he felt a speeding bullet pass just over his back.

"I didn't forget nothin'," the man whispered between shallow gasps.

Casper pulled off the man's helmet. Hoping to get him more air.

"I didn't forget... nothin'," he repeated.

And then the kid's eyes just glazed over, watching the twilight above. He was gone.

His name, according to the unit roster in the HUD, was Private Gordon.

And that was when the ground began to shake. Once. Twice. Again. And again. And in the dream, it's almost familiar to Casper. And he remembers that, in the distant future, his ship will be destroyed by a monster who makes those same sounds. The ponderous artillery strike footsteps of something giant coming this way, one after the other.

So I am *dreaming*, he thinks in the dream. *This is all just a dream.*

And that's when the infantry saw the huge mech coming for them above the dead fields of a dead world traveling through the Dead Zone of outer space.

The mechanized armor was huge. Frankensteinian. A monstrosity of machine and nightmare. And it was coming from the opposite direction, as though all the gunfire was merely a trap intended to distract the Martian light infantry, and now came the coup de grâce. It hit them in their flank, and Casper barely scrambled away before it tore the heavy weapons team to shreds with claws and spinning saws.

Rex was screaming orders over the comm to be heard and obeyed. He knew the mech made the infantrymen feel helpless, and that without orders the mindless fear would take hold and send them all in a hundred useless directions. In seconds he had the infantry falling back, with teams providing covering fire. Running. A full retreat through the dry dead fields.

The towering mech nightmare chased them through the twilight world of the ship. A nightmare at their heels.

Casper awoke with a start.

In the dream he was screaming. Because the hulking mech had caught him and pulled him apart by the limbs. He saw everyone racing away from him. Leaving him. Even Rex. The looks in their eyes, behind their faceplates, had told him how hopeless his situation was.

Now awake, he saw the campfire on the beach. Saw Urmo sitting before it, the smoke rising up to meet his dreaming monster face. The little goblin looked peaceful, as if his dreams were good to him.

As if dreams ever could be, thought Casper.

And he fell back to watch the rest of the night pass through the shattered glass of the canopy of the ruined ship.

13

They left the river the next day. Casper carried the bag with the medical supplies, which now also held a few tools he'd managed to scavenge from the wreckage, a small tarp, and a hatchet. He wore his holdout blaster and carried his hunting rifle. He'd strapped a survival knife to his hip. THK-133 carried the heavy blaster and a rucksack overloaded with survival rations. Rations that would last for up to five years, unless they were relied upon as the sole food source, in which case they'd last for about thirty days.

Before they left the beach, Casper oriented himself. He established north and was pleased to find that great hairy ropes of black moss tended to gather along the north sides of the massive swamp trees. They would follow the ship's trail of ruin backward, away from the crash, toward the enigmatic statue on the high desert plateau.

He considered climbing up into the trees to get the lay of the land and possibly see some features to navigate by, but the thought of falling and ending up with a broken leg or arm dissuaded him. And this planet was so far beyond the galactic lens that navigating by the stars was all but impossible.

With a final sigh that expressed both resignation and frustration, he hefted the hunting rifle blaster and announced, "Time to move out, 133."

The bot turned and headed off. "You've probably forgotten that my internal navigation system can establish a reliable course to take us back to the statue you wish to look at, master. I could sense you feebly attempting to plan your way across this planet... and while it was fun to watch, your very pathetic odds of survival were made abundantly clear. Allow me to lead you to your destiny, master."

He'd forgotten the bot had that capability, and for a moment it comforted him. But the comfort soon passed, and he found himself unable to totally trust the bot. He'd follow it, but he vowed to keep his own dead reckoning running. Cross-checking everything for reasons he couldn't put his finger on. It just felt like the safe thing to do.

Casper scanned his temporary campsite once more, and his gaze fell on the little creature. Urmo. Casper had almost completely forgotten about the thing. While Casper and the bot had made their preparations, the strange red-haired beast had simply sat before the cold fire, his tiny little walking stick across his knobby knees. As always, he seemed interested, in an incomprehensible way, in anything they were doing.

Casper wondered what Urmo would do once they began to leave.

And then, without prompting, Urmo hopped off the log, grunted, and began to follow the bot, muttering, "Urmo."

Casper shook his head and not for the first time asked himself what he was doing here. He'd planned this expedition to the last detail. He'd had to. And now, at the very doorstep of his prize, he feared his plans were for naught. The idea of finding the Temple of Morghul on foot, of exploring an entire planet of whose geography he had not the slightest clue, never mind the giant lizards and whatever else was out there... it all seemed just a little too impossible. He might as well have been on the other side of the galaxy.

Ahead, the tactical hunter-killer bot disappeared into the dense jungle foliage like it was stalking something, or on patrol in some terrible conflict where mercilessness was ever the order of the day. It was followed by a creature that looked more like a child's puppet than an actual living being, walking stick in hand, just out for a morning stroll.

Casper took the first step.

The first step is always the hardest, he reminded himself. Especially if you were someone like him. Someone who had to finish what was started. Had to know what was out there on the other side of all the unknowns. Once you'd taken that first step, committed, then the ten thousand that followed were easy. Because you knew you'd never stop. Never. Ever.

That just wasn't you.

THE LESSON OF FOCUS

The Master has brought the student into a howling wilderness. A place of cold ice, cutting snow, and howling wind.

Whether this lesson has happened before, or after, or at any time is irrelevant. Again, time has no meaning in the temple, and reality is best thought of as a candy store, in that there are many selections to choose from.

The student stands before the Master, shivering on the frozen ice. They are on some kind of glacier. The air bites cruelly into the skin and stings at the eyes with its frost. It hurts to breathe. The lungs ache because the oxygen is so very cold.

Within moments the student knows that to stay here is to die. He doubts he can last much longer than the few minutes he foresees.

"Live..." says the Master in his swallowed and gravelly voice. "Moment to moment... live one must. Other things... things that cloud and haunt our minds... those things must be pushed away in order to focus. And to live... is to focus. When you have blocked out all the distractions... live you will then."

The storm surges on a banshee's cry, casting snow and ice in whirlwinds all about, only to die down and reveal that the student is alone on the icy glacier. Alone in all its vast cruel emptiness.

The student turns. Turns looking for the Master, and does not find him. It is so cold that though the panic of being suddenly abandoned has caused his adrenaline to spike, the feeling dies off in seconds, and the student thinks of just lying down on the ice and going to sleep. It is that intensely cold. It is the cold of despairing for your life.

And of course the wind is a constant howl that sets his nerves of edge. A shrill whistle from far off within this featureless frozen waste that says warmer places of friendship and love are just lies told to wicked children abandoned in the dark.

Move, thinks the student to himself. Move and stay warm.

And so he does. If just to stay warm.

He has only his clothes and the old jacket from that other life, and they are poor defenses against the howling icy wind that is both constant and relentless here on the glacier.

He goes upslope, into the blinding white snowstorm, at times unable to distinguish between the land and the sky. He climbs because he feels that down must lead to some icy canyon or unseen crevasse that he might slide into helplessly.

And if that were to happen?

This is a serious question.

There are things in the temple that have been revealed to be a simulation. He *felt* himself being stomped to death, and cut, and burned, only to find it wasn't true. But not everything is a simulation. He has seen things within the temple that indicate there have been other students—many of whom failed.

And if the Master's ambivalence toward him can be used as an indicator, then his own failure is definitely a possibility. The Master seems to care little for his student's survival. And maybe, possibly, there is even more to this. Maybe the Master thinks the student is arrogant in the extreme for trying to learn. And so the Master is daring him to try, while knowing the inevitable failure that is to come.

The student is thinking these things as he crawls on numb hands and frozen knees up the icy glacier. And now the wind is howling so high up in the upper registers of sound that he can no longer think the thoughts he was trying to distract himself with.

At the top of the glacier he reaches an icy bowl. The wind is howling over the lip, and flying debris nicks the student's face. All about the bowl are strange stones, and as the wind whips through these stones, it wails—a high, tortured soprano.

The sticks.

It is his mind that focuses on the debris. Broken pieces of wood, sticks, carried here from some forest beyond the other side of the glacier. Their presence conveys so much. But the element that means the most in this freezing moment of imminent death is... *heat.*

He begins to race about, gathering up the sticks, ignoring the shrill cry of the wind while he tries to remember how to start a fire with snow.

He has done this before. Once. A long time ago, in a life that doesn't matter anymore. Not when one has become lost within the temple.

One must come to the end of one's self in the temple. That was the first lesson.

When he has a pile of sticks, he throws himself to the snow in the lee of the bowl, where the wind is the least brutal. Ignoring the painful burning of the ice on his frozen hands, he begins to burrow into the side of the drift. Pulling, pushing, packing, the work progresses steadily. In no time he has an ice cave, and he wonders if it will fall in and crush him...

But he is freezing.

And the wind is howling.

He has forgotten why he is here. That is how desperate this moment is. There is no larger picture of all the things that brought him to this moment. That brought him into the temple.

There is only survival.

He gets the fire started by tearing off a piece of his jacket and using his body to shield it from the wind. He cups some ice, forms it, molds it into a lens of compacted snow.

A sun floats high above. Somewhere above the howling winds and the wan, overcast sky, a star burns down on this nameless world. Lying here, feeling himself go numb and drifting into a sleep that promises so much more than just rest, he despairs. He will never get the kindling to ignite. It seems like some miracle that has never happened, could never happen. Or only happens for other people.

He has closed one eye and the other is just a slit when it ignites. Smoking gently.

As carefully and as quickly as he can, the student moves to the woodpile just inside the cave. And yes... he gets a fire going. And very carefully he gets deeper inside the cave, into a grotto of ice where he can stay warm.

For the next few days the student's life is nothing but gathering sticks that were once wind-driven debris, melting water to drink, and trying to drown out the shifting, howling wind that never lets up and never dies down.

But soon the hunger screams deep inside him. It is the hunger, much more than the wind, that is on the verge of driving him insane. He hears the voice of the Master... but he has forgotten the meaning of words.

He makes a spear and goes out to hunt.

To kill and find food. Any food.

And he finds the three-headed snow leopard. He is so hungry and tired he cares not whether he lives or dies, only that he eats. So when the three-headed cat comes at him, all jaws and saber teeth, he attacks with the fire-hardened spear, thrusting it straight for the body of the charging leopard.

The leopard raises one snow-white paw and bats the sharpened stick aside, snapping it in two.

Then the three-headed cat comes after the student. One head rears back to yowl in victory, while the other two, open-jawed, lunge for his throat in killer fury.

Because the student has learned the Lesson of Flying at some other point of never-time within the temple, he leaps away to a fantastic height. It's a short trick—and a trick is all it is.

The leopard scrambles in a flurry of claw-thrown snow and comes for him in a tremendous burst of speed and screeching. As the leopard leaps, the student dives. His fatigue is gone, replaced by a sudden awareness that death is indeed imminent. He doubts it will be a tableau this time. An endless tableau he will be allowed to repeat.

There are no do-overs.

The leopard drags a claw through his jacket, and the student reaches the broken spear, half-buried in the drifting snow. Because it is broken, it is now more knife than spear, and a knife it must be. He pivots, sees the leopard leaping, and falls back.

The cat embraces him with its paws and fetid breath.

But by then he has jammed the knife up and into the wild animal's belly. The student twists it and drags the stake as much as he can. All three of the cat's heads yowl pitifully.

It dies there on the ice.

He drags the beast back to his cave, his ears beaten almost to deafness by the howling wind. He skins the cat, then eats the meat.

His days after that become the gathering of sticks, the melting of ice, the hunting of three-headed snow leopards, and the scraping and curing of the hides. In time the cave is close and cozy. Warm and safe.

But he can never block out the howling wind.

And he despairs that he will ever leave this place.

Three years pass.

For the most part he has forgotten the Master, though there are some nights he remembers the temple. Its bells and smoke and silences. And that voice. He has dreams and sometimes nightmares of his other life. That life forgotten before.

But now...

Now it is wind.

Ice.

And death.

He walks the glacier dressed in skins. A great moving bear of a man. He walks the glacier looking for a way off of it. As though that is somehow important. And he knows there must be a forest somewhere. A forest that brings the dead wood to his cave in his bowl with the stones that make the wind howl and keen. The wind is passing over the graves of ghosts, drawing out their hysteria and misery. Reminding them that their torment is never-ending. That there is no peace for the wicked.

But he finds no way off the high glacier. Every pass and path is too dangerous.

He searches along a jagged crevasse that looks so deep in its iridescent blue bottoms that he wonders if it is depthless. He wonders, if he should decide to step off into its nothingness... he wonders how long he'll fall.

He never finds the edge of the glacier at the bottom of the descent. It just seems to go on and on, and he is reluctant to tread any farther from his cave. But the cats come from somewhere. He thinks they live in long-ranging tunnel systems beneath the ice. He will not go down into these. He would not be able to fight well down there. And there might be many of the nightmare cats with three heads and long saber-tooth fangs.

One cat badly mauls him across his back.

It's a vicious battle, and he barely survives. He won't be able to hunt for a week after.

But he wins.

And he never doesn't hear the wind. Never doesn't hear its howl. If he gets used to one pitch, it changes to another that bothers him even worse than the last.

One day, when he has meat for the week, and water for the day, when the sound of the wind bothers him so much he can't stand it anymore, he goes out from his cave.

If he buries the stones, the wind won't be able to pass over, and the disconcerting notes and tones won't sound. He hopes this. Sweet perfect silence seems like a kind of salvation to him. To even imagine it reminds him that there are other worlds than this.

He tries to bury the stones, but the wind fights him. It sweeps the sleet and ice from them before he can bury more than a few.

But he does notice something.

He notices that, for a moment, the pitch changed.

He bends to one crescent-shaped stone and wonders if he can't pick it up and move it inside the cave where the wind can't pass over it.

But it has a weight beyond its size. Like it's some trick weight at a carnival run by cheaters and hucksters who not only take your money but also like to make you feel weak and stupid. The rock cannot be lifted.

But it can be easily turned. He pivots the stone—and notices the barest change in the howl of the wind.

For a while he plays with the stones. Randomly shifting them. In brief moments there seems almost to be a harmony emerging. But inevitably the music turns discordant and drives a fresh spike into his brain.

In time the student returns to his ice cave. Throughout that long wind-howling night he listens and thinks. Remembering that certain stones made certain notes, pitches, tones, even timbres.

He lies awake, thinking.

In the morning he returns to the field of stones and begins to adjust them once more. There are hundreds of stones. He tries random configurations and never lucks out. Never gets it just right. But the wind teases him, hinting that there's a key to be unlocked if he can just find it. Each new combination reminds him that he never will.

The day passes and turns to night, but his new obsession takes him right into the long darkness. He continues adjusting stones and listening for the differences made. He makes a horrible wind-burnt sour face if a note is wrong, and he laughs triumphantly if somehow a little chorus of stones, or a snatch of harmony, comes to him in a sudden gust atop the icy plateau.

It is late when he remembers that he has not had a drink of water all day. He crawls into his cave, tired and dehydrated, because the cold and the wind can dehydrate much worse than any desert.

He drinks the melted water and lies next to the fire, listening to the wind in his dreams.

In the morning he chews some cold meat absently and returns to the stones. Now he tries systems and patterns. He works all day at this and into the night, remembering, just barely, to drink and eat as he does so.

On the fourth day he goes out to stare at the stones. The wind taunts him. Lies to him. Tells him that there is a solution to be found. Promises that this will waste his time. That this will kill him. That it will lead him too far into hunger and thirst to survive.

If he keeps this up he will be too weak to fight the cats.

But like a slave to addiction, he bends to his task once again, expecting a different outcome, and he is soon lost in the insanity of the puzzle.

Days pass.

The meat is gone.

He only barely remembers to drink melted snow water.

Now he takes the snow and melts it in his mouth. It burns his raw and ragged wind-burnt throat.

His voice is a croak. A hollow croak. It is a cracking croak on the morning he finally harmonizes the last stone and the howl of the wind reaches its perfect harmony, a multi-tone chorus vibrating on a single note...

... and the howl fades to nothing.

Silence.

Beautiful.

Sweet.

Silence.

He falls to his knees and hears the croak that his dry husky coughing laugh has become. He hears that and only that in the yawning sweet silence.

He basks in that silence.

And then sound returns.

A white noise hush. The wind, far off, distant, moving through... trees.

He stands and stumbles away from the bowl, never to return.

He follows the soft broom whisk noise beyond a crevasse he'd always been wary of. And hours later he stumbles down into a high alpine forest. Here there are trees. Water. Game. And the land leads down into a valley that seems, from this great height, to be blossoming into coming spring.

He will live.

He falls back against a warm tree and smiles. He sinks onto the twig-laden forest floor and listens to the sweet sound of the quiet wind whispering in the treetops above him.

And the Master comes.

In the forest dark, in the night, the Master comes. The student has built a fire of sweet-smelling woods.

He recognizes the Master.

It has been many years.

He remembers the command. The lesson required of him.

And the Master speaks, for the Lesson of Focus is now done.

"Live moment to moment... one must. Haunt our minds things do. Unimportant these are. Focus, or you will die."

The Master smiles. But it is not a warm smile, or a friendly smile. It is a smile that knows worse things are coming. A cruel smile that delights to see what may become, or not become.

14

The fetid jungle was already reclaiming the scorched earth the falling starship had carved in its wake. They followed the long burnt scar, and within an hour they'd passed beyond the point of initial impact, where the ship's repulsor fields had first smashed the treetops.

They continued walking for the rest of the day, and it was hard going because there were no trails. They had to weave around murky pools of green, moss-laden swamp water, and maneuver past giant trees that had fallen and lay rotting. The heat grew, and the air became like an oven. Casper's shirt and pants were soaked with sweat.

They found a stream miles from the crash, and Casper tested it with a small survival scanner. It was good, or at least its burbling course contained nothing *known* to kill anyone back in the galaxy.

Casper dropped his pack and got down on all fours to dip his canteen cup into its coolness. The cup would also attempt to purify the water. Its advanced nano-forged construction could purify, chill, or heat liquids to a boil. None of this was needed though.

As Casper sat drinking the cool water, he ruminated on the fact that there were no trails. No animal trails. No trails left by hunter-gatherer-type civilizations. Other than the insects, and the strange unseen birds that cried out at soul-chilling moments, there were no other life forms here.

And then he remembered the giant lizard that had destroyed what was left of his ship. It had left a trail. A trail of flattened trees and wanton destruction. A single trail that led away from the crash site, as though, having done what it had come for, the beast had retraced its steps.

Despite the cleared path, Casper had chosen not to follow that trail. For reasons of self-preservation.

A sudden hopelessness caught him as he once more considered the desperateness of his situation. He raised the cup to his lips, breathed in the iron sharpness of the water, and concentrated on solving the problem. He'd learned that back in NASA. There was always a solution. Or so they'd taught him.

But what if he finally found what he'd come for... and there was no way off this planet? No way back to the galaxy proper. What if he was doomed to live here on this planet, lost between the galaxies, for as long as his body's machinery allowed him to live? And even the members of the Pantheon of the *Obsidia* had no idea how long that would be. As extensionists, their only goal had ever been for more life, regardless of the cost and no matter the length. *A little bit more* was all that mattered to the mummies of that hell ship.

That's what Rex had called them when they led the rebellion on that ship. He'd called the Pantheon "soul-sucking mummies."

He'd been right.

And that was when Casper saw it. In the stream bed.

He was tranced out, back there on the *Obsidia* once more. Trying not think about anything other than the absolute hopeless folly this expedition had become. Trying not to think that he'd turned his life into a long-lived hell trapped forever on a planet no one would ever find.

And he saw a carved stone.

A *shaped* stone. Something that evidenced tools, construction, and therefore... a civilization. Which was what he'd come here to find. A lost civilization that held the secrets of a great power beyond anything the Republic, and the galaxy, could ever imagine.

He put one hand down into the cold water and felt the ancient stone. It was only one of many—the stream was lined with them. Perhaps they'd once been part of some canal or aqueduct. Some redirected course of water. A common thing for any civilization.

He cast his eyes across the jungle. The ground was covered in gnarled and warped trees, moss, vines, and strange red ferns. But he knew—he knew—that underneath the undergrowth were other carved stones. That this, once, long ago, had been something that someone had *built*.

The stream flowed from a hill above. A hill implied a temple. And even if it wasn't *the* temple, it would, most likely, contain a clue that led to it.

He pulled his hatchet off his ruck and went to a large clump of vines. He hacked at them, clearing them away. Underneath the clustering mass he found more shaped stones: the remains of a pedestal and the barest portion of a rising column that had been broken off who knew how long ago.

Ancient runes were carved around the pedestal. He threw the hatchet down and pulled at the clutching vines, revealing more of the runes. He heard himself shrieking and felt his hope returning.

He knew these runes. Knew them well.

He'd seen them in the *Moirai*.

He'd chased them in all the years since.

In an ancient library on the desert world of Uraam, he'd found an actual book. An old-school, ink-printed-on-page book that no one in the library had even known was there. Runes just like these had been copied on the brittle pages within. None of it was intelligible. Nothing beyond a note left in the front of the book, written in semi-modern ink.

Found in the wreck of the Halstead's Rhone out in Jumai. –T. Noc

Halstead's Rhone had been one of the ships someone had built during the Exodus. Who Halstead was, Casper didn't know. Just another kid, probably, much like he'd been, with the gumption to put together a hyperdrive and get off planet using a prefab ceramic hull. And where Halstead had found the book was also unknown.

T. Noc, on the other hand, was known. He had been a scout in the Republic Scout Service seven hundred and fifty years ago. At some point he'd found the book, and at some point after that, it had found its way to the library on Uraam.

Casper kept the book. Had it analyzed. Transcribed.

And in time, translated.

It was a long form epic of an ancient warrior known as Gogamoth. It was striking in its similarity to other ancient epics, from *Beowulf* to *Gilgamesh*.

The translation was imperfect, as all translations are. There was a chance that every time the epic mentioned "the Sea," what was really meant was "the Stars." And other translation options might have put a different spin altogether on the ancient fable. But as best as Casper understood, the original had begun as follows...

Gogamoth Sailed the Seas from the Lost Home Beyond the World and came to Land of Angry Kraken.

And Gogamoth did battle against Ur-Zyxgar and subdued the Behemoth-Leviathan with his Invisible Hammer. Many-armed People did obeisance at his great powers of Chankar and in time he leaped across the Sea to Lost Home Beyond the World once again.

Casper had, of course, tweaked the translation options, analyzed for deeper meaning, and drawn his own conclusions. Had he taken the time, at this moment, to reference his research, he would have found the following annotated version...

Gogamoth Sailed the Seas (Stars) *from the Lost Home Beyond the World* (a planet beyond the Galactic Lens) *and came to Land of Angry Kraken* (Tennar).

And Gogamoth did battle against Ur-Zyxgar (the Tennar deity known as Ash-Kaxor) *and subdued the Behemoth-Leviathan* (ancient Tennarian records use this as an early name for the legendary tyrannasquid) *with his Invisible Hammer* (psionics?). *Many-armed People* (Tennar) *did obeisance* (became mindless slaves like thralls) *at his great powers of Chankar* (Tennarian name for the mysterious pyramids left by the Ancients on most planets across the galaxy) *and in time he leaped* (faster-than-light travel) *across the Sea* (Stars) *to the Unknown* (not part of the stellar map) *Lost Home Beyond the World once again.*

And now, here on this forsaken planet, were more of those same runes. And along with these were pictoglyphs depicting humanoid lizards battling against other alien humanoids. Insect people. Possibly.

That ancient book had contained the first reference to the Temple of Morghul. It had placed it at "*across the Sea to Lost Home Beyond the World.*"

The place of ancient power that Gogamoth had made his own.

But it was the mention of the Dark Wanderer that first told Casper he was on the right trail. Deep within the book's brittle pages, a book bound in some kind of leather that had resisted categorical analysis, he'd found these words.

And Gogamoth was a servant of the Dark Wanderer, whose power was his and his alone. And even Gogamoth did tremble at the terribleness of the un-named demon.

On the *Moirai*, all those years ago, they would meet the Dark Wanderer. The possessor of the power the prophetesses had barely been able to wield. Finding that book with its crazed and snake-like runes, and then later a direct mention of an entity he had personally seen within the worst and last moments of the ancient lighthugger, had sent a cold chill up his spine within the deeps of the dark and warm library. And... it had confirmed that there was a trail that led to this planet, a place beyond the known. *The Lost Home*. It confirmed that there was a place where the power he sought... waited to be found.

"133," said Casper breathlessly as he sat back on his haunches and stared in disbelief at the runes he'd uncovered. Runes just like those he'd found in a forgotten library long ago. Letting their weirdness wash over him. Letting their unbelievable realness comfort him. "Scout the hill. We'll camp here tonight."

"As you command, master. Though I can tell from my sensors that that there are no life forms here for me to kill. Other than you and the Urmo. It seems a rather boring place, though I am always open to surprise attacks by hordes of combatants who are willing to die badly for some cause they desperately believe in. I have always found that quite amusing. I doubt I will get that opportunity today. Still, one can hope."

The homicidal bot went off, heavy blaster rifle at the ready, stalking through the undergrowth, on alert for anything from a MK9 main battle tank to the fabled OGRE mech of the Krogon Reich.

Casper cleared away more vines from other stones, relishing in each new discovery. Watching the story of the carved lizard people come to life. Seeing the symbol that represented the enigmatic pyramids. Remembering the one he'd seen inside the lighthugger—on the night battle with the crazies that came for the rest of the light infantry in that abandoned city on the curving plain.

15

Fifteen of them had made it to the abandoned city. Out there, across that insane landscape no sentient mind failed to struggle with, were other structures. Abandoned cities. Enigmatic ruins. And halfway up the cylinder from their current position lay a strange pyramid. Just like the pyramids the first star travelers of the Exodus had seen on so many other worlds.

Everyone had ended up calling them the ruins of the Ancients. They defied explanation, and their secrets remained undiscovered.

On every planet where they were found, the pyramids were formed of local rock and organized in complexes that involved one massive pyramid and three smaller ones. They were usually located in the deepest and most forsaken wastes, and they were in no way connected with any other planetary civilizations, modern or ancient. They served no apparent purpose.

And... the pyramids were impenetrable. Unreadable by the most powerful of sensors, even by deep-scan radar. They could not be destroyed or damaged. Not even the heaviest cutting tools had marred them in the slightest.

The galactic excitement at their discovery died down when they refused to reveal their secrets. Now they were merely there, everywhere, and no one really much cared.

Theories, and that's all they were, posited that they had existed long before the Galactic Republic—on the order of possibly millions of years. It was assumed that they were created by some ancient civilization that had also once spanned the galaxy. This other galactic civilization had had their heyday, and then they'd mysteriously died out, for no known reason. That dead civilization was the living embodiment of the argument against the Fermi Paradox, which anyway had pretty much been destroyed with the advent of the hyperdrive. The answer to "Where is everyone?" had been: *everywhere*. They just didn't have faster-than-light travel.

Not until mankind came along.

Everywhere humanity went, they found life. And not just bizarre and hard-to-understand alien life, though they found that too. Humanity also found a multitude of humanoid life forms much like themselves. This had been the source of endless discussion in the field of xenobiology.

But the ruins of the Ancients, the strange pyramids that seemed almost to curl, though the math and measurements said they did not, were the real response to the Fermi Paradox. They served as proof that there *had* been a galaxy-spanning civilization before our own—a civilization that had come and gone. The Ancients were a Galactic Republic from long ago.

Yet here, in an Exodus lighthugger, was one of those pyramids. How could that be? The last thing Casper expected, as he ran for his life, old-school Savage bullets whipping past him through the dry brown bio-engineered corn still growing in the fields outside the dead city on the curving plain inside a massive ship, was to see an Ancients' pyramid inside the main hab.

All Casper could hear was his heavy breathing, coming in ragged gasps, as he dashed forward. In the moment before he saw that pyramid up above him, hanging in the sky that was merely more of the dark plain they were fleeing across, he would've told you that they were all about to die. They were too deep inside the ship. Too outnumbered. And heading into more of the unknown.

This was how everyone got killed.

They were at least four miles from the entrance that could take them back up through the outer decks to the only ship that could get them out of the Dead Zone. A Dead Zone no one had ever gotten out of.

And those four miles between them and the *Lex* were overrun with long-running science experiments gone horribly awry. On this ship, man had left his humanity at the door and opted for the next step—seeking some kind of godhood, ripe for the taking, if we would just let go of ourselves and grasp it. If we were willing to become monsters in the process.

Casper threw himself onto the dry dirt below the field of wild dead corn. He sucked in lungfuls of the cold, stale air as though there were little and less of it in each frantic second. All around, the electric fire of the Martian infantry mixed with the hiss and whip of Savage bullets, actual bullets like those used by ancient bands of tribal jihadis back on Earth. Hundreds of enemies closed on their position.

"Sergeant Trask!" shouted Rex over the comm, his voice mixing with the sound of automatic weapons fire up close and personal. "Fall back to the city and secure a perimeter. First Squad will hold here until you do. Standing by for your confirmation."

Trask's fear was evident in his voice as he responded. "Roger that, sir, will have a perimeter set up in the next five. Trask out."

Casper listened to all this and was struck by a thought.

Who was their Prometheus?

Who would bring the gift of godhood to the savages seeking it?

Who gave them the prophetesses?

Because... didn't there have to be someone to *give* the gift? It couldn't just be taken. Could it? They hadn't just made that. Made a human who could do real live magic? Someone had come. Someone had shown them the trick of space magic.

Private LeRoy threw himself down next to Casper.

"Dig in, sir. 'Bout to get real hairy and all."

A moment later a wall of screaming Savages came charging through the stands of corn like demons howling for living flesh. A second after that a hot jet of flaming liquid fuel lanced out across their axis of advance.

LeRoy screamed and whooped.

Casper recoiled in horror. Fire aboard a ship, as every astronaut knew since time immemorial, was the devil's friend. It was the worst thing that could happen in an oxygen-rich environment. It could consume all your breathable air in moments. And though the *Moirai* was like a world unto itself, it was still, at its basest definition, just a ship in the void. Its oxygen was a finite thing in a bottle.

"When you got to kill everyone in the most gruesome way possible... always pick the flamethrower!" LeRoy whooped and shouted. Then he opened up with his KS, shooting into the flaming corpses that wandered about, writhing in pain and eternal agony, their flesh and machinery melting.

The energy blasts punched gaping holes in them, carrying away flaming debris to ignite the fields beyond. Out there, other Savages could be seen in the firelight, their advance checked. Some ran off back into the darkness. And off to Casper's left stood Rex, pumping out short spurts of flaming fuel from a small but heavy rifle, creating a barrier of leaping flames between them and the Savages. The Savages' keening wail rose into a howl of torment.

The mech loomed above the firefight, its guns pivoting to some other section of the field, spooling up and hosing everything over there with bright bursts of gunfire in excess. Giant brass ejecting shells gleamed in the hellish light of Rex's flamethrower as they showered down into the corn.

Rex sprayed the mech with a hot liquid jet of burning napalm. Flames raced across the thing as they connected with some badly maintained oil-laden section. The pilot tried to back away from the fight, but within seconds the entire piece of equipment was crawling with racing fire. A hatch popped open and a figure crawled from the mech, but it was consumed by the greedy flames and collapsed half in and half out of the burning armored walker.

From Casper's view among the igniting cornstalks, it was like watching some mythical giant being burned in effigy at Fall's End.

And then, above all this, he came.

The Dark Wanderer.

They'd find out later that's what he—not *it*, but definitely *he*—was called.

He came through the press of Savages beyond the leaping Halloween fire that turned everything on the dark shadowy plain into a hellish orange. He passed through the drifting smoke and strode past creatures that screamed while being roasted alive, once-men beasts that howled in a torment that seemed eternal. The Dark

Wanderer came through all this battle mayhem turned autumnal festival. He came in seemingly above them.

Not as though he was merely taller than them, which he was, but above them, as though he were floating. A dark angel that ruled over these wicked half-human, half-machine goblins in a fantasy not written by a sane or rational mind. He ignored their mad press to get away from the flame-spitting devil Rex had become.

The Dark Wanderer came through the flames.

Rex cut the bursts of pumping fuel igniting into flame and issued a command over the squad comm. As though he, Tyrus Rex, a murder machine if the galaxy had ever created one, knew in that second that what came for them was beyond his power to resist.

As though this was the fabled Balrog to their Gandalf.

"Run! Now!" Rex shouted.

Not *Fall back*. But... *Run! Run for your lives.*

Casper heard someone fire. Full auto. A whole charge pack on those old trusty KSs they'd used for so long. They were ancient compared to the weapons the Legion used now, but back then they'd been state-of-the-art. It was Rex who laid down the cover fire, long enough for all of them, what remained of First Squad, to get up and run for their lives.

LeRoy literally pulled Casper to his feet as he started running. Firelight danced across his Martian armor.

"Come on, sir!" he shouted. "We gotta didi!"

Casper had never heard that word before. Didi. But the meaning was clear. They were running, full out, full tilt, for their lives. Why?

Because they'd been ordered to?

Because it was their only chance to go on living one minute more?

No.

Because they could feel the fear, the palpable fear at their backs, chasing them through the flaming darkness of the field of corn. They could feel the Dark Wanderer coming for them.

That strange corn born in the dark between the stars, modified to grow and live in the shadows of a permanent twilight, tore at his gear as though trying to prevent him from escaping the Dark Wanderer who must surely be at his heels.

Casper remembered thinking that Rex was dead now. Gone. And that he'd been only barely able to care about that over his overriding desire to save his own life.

Who could stand against something so... weird?

They reached the streets of the abandoned city.

Shadowy towers with windows like gaping eye sockets rose up in the twilight darkness all about them. Gazed down in horror at them. The streets were bare, and yet there was a feeling of dust and disuse about everything. The buildings revealed inner darknesses beyond their facades that seemed to scream out at them in a permanent silent horror.

They had run from a burning hell, chased by an unknown demon they'd been too afraid to even remember from childhood, to a lonely and forgotten place that was somehow far worse than the horror at their heels.

Trask sidestepped out from an anonymous building and signaled them over. Casper heard LeRoy's boots behind him as he pounded across the empty street, racing for the darkness inside the building.

They numbered only nine.

They were the only ones from First Squad to have reached the city. The only ones to have survived the horror in the dead cornfield.

They could hear the Savages out there in the darkness, coming for the city. The half-human, half-machine beasts' passage through the mutant corn was a symphony of rasping white noise that was both discordant and darkly hypnotic in the same moment.

Like it was a promise.

As though they too would soon be running through the corn.

"Take a position," Trask ordered. He was afraid, but there was a resolve in his voice, like steel that wouldn't easily break. "We're holding here. Last stand, gentlemen."

It was dark when Casper found the altar beneath the vines.

Long had it lain, covered in snake-like growths that had not easily relented beneath the onslaught of Casper's hatchet. He'd cleared them away with ragged heaving breaths and a fury that belied his weary muscles. He'd cleared pillars, pedestals, even some sort of chair. And beneath all of that he'd found the ancient paving. Every stone denoting that this was a special place. It was a small place—not what he'd expected the Temple of Morghul to be. Perhaps it was a shrine. Some waypoint that led to where he must go.

But it was the altar that showed him what this place was.

The lizards were shown in bas-relief, carved like pictoglyphs on some ancient wall, dragging prisoners forward. Harvesting them with terrible dark scythes. Offering them up to the thing they worshipped.

Casper pulled the remaining dead vines from atop the altar. Revealing the last carvings. Revealing the outline and image of that nightmare in the corn.

And here too was the Dark Wanderer.

Except this time the Dark Wanderer was reaching out, opening his arms to embrace and receive the sacrifices that had been laid atop this table long ago. And in return, he offered... power.

So, thought Casper. *We meet again.*

16

The next morning, standing atop the vine-covered jungle hill in the soft light of daybreak, Casper looked west and saw other hills rising above the trees. In the distance—and who could tell how far the horizon was in the steaming jungle—were the jagged mountains where that monolithic statue should be.

An hour later, after a thin breakfast—nutrition bars for Casper, some strange jungle fruit for Urmo—they started off again, following their course, leaving behind the vine-covered temple of the Dark Wanderer.

As they descended the leafy hill they were swallowed once again by the dense dark jungle. Surrounded by a chiaroscuro of red light from the dying star filtering through the high leaves, they traveled among the bogs. Alien branches grew and twisted like many-tentacled squids reaching out to clutch and take as much of the jungle as they possibly could, never mind the time it might take.

THK-133 wove around these spider-like trees and always returned once more to its true course. Its heavy blaster at port arms, it scanned the darkness between the shafts of bloody light that fell down in great pylons.

As the day progressed, Casper began to feel better. Much better. Not that he'd felt bad—he'd just been hot and tired. And again he wondered how much of this planet he would need to search in order to find the Temple of

Morghul. The excitement of finding the pictoglyphs of the Dark Wanderer had faded.

They passed deep dark pools that might have offered a cooling dip, or perhaps the sunken remains of lost civilizations, but even Urmo avoided these, muttering his only word nervously, casting large wary eyes about as though expecting danger from all quarters at any second.

Casper used the little beast as a kind of planetary guide. He vowed to try some of the orange-like jungle fruit Urmo had consumed for breakfast. It hadn't killed the creature, and thus the chances that it wouldn't kill him were... possibly even acceptable.

And so, as he watched Urmo give those deep dark jungle pools a wide berth, he decided it was probably best for him to do the same.

At times, THK-133 would deploy his carbon-forged machete to hack through the denser areas. "In lieu of killing your enemies, master," the bot always began in its droll English butler voice, "I shall murder the local flora and fauna, so that your passage may be made easier. Rest easy, and I shall commence the slaughter, my liege."

Casper would sit, sweat dripping from his hair, which had turned prematurely iron gray the year he made captain, and listen to the monotonous chop of the bot's war against the jungle. His shirt was drenched. He drank some of the water, telling the canteen to chill it.

He'd been in a lot of jungles, and he'd never heard one as quiet as this. And that was strange. Jungles were alive with the sounds of birds, insects, and predators. Here? There was nothing. Just a dull, brooding silence that hung over everything.

It was then that he began to notice the mushrooms. They were a deep purple, and though they were beautiful in a dark and sinister way, they were clearly, or most likely, poisonous. Their very look seemed to promise death. Some things, Casper thought to himself as he took another swig from the canteen and felt better, cooler, more refreshed... some things just *looked* deadly—because they *were* deadly.

He swirled the water as he eyed the mushrooms clustered on the dark loamy ground. They gathered primarily near the rough trees that arched and spread out over the jungle deep He could hear THK-133 up ahead, hacking his way through the dense overgrowth. Rhythmically, methodically. Hacking and slicing at the dense vegetation that seemed to grow and expand as Casper watched.

He began to notice that there were mushrooms everywhere. They seemed to reveal themselves, as though appearing from one moment to the next.

Everywhere...

There was Trask.

LeRoy.

Dunbartty.

Nogle.

Barr.

Esmail.

Duhrawski.

And a medic. A young girl the team called *Bones*.

Eight of them and Casper.

For the next hour the Savages would probe the abandoned city on the dark curving plain, trying to locate their position. But the Martian infantry were not so easily dislodged. Based on the old Rangers of the ancient and long-forgotten American military, of which Rex had been one of the last, the Martian infantrymen were far more highly trained and had seen much more actual combat than the Savages.

Probably.

The Savage marines, as they would come to be known over the millennia of warfare to come, were at that point used to being mere enforcers of the lighthugger's oligarchical ruling elite. Perhaps they occasionally served as raiders against a frontier outpost. But the Martian Light Infantry had fought the collective forces of the UN to a standstill in the War for Martian Independence. They had even counter-invaded and taken the entire West Coast of North America, all while being heavily outnumbered.

The next hour was as bloody as it ever gets, remembered Casper as he watched the memories unfold.

And as close.

The first ten minutes were quiet. Trask leaned against one of the walls of the abandoned building and peered out through the shattered glass at the empty twilight street. Every other soldier had a point and a field of fire. There was only one exit, in the back. They'd put Esmail on that. The rest watched the two streets that intersected beside the building, just a little ways into the city.

"It's creepy how it's all dark in here," whispered LeRoy over the comm. "Think it's like that all the time, Sergeant?"

Except, Casper noticed, they never pronounced *sergeant* as "sergeant." It always came out sounding more like "sarn't." Some distant part of Casper's mind that had always been interested in history and etymology wondered how that had come about. Was it particular to the Martian military forces, or had it come from some old American military NCO who'd fled Earth during the Exodus to be part of the Grand Martian Experiment? New America, as some had called it for its short-lived existence.

"Contact," whispered Private First Class Nogle. Then, "Three hundred meters down the main street. Team of four moving close to the buildings. Light 'em up, Sarn't?"

"Wait..." whispered Trask. His gravelly voice was almost trance-like as he craned his head around the dark spaces inside the building, staying out of the window's frame. "Might be tryin' to get us to show 'em where we're at. Don't do nothin'. They're tryin' to find us."

Silence.

Casper heard one of the soldiers in the darkness spit, snuffle his nose, then spit again.

"Two fifty," whispered Nogle, calling out the distance.

Casper pulled his sidearm and checked it. Full charge. He clicked the safety off. They would need him too if it turned into a full-blown firefight.

"Two hunert, Sarn't."

"Don't do anything!" hissed Trask.

Silence.

Then, "Crossin' the street, Sarn't. Our side now. Got 'em lined up. One burst and they all go down."

Trask didn't reply.

Again, it was a testament to the training of the Martian light infantry that they held their fire despite a palpable nervous undercurrent of tension. The desire to unload and blast their way out of there... it was something even Casper could feel.

"Hunnert."

"Anybody see anything else?" Trask asked nervously.

Negatives all around.

"Sarn't… they're comin' straight at us. Like they know we're here. Thirty seconds and they'll reach the intersection."

"Be cool," whispered Trask.

A second later PFC Nogle announced the Savage scout team had stopped. Then, "They're doin' somethin', Sarn't."

"Can you tell what?" asked Trask. "Switch to low-light imaging."

"Already there, Sarn't," replied Nogle testily. "Comm, maybe. I don't know—maybe they got some close-range tracking juju… like a radar that triangulates heartbeats… and they had to be close enough to get a read on us…"

"That's crazy," replied one of the other soldiers in the shadowy darkness. "Ain't no such thing."

"Yeah, that's what everyone says, Dunbartty. Till there is. Whatever they're doin', I'm bettin' next month's pay they know we're here exactly, and they're callin' in a strike. I say light 'em up and shift positions. Sarn't?"

"Nah," said the other soldier, "tha's crazy. We just hunker and they—"

In an instant, incoming rounds came at them from everywhere. Mainly from the buildings and alley located diagonally across the intersection. Dunbarrty got hit in the chest by a round that zipped straight through the door that guarded the street entrance.

"Bones!" someone shouted out over comm. "DB's hit!"

What remained of the Martian infantry opened up and returned fire. The once-shadowy room was filled with the staccato pulse of the KS rifles' green-hued energy bursts.

Trask shouted out orders. "Suppress that alley on the right!" He duck-walked beneath a window, held his rifle above his head, and unloaded on the street where the scout team had been.

"Anti-armor!" someone shrieked.

Casper was crawling across the floor to reach Dunbartty and assist the medic when he passed the space where the door had been. Now he had a perfect view of a smoke trail sidewinding from down the street. Leading the curling snake of smoke was a micro-missile of some sort. It bounced off the street mid-intersection, skipped, then curled off in a whole new direction, smashing into another building across the way.

"Got it!" shouted Barr. "Old-school smarty RPG from Third Iran just before the Exodus. I had some ECM codes loaded up in my HUD just in case they brought out their old caveman sticks and stones from back in the day!" He said all this while firing on full auto.

"They movin' up on us in teams. Looks like a rush!" cried Nogle. He unloaded a blur of charged hyper-destabilized energy on some unseen target.

By the time Casper reached Dunbartty, he was dead. His eyes had glazed over, reflecting the bright fire all around, staring skyward. The medic shook her head and high-crawled away.

"He's dead," Casper announced to no one as the Martian infantry squad engaged targets from almost all points of the compass.

No one replied.

Instead they just kept killing everything out there on the streets for as long as they could in the time that remained to them.

Within minutes, that first Savage assault stalled. The Savages pulled back, leaving their dying to moan in the streets. But the respite was brief. Five minutes later they tried a diversion, a feint at the left flank. Meanwhile at least a platoon of them tried to take the rear alley leading into the building. An alleyway where Esmail had set up micro-mines and a kill zone.

The Savages were almost right up on the door when Esmail detonated the smart mines. Graphene tape that mimicked any surface it was attached to suddenly sprayed an explosive mist across the alley. A picosecond later the mixture ignited.

A smell of burnt flesh mixed with micro-circuitry flooded the building as the waves of heat pushed the hot air in at the defenders. The attackers had been roasted.

But two more platoons of Savages were already stacked and ready to overrun the alley. They came into the tight passage, firing hard and pushing behind a screen of something that shifted and blurred.

"It's their peripherals!" whispered Casper, watching a live video feed of Esmail's HUD. A wall of steel butterflies was blocking Esmail's fire. A few shots were getting through, but not enough. The Savages were closing in.

"Duhrawski!" shouted Trask to the squad's heavy gunner. "Redeploy the pig to assist Es!"

Sniper fire zipped from the rooftops while more Savages tried to take the streets out front. They moved from cover to cover, sometimes taking up positions behind groups of dead comrades.

Duhrawski heaved the massive KS-249 up from the position he'd taken at the front. He hustled back to the dark rear rooms that opened onto the alley. A moment later Casper heard the heavy weapon spooling up.

Normally they'd fire the weapon in bursts. Now, within the tight passage of the alley, no targeting would be needed. The Savages had bunched up behind their butterfly shield and were trying to surge for the door all at once, stumbling over the dying and ventilated to get at Esmail. Esmail had been hit, but still he fought back, holding his KS out beyond the frame of the door and spraying the alley. The wild and erratic fire was chewing up the Savages and their shifting shield.

It wouldn't be enough. The monsters were determined to get through.

And then the 249 opened up, and it was all over for them.

The heavy weapon shredded the butterfly shield and tore through both bunched-up platoons. The voluminous fire worked the dead and the running over without distinction. Duhrawski was thorough. In the end, nothing moved in the narrow rear alley.

"They done, Sarn't," he said over comm in the silence that followed. His voice was flat, even, as though one hundred and twenty-odd corpses, some on fire, and most of which he had personally eviscerated, wasn't as terrible a thing as it actually was.

In addition to Esmail—who wouldn't let anyone check him—Trask and Nogle were also hit. As the medic rushed over to Nogle, Casper made it to Trask. A bullet had smashed into the sergeant's forearm, which now hung limply against his armor. Casper placed a medical cuff over the elbow, just above the wound, and expanded it. The pumping blood that indicated a destroyed artery trickled to a stop. The cuff also flooded the local area with pain tranqs, leaving behind only a dull ache in the pain receptors.

"You want some Chill?" Casper asked. He'd heard the slang the Martian infantrymen used for their anti-shock/anti-anxiety meds.

Trask shook it off, breathing heavily. "Nah," he waved. He gritted his teeth and breathed through his nose as the pain began to disappear. "Stuff makes you sloppy. Ain't got time for that. We're getting out of here. Promised my wife..."

He closed his eyes and swallowed hard. Though Trask couldn't use his left arm, Casper could see that the sergeant had pushed the pain aside. His face regained a look of desperate fear.

"They comin' at us again, Sarn't," said Nogle over comm.

Trask hobbled over to the window and peered past the few shards of shattered night-blue glass that remained in the dusty frame. Down the street, a large mass of Savage marines were coming for them again. As though they hadn't just taken severe losses. As though they hadn't been checked in the least.

"Movement over here too," said Duhrawski, who'd repositioned the pig back into the main room.

"Here too," said Barr. "Right down our throats."

The Savages were coming at them from both flanks and right into the front entrance. Three directions at once.

"Light 'em up!" screamed Trask. He fired on full auto out the front door.

Duhrawski cut down wide swathes of the incoming Savages on his side. Green-hued bursts illuminated the faces of the buildings across the debris-littered street like tram cars racing by in the night. But the other two groups closed faster than the surrounded infantrymen could return fire.

"Comin' at me again," whispered Esmail over the comm. His voice betrayed no emotion.

"Can you hold?" shouted Trask between bursts.

"Do my best, Sarn't."

Casper raced back through the shadows, sidearm out. In no time he was alternating fire down the alley, covering Esmail as the wounded man struggled to reload his rifle. The soldier had been hit worse than anyone thought. Now his fingers trembled as he tried to rack fresh charge packs.

Over comm, Duhrawski said, "Pack swap!"

"Covering!" shouted Trask.

A violent explosion shook the building.

One of the Savage marines in the alley got close enough to lob a grenade into the small room where Casper and Esmail were holding out. For a brief second they looked at each other in disbelief.

Which was all wrong, Casper would think years later on the mushroom trail, lucidly hallucinating in the depths of the jungle. Esmail hadn't looked at him at all. They hadn't checked in with each other. Instead Esmail, who'd been sitting splay-legged, his back to the wall, merely stared at the rolling grenade in utter disgust. Then he turned over on his side and executed a near perfect soccer sliding kick, sending the grenade back out into the alley.

It exploded in the Savage marines' faces.

A shockwave of noise and dust stunned Casper, who was crouched near the door. The force of the blast, which the Savage marines' swirling mechanical butterfly field had attempted to contain, pushed Casper onto his back.

Two more Savages tried to rush the door with the explosion still ringing in Casper's ears.

Casper fired his sidearm. He'd always been a steady shot. Always qualified. Been in tight spots before. Both screaming Savages, howling like ghosts behind their mirror masks, went down.

And more appeared in the doorway.

Esmail got the mag in, pulled the charging handle, and practically lunged toward the doorway, firing on full auto. Casper didn't see who he hit, but Esmail kept firing until the charge pack was burned through. Then he popped the industrial diamond-tipped blade from beneath the barrel of his weapon and started stabbing and slashing.

Casper regained his knees, then his feet, and followed Esmail out the door, blasting at the attacking marines, who seemed to not yet comprehend that they were being counterattacked.

Now, almost unconsciously, Casper and Esmail were pushing into the alley, unable to go back, Casper shooting down Savages and Esmail working his bayonet-led rifle like a jackhammer on the post-humans.

Miraculously, they cleared the first alley and came to a wider alley that ran parallel to the main street. Through the buildings they could hear the fury of gunfire mixing into a discordant symphony of violence and chaos.

"Too far!" Casper gasped. "Gotta pull back and protect the rear."

Esmail stopped as though only now suddenly coming to himself. He'd gone a little berserk. Or a lot berserk, judging by all the dead in the alley.

Then Casper spied something farther down—something that didn't make sense. The corpses of Savages lying farther down the alley, just visible in the half-light thrown from the enigmatic sources of the main hab.

"We didn't kill those," he whispered.

Esmail threw his rifle down and picked up one of the Savage rifles. It was long, vented along the barrel, and had a semi-triangular drum magazine and a pistol grip instead of a stock. "I'm out of charge packs." He bent to a few of the corpses, searching them for more magazines.

Casper walked down the alley, crabbing, alternating scans to check his six. When he reached the bodies, he found they'd been killed by KS fire. Telltale charred flesh wounds dotted their flesh/mechanical corpses.

Esmail came up with the Savage slug thrower he'd commandeered. "No wonder they're such bad shots. This beauty is all spray and pray."

Casper ignored the comment. "Look. One of ours must've made it out of the cornfields. We didn't kill these guys."

Esmail scanned the area. "Getting nothing on our HUDs... can't tell you who's still active in the unit roster."

Casper spotted a small alley to one side, so narrow that one would have to move through it sideways. He activated his searchlight and shined it into the darkness.

Esmail cursed and told him to shut it off. Casper knew that soldiers were serious about noise and light discipline. But if one of their men was out here, they needed to find him and get him back inside the perimeter.

Down the narrow alley were two more bodies. Savages. Heads hung at odd angles. Dead metallic butterflies around them like discarded toys.

"Whoever it was... they went that way?" Casper whispered, turning off his light.

"How do you know they didn't *come* from that way?" Esmail asked.

I don't, thought Casper.

"You head back, Sergeant. Secure the rear entrance. I'm gonna find our lost soldier and get him back inside. I'll give a low whistle when we come down the alley. Signal back with one so I'll know it's clear."

Esmail acknowledged with a subdued yet typical Martian infantry "Oorah," then limped back down the alley and disappeared into the wan darkness.

Casper adjusted his gear, swapped charge packs on his sidearm, and squeezed into the narrow alley.

As he stepped over the dead Savages, he saw that one of their mirror masks had fallen off. The face that stared up at him was elfin and beautiful. Almost perfect, if not for the lolling purple tongue. The eyes, though... they were not the eyes of a human. They had been replaced by bio-circuitry that, theorized Casper as he passed, must somehow interface with the mirror masks. It was like looking at a lonely high mountain lake, and finding a face beneath the calm water staring back at you with dead eyes.

17

As the alley widened, Casper found more corpses along its length. All of them had their necks broken. The alley twisted and turned, but it was generally heading back toward the cacophony of battle noise along the main street.

Duhrawski's 249 was working the street in high-pitched close bursts of hectic fire. Savage weapons were obnoxiously burping out their sprays of lead in terse replies. Explosions sounded sporadically, concussive strikes, some clearly from grenades, others more like mortar rounds being called in on the building. But inside the tight alley sound bounced about, masking much of the directional information.

Finally, up ahead, the alley opened out onto the main street. Remaining in the darkness, Casper peered ahead at some Savages who were setting up a tripod-mounted assault gun.

One of the Martian infantrymen was mixed in among them.

The soldier kicked one Savage, sending him flying backwards out of sight. The infantryman then lunged forward, reached right through a second Savage's shifting hypnotic butterfly net, and pulled the post-human's head toward his own. In the same motion, he lowered his bucket and slammed it into the Savage marine's head. Even above the circus of battle, Casper heard the sickening crunch of bone. The Savage went lifeless and slumped to the dark street.

The third Savage marine, who'd been smart enough to grab a slug thrower, brought it to bear at just the moment the Martian soldier pulled the machete from his back with his off hand and made a quick clean slice through the Savage's unprotected neck.

The head came off. Mostly.

Casper ran down the alley, following the barrel of his sidearm onto the main street. The Martian soldier paid him no heed. Already he'd secured a Savage weapon and was unloading a full magazine on a nearby group cowering behind what might have been an overturned dumpster. The targets of his fire twisted and slumped. Blood sprayed in the gray twilight, looking dark and final, like some artist's commentary on everything that was wrong with how wars are won.

In the dim twilight of the street battle, all was chaos and confusion. Green fire spat from the surrounded defenders, while the Savages stopped to fire short bursts of bright gunfire and shift positions for new cover. But in the light of an explosion, the soldier turned, and Casper saw that it was Rex. His oldest friend, who he thought had most likely died only an hour ago. An hour in which he'd pushed those mortal thoughts away, because there wasn't time to deal with it, what with all the running, hiding, firefight, dying, and assaulting from a dark alley into the flank of an enemy assault.

Rex didn't even bother to question how Casper had ended up on his six, Terran Navy sidearm in hand. The even-then-legendary Tyrus Rex acted as though this too was just as normal as any of the other millions of minutiae that made up his life of fable and myth.

Some of the Savages turned back to see why their heavy weapons assault team wasn't putting rounds on target anymore. One of them spotted Rex and Casper and howled. Casper shot the post-human in the chest, and the Savage went down. But other Savages were already seeking out the targets who'd invaded their flank.

Rex ran to his right, strafing a large group as he went, drawing them away from Casper, who continued to shoot down Savages all around them like some defiant hero making a last noble stand despite the overwhelming odds.

Surely someone had done this at least once before.

Surely there was still a thing called bravery somewhere in the darkness of history.

Rex moved quickly, firing short bursts into the charging waves, avoiding fire from the defenders, surprising the attackers and cutting them down. In seconds a mad crossfire had stalled the Savage attack. The Savages in the center—thrown into confusion, sensing the loss of forward momentum, denied an exit, and unsure of their orders—broke.

Trask by that time had line-of-sight comm with Rex. He shifted the light infantry's fire and brought the full weight of it to bear on the mass of Savages moving in to breach. Another crossfire hurricane evolved between Casper/Rex and the besieged light infantrymen. The Savages were being smashed between hammer and anvil, until at last they fell back and scattered, disappearing out into the strange forever-midnight cornfields.

In the aftermath of the battle, the street was littered with bodies. Rex began collecting magazines and rifles. Casper did the same, ignoring the mirrored faces of the dead Savages staring up at him as he liberated them of their ammunition. Thinking not of the strangely beautiful faces hiding beneath their soulless masks.

Soon he and Rex were hustling back inside the building, and Rex was issuing new orders. They were ditching their issue rifles. Which was fine; most of them were down to one or two charge packs at best anyway, and the 249 had fired dry in the last moments of the slaughter.

"It's time to exit this area. We'll make toward that pyramid up-cylinder. If we can find a terminal and hack into the ship's operating system, we should be able to find out where they've taken Red Queen."

In all the mission briefings, Reina Benedetti had been referred to as "Red Queen."

As the soldiers gathered their gear, redistributed ammo, and patched up as much of their wounds as they could, Rex turned to Casper. His face was blank, like a bot's mockery of human expression. Except those sorts of bots wouldn't exist for another several hundred years.

"You're having a hallucinogenic reaction to the mushrooms, master."

THK-133 was leaning down over him. Casper was on his back, watching the jungle light undulate in the treetops above.

It looked like afternoon light.

They were deep inside a beautiful emerald jungle. Flowers were exploding, popping and spraying prismatically all across the lush landscape. Every palm leaf seemed to curl or twist, to wave gently at him. Lush trees stared down at him, smiling their wizened smiles.

Casper looked up at the milkshake sky and saw an emerald dragon wandering through the vibrant trees. It turned and stared down at him like it was a real thing. As though wisps of smoke were truly rising up from its flaring nostrils.

Well, thought Casper. *I've gone completely mad.*

"The local flora and fauna," lectured THK-133, "seem to have infected you with some sort of contact poison, master. It may even be an inhalant, though I don't possess a sensor array configured in a way to detect such particulates. But we've been marching for hours and you haven't said a word... master. Unless moaning like a Syclopian rotuaro counts as words. Languages are not my specialty. So possibly it does. Nevertheless, you seem to be suffering from ill effects."

Casper came to himself, experienced a brief moment of clarity. There was no dragon in the treetops. It was merely the taller trees shifting back and forth, making a shape like something his drug-addled mind might contrive to be a dragon.

I'm hallucinating.

And why the dragon? he asked himself.

And it was black.

It was coming for him just as it had in the Quantum Palace. Just like the nightmares of the prophetesses in that permanent midnight. Except it hadn't been a black dragon... it had been the Dark Wanderer.

"We shall stop and rest, master," announced THK-133 without fanfare or sympathy. "Perhaps you will feel better by tomorrow."

And just before Casper fell once more into that reality-turned-hallucinogenic nightmare, he saw all the mushrooms everywhere, spreading like wildfire. They were big and pulsing, at times beautiful and luscious, like sugary candy in a candy store to end all candy stores, at other times like big corpulent Cheshire spiders, swollen with sinister menace, biding their time until they might scurry forward and fill him with their strange poisons and intoxicating nightmares.

He heard himself screaming as he went down the well of darkness.

He wouldn't come out of the drug-fueled nightmare until they'd reached the mountains in the numberless days to come, where the giant statue watched over the desert wastes.

For now, as he lay in the dirt, howling like a wounded animal, Urmo smiled and offered him a small stone.

18

What remained of First Squad left by the body-filled back alley in patrol formation. Nogle, Rex, Barr, Duhrawksi, Casper, Esmail, Bones, and Trask, with LeRoy bringing up the rear. They threaded the alley, picked up the larger one that paralleled the main road, and headed in the direction opposite the way the Savages had retreated. In time they left the small city, each of them wondering at its enigmatic purpose, its lost history that would never be known.

"What was it?" asked LeRoy as they moved down a lonely road that ran roughly toward the pyramid.

"A city," whispered Casper.

Trask was probably in too much pain to tell them to shut up. The cuff's meds would be wearing off by now. Soon Casper would have to give him something from the medical bag. Something that would definitely take the edge off.

"Why ain't there anyone livin' in it?"

"Dunno," answered Trask matter-of-factly.

Casper turned to see the sergeant's face. It was ghostly white in the near darkness. Even though Casper's medical training was the bare minimum required by the Terran Navy for damage control operations, he knew things did not look good for Trask if they didn't get to a medical facility soon.

Then again, things didn't look good for any of them. And as Casper knew, when it came to the Savages, there were fates far worse than death. To be enslaved by them was a kind of living death that made one wish for the real thing. And so who was to say that Trask, dying of his wounds out here in the dark, might not be better off in the long run?

And even if they weren't captured by the Savages, what then? What were the odds the *Moirai* would survive contact with the Dead Zone?

But… maybe they weren't even in the Dead Zone. Maybe they'd changed course. Maybe the *Lex* was still on the hangar deck. Maybe they could find their way back. Maybe the Savages would remain in retreat. Maybe there was a way out of this in the end.

Or maybe not. As his mother had always said, if wishes were fishes, beggars would ride.

Casper pushed thoughts of other places, safer than this one, away. He tried to move as quietly as the soldiers in front of and behind him. They moved off into the fields, keeping low, following ancient canals that were sometimes bone dry, sometimes filled with a foul-smelling water. After four hours, far out into the middle of nowhere, seemingly no closer to the distant pyramid above their heads on a land with no horizon, they halted and formed a small perimeter. They took turns sleeping in an enigmatic depression near a maintenance road.

Nothing moved. All was silent.

Rex and Casper took the first watch. They lay on their backs and listened to the nothing of the ambient night. There was no need to stand, to look. If anything came at them, its sound would be heard in the fields, or out across the still air.

Casper lay there, telling his mind to stop searching for stars above, because there weren't any. He told his mind to just accept the dead cities, roads, and stranger structures that hung above him where a night sky should be. Occasionally, out across the distance above, ghostly lights came on and went off just as abruptly as they had appeared.

"You think she's still alive?" asked Rex.

Casper knew exactly who his friend was talking about. Some part of his mind had been wondering the same thing.

Long ago the three of them, and many others, had been captured attempting to make contact with an old lighthugger. The members of that ship weren't called Savages then. Some called them the Lost Children, affectionately forgetting that they had been the elites who'd abandoned Earth, and their fellow human beings, at the most dire of hours in human history.

But, as some say, time heals all wounds.

Casper had never agreed with that. Hadn't found it to be true. Some wounds never healed. Some things were never forgotten. No matter how long one lived, some hurts remained fresh.

"We won't leave until we know," he whispered in the darkness.

He felt Rex, who Casper would've described as the most immovable object in the universe, relax. Just a bit. Just a little. Imperceptibly... unless you'd been through what they'd been through together. Had known one another in what some measured as lifetimes.

She had rescued them both. She'd broken through the mental desert their minds had been cast into by the Pantheon aboard the *Obsidia*. She'd awoken them to their condition as slaves. When they'd come back to themselves, they would have told you they'd been wandering a desert with no nights. That their minds had thought of only one thing for all the years they'd been slaves inside that slow-moving ship. In those years when their bodies were alive and active—fighting wars, being experimented on, used—their minds thought only of putting one foot in front of the other, of crossing that endless, featureless desert in which they had lost themselves.

Casper shuddered in the vast cornfield traveling through space. Yes, there were fates worse than death.

The endless desert one's mind can wander in.

Mindless servitude.

Loss of self.

Better death than any of those. And not for the first time since he'd decided to go forward with the infantry to maintain communication, he reminded himself that he would not allow himself to be captured again. That if there was at least one shot left in his sidearm... he would choose that.

As an ensign aboard the *Challenger*, chasing the *Obsidia* out into the big dark empty, hoping to rescue the "Lost Children" who'd abandoned Earth in its hour of need, he had *not* chosen that when everything went to hell in a handbasket. He'd opted to try and live. To survive for just a little bit longer.

And so he'd spent fifteen years as a mindless slave aboard the *Obsidia*. Wandering a simulated desert inside his head, punctuated by nightmares of the real world in real time at the cruel pleasure of the Pantheon.

Gifted or cursed with long—a very long—life.

Reina Benedetti set them free from that slavery.

You could put "free" in quotation marks, he thought as he tried to stop staring at the cities on the plain above his head. Instead of being free, they had merely awoken to what their bodies were doing. They'd still had to fight, quietly, silently, resisting the programming and insanity of the cubes, to regain the ability to control their own bodies. And even then they'd had to go through the motions of continuing to do all the horrible things they were required by the Pantheon to do, lest their self-awareness be discovered.

Because the Pantheon couldn't know that their slaves had woken up. Not yet. Not then. So they went through the motions. Played the game. Waited as Reina woke an army up one by one. And in time, when their numbers were sufficient, they revolted. They slew the Pantheon. Regained the ship. And those who survived fled in the old *Challenger*. One last flight. One last jump. Leaping away as the entire *Obsidia* went up like a bright supernova.

There had been only three survivors. Two of them owed Reina everything.

So of course they'd come to rescue her. Of course they wouldn't fight their way back to the *Lex* until they knew if she was still alive, or dead.

They owed her that much. They owed her at least that. Because they owed her so much more.

Before their capture, their slavery, Rex had been the platoon leader in the *Challenger*'s security detail. He was a member of the new UN naval force's own army, formed out of what was left of the North American and European militaries. But as a slave aboard the *Obsidia,* Rex had become a gladiator. Fighting other slaves. Fighting chimeras the Pantheon either made or abducted from the worlds they passed along the way. All for amusement. *Their* amusement.

Because death was an amusement to the deathless.

Casper, on the other hand, had been turned into the personal slave of a high lady. Some evil witch who'd once been an entertainer back on Earth. A pop star twenty years gone to seed before Casper was born. Part of the elite, chosen because she'd won the genetic lottery of being beautiful, and therefore connected, and now, thanks to the discoveries of the Pantheon, she was eternally young. Once again.

And she was insane.

Hurting people for pleasure was her taste.

All those lost and horrible times came rushing into Casper's mind unbidden as he lay there in the dirt of the dead cornfield. And so he changed the conversation, as he'd done so many times before.

"One of the men who died back there..." he began, knowing Rex was listening in the deep stillness. It would have been inconceivable for Rex to be derelict in his duty to others. "He said, tell them I didn't forget nothin'."

Silence.

Then Rex asked, "What was his name?"

Casper told him.

Rex seemed satisfied with that. Which was so like him. Never to understand that the rest of humanity had further questions. Wanted answers to those questions. Why else had they gone out into the stars?

Rex was the opposite of everyone in that he never seemed to need answers to the big questions. There were no mysteries to Rex. To him, life was nothing more than surviving this day to the next. And he was the best at surviving.

Bar. None.

Casper, on the other hand... had nothing but questions. Nothing but curiosity. He was a great reader. A student of history. A man always asking: *Why?* Why couldn't things be better? Why this way and not that? Why don't we go where we haven't been?

And... why did some things have to happen?

That was what had driven him out into the stars.

That was what urged him forward day after day.

The desire to know. That was the quest.

And when will enough be enough? he'd asked himself many times before. When will all be known?

When?

"What did that mean?" asked Casper in the barest of whispers. "'I didn't forget nothin'.'"

A breeze, probably urged on by a climate control system, passed through the dead corn, causing the husks to whisper as they brushed against one another in the darkness.

"What?" Rex replied. As though he had not been a part of the previous exchange.

"What did, 'Tell them I didn't forget' mean?"

Rex sighed. Just barely.

The wind passed on through the corn and was gone, and once more the night was still.

"It's from Rogers' Orders. In the Martian Light Infantry we promise each other never to forget our orders, and to remember the fallen who died doing their job. It's the last honor we pay each other. To say we didn't forget our orders."

"Who was Roger?"

"Rogers. Don't know. Never cared."

Typical, thought Casper. And that thought made him happy. The galaxy got weirder by the day, and Rex never changed. It was good that there was at least one constant thing on which all compasses and timepieces could be set. Rex was a lodestone, a true north. An atomic clock that never ran late despite the forces that sought to shake everything apart. Without him... Casper imagined all would be madness.

"Where do the orders come from?"

This seemed to stall Rex. His silence indicated he didn't totally understand the intent of the question.

"How do you know them?" Casper clarified.

"Rangers. Back on Earth. They make you memorize the orders. They're good. They make sense. You can apply them to a lot of situations. That and a five-paragraph op order, and you can lead just about anything into a fight."

This had already been one of the longest conversations Casper had ever had with the man. It almost qualified as Rex baring his soul. Almost.

Except what happened next was downright stunning. In the dark, Rex began to recite and comment on the orders.

"Let's see... there's *Don't forget nothing.* That's the first. Then there's the second order: *Have your musket clean as a whistle, hatchet scoured, sixty rounds powder and ball, and be ready to march at a minute's warning.* That's all good, though I have no idea what a musket is. But being ready to move at a moment's notice... that's crucial. Three is, *When you are on the march, act the way you would if you were sneaking up on a deer. See the enemy first.* I knew that one before I was in the army. We ate deer when we could back before the Exodus. My father taught me that. *Tell the truth about what you see and what you do. There is an army depending on you for correct information. You can lie all you please when you tell other folks about the Rangers, but don't never lie to a Ranger or officer*. Goes without saying, of course. Five is, *Don't never take a chance you don't have to*."

Rex chuckled in the darkness at that one.

"Combat is nothing but chances. Especially if you want to seize the momentum and maintain it. So that one was always ridiculous. To me.

"Six was..." He thought for a moment. "*When we're on patrol, march single file, far enough apart so no one shot can go through two men*. Which I have seen happen. Seven... *If you hit swamps, or soft terrain, spread out in a line, so it's hard to track you*. Then there's, *When you march, keep moving until dark, so as to give the enemy the least possible chance to shoot at you*. That one seemed old because most modern fighting takes place at night anyway. Especially asymmetrical warfare operations. And *When you camp, half the party stays awake while the other half sleeps*. But these guys are on their last legs, so..." He let that last word slip off into the dark and the cornfields.

"*Keep prisoners separate until interrogations*. That's ten. And eleven, *Don't take the same route twice. Take a different route to avoid being ambushed*. Twelve, *No matter whether we travel in big parties or little ones, each party has to keep a scout twenty yards ahead, twenty yards on each flank, and twenty yards in the rear, so the main body can't be surprised and wiped out*. Makes sense. Thirteen: *Always have a rally point*. Didn't set one tonight. There's no place to fall back to. And fourteen is, *Don't sit down to eat without posting sentries*. Naturally. *Don't sleep beyond dawn. Dawn's when the French and Indians attack*. French used to be our enemies just like they were when they went full-Islam before World War III.

I always thought that was crazy. Showed that Rogers was one smart soldier. And that things never change."

Silence.

Casper wondered if Rex would go on. He didn't dare speak; he didn't want to break whatever spell had overcome his friend.

"*Don't cross a river at a regular ford,*" Rex said. "The funny thing is that back in Ranger school, this sergeant had to explain to me what a ford was. Basically don't use bridges or places where cattle cross. It's usually mined. *If somebody's trailing you, make a circle, come back onto your own tracks, and ambush the folks that aim to ambush you.*"

Rex paused. Was he thinking about that one? Did he anticipate it was applicable to what needed to happen when they took up their march in a few hours? As though some ancient bit of wisdom might just get them all out of this jam alive.

Casper sensed his friend was testing that rule, seeing if it still held true on a battlefield stranger than what old Rogers could ever have imagined when that rule was first put forth.

"Eighteen, *Don't stand up when the enemy's coming against you. Kneel down, lie down, hide behind a tree.* Or, cover first, then fire. I've found that to be good, when you can apply it. But sometimes in CQB it's better just to put as many bullets between you and the enemy as possible in the shortest amount of time. And nineteen was, *Let the enemy come till he's almost close enough to touch. Then let him have it and jump out and finish him up with your hatchet.* I prefer these machetes we started using back on Mars at Saffron City. Wouldn't trade it for nothing. Axe is a bad weapon. You get one chance with it. That's all. So you better do all the damage you can do in that one swing. With a machete you can just keep chopping and slicing."

Casper lay there in stunned silence. He wondered if Rex, too, felt that they were at the end of themselves. If maybe his old friend knew as well as he did that they weren't getting out of this one alive. And maybe the old memories, the important things, maybe they were coming around for one last visit before it was closing time for the both of them.

"If I ever form any fighting force," said Rex in the silence, as though reading Casper's thoughts and promising him there would be a future in which they played a part, "they'll memorize all those orders. They'll be the one percent of the one percent of the one percent who try to make the galaxy a better place. Most people just want to burn it all down. My men will be that line between those who are trying to go on, and those who want to watch it burn to nothing. They won't forget nothin'... and we won't forget them."

19

They moved out a few hours later, following the old dirt-carved service road that cut through the cornfields. An hour into the march, Nogle held up one fist. They were using hand signals in the event comms had been somehow compromised by the Savages' predilection for developing next-gen tech. Also, they'd left a lot of their own dead behind, and it wasn't impossible for the tech-hungry Savages to have hacked the captured comm devices. They could be listening in. Or even tracking them.

So Rex had ordered them to disable their telemetry and transponders.

Nogle's hand signal came down the column. In the distance, a small structure lay between the rows of corn. Rex ordered a wedge, and the Martian infantry slid through the cornfield and came out in a quiet clearing before an ancient and leaning wooden barn.

Casper had fallen in behind the wedge.

Rex raised a fist, and they waited. Listening. Then he signaled Nogle and Barr to move forward and search the building. The two moved forward, stacked at the open entrances on either side, and moved in as one, sweeping the darkness with their weapons. No doubt they were imaging on low light.

Before the march had started, the command team—Rex, Trask, and Casper—had discussed finding another structure. Rex and Casper, having been prisoners on just such a ship as this, knew that four rail systems ran the length of the long cylinder, from bow to engines, on these Rama-class vessels. Below the "earth" of the cylinder, or the main hab, lay a network of supply and maintenance tunnels, storage warehouses and lifts that allowed cargo to be moved about. Finding an entrance into this subterranean network, and ultimately the rail system, was the priority. Out here on the open plain of the cylinder, they were needlessly exposed and quite possibly under some kind of drone surveillance, though they'd detected none thus far.

Nogle gave the move-forward hand signal, and the rest of the soldiers, including Casper, moved in.

The barn was open and empty. The floor was covered with old straw, and the faint scent of animals hung in the air, but that was all. Rex was immediately down on his hands and knees, sweeping aside the straw, and within moments he'd located the gates to an old service lift that accessed the maintenance levels. Finding the control mechanism to open the gates and call the lift took a bit more time, so while the others worked at getting it operational, Casper walked the rest of the barn.

He felt uneasy. There was something here that was bothering him. Except... it wasn't obvious to the eye. It was something that needed to be discovered.

Rex and his men managed to raise the lift gates that barred access to the lift. The platform itself was somewhere far below. Someone found the controls and called it up from the lower levels. Unsure how far away it was—or how long it would take to arrive.

Casper was only dimly aware of this activity. With his light, he was scanning the wooden walls. At first there was nothing. But then, low in a corner, he discovered writing.

This writing wasn't in the same hand that had written the madness on the walls of the outer hull corridors. This seemed almost sane. Rational, at the start.

It was different. It was like a log, a diary.

And it would prove to be a warning they should have listened to.

Beware the Dark Wanderer. He ain't human. Ain't from Earth like he claims. He's a demon. A demon who walks like a man. Whole command team is dead. Whip ain't himself anymore. This ship is a hell ship. And beware of his spooky women. Get off this ship while you still can. But if you're reading this you're probably already dead. —Dobbs

There was more. Much more. But none of it made sense. Some of it was a supplies list. Another section was a kind of roster, with names that had been crossed off. If they'd had the time, they might have learned more. They might have heeded the warnings. They might have... done what? What could they have done differently?

It didn't matter what they might have done. Because they didn't do it.

Because the prophetesses came at them.

They surrounded the barn as if they had known all along that the little soldiers would hide within like frightened animals. A strange, almost hypnotic music—like some composer's take on a siren's call—announced their arrival. It floated out there in the darkness, haunting them. Taunting them. *Come and see.*

Rex's soldiers took up their rifles. They were not going down without a fight.

In the end, each and every one of them would deliver that much.

"Come out," whispered three voices together but not in unison.

Casper heard the voices inside his head... and as clear as day. As though the women were in the same room and spoke as gently as possible. Coaxing and commanding all at once. The meaning was clear. And the audible sound, it too had been clear. Like a bell. A perfect pitched bell ringing inside his head, communicating the command, the request, the threat.

Casper turned and saw that the others had heard the same thing. The same three discordant voices. The women. Everyone scanned the dark barn, but there was no one there. Just that haunting music that probably wasn't even real.

They were still waiting for the lift platform to arrive. If it ever would.

Casper glanced over at Trask. The man's face was pale, and the look in his eyes made his feelings clear: it was time to run. Or perhaps Casper was just projecting. Because he felt it too, deep in his gut, a feeling that had to be true whether it was or it wasn't.

Nogle, who'd been watching the wide barn door entrance, was suddenly yanked from their presence and out into the darkness. Out into the twilight of the corn. His weapon went off with a short, high-pitched staccato burst. And then it fell dead silent.

By the time Casper had taken the mere strides it took to cross the empty building to the other side, Barr, Trask, Duhrawski, and Rex had already opened up with their weapons on what was out there.

The prophetesses were out there.

And what Casper saw in that moment changed him forever.

It was not the three women, ethereal, wan, and pale, wisps of shrouds covering their emaciated frames. It was not that.

It was not the fact that Nogle was suspended in midair, feet dangling helplessly. Humans don't hang in midair unless some type of anti-gravity system is in place, and at that moment in galactic technological history, anti-grav was mostly theoretical. Repulsors were still a long way off. But that was not what changed Casper.

It was the look in Nogle's eyes. The desperation to be set free of what had him, the conviction that he never would be free, the desire to have never been born... it was all there in one horribly twisted mask-of-pain moment. His head was canted back in a silent horrible scream as though he was in an eternal torment that might never end. And maybe, thought Casper at that moment, it wouldn't.

And the prophetesses were somehow controlling all this with their minds.

The next thing that every soldier, including Casper, was about to find deeply disturbing, was the fact that their gunfire wasn't getting anywhere near the three women, the three girls, the three... prophetesses.

There *were* three of them, whatever they were. One was holding a long and spidery-fingered hand to her head, just like that first prophetess had done. Right before she popped a soldier's head like a swollen pimple. The other two had their arms spread wide, as if they were holding Nogle up.

With a quick motion, one of the two flicked her wrist, and Nogle's neck emitted a sickening crack. His head flopped to the side, and his tongue hung thickly from his mouth. His hands and legs began to twitch.

And then his body hit the dead comet dust–collecting earth of the main hab cylinder.

None of the soldiers were firing now. Perhaps they'd fired dry on their magazines. Perhaps they'd recognized the futility of their attack. Perhaps they, like Casper, were almost too stunned by the raw power they'd just witnessed.

Then Sergeant Trask was yanked off his feet just like Nogle had been, forward and into the prophetesses' midst. He screamed.

"Move! Fall back to the shaft!" Rex shouted. He stepped forward to fire another burst at the three girls, as if that might achieve something it had so far shown no signs of achieving.

Casper did not retreat to the shaft as ordered. His eyes refused to look away from Trask as the NCO was spun and rotated in sudden torment. The chorus of witches chanted some unknown word inside Casper's mind like a bare harmony of whispers in the background. He felt, more than knew, that they were telling Trask in their chant that he, and they, were all about to die. Telling the sergeant he would be the first, but not the last of the men he'd been given sacred charge over.

He might have been frightened. He might not have been the most high-speed, low-drag, hardcore soldier who'd ever served. But Trask was brave. That was for sure. And he proved it in his last action.

He fought their iron will and somehow reached his good hand across the load-bearing harness that covered his Martian armor. He pulled the pins on two matte-gray grenades, leaving them attached to his body.

Rex might not have even seen this.

Casper was distantly aware that his friend had gone to that old place inside himself. That place he'd needed in order to survive the gladiatorial pits of the *Obsidia*. That place of the ancient warrior. A place of mindless rage, where there was nothing left but to do as much damage to your enemy as you could. To keep fighting until they couldn't fight back.

It was entirely possible that Rex, in that mindless place, had not seen Trask pulling the pins in this last action of his life.

Casper hurled himself at his friend, yanking him behind the barn doors just before the explosives went off and sent thousands of jagged shards in every direction. The barn's wall on that side was torn to splinters, but Rex's armor absorbed most of the damage, protecting both men as they crashed down on the stale-smelling straw.

When they recovered their feet, weapons out, they saw that the prophetesses, all three of them, were dead. Their bodies had been savaged by the mercilessness of physics and explosively released energy.

Rex raced forward, picked one girl up, and hurled her bloody body into the side of the barn. Then he shot it several times. When he was finished, he stood over it, a savage sneer across his face, his chest armor heaving like a blacksmith's bellows.

Casper realized then, in some sad and distantly ironic commentary on his life, that only they, of all the galaxy's fools, had been *so* foolish as to come to this terrible relic of a ship. They came willingly, like rubes unsure what horrors and mirrors the funhouse might offer. Now their dead were strung out behind them, discarded tickets between the booths the carnies hectored them from, in a forgotten amusement park on some lost back alley street that was always too hard to find. This ship was that amusement park. A museum floating off into the dark of the cosmos.

Casper had all these hopeless thoughts of melancholy as his feet carried him forward and his light shined on the faces of the two prophetesses who remained.

One had been horribly marred, her face torn to shreds. But the other didn't even look that badly hurt. Instead there was a look on her face of... found peace. Finally. And that was somehow much more terrible than the girl who'd been blown half away.

Casper wondered if there was still some part of the dead girl's mind that was whispering.

Still whispering that phrase.

"I embrace the Quantum... and it embraces me."

Some part of him knew that she was. That there were other worlds than these. Other worlds of powers like they ones he'd just seen displayed. And that those worlds had been there all along, and he'd just had a first glimpse of them through the funhouse mirror of this nightmare ship wandering the cosmic dark.

He thought about the prophetesses' powers. There was nothing like them in the entire universe. Nothing at all.

And yet, there was.

THE LESSON OF LISTENING

"Listen to it," says the Master to the student. "Hear it first... then... yours it is to command."

The silence within the temple is so deafening that it has become like a physical thing to the student. A thing that seems a wall, or a wave, or a blanket that covers and smothers everything.

The student holds the stone.

The stone is his focus.

The stone is the invitation.

The student waits, listening for the music the Master has instructed him to hear.

But it does not come that day.

And the student opens his eyes to see the Master floating, floating above the debris-littered floor of this ancient place. Shafts of bloody light stab down into the darkness around him. But there is more...

All about the Master, rocks that have long lain forgotten among the ruins of the temple now hang like planets, circling the Master in concentric rings. Orbiting their sun. One explodes, and like some moon hit by a planet killer from an Ohio-class battleship, its debris field expands outward. Except in slow motion.

The student watches... fascinated. Always fascinated.

Beyond the Master, the ancient idol that was toppled long ago in this room, an idol that reflects the image of something that never should have been, grinds and rises up from its eons-long resting place on the floor.

The Master's face is neither beatific nor straining... it just is. As though this too is the way of all things.

The student watches this raw display of power. He has seen the Master perform many such wonders, and always they have struck him to the point of dumbfounded amazement.

"Do... you cannot," hisses the Master as the multi-ton idol begins its circle, joining the tiny inner worlds that were once rocks. "Deafened by your blindness you always will be."

Later...

Later...

Another lesson.

The student follows the Master across a deep, possibly bottomless chasm far beneath the temple. A central stair leads down to an incredible depth, and the waters from the sea fall down into it.

The Endless Well never fills.

And the waters fall into it endlessly.

What has become a typical daily exercise of balance and combat becomes something else. Down here, far down the depth of the shadowy well, the student follows the Master across a thin strand of ancient stone that crosses over the void. Water cascades all around them, down the sides of the immense cistern, onto the stairs, across the narrow rock on which they stand. Its bombastic thunder is deafening.

"Deafened by your blindness always you will be," says the Master, though the student only hears this in his mind.

And then... he is actually blind.

He has practiced this before. Moving while blinded by a tied strip of cloth. Moving in the dark. But never here, above a bottomless well where death waits to pull him down into its unknown. And never *actually* blind.

"Master!"

He hears himself. Hears himself desperately asking for the voice of the teacher to come back to him. To reassure him. He repeats the word, over and over, his voice rising. Rising to the point of hysteria.

He knows that if he reaches that point, he will surely fall. Balance will flee him.

He *will* fall.

So he stops.

Stops his mind.

Slows his breathing. In through the nose. Out through the mouth.

He can feel the rock in his pocket. Or rather, he knows it's there. And that is a comfort to him. A wild and reckless thought surges to the front of his panicked mind...

Take the rock out. Hold it in your hand. Comfort you will have.

But of course here, on a slender beam deep down in the Endless Well, the act of fishing around in his rags for the rock will cause him to lose focus and fall. And so he does not.

"Master?" he tries again.

His voice is forlorn and lost. Like some child abandoned by the wayside. That small and helpless voice is carried away by the weight of all the waters falling down and down the steps of the deep well.

That way lies madness.

In that moment the student knows that this too is a lesson. Knows that this is the *next* harsh lesson. He must hear the music. That is the power. He must find it. And once he hears it... then he will control it.

Except the noise of the well is deafening. In fact it is so deafening that even hearing his own thoughts requires a supreme act of focus and concentration.

It so deafening that its constant thunder is all he can hear.

His legs are getting tired. The beam he stands on is so slender that he cannot even crouch down to his hands and knees so that he might begin to crawl back to safety.

Hear it! his mind roars. Because he knows that if he doesn't... he will soon fall. And the student is convinced that the fall will be endless. And so he must learn. Now or never.

But all he hears is the noise of the falls. Cascading and rumbling. Falling from the ocean that presses against the temple above. Washing in across the lower levels where he has trained with the stick and the sword to perfect his body. Cascading across carved stones that might have been shaped before the ancient pyramids that litter the galaxy he has passed beyond.

Then those waters pass into the four channels that serve the well. There, the water turns smooth. It forms a powerful flow that makes a different sound. Not the rush of the tidal wash that flows beneath the temple.

Each physical object makes a music all its...

... own.

He forgets his body. The pain and fatigue. The crying muscles and stiff bones. He listens to the music of water falling on stone. It is like a living thing.

Pictures form in his mind.

He sees the well as though he is looking at something with what his mind poorly describes as a powerful deep-scan sensor. But it is really so much more than the most powerful detecting device the Galactic Republic has ever conceived of.

He sees *all* the stones.

All the falls.

All the waters.

Every drop.

He sees his place within it all.

He sees it interacting with itself.

And...

He senses the Master, watching him, just in front of his face. Just beyond his reach. His look is neither strained nor beatific.

Just...

Existing within it all.

The Master lashes out suddenly with his staff. He smacks the student in the head with a terrific crack. Bells ring, klaxons erupt, and the student is going over and off the slender beam.

He is blind.

Yet he sees himself departing the narrow walk that crosses the bottomless chasm. And without flailing he twists, knowing exactly where he is within the well and the falls, and everything around him slows, just like that tiny rock that had become a planet orbiting the Master. A rock exploding outward in slow motion.

The student twists as he falls.

He grabs the beam with both hands.

He swings back up into the air above the plank, and for uncounted moments he hangs in the nothingness above the place where he must either land... or fall.

He lands back on the plank.

The Master comes at him with another strike from his staff. Surefooted, the student gives ground, step by step, weaving to avoid each impossibly terrific blow. The radar beyond his blindness shows him every swing in a series of furious attacks.

The pace of the strikes increases, and soon the student is not only weaving and backing up step by step, but also hopping and at times jumping, really flying backward to avoid blows that will send him off and down into the nothing. Yet with each flip and turn he knows where the beam is and where his feet must be.

The student deftly avoids sudden extermination.

The Master whirls the staff and brings it down hard. It will surely crack the student's skull. There is no question of this.

But the student sees this happen before it happens. As though some tell has telegraphed the move. His cross-handed block comes up, and he catches the staff inches from his own forehead.

The Master holds the staff, forcing down against the block. Forcing his will down onto the student who must yield.

And now the student can sense the Master's face close to his. The Master's eyes are closed.

And beyond that, he sees thoughts.

The thoughts of the Master.

Rage.

Darkness.

Destruction.

There are some who want to watch the galaxy burn...

In the student's blindness, the Master smiles. The student sees the textures form and evolve across the ancient face above his own.

"Listen to the music of it," says the Master in the deep silence that has enveloped them both, for the noise of the falls has ceased, and perhaps the waters have ceased their fall. "It is me... and I am it."

Thus ends the lesson.

20

The lift was a slow, creaking descent into darkness. The old piece of equipment had obviously not been maintained, which to Casper, as a starship captain, seemed a crime more sinful than dereliction.

Now it was just Rex, Esmail, Duhrowski, Barr, LeRoy, and Bones.

And you, that other voice reminded Casper as he watched all this from his disembodied vantage point on that lost island. No, it was a lost world, not an island. Not an isthmus or a peninsula. It was connected to nothing known.

In that way it was like the things we call "Quantum." In that the unknown was the only known. And what you knew... wasn't what it was. At least not anymore.

But it *felt* like an island. The crash had been a shipwreck, and the planet was an island of madness and riddles. An island with no ocean—just jungle and desert. And mushrooms.

He looked around the ancient lift. Its panels had been knocked out of place, taken away. And used for what? *Shields,* said that voice. The Savages of this place carried them as shields into battle against the ruined cities on the curving plains. Or have you been ignoring the bones and piles of skulls almost everywhere on this little quantum jaunt into the past? In the cornfields, buried in that strange interstellar dirt. In neat stacks back in the cities. Along the roads. Filling the canals.

Oh—but you've been editing out all the bones and skulls.

Haven't you?

This is what he asked himself as mushrooms grew and sprouted behind Bones's helmet. He mumbled something about this, and the medic turned. Her eyes were wide and cat-like, as though the fear she'd been hiding was blossoming into wonder.

Piles of skulls as big as a mountain.

The Mongol Khans had laid waste to entire cities back on lost and ancient Earth. Caravans traveling across the windswept wastes would find silent cities on the plain, and not just piles of skulls... but mountains of them.

History, his mind chuckled. It's been there all along for you, hasn't it?

"You've been ignoring the skulls!" said Esmail as they reached the bottom of the lift. His voice was slow and drippy, like syrup taken from the Murinar tree on Deglastani. It's one of the most expensive commodities in the galaxy because of its rumored aphrodisiac qualities.

The soldier laughed, the laugh turned hideous, and the lift descended into hell even though it had already jittered to a halt.

You've been ignoring the skulls.

Ancient locks snapped into place beyond the skeletal walls where the panels had been parted out to make weapons and armor for the Savages in their unknown wars for mastery of the ship and its crew. The doors opened onto a torch-lit platform where a battered monorail waited.

THK-133 stepped forward with a hypo and med patch.

"Master, the hallucinogenic properties of these fungi are too much for your pitiful system. You are close to having a heart attack. I'm sedating you."

Rex and the soldiers stood aside as the bot walked forward and reverently placed the med patch on Casper's fevered forehead.

He was burning up.

The patch felt cool and calm, and he surrendered to the nano-sedatives, closing his eyes and falling through the bottom of the lift to the jungle dirt below. His last vision of that lost history inside the ghost ship *Moirai* was one of pulsing iridescent mushrooms sending forth sweet clouds of green tasty cotton candy poison across his fever-drenched mind.

There were drums. Tribal drums beating in the distant darkness. Close and all around. He lay on the moist jungle floor.

He could hear a tiny furious animal repeating something. Thumps and grunts were followed by the smash of crushed foliage and the agony of some saurian hissing in pain. One of Casper's eyes scanned a horizon that reached from ground to night sky at a perpendicular angle. He was lying on his side. He saw a hypodermic injector in the foreground, and beyond that THK-133 firing its heavy blaster into the jungle. Strange shapes wielding sharp-toothed weapons surged out of the darkness.

THK-133 turned between bright flares of the blaster and said, "Don't worry, master, I'll kill them all!"

With something like glee.

And was that a smile on the machine's face?

Casper wondered this as he surrendered once more to the darkness that took him down where there were no more dreams. No visions. No memories. Down there was only nothing. And nothing more.

Not even himself.

Was there such a place? he asked.

And then he arrived there.

21

Casper found himself in a decrepit and rattling transit car speeding down a dark tunnel. Eight cars made up the once-train-of-the-future—three smashed and gutted passenger cars, five pitch-black freight. Rex chose the forward car, as it was both the easiest to defend and the only car with a working light. It was LeRoy who figured the system out and sent the train moving forward into the dark of the tunnel that ran the length of the massive ship.

They approached a platform that first appeared as a tiny light in the blackness ahead. LeRoy slowed the train, and everyone readied weapons and ducked behind what little cover could be had within the beaten rail car. But all they saw as the train whipped past was a lonely platform. Unused, abandoned for who knew how long. A few sporadic lights managed to effect the opposite of illumination, instead creating more shadows and a mood of forlorn hopelessness that made one glad for the speeding dark of the tunnel.

A few skulls were scattered across the platform. Casper did not ignore them.

"Notice the graffiti," he said to Rex over the command comm.

It was scrawled everywhere.

Every Stop is the Last Stop.

All Prisoners must be taken to Cog for Dissection. Stop Nine.

The Dark Wanderer is always watching you.

"Yeah," grunted Rex. "I see it. We'll try and pick up her trail there, at Stop Nine, if that's where they take the prisoners." He looked toward some markings on the wall. "This is Stop Four."

"We started at Two," said LeRoy. He was hunkered down below the controls at the front of the car. Everybody was keeping a low profile. No one was taking any chances. "But I didn't see no Stop Three unless we just missed it in the dark."

It would've been impossible to miss Stop Three. No doubt they'd all been running their low-light imaging systems. And yet here they were at Stop Four. Nothing aboard the *Moirai* made sense. As though the eradication of meaning had become some sort of state-mandated religion when they'd all lost their minds in the long sub-light crawl through the void.

"Take us forward," said Rex.

"Yes, sir," replied LeRoy.

It was good to be moving away from the mystery of Stop Three's screaming absence. A mystery that proclaimed non-existence might also be an option, or a fate, awaiting them just a little farther down the line.

They had traveled only a short way through the darkness past Stop Four when a sound rang out above their heads, like a locking clamp grabbing hold of the car. And then more such titanic and hollow strikes sounded out at points along the rattle-y train, back in the trailing cars.

LeRoy had already added motive power, and the monorail, rickety-racketing its way through the tunnels between stations, surged ahead into the seemingly eternal darkness as more and more of the "locking clamp" sounds resounded out across the ceiling of the car.

Esmail stood and scanned their six. "See something..." he half-muttered.

The low-light imaging in Casper's SmartEye fritzed out in a wash of electronic distortion. Using the interface on his sleeve, he cycled through night vision and thermal. Both were a snowstorm of static, effectively blinding him. And it quickly became clear that everyone else was having the same problem—even though Martian and Terran tech ran on different operating systems.

Esmail tapped the high-powered searchlight atop his combat helmet and turned it toward the cars behind them. As the bright beam fell upon the dark cars, it illuminated a gruesome sight. Gleaming steel spiders were everywhere, skittering forward for them.

Mechanical spiders.

But with human torsos and gray human horror-show heads.

Bones screamed and fired a burst from the Savage weapon she'd picked up. Bullets danced along the beasts' horrible metal carapaces and articulating mechanical legs. Subsonic rounds smoked through the pulpy steaming gray flesh of their upper torsos and ricocheted off into the darkness.

As Bones's weapons fired dry, the rest of the team engaged the closing targets. There were at least a dozen human-spider hybrids climbing forward over their dead biomechanical brethren. Their eyes glowed with insane green circuitry, and their mouths were filled with once-human teeth that had been filed into gleaming needles. Their very nature was a monstrosity the human mind didn't want to look upon.

One of them, a male, smashed through the glass at the side of the car, hauled Duhrawski out through the shattered glass with four of its hydraulically driven legs and claws, then fell to the tracks. All that was left of Duhrawski was the sound of him firing into the darkness as the motion of the train carried nightmare spider and soldier away, leaving them alone in the dark of the tunnel.

Another spider, its human mouth working savagely, even though it had been hit several times and blood was pumping from arteries where there shouldn't be arteries, made a grab for Bones. The medic had been struggling to get a new magazine into her scavenged weapon, but now she let go of it and scrambled backwards, her combat boots pistoning to keep her away from the drooling and gore-draped monster.

Emergency horns blared across the car, and some kind of over-speed terminal approach warning sounded. Uncaring, the spider-overrun train shot through a station at high speed.

Casper raced forward to cover Bones, firing point blank at the thing that was trying to drag her back into the darkness of the other cars, where other biomechanical spiders clustered. It wasn't until the gray human head of the biomech spider disintegrated from three direct hits that the main bulb of its body fell over awkwardly and died.

And still more were coming in through the windows and up along the corridor that ran between the dirty seats. It was like watching the horror of all horrors made suddenly all too real.

Rex ran out of ammo. Barr yelled "Mag out!" and bent to one knee to load a new mag. LeRoy shoved the monorail throttle full forward, and the unseen engine rose to an ethereal demonic hum. The cars began to wobble and shake as though they might just decide to leave the track altogether. Casper continued firing at the looming spiders now moving forward en masse. LeRoy turned away from the controls and swung the barrel of his automatic rifle up with one motion, pulled the sling around his shoulder tight, and fired.

It was then that Rex dropped the savage slug thrower, raced forward, and pulled his plate cutter. He danced forward, dodging the frail once-human arms that reached out to embrace or tear, and lopped off the biological head of one of the spiders. Pivoting on one foot, he and slashed through another spider's rib cage with the spinning blade of the plate cutter. The beast reared back on its mechanical hind legs, vomited blood and oil, and died screeching. Its voice was like some ancient eight-bit arcade machine gone tilt.

Bones brought her now-loaded weapon up to bear and shot three spiders dead in succession, using most of a mag to do so. Casper followed this up with rapid-fire double taps from his Terran Navy sidearm, making sure all the dead spiders were truly dead.

Rex cut his way down to the linkage that connected the trailing cars to this one. He slashed into a thick rubberized connector, reared back, and severed the connection with a mighty blow that sent sparks flying into the night.

One spider, on the trailing car now falling away, leapt across the new void at Rex, knocking him backward. But the thing impaled itself on the spinning plate cutter and fell onto the tracks, dragging the tool with it into the darkness of the tunnel.

Without the weight of the trailing cars to hold it back, the over-speeding monorail finally left the track as it had long been promising to do. It turned over onto its side and sent them all sprawling across the cabin. Casper slammed face first into the side of the car, which was now the floor, and watched as the smooth concrete of the tunnel slid just beneath his eyes on the other side of a cracked window.

A moment later the monorail wedged hard into the tunnel, refusing to go further, and they were all thrown forward, tumbling over one another.

And all was darkness.

It was Casper who got his light on first. He was surprised he hadn't broken any of his bones, though his shoulder was definitely dislocated. He screamed as he forced himself to pull his light off his belt and scan the cabin.

In the bright, unforgiving glare it was impossible to tell the difference between the living and the dead.

"Everyone okay?" he asked. It sounded pitiful, and he knew it.

"Don't move anything until you're sure it's not broken," Bones shouted. "Especially your necks and heads."

Someone else groaned.

Then LeRoy spoke up. "All right, guys, sound off," he said, like they'd just formed up for some work detail. "Who we got?"

Bones.

Barr.

Esmail.

Casper.

That was all.

A quick search also revealed Rex. He'd slammed so hard into the front of the car that his bucket had cracked in half. He was unconscious.

"In addition to the rapid deceleration trauma," Bones said after inspecting him, "someone shot him. Probably LeRoy."

"Nah... wasn't me. My grouping's always tight, little sister."

Barr had taken a nasty blow to the head too, although his bucket hadn't cracked. "Yeah, it was probably you. You got the jitters and all, Leroy. Remember Tankersly?"

Bones patched Rex's bullet wound with a med patch. The slug had gone right through the meat of one thigh, and there was no artery damage.

Barr loaded his weapon. "We ain't gettin' no medals now. Not after shootin' the major."

LeRoy grumbled, "I don't think we're gettin' out of this to get any medals, Barr."

Casper pulled himself out of the crashed train car. The smooth concrete of the tunnel felt gritty and dust-laden under his feet. He peered down the tunnel. A clean white light was just visible in the distance, though it was hard to judge how far. It was brilliantly fluorescent compared to the overwhelming darkness they'd suffered ever since the moment the *Lex* had set down on the hangar deck.

He turned back to the others. "I see a light up ahead. Got to be the next stop. I'm going forward to scout. Get Major Rex up and out of the car, then wait here. Back in five minutes."

He pulled his sidearm and began to walk. He had one charge pack left.

Within a few minutes he neared the broad blanket of light. It was, as he'd expected, another platform. He took a knee and waited, listening.

He checked his six. From here he could see no sight of the ruined car. Or the spiders. Maybe they, too, had died in the wreck. Or maybe they'd taken too many losses to continue on and had gone off to...

Caves?

Warrens?

Labs?

His mind didn't want to think about what those things might call home, so he left the thought alone.

But whatever had happened... they hadn't continued their attack. They'd disappeared with the victims they'd managed to snatch. And maybe for them... that was enough of a victory.

When nothing changed in the local soundscape, he proceeded forward cautiously. Unlike the other platforms they'd passed in their helter-skelter journey along the rail line, this one was pristine, almost new. It waited as though at any moment some sleek monorail train might appear in a rush and disgorge chattering and harried scientists, crew, and colonists from that long-ago era that was Earth outward bound and hopeful. Casper imagined that the big ship, when it pulled away from low Earth orbit all those years ago, must have looked a lot like this platform did now: a cross between a state-of-the-art gadget store of slate-gray chrome and glass, and a medical facility with all the latest longevity techniques promised to those who could afford them.

For Casper it was like stepping back in time. Or stepping back into a time before time as he knew it. For him there were those kinds of memories too. The memory of wandering other people's memories. Of uncovering what once was. It was part of his nature, that constant archeologist he'd always been. The wondering wanderer who'd asked all those questions across all those worlds.

Who were these people?

Why is this here?

What do these pictures mean?

He remembered, as a child, maybe seven or eight years old, wandering the ruins of a wrecked Los Angeles as a kind of playtime after the daily chores. That year his father was raising a herd of pigs in the ruins of their farm on La Brea Boulevard, and Casper would often go out to the big old silent street and look down it, morning and evening, and wondered what had become of all the cars that had once raced up and down the broad avenue. All the movie stars who had died before, and during, the war. And maybe even after, in the ruins and long winter.

In the afternoons, when his father went copper mining, Casper often went with him. They'd head for the wreckage of some old building where his father would extract all the copper wire he could wrap and bundle and sell at the swap meet in Santa Fe Springs.

Casper never went inside the shotgunned and barely standing buildings. *It's too dangerous.* The buildings his father worked in were on the verge of constant collapse. Old rotten floors could give way, and often did. Weakened walls would collapse inward. And raiders might be hiding in there in the darkness. Waiting for the night and their wildings.

And so Casper as a child wandered La Brea, allowed only to look from a distance at all the "once was" that once was. He spent many a long hour watching those stores, trying to see what life had looked like before the world had gone ruined. Trying to imagine it all. Sometimes he could form an image, an understanding. Other times things were so tumbledown that they were beyond the knowing. But sometimes there were pictures that made the work of imagining what everything once looked like much easier.

His father had been a cop in the times of those pictures. LAPD. All through the food riots and during the Vegas War, as he called it. Even then, on La Brea, the other farmers had made his father a kind of sheriff and judge, and sometimes an executioner too, when it needed to be done.

"We do what we have to," his father remarked sadly one evening after returning from Beverly Hills where he'd had to hang a rapist. And then he'd said no more as they thanked God for their lima beans and cornbread. There was bacon that night too.

Casper recalled all those memories as he stood there looking at the platform on the ship from the past that had hurtled off into the future. Memories of a pristine golden age when the world was a better place of abundance and technology, and the celebrities and politicians and thinkers had seemed like gods among men.

A particular memory came back to him, distinct. He was staring into the grit and debris of a store on La Brea. A high-end gadget store named after a fruit. Which seemed dumb to Casper. The picture had been thrown to the floor by some looter in the time of looting, left to lie abandoned among the smashed glass and shattered furniture.

It was a picture of a family. Obviously they were getting a smartphone. A gadget. A toy to them in that lost age of abundance. They'd used that fantastic device to amuse themselves from moment to moment. With games. Or pictures. Or commercials of endlessly available goods and services. Or meaningless conversations that paled in importance to what was on the horizon and headed straight at them like a bullet.

In the age after that, everything was precious, and nothing, not even smartphones when they came back, was used to play. Instead, when technology returned, it was used to work, make, and grow. All the noble things. Everything the Galactic Republic used to be before the House of Reason took it upon itself to steer the ship of culture right back to what had ruined everything in the last days of Earth.

When no one had hired it to murder another civilization, the House of Reason had taken it upon itself and returned to its old tricks, expecting a different outcome this time rather than all the failures they'd ended up with before. And they were always surprised when the same results of failure, starvation, and revolt came up again and again.

Insanity.

But on the eight-year-old child's day, when he looked at the family in that picture he'd found among the grit and rubble, getting that wonderful device and all the pleasures it promised, things were different. Better than what they had become.

In the picture they were all clean. Some weeks Casper's family did not bathe at the farm.

In the picture, they all looked healthy. Casper's little sister had died of the plague at two.

And they had new clothes in the picture. The eight-year-old Casper had never owned new clothes. The first set of new clothes he would ever own that weren't salvaged or found, or put together from the scraps of lost things, was the plebe uniform that NASA issued him at the academy in his first year. Blue coveralls. Boots. A nylon jacket. And the next new clothing he would own was his issued uniform the week before graduation four years later.

On that day, his mother and father, the sheriff of La Brea, drove six hundred miles in an old truck that was his dad's pride and joy. His father was wordless that whole windy sun-swept day in Houston. And then, finally, he said to Casper in a low voice made hoarse by wind, dirt, and fallout: "Make the galaxy better than what we gave you, son. Make it better out there."

Yes. That's how it should've been.

Casper hauled himself up onto the platform.

The slate-gray floor was polished to a high sheen, and the back wall was polished chrome. Space Age lettering on frosted white glass, backlit with a soft green glow, announced this platform as "Platform Nine."

Casper studied everything. A high-tech security hatch was set in the wall, and next to it was a glass plaque with embossed black lettering that read:

Welcome to the Moirai Center for
Advanced Cognition.
Within all will be known.

22

There was the man, the bot, and the little beast.

Casper came to himself as the three of them struggled up through the shattered granite scree of the jagged ridge that separated the jungle and all its narcotic madness from the desert that lay ahead with all its unknowns.

The effects of the psychotropic mushrooms were fading, and in those moments he slowly awoke from the nightmares. They seemed now more like dreams than the stark raving terrors they had been. Even now all the horrors of his memories, mixing with the dark rivers, strange stones, and wild clutches of that spreading jungle, were like something that had happened to someone else. Someone not him. Someone he'd only been half-watching.

The first thing Casper heard as he came out of that day's long waking dream was the sound of his own boots crunching against tiny broken rock. The *Moirai* and its horrors lurked within that sound. The screams. The staccato bursts of automatic weapons. The half-remembered conversations. The running. Running through the darkness in fear and terror. The Savages always at your back. And all the unknown tunnels surrounding you as you made your way through that ghost ship.

The next thing he heard was the little beast huffing and puffing up the ridge behind him, muttering.

"Urmo. Urmo. Urmo."

Casper looked up and saw the tactical hunter killer bot, a dark shadow against the rays of red light that cast themselves out beyond the ridge. And beyond the lethal killing machine rose the ancient edifice.

The statue of a lizard king.

In his mind, during the terrors, he remembered it hovering ever above him, watching with those soulless saurian eyes and that hungry wide smile. It had been there too, on the *Moirai*, watching him like the piles of skulls.

But now it faced away from them, out over the desert. Looking toward some unknown place that couldn't be found on any maps back in the galaxy. Casper had a feeling that this place, this planet, was far more ancient than anyone could have suspected. Ancient by orders of magnitude.

He began to shiver.

Or maybe he had been shivering. His teeth rattling in his skull. Every muscle ached. Especially his eyeballs. And his jaw. As though his eyes had been pinned wide open and his jaw set in some grim yet furious decision to see the end of the drug trip through to its fatal end. As though he hadn't been able to take his mind or eyes off the hallucinations that had ravaged him in the long and lost trek through the jungle.

He turned, just below the ridge, to stare back at the jungle one last time. He would probably never see it again. It covered everything, swallowed everything. The ship. The rivers. The memories. His arrival. He scanned the hazy alien treetops that rose up like statues in their own right. Clustered among those great trees he saw finally the unseen birds that had howled and moaned and always stayed just out of sight. From this distance they seemed to swim through the red-and-yellow-hued haze as though it were a sea, and the trees were great coral reefs, shimmering and waving.

And then Casper turned his back on it all and climbed the pass between two summits.

Beyond the statue that seemed to stare down at them once they crossed from jungle to high desert waste, its expression one of anticipation and contempt, a vast desert fell away from the sharp iron ridges turned blood red by the fading red dwarf sinking into the horizon. Casper saw jagged canyons, a sea of dunes, and nothing... endless nothing. If the desert had once had a name, it was long lost now. It was the quintessence of nothingness.

A desert of nothingness.

For there was nothing in it.

PART TWO

THE DESERT IN WHICH YOU MUST COME TO THE END OF YOURSELF

23

That night they made camp beneath the statue. THK-133 had gathered dead wood to make a fire while Casper sat beneath a survival blanket. His body felt drained, his mind cottony and distant, as though it had been through a great sickness and had only just survived. In other words... he felt thin.

There was little food left in his ruck, and THK-133's pack carried only charge packs for the heavy blaster. This was odd, because Casper remembered loading that pack with survival rations.

The state of Casper's gear was a question unto itself. Many things were simply missing. Some were not. There was no rhyme nor reason as to why one piece of equipment had survived the trek through the jungle and another had disappeared. Try as he might to remember what had happened in the jungle, Casper could find nothing in his mind to give him a coherent picture of the journey. His boots had been ravaged. His pants were muddy and torn. His shirt had been so badly ruined through sweat and damage that he'd used it as kindling to start the fire that night. He had only the jacket now. That had remained strangely pristine, folded and strapped to the top of his ruck. For all the damage everything else had taken, the heavy-duty survival jacket looked like it hadn't even gone on the terrible journey that had brought them beneath the glare of the desert statue.

The hunting blaster rifle was gone too. And he had no memory of losing it.

He looked at THK-133. The bot merely stared into the fire. Urmo had caught some desert rat and was busy skinning it in the darkness away from the fire.

"How long?" Casper croaked. From the sound of his voice, he guessed he hadn't used it much in the time he'd been under the influence of the strange mushrooms. Or perhaps he'd screamed and screamed it into uselessness.

The bot swiveled its head mechanically, landing its gaze on Casper.

"Ah, you can speak coherently again, master. Excellent. This is quite a change from your constant nonsensical raving and general lunacy. I look forward to a return to your more lucid conversations, which I have occasionally enjoyed."

Raving.

Casper drank some water. He still had the canteen. It didn't cool things now—somehow it had malfunctioned with regard to only that one feature—but even the tepid water felt good on his raw throat.

Little Urmo returned with the spitted rat. It had two heads. The tiny creature thrust it into the fire with evil delight and watched the flames leap up around it, muttering its one, oft-repeated word over and over to itself.

"Raving?" Casper asked. His voice was still hoarse.

"Yes, raving," answered the bot drolly.

Pause.

"What I was I raving about?"

"Oh... everything. You gave a running commentary of everything we saw. Often objectifying trees or rocks and turning them into persons. You had cute names for them.

It was like going on a long walk with a primeval tribesman who explained everything with the catchall word 'magic.' It was quite ridiculous."

Casper thought about this. Again, there were no memories of any of these events inside his brain. Instead he felt that the ancient memories of his time aboard the *Moirai* had been the subject of his waking hallucinations. In the past, in the years since those events, he'd often returned in nightmares to that haunted ship, awakening and feeling as though he were suffocating, or screaming out with night terrors as the *Moirai* exploded around him once more.

"What did I say?" he asked the bot nonchalantly.

Urmo's coal-dark eyes glistened greedily as the two-headed rat began to roast and sizzle. The little beast hopped gently back and forth from one tiny furry leg to the other as flames licked at the desert rat's flesh.

"Oh..." began the bot, staring upward as if in deep thought.

There were no stars above; this planet was too far from the galaxy. Casper found that deeply unnerving, both with regard to navigation and basic humanity. But his system was too shot to even consider how lost beyond the known he was, so he focused on the flames consuming the dead wood.

Dead for how long, he wondered absently. This wood had once been some kind of tree. Now it had arrived here in a treeless desert.

"Well... you talked about your parents," said THK-133. "How very proud they were of you. Graduating from something you called 'NASA' seemed to have been a big moment for them. For your male biological progenitor especially. You were very proud of that. So proud that you talked about it endlessly for days—when you weren't tearing through the rations every time I turned back to make sure you hadn't fallen into another pit."

That doesn't seem right, thought Casper. His parents had been murdered by raiders. A biker gang called the... *Goths*. And that was well before he'd ever been accepted into NASA. No one had come to his graduation because there had been no one. He didn't think about his parents much; their deaths formed one of the most painful memories of his life.

And yet he'd been luridly fascinated by Goths. As though they were the source of all his fears. He'd been driven to learn about them, to make them less... powerful. Less of a nightmare figure, always on the edge of his vision. Always waiting in the shadows. And instead... the very word *Goth* inspired a sense of dread darkness inside his mind despite all his efforts to haul it into the light.

So he had researched them, the Goths. The original ones, found in the history books, from which the bikers must've taken their gang's name. The Goths of history had destroyed the known world, such as it was back then. Just like the later Goths who killed his parents... and destroyed his *own* known world.

When he suffocated... at night, in his nightmares of the *Moirai*... the painful sound he made as the air refused to come sounded like... *Gothhhhh*. It felt like a hand gripping his throat.

Painful... like Reina? asked that observer who watched all the dreams and nightmares in his mind.

"Yes," he whispered aloud, answering the question as though it were his own thought, when it had so clearly been a voice inside his head. "And that was somehow worse in its way. Which, even after two thousand years, is a terrible thing to think about your parents. That losing the love of your life is somehow worse than losing the people who gave you life and unconditional love. But I'm too strung out from the mushrooms to be anything but honest with myself. It's too late for comfortable lies."

He was talking to himself. He was aware of that. But the bot didn't seem to care, or so its programming indicated, and Urmo remained only "Urmo" and nothing more.

"And so where do we go now, master, now that you've reached your... 'lizard king statue'?"

The bot's question broke Casper's reverie. He'd been close to completing some thought that meant something. That might unlock the mysteries of the universe that surrounded him. But now it was gone.

"*The lizard king will tell us where to go next!*" erupted the bot. "You screamed that over and over back in the jungle, master. No matter how I tried to quiet you, you would not relent from proclaiming that hope as loudly as your pitiful lung capacity would allow. That's what drew those Bronze Age apes out. Your maniacal screaming. Which was a good thing, of course—it's been so many years in flight time since I have killed anything in mass quantities. It was nice to know I hadn't lost the touch."

"Apes?"

"Only vaguely. Definitely simianoid, master. But giant. Four arms. Savage brutes. Some tools. If they had gotten ahold of you they would've torn you to shreds. It was all I could do to save your life, master. And I enjoyed the challenge. So there was that."

Urmo apparently deemed the rat sufficiently cooked, as it fell upon its flesh, tearing and grunting with delight, ever murmuring its own name. It was as if the little creature were killing it all over again with each gusty bite.

"And so I return your drug-ravaged brain to my original query: where do we go now, master? Now that we have reached your lizard king, where shall we spend your few remaining days wandering endlessly on this planet where no one will ever find your body?"

Casper didn't know. Now, bereft of anything, any idea, of even the basic ability to feel anything other than empty, he had no idea why it had been so important to find the statue—other than that it had been the only observable landmark in the moments before the crash. But a planet, even a small planet, was large. And no man, even over several lifetimes, could search an entire planet for a place no one had ever been to. When he thought about it... it was like looking for a needle in a haystack the size of a planet. On foot. Day after day. Surrounded by predators. No sustainable food, water, medicine. The chances that he would die badly were suddenly overwhelming.

He had crossed all the boundaries he'd sworn never to cross, and now... he had no idea where he would find what needed finding. What he had traded everything to find.

The Temple of Morghul was somewhere on this planet... but the *words needle in a haystack* seemed like the truest words he'd ever heard.

Urmo burped loudly. The sound startled Casper. His nerves were still on edge. When he turned, he saw the little beast looking up reverently at the great statue that loomed over them in the night.

Casper followed the creature's gaze.

And paused.

He would've sworn the statue had been head down, staring at some focus point on the ground just beneath it, ready to greedily receive some sacrifice due to it long ago, its arms stretched out to receive whatever had been offered. But now the flickering firelight and shifting shadows showed the giant half-man, half-lizard staring out across the desert. One long and muscled arm pointed toward the distant horizon, unseen in the starless and wan moonlit night.

At any other time in his life Casper would've sworn that it had always been that way. For how could it have been otherwise? Even in the brief moments before the stricken freighter had almost smacked into it dead center...

Which had been an odd thing.

On a vast and empty planet, his freighter, falling out of hyperspace off course and out of control—for no reason that he could diagnose, other than nav and engine failure—in those desperate bare seconds, somehow that freighter had aimed itself straight for the monument.

A monument whose arms were outstretched and waiting to receive a sacrifice. Yes, that's exactly how it had been.

Except now everything was different.

Now the monolithic edifice was pointing like a signpost on a lost and lonely highway, when the lights have all gone dark and the good people of the galaxy have hidden themselves behind their walls and blast doors. Just as they always had. The statue pointed off into the unknown, disturbing the mind with its promise of a location not yet considered.

Except you, Casper. You're out here, beyond the perimeter of the known, lost in the dark, and you encounter a sign. A signpost along the road.

But am I at an intersection? he wondered. *Is there another choice I'm not seeing? Another option I'm missing? Or is this merely something to remind me where*

I've been headed all along? As if I've had no other choice all along.

"I guess we go that way," he murmured when no other answer called itself out across the high desert night.

The bot clicked and whirred, indicating that it was satisfied with the shape of the next event concerning it.

Casper studied the strange little creature that had found them in the jungle alongside the river, after the behemoth of a lizard had destroyed everything. And for the first time, he sensed something other than just a tribal prehistoric creature with a bare intelligence.

He sensed knowing behind the little creature's eyes.

And that was when Urmo nodded at him, there in the night, beneath the lizard king, on the high desert ridge, out beyond the known of the galaxy. Nodded as if confirming all the fears Casper had never considered until that moment.

24

They set off at dawn. Throughout the long night before, the wind had howled and moaned, keening like some wounded animal that could never be comforted in its grief. In the morning they followed the fall of the ridge down onto the dry desert plain, and for a time, by the light of the rising yet dying red dwarf star at their back, everything was revealed with an almost pristine clarity. There was no sign of life, no track, no ruins of the creatures that had long ago erected the enigmatic monument falling away behind them. No ancient road, no structural remains seen through the wind-driven dust. No desert plants, resilient and dangerous. There was only the silence and the distant low moan of the wind as it raced through the broken arroyos and ancient red rock canyons, coming up off a sea of dust that seemed never-ending.

Within hours the desert cool of the night was a thing forgotten, and the air was a dry furnace. As the furious red dwarf neared its zenith, they stopped in the shade of a giant boulder found out on the desert plain. Ahead lay only dunes. Dunes that most likely wandered in their own way back and forth across the wastes, covering anything that ever was. If there had once been landmarks, guideposts, anything at all that might have helped them navigate, it was now buried somewhere out in the sea of sand.

Survival.

He had a day's worth of water.

"This is madness," he whispered as he ate one of the few stale nutrition bars that remained.

"What is madness, master? Are you feeling the return of your lunacy? Shall I restrain you? Place my arm in your mouth so that you do not swallow your tongue when you begin to froth in feral madness? It might be best to discuss at what point I should end your suffering. At least while you still retain your limited faculties."

He ignored the bot.

When the blazing red orb was directly overhead, they headed out again. Casper had instructed THK-133 to maintain the same compass heading, an easy thing for any bot to do. Even now, it seemed to be holding course without the slightest bit of trouble.

Hours passed, and eventually the sun fell toward the horizon. Urmo was content to trudge through the thick dust behind them, following their trail closely. When Casper looked back, he could see that they had mixed all their tracks one after the other. He felt good about that.

And he felt better. He was tired. Thirsty. Burnt. But better. The poisons of the mushrooms had faded, and his rest beneath the giant statue had been so untroubled he hardly remembered dreaming, or even waking.

Darkness fell, and just before it did, Casper climbed to the top of a tall dune. He stared out across the dusty sea and searched for anything. Any sign of habitation or landmark. But there was nothing. Nothing but endless desert and a distant haze brought on by some windstorm that obscured what lay beyond.

He sighed and tramped back down the hill.

"Shall we camp here?" asked THK-133. "Full dark will come soon, master. Both moons will be gibbous."

Casper wasn't tired. Not yet. And possibly it was better to continue on in the cool of the night. He pulled out his canteen and shook it. Half full. Then he remembered the medical kit. There were hydration tabs in there.

He pulled the medical bag from his ruck. He'd done an inventory at the camp last night, and he couldn't recall seeing the tabs. Sure enough, they were gone. The soft blue cylinder they came in was empty. In frustration, he flung the useless item away, and the wind came up and carried it into the shadow of a dune. Within seconds, the gently drifting sand had buried it.

If they stopped, he thought, if he gave up, the sand would bury him, too, in just that manner. Softly. Slowly. But steadily. This world would bury him. As though that's what it had been waiting to do all along.

"Let's keep moving."

They set off once more. Into the night, swallowed by the dust and the darkness. Following the barest glint of moonlight reflecting off the killing machine's armor.

THE LESSON OF NAMES

Long has the student trained within the temple. Years have passed, and whoever he once was is gone now. Washed away. Who he is... or rather who he is becoming... that's becoming clearer and clearer every day. Like a body of water, once disturbed by a thrown rock, settling back to its equilibrium, revealing not just the mountains and forest that surround the high lake, but the sky above and even the stars beyond.

The waters are settling.

A new picture is being revealed.

As has been said before... time does not matter within the temple. All the years in which the student has trained seem like days. And some days seem like centuries. The temple is not a safe place. There are in fact many places in which one can become lost—forever, notes the Master on occasion. The sanctuaries, the lowers halls, and the "other" places the temple connects to.

On the day the student learned what this power was actually called, he was following the Master out into the crumbling reaches of the Cathari Tombs. They had been walking for days down the Hall of Lost Kings. The student knew that days had passed because in the crumbling roof above he could see the night sky, then the daylight, and then the night again, several times over.

He knows how to read the runes now.

Knows what they mean.

He has, on this long journey through the crumbling tombs of the Hall of Kings, long since given up on reading their names, stamped upon their sealed tombs.

Xur Ilgon the Unquenchable.

Xur Slighyth the Wounded.

X'ao Moloth the Damned.

X'ao Byyal the Ruiner of Stars.

X-unth Tigla Polazaar the Defiler of the Central Core.

X-Um Hadezzarrix the Vanquisher of Light.

And so on and so on.

"Who are these?" asks the student in the almost reverential silence of the place. Only the padding of their bare feet makes any sound here.

"Who is anyone?" mumbles the Master as he continues forward into the darkness.

In the night they make a fire, breaking up a once-ornate carving of the obscene sacking of some lost city. Lizard warriors, wielding ebony blades of darkness and carrying something that reminds the student of the heavy blaster carried by the Legion at Karthae, rape and pillage a race unknown. The student studies as much of this as he can before the flames consume the ornate carving the size of a door.

Who is anyone? he thinks, and wonders who they all once were.

In the silence, eating the bread they baked three days ago within the Master's sanctum, the student wonders at the meaning of their titles.

He hears the Master, who is intent over his dry and tasteless bread, chuckle softly to himself. It is the sound of dry leaves crossing the graves of the dead under a harvest moon.

"Close you are to becoming what you will be?"

The student lays down the bread at his feet and stares about at the tombs. He considers the Master's question and statement all in one. And he knows an answer is expected of him if the lesson is to continue. Perhaps that is the reason they have gone so deep into the tombs. A place the Master warned him, early on, to stay away from.

He looks around.

There are only two things that have a connection with all the things in this place, he thinks to himself. And so the answer must be one of those two things.

Death?

Or...

Kings?

He tries to remember why he has come here. But even that, in its own way, has lost meaning. He came here to do something. To set right some wrong. But the cruel lessons of the Master... and the power... have stripped such lies away.

He came only for the Power.

"I see only two things here, Master," says the student. He waits to be struck, chastised... or for the lesson to continue.

"See what?" grumbles the Master, intent on his bread.

Once more the student stares about at the precinct of waiting, silent tombs, stretching off into the shadows in every direction for days at a time.

There are places within the temple where one can become lost forever. "Other" places from which one never returns.

"I see Death and Kings... Master."

Silence.

And then...

"Fool," mutters the Master, still intent on his dry and tasteless bread. "See only that which you want to. Fear that which you do not see."

The student tenses his body and readies for action. To the casual observer, of which there are none, no change in posture would have been noticed—but the student is ready for battle. The mention of fear has warned him. He reaches out to sense menace or attack, and finds nothing.

Again the Master chuckles and continues on with his meal.

"Fear nothing always. And yet fear makes us strong once master it we do. Death... inevitable it has always been. Even for you. And for me. A king is everyone unto himself. Those who mastered their fears... this the Hall of the Kings is marked by."

The Master lays down his bread and closes his eyes.

"Names are meaningless. But meaning... words have. A Kogon death giant was Xur, Warlord of Ten Thousand Worlds. All feared him. Terrible was he to behold. The mind, they say, shattered when one looked upon his insane visage. Slew him did Ilgon. Frightened he was. King he became. Fear he did master."

All around them the temple begins to tremble. Dust and grit fall from the ceiling.

"Kogon menaced the Spiral Kings for ages untold."

Nearby, one of the entrances to a tomb slowly slides away from its foundations, revealing a growing dark beyond.

"X'ao, X-unth, X-Um, and Xur. Among the Kogon giants these were. Others too. Conquered them the Spiral Kings did. Powerful they became. Fear they became. Power is fear."

Now the Master is looking at the student with a malevolent gleam in his eye.

"Soon you will be ready. Fear must you conquer. Then you will know. Powerful you may yet still be."

The student watches the darkness beyond the tomb the Master has opened. And it is not just darkness there that waits for him. It is cold. It is lost. It is death.

And so much worse.

"Afraid of what you... you will become," chuckles the Master with no humor. "Enter the darkness and face your fears you will. Die or die not, then powerful you will become, my student."

25

At midnight, or as close as he could come to guessing what might pass for that hour, they stopped in the lee of a massive dune. Casper simply muttered "Patrol" and fell to his knees. He wrapped himself up in the jacket he'd put on as the night got colder, and he used the near-empty ruck as a pillow.

Urmo sat down in the sand near him. Cross-legged. Eyes closed. The moaning wind tossing sand into the creature's fur. And Casper remembered something. He patted his leg where he'd strapped his knife, back before the giant monster had wrecked the ship. He only remembered that now, as sleep dragged him down and under.

The knife, too, was gone.

Most likely lost somewhere in the jungle.

Rechs, limping, led the rest of the soldiers forward. Casper was still standing on the platform of Stop Nine. Staring at the letters stamped into the wall.

Welcome to the Moirai Center for
Advanced Cognition.
Within all will be known.

Casper had been trying to hack some ancient operating system running on a console that seemed to be the administrative center for the platform. It was an old OS, so he had no problems getting around it and finding an admin back door. Unfortunately, the system merely tracked the access times the security locks on the doors had been opened, along with the encrypted passwords and associated usernames. All of them were weird.

windlooker

fategatherer

spiritmama

Typical Savages. He'd seen it before. When those massive ships left Earth in the bitter harvest of a thousand different dogmas colliding with each other head-on, they were each the embodiment of some singular philosophy that would prove them right in the vacuum. A fully contained world in which to experiment, refine, and perfect their ideal society. But every time the Terran Navy cracked a lighthugger, they went in to find not utopia found, but something much worse. Worse... yet still related to the original dream. Like some horrible doll with its head missing, replaced by something dead found along the highway.

Casper borrowed a username and ran some encryption from his smart device. He kept apps that interfaced with the old systems, because part of the navy's job had been to deal with the eventuality of a Savage encounter—which meant encountering the old-timey operating systems used by the formerly state-of-the-art lighthuggers.

In thirty seconds, the app had decrypted the password and gotten him access to the logs.

Twelve standard days ago, he learned from the system, the doors had been opened for a prisoner transfer.

Casper already knew that thirteen days ago, the *Moirai* had raided a science colony at Al-Baquar Seven, taking Reina hostage.

He beckoned Rechs over and pointed toward the entry. "Could be her?" he whispered.

For a long moment Rechs stared at the highlighted log entry on the screen. Then he nodded.

As one, what remained of the Martian infantry stacked itself against the security door that led into the complex beyond. LeRoy hacked the lock, the door *shhusss-hed* open, and weapons out, they entered the brightly lit halls beyond.

26

In the days that followed their long trek through the depths of the unforgiving desert, there was only the sun, the wind, and the memories. And at night, the moons, the cold, and the nightmares.

Two days into the wastes, with the water in the canteen long gone, they found a well. An ancient well. There was no bucket or rope, for how long could those things survive? A hundred years? Maybe two. But not more. Not eons. All that remained now was the well's shallow sandblasted stone lip.

Casper, lips chapped and skin scorched, peeled off his jacket and fell to his knees, wondering briefly if he would ever get up again. Even little Urmo seemed on the edge of being finished. THK-133 watched all this from the default position of passive judgment inherent to all bots.

On the distant horizon lay the bleached skeletons of massive monsters seemingly drowning in the sand.

Casper pulled off his ruck and dug through it. He had a memory of there being a knotted length of survival cord. All legionnaires carried the stuff in the same spot, and Casper had once been a legionnaire. One of the first, in fact, when Rechs was building his famous fighting unit to stop the Savage Tide that was on the verge of conquering the known galaxy. Casper had gone through Rechs's hellish training. He and Rechs had been well aware that if the Savages won, it would be Earth all over again.

He felt one hand find the almost silken knots of the survival cord. He pulled it out clumsily and held it aloft in triumph.

Urmo stared at him in incomprehension.

"This!" croak-shouted Casper over the howling wind that had come up in the afternoon. "We're not finished yet!" he added triumphantly. And then he laughed. He didn't know when—maybe he'd begun doing it in the swamp of hallucinogenic mushrooms—but he'd begun to talk to Urmo, to converse with him. His sun-blasted brain ignored the creature's inevitable one-word replies, instead making up its own responses. And thus a conversation had followed.

"Urmo! Urmo! Urmo!" the little beast shouted above the wind's moan.

"That's right," said Casper. "With this, and..." He turned wildly about, seeking THK-133. "And with him holding it, I can go down and see if there's water for us at the bottom."

"Urmo! Urmo! Urmo!"

And so, with the survival cord unknotted and at length, THK-133 lowered Casper down into the dark well rather easily.

In was cool and quiet down there, and only a small patch of sunlight-illuminated red dirt could be seen at the bottom. The constant hurl of the wind across the dune sea found the circular opening in the well and caused a single deep note, wavering, but always on pitch. To Casper it was like being lowered into some quiet temple—some place of peace and reflection beyond the assault of heat, light, and wind above.

The first thing he saw was the skeleton. The bottom of the well widened into a shallow cave, low-ceilinged, and the skeleton lay within it, on its side. It was fully intact, with only a few shreds of ancient disintegrating rags draped across its chalky white bones.

Casper felt the sand beneath his dry fingers. It was wet. He checked his surroundings, felt it was safe enough, and began to dig, breathing heavily in ragged, desperate gasps. Soon water began to collect inside his small depression. He filled his canteen cup, letting it analyze and remove anything harmful that it could detect, then raised it to his lips.

It was cold.

He tasted iron with a hint of sulfur.

But it was water.

"Water!" he shouted up the tube to the well's mouth. "We found water!"

He heard Urmo triumphantly repeating his own name.

And then Casper drank more.

Urmo shinnied down the rope, Casper handed the little thing his cup, and the creature drank greedily, slurping at the water. When it was finished, it sat down on its butt and burped. It held out the canteen cup, and again Casper was amazed that it was, in some way, intelligent. Very much like some kind of house pet, some barely domesticated animal that required only sustenance and company.

Casper refilled the cup, processed it, and handed it over. And as Urmo slurped once more, Casper crawled over to the skeleton on his hands and knees.

Although it was curled up and lying on its side, he could see that it was immense—nine feet tall at least. Its one lone eye socket stared out from beneath a bony forehead ridge. And that was what made the skeleton unusual. Yes, there were some intelligent races within the galaxy that reached a height of over nine feet, but none of them had one eye.

So perhaps this skeleton belonged to a race that was extra-galactic?

Casper leaned closer to study the eye socket, to make sure it wasn't actually some kind of wound that had opened a big hole in the skeleton's head. It was not. It was a massive orbital socket where once some eye had looked out upon the galaxy—and of course, in the end, had looked upon this cave beneath this well.

"It's like a Cyclops," whispered Casper, remembering his ancient myths from Earth's lost past.

"Urmo!" said Urmo, then burped.

Casper cast a quick look back at his companion. The little monster's belly was tight and swollen with water.

"Don't drink too much or you'll get a tummyache. And you're right. No such thing as a Cyclops ever existed. No known race in the galaxy fits this profile. And yet... here we are. Staring at the skeleton of something that once was."

He touched one of the bones. It wasn't just dry and brittle, it was turning to chalk.

Casper sat back and stared at the amazing skeleton, wondering who, or what, it had once been. And inevitably he thought of the mystery that had plagued the galaxy since the discovery of the pyramids on almost every world. The mystery of the Ancients. Was Casper looking at the skeleton of a member of that race? About which nothing was known.

Not *almost* nothing.

But *actual* nothing.

He liked thinking about this for the few minutes he sat staring at the bones found in the bottom of a lost well. It was a break from the examination of his memory of the *Moirai* that all his dreams and almost every waking thought had become fixated on. As though he were being tested in order to be found worthy, or wanting, as his memories were trawled and held out to the light of examination.

As though this needed to be done if he were to...

Continue?

Survive?

Find the Temple of Morghul?

But this mystery, the mystery of the ancient one-eyed skeleton that might or might not be the answer to the greatest question that had plagued the galaxy, collectively, since the dawn of light speed... this mystery seemed to be part of the *something* that had lured Casper to this lost planet far beyond galaxy's edge.

He lay back in the cool dark and closed his eyes.

He heard Urmo gurgling at more of the water, apparently having figured out the cup between mutterings of his own name.

Casper was tired, and as he drifted off to sleep, he tried to think about the Cyclops instead of the *Moirai* and...

Casper found himself in the dream once more. Following Rechs and his soldiers, moving tactically, hall by hall, corner to corner, clearing pristine rooms full of ancient medical and science equipment. Vintage terminals a couple of hundred years old and working as though they'd just been installed by the shipbuilders. All the rooms empty of life, yet humming with current as long as the ship's reactors kept generating power.

They found her, as easy as that.

They found Reina Benedetti.

It was Barr, on point, who moved first onto a balcony that overlooked an open level. Below, massive processors, lit blue and humming so powerfully that the electricity within them could be felt on one's skin, stood on the edges of a vast medical operating theater.

She was down there.

Reina Benedetti.

The woman who'd led the revolt on the *Obsidia*. The woman who'd freed Rechs and Casper and so many others from a dreamy hell that was all too real in moments of horrible stark screaming madness.

Like Casper and Rechs, Reina was old. But she barely looked to be approaching a fit and vivacious forty, for she, too, had been a victim of the longevity experiments aboard the *Obsidia*. It was hard to tell what she was doing down there, center stage, but she definitely wasn't afraid. In fact, it looked like she was organizing things.

It looked like she was in charge.

Seeing her down there, among the Savages, took Casper instantly back to memories of the *Obsidia*. Memories he'd worked hard to bury, deal with, or even erase through therapy. He'd tried it all. And yet they were still there. Taunting him with what should never be. Convincing him to cross a line he'd sworn on his life he'd never cross.

The memories of that ancient celebrity who'd wanted to be a god, turning herself into a horror show of beauty and desire, mindlessly drugging her thralls so they'd worship her, validate her, and of course obey her every whim. He'd been a puppet, and nothing more.

The shame of it had never left him.

And then he remembered that Reina had freed him. He told himself that. Reminded himself that he was no longer a slave, but free.

"It's her," whispered Rechs over the comm. Casper and Rechs had hung back with the others, but they were all watching Barr's feed via HUD. "Scan for entrances," Rechs ordered the hidden soldier on point. "Slow pan."

The image shifted across the room below.

There were easily ten Savages in there. And they were wearing some type of advanced armor system like nothing Casper had ever seen before. *Because*, thought Casper as he watched himself watching all this once more from the future in the desert, *because this is the version of armor that came before the Mark I legionnaire armor*. The legendary armor Rechs would take for his own. The armor the Legion techs and scientists would try to reproduce, but would never really be able to.

There it was.

It was like some ancient mythical artifact from a time of legends and heroes long gone. Armor they'd forged inside the Quantum Palace.

Maybe that was the reason it could never be reproduced. Because it had been built inside a place that existed in a different reality. A reality that was like a universe constructed totally of information and data.

Rechs relayed the plan over comm. They would sweep in, double-tap as many of the Savages as they could, grab Reina, then exit the complex, making best speed back to the *Lex*.

As he spoke, two lesser Savages, obviously some kind of tech class, wheeled in a prophetess on a stainless steel gurney. She was strapped down, and they quickly hooked her up to crude biometric contacts—things that would've been state-of-the-art in the years before the Exodus.

She looked like... just a girl. A skinny, underfed waif. Nothing like the terrible prophetesses who'd tried to flay them alive with their witchy mental powers. This one looked frightened, even—and resigned to some fate in the offing.

A voice came across the speakers below. "Are we ready, Doctor?"

The voice was rich. Powerful. And yet full of some cold and inhuman menace that knew neither sympathy nor mercy.

The girl they once knew stepped back from the table and nodded as she took up a tablet of some sort.

Casper asked Barr to pan back to the girl on the table. Barr zoomed in. Her lips were moving, and Casper had a pretty good idea what she was saying, over and over.

"I embrace the Quantum... and it embraces me."

A surgery bot like some mechanical spider lowered itself from the ceiling high overhead. Blades and hacksaws deployed, as did the barrel of a surgery laser.

Reina looked up from her tablet and studied the girl on the gurney for a long moment.

"Are they going to...?" whispered the medic.

"Yeah, girl," answered LeRoy over the comm. "They gonna do somethin' real bad."

"We goin' in, Major?" Barr asked. As though half a squad and one naval officer were some kind of cavalry that had to ride in at the last moment and rescue the damsel on the table.

Casper knew the answer, because he knew Rechs. A man some had called "hard to know" and others had called "cold."

The witch on the table was no damsel.

And they weren't here for her.

"She's not our target. We're here for Red Queen." Rechs tagged her in the HUD.

"Uh, yeah," said LeRoy slowly. "But Red Queen looks like she in on it and stuff, Major."

"Stand by. We might get a moment to snatch her once they start whatever it is they're going to do."

But they didn't. What happened next was so beyond conception that it seemed to mesmerize them into inaction. The plan they'd been ready to enact simply faded away.

The show commenced via Barr's HUD feed. And what a horror show it was. The gleaming robot spider surgeon lowered one of its cutting saws and severed the girl's head from her neck in an instant. There was no hesitation once it began. The cutting laser followed, cauterizing and touching up any bleeding with short, bright bursts of fire.

Even here, up in the balcony, a terrible stench rose up in their nostrils. The stench of burning flesh.

Casper tried to forget the moment, just before the cutting saw had begun to cut, when the restrained girl opened her mouth to scream. The cut had been made so fast no sound had come out.

The laser couldn't cauterize the wound quickly enough, and now other arms moved in, holding loud whirring vacuums at the ends of industrial-grade suction pucker-tentacles. They greedily cleaned the mess of the girl's lifeblood while the laser finished its work.

Barr's cam zoomed in for an extreme close-up of the girl's head, and they could see only Reina's torso and hands diving in and out of frame.

"What the hell are they doing, Major?" asked someone over comm. Casper couldn't tell who it was. He too was too horrified at what they were seeing to pay attention to the notifications coming up.

Then something happened.

The girl blinked.

Once, twice. Then rapidly.

"We have consciousness," said Reina in her heavily accented English. She'd been Italian, once, long ago. But what did that mean anymore out here in the galaxy?

She rattled off a few vitals, and Casper knew she was speaking to that voice—the voice that had spoken so loud and clear across the surgery amphitheater—and what she was saying was that, for all intents and purposes... the girl on the table was alive. The head. The body. Separately.

"My child," erupted the cold and imperious voice out of the ether. Its low baritone made one of the speakers pop and whine on a pitch that became a hum fading into nothingness. "Do you know where you are?"

The girl's lips moved. But there was no sound.

"She said, 'I'm here,'" Reina said.

Reina must be using an app to read lips, Casper thought. Of course the head on the table couldn't speak—her vocal cords were severed.

Casper wondered what in the hell, exactly, was going on.

Reina Benedetti had been a science officer aboard the *Challenger*. She'd specialized in xenopsychiatry. After their escape from the *Obsidia*, she'd devoted herself to research, but Casper hadn't paid all that much attention to the details. He'd had only brief contacts with her over the years.

Reina and *Rechs*, on the other hand… they'd been something more. Something Casper had needed to force himself to stop imagining, for his own sanity.

Casper had loved her, and had known they would only ever be friends.

And now, watching her, he wondered if he'd ever *really* known her. The woman he'd known had been a champion of freedom. And what he was seeing here was a monster, a ghoul, slicing up a living, breathing person. No matter how terrible that person was, or had become, it was still a person. And the woman he'd known, the woman who'd rescued them all, never would have willingly taken part in something like this.

"What do you think is going on here?" he asked Rechs over the command comm, away from the ears of what remained of their unit. "This isn't her."

"No, it isn't," Rechs replied.

And then the carnival of horrors moved into its next act. An act that would be far worse than the sword-swallowing girl or the monkey-faced boy.

Reina leaned forward with a hypo.

"Injecting now," she announced.

And that, too, to Casper then, and to the Casper of now watching as he tramped across the moonlit desert beyond the well, was as much a part of this quest as the Cyclops skeleton. The injection had been the revelation of something much larger than he'd ever considered. Like that skeleton in the well, it was a simple bit of evidence that revealed so much. The injection had opened up the invisible world of a power no one had ever known.

They camped in the well for three days. Rehydrating and allowing Casper's skin to recover from the almost first-degree burns it had received from the glare of the sun. And as he rested, the nightmare of the *Moirai* continued to unfold, like some grim trial testimony being read out for a jury to listen to, to judge him by. The skeleton that lay beside him was just as tantalizing now as the injection and what came next in the surgery amphitheater was all those years ago. But somehow the skeleton was another quest. A different story. Not this one. And so he let it go... because there was only the temple for him. All other mysteries paled in comparison.

They continued on across the desert by night. Moving forward. Following the course THK-133 was either keeping, or wasn't keeping.

"It's in," Reina announced as she stepped away from the gleaming stainless steel operating table. She moved to a rolling tray and dropped the hypo with a clatter. "Thirty seconds to take effect. Then we can start phase six."

It was a long thirty seconds. And when it was over, Reina leaned in and checked the girl's pupils with a small flashlight.

"We have a reaction. Shall I continue?"

Over the ether, the voice answered. "You may, Doctor."

Reina stepped back and laid her tablet on the surgery tray. "Moonsong," she said softly.

Then waited.

"Are the girl's lips moving?" asked Casper. "Barr. Close-up on the girl."

The camera shifted and moved abruptly.

The lips were moving.

"Good," said Reina. "Don't worry, you won't be afraid much longer. Start your mantra and let go."

The girl's lips moved again. And as before, Casper had a pretty good idea what the girl was saying.

"Let go, Moonsong," cooed Reina softly. "Try to visualize yourself hanging from a rope bridge that has snapped on just one side. You're hanging there and you have no hope of rescue. You can only let go."

Moonsong continued to move her lips, repeating that phrase over and over as though it were some final rite, some savored prayer, some ward against all things that consume and destroy. The operating theater was so still and quiet they could hear everything clearly, including the small papery smack of the girl's lips. Or at least, so they imagined.

Barr must be using his sound detection mic to focus in, thought Casper. That's why they were hearing it all so clearly.

"Good," replied Reina. And then, "You're holding on as tight as you can, but you know it's futile. You know you can't hold on much longer, Moonsong. You know, eventually, you're going to fall, little girl."

Over the speakers, a new voice, the voice of a girl, spoke. Just one word, or maybe it was a syllable. It was so sudden, they barely registered it. Maybe it had been an "a" or something like it.

Impossible, thought Casper. Impossible because the threads were coming together as he watched. He knew what was happening, and at the same time he didn't want to know.

Advanced cognition.

I am the Quantum and the Quantum is me.

"You've done so well, Moonsong." Reina spoke like she was addressing a small child that was trying hard to learn some basic task. Her voice expressed encouragement and admiration all at the same time. Hopefulness, too. "But wouldn't it be so good to let go of the rope?" she continued. "Y'know... the bridge is gone now. You can never come back to this side. You must let go now. You must fall. Let go, and embrace the Quantum to its fullest."

"... SEE THE FOG ..." erupted the girl's panicked voice across the speakers. "I don't want to. There're things down there in it. Monsters..." She was whimpering now. Frightened. Scared. On the verge of hysteria.

"You don't have to worry about those things anymore," cooed Reina. "They won't hurt you down there. You'll float... once you're down there. Trust me. You'll float."

Casper felt a shiver run up his spine, like the cold claws of rat's feet scurrying in the dark. The galaxy, even at that time, was a scary place, and there were a lot of weird things from one end to the other—but he'd never seen anything as creepy as this. The girl's head was clearly detached from her body. She was communicating without voice or detectable instrument. And she was... some place, seeing some thing that frightened her.

In that moment there was a part of Casper's mind that said, *Back away from this. There are things that aren't meant to be known, and this is one of them. Here be monsters.*

"*I don't want to fall down there!*" the girl screamed. The speakers popped with feedback, and the overhead lighting flickered. Went off and came back just as suddenly. But somehow the quality of the light wasn't the same. It was colder somehow. Like a ghost from the darkness trying to imagine what light must be like.

"Trust me," whispered Reina in the deafening silence that followed. "You'll float. Just let go now, Moonsong. You are the Quantum. The Quantum is in you. Embrace it."

That's what they thought it was, Casper whispered in his own mind from the future. Watching the memory play out once more. Standing in a garden of strange stones. They'd passed from the endless dunes, and here the desert floor was littered with these oddly shaped rocks that were definitely volcanic.

There was only one moon visible overhead, oblong and swollen. Wrong, somehow. He wondered how much water was left. In the distance, far ahead, he could see mountains. Another low, jagged range. *And then what?* he asked himself. More desert? More endless desert?

What if this is the shape of the rest of my very long days? What if I wander this desert forever?

Which was a kind of horror the mind instinctively reeled away from.

He drew back to the operating theater aboard the *Moirai*. So long ago. Watched the dead girl speak from between the knowns.

They, the Savages of the *Moirai*, had called it the Quantum. Like monkeys grasping a bone to use as a weapon, they'd given it some ancient monkey-name.

Ea for earth.

Fa for friend.

Da for darkness.

Quantum for... something far greater.

But they'd had no idea what they were really messing with. Power. Plain and simple. But unlike anything the galaxy had ever seen before.

They were like animals seeing fire for the first time, Casper thought all those years later.

Which raised the question once more...

Who was their Prometheus?

Who had brought them the power?

Is.

Who *is* Prometheus?

The girl screamed over the loudspeakers. A sharp, sudden, soul-tortured shriek. She screamed like she was falling from some great height toward a certain death far below. Or worse.

What is worse?

Hell.

Eternity in hell.

You'll float.

In the past, the girl screamed and fell again and again as he crossed the seemingly endless desert. All those years ago she went to a place he'd come to this lost planet to find.

A place where intelligence precedes physicality.

Where the invisible power waits to be taken up.

In the desert, he continued on toward the mountains in the night. Crossing silent gardens full of lost stones.

27

They were in some gentle hills now, late in the night, beyond the desert. There had been an oasis along the way. It had made him uneasy, but they took water there anyway. Farther along there had been plants like spiny palms; Urmo had scrabbled at these furiously, cut them open with his sharp tiny biting teeth, and gulped like a vampire at the thin moisture they provided. With enough of these, there was at least some hydration for the day. And there had been other ancient wells. Some dead and dry. Some with moisture that could be had for the digging.

The air felt slightly less dry, slightly less hostile, as they passed through these low hills. The last of the two moons had just gone down behind the foreboding mountains ahead of them, mountains they were heading straight into the teeth of, when they heard the titanic roar far off across the desert wastes. It was a hollow bellow that cast itself along the chalky passages of the narrow draws and made Casper feel small in the hearing of it.

And then there was nothing but the sound of the wind skirling along these dry places.

They stood there for a long time, the bot, the tiny creature known as Urmo, and Casper, waiting for the doom that lay behind the monstrous roar that had echoed and faded forever out across the lost canyons in the hills. But nothing came beyond that one mighty titanic bellow.

That night, curled up in a small niche within the walls of a canyon, Casper dreamt of other monsters he'd once known.

"Where are you?" Reina asked the head on the table.

Barr was still forward, crouched down behind ancient machinery on the platform above all this, panning his helmet slowly back and forth across the scene. Focusing in on the moments for the rest of the team to watch via HUD. The Martian light infantrymen remained stacked in the dark passage behind him.

Casper and Rechs had just watched an old friend behead a young girl in an act more befitting Frankensteinian sci-fi than science itself.

"I am in the Quantum," came the girl's voice from some other place not this amphitheater, or ship, or even possibly this reality. "I am in the Quantum," she repeated, then added, "now."

There was no horror in the decapitated girl's voice now. No fright. No fear. No realization that her life—whatever it had been aboard the nightmare generational ship known as the *Moirai*—was about to come to an end. Even though they'd cut off her head, there was no screaming. No endless torment like the moments before.

None of that.

Just an ethereal calm that verged on eerie. A peacefulness, someone might have mislabeled it. Like the moment of horrific realization the victims of accident have just seconds before their ends.

Barr's camera captured Dr. Reina Benedetti, making notes on her tablet, and the now twenty strangely armored Savage marines standing guard around the amphitheater. Like iron sentinels from some lost age when heroes wore armor and did battle on mounted steeds with barbed lances against mythic monsters.

"Good," said that other voice. The voice that was cold and cruel, yet rich and resonant. Casper had a feeling this was the voice of the Dark Wanderer all the graffiti had warned them of. And in the hearing of it, he wished he'd been warned more urgently—or had heeded those now not-dire-enough warnings. There was something so not human, so not even alien, about the voice. There was something "other" about it. Something that bothered Casper on levels that felt too primal to be addressed. Deep down there in the fight-or-flight reaction of human hardwiring. A place his ancestors might have called the soul.

And whereas his old friend Rechs would've chosen "fight"—he would have fought the devil himself, and Casper could make the argument that Rechs *had* fought many devils playing at men—there was something about the voice that flipped the "flight" switch on the control panel in Casper's wiring.

"Then I think it's time we test the interaction between both states," said the cold and imperious voice. It wasn't a request. It was a command. "Have her kill the guards."

Without hesitation, Reina leaned in close to the girl and said, "Kill the guards."

The Savages weren't mindless, even though at times, despite their high-tech augmentation and biogenetic engineering, they seemed more like vicious pack animals than combat personnel. So when the voice instructed Reina to have them killed... they reacted. In disbelief at first. Looking one to another. Some raised their ancient slug-throwing automatic weapons, clearly indicating they weren't about to just roll over and die. Others did not. Because, after all, what did they have to fear? A headless girl on a table? Some pure-strain inferior they'd captured on a colony raid?

Certainly not. They'd been born, designed, and modified to rule.

The first of the twenty armored guards was hauled into the air as though he had repulsor technology in his boots. That Savage was hauled so fast, and so high, that he had no time to react—no time to even realize that his head was about to meet the ceiling of the amphitheater.

There was a sickening crunch, never mind the heavy-duty armor.

His lifeless body hit the floor.

Now there were nineteen.

To their credit, the rest of the Savages reacted quickly, almost mindlessly dividing into two supportive teams in which to engage the threat.

The threat being the headless girl on the operating table.

Team Alpha, as it was tagged by Rechs's command prompt in everyone's HUD, was composed of ten Savage marines in heavy armor. All of them were simultaneously swept off their feet and into the wall at their backs. Surgery trays, chairs, and other equipment followed them, and the cacophony of everything colliding was like some postmodern symphony on themes of madness and destruction.

Team Bravo started firing at the head on the surgery table.

Nothing hit. Those mercilessly brutal ancient slug-throwing weapons found it impossible to hit their mark. Ricochets rebounded off some unseen shield and spent themselves along the walls in bright impact flashes, throwing explosion of sparks across the theater. Other rounds skipped off down unseen halls and passages, making strange twanging notes as they hit deck, wall, and bulkheads in the ship's darkness beyond the surgery theater.

Casper was fascinated by the raw power and the total invulnerability of the head on the table. He watched in awe as a heavy-duty bulkhead was effortlessly torn from its mountings and hurled into one of the firing Savages. The man was crushed beneath its incredible weight and the force of its terrible impact.

Nothing had actually *touched* the door. It just tore away from its mounts on its own, as though some invisible force had reached out and tugged it from its mountings.

Another Savage grabbed at his head as though he was suffering a sudden migraine of apocalyptic proportions. His weapon, a lethal matte-black light machine gun, fell forgotten at his boots. A mere second later he pitched over dead.

The Martian infantry moved quickly and quietly into position on the balcony above the surgery amphitheater, weapons ready. It was Rechs who moved first, apparently sensing a moment to act, and his action broke the stupor that had infected his men.

Rechs duck-walked over to Casper, rifle held out at port arms for balance. "Now," he whispered. "We snatch her and get out of here."

Casper felt both confusion and disbelief. As in, *How, exactly, in the middle of a supernatural firefight between a heavily armed superior force and... well, the unknown... is that supposed to happen?*

"I'm going down there. You lead the covering fire from the balcony. We'll link up back at the platform. Roger?"

Rechs had already rigged himself for fast-roping down to the next level. D-clips and a knotted length of the Martian infantry's graphene-cord had been attached to the rail that guarded the balcony. The rope was already tied off to a secure mount at the rear of the balcony.

Casper chanced a quick look down. Amid the chaos of Savages being held in the air, their heavy armor suddenly imploding as though being squeezed by a giant and unseen invisible hand, and the voluminous return fire from the first group that was recovering after having been thrown back into the medical equipment along the far wall, Reina was crouched down and off to one side of the fight. Almost directly below. Almost in the middle of it all.

Casper nodded. It was the only way. And they owed her whatever it took to get her out of there. Even if he wasn't actually sure she *wanted* out.

It was crazy, but right now it was the only escape from this constantly unfolding nightmare. Like some Escher-scape that never ended and only ever led to some new perspective that changed the whole game.

Rechs gave the order.

"Go."

Barr, LeRoy, and even the medic popped up and opened fire, spraying the room below with fire from the automatic Savage weapons they'd commandeered, their loud chatter mixing with the confusion below. Rechs popped a grenade off his belt, cooked the spool, and tossed it as he called, "Banger out!"

Casper knew to turn and look away.

The grenade went off, but its dull explosion was lost in the merciless hammer of gunfire from all sides. And the screaming. The Savage marines were screaming as the headless girl murdered them one by one.

When the flashbang went off, it fritzed out everyone's HUD, leaving a small tinkling of broken-glass static wash in the comm for the few seconds it took the EMP-hardened systems to reboot and come back online. But that didn't matter to the Martian infantry; they'd switched to iron sights and were raking both groups with fire.

Casper stood up and drew a bead with his sidearm on one of the Savages. But in the same instant the man lifted one armored gauntlet from his automatic rifle and raised it to his neck. Casper stared in stark disbelief as the man tried to pull at the metal collar below his bucket—as though the collar itself was choking the life out of him. Casper was only secondarily horrified by the fact that the man was standing, impossibly, on the tiptoes of his heavy boots. He was being hauled upward by an invisible strangler who needed that nuance to make the kill complete.

And then Rechs was pushing past Casper, mounting the barrier that guarded the balcony. He had one hand on the rope at his midsection and the other on his rifle. He leapt out into the open space above the fight, firing at targets as he fast-roped facedown into the midst of battle.

Below him, two Savages, each standing their ground and sending copious amounts of fire at the severed head, were suddenly slammed into one another.

Rechs hit the deck, ventilated a nearby Savage with a spray of hip-fire from the Savage weapon, and disengaged from the ropes. He took two steps, grabbed the doctor, and threw her over his shoulder. Then he disappeared underneath the balcony, firing at Savages as he went.

"Give him time to get clear!" yelled Barr as he ejected a mag and fished around in his ruck for another. Then Barr was pulled off the balcony and thrown to the floor below. The medic tried to grab him as he went over, but he was hauled as though dragged by some line pulled by a great engine.

LeRoy popped a grenade off his belt, shouted, "Heads up, chumps!" and threw it into the melee below. The medic regained her feet and fired down into the madness. Her face was one of fatalistic determination. As though she and Barr had been more than just squaddies.

Time slowed in Casper's memory.

Slowed to a crawl as he watched bright flying brass trailing from their weapons. As he watched his own sidearm cycle energy and charge between each shot. As he saw some Savage from below rocketing toward the ceiling, arms and legs flailing as though he were at the zenith of a trampoline's bounce.

The grenade flared explosively, sending a wave of sudden debris in all directions.

At the same moment, the medic was lifted off her feet. Casper lunged, reached for her, and in that moment he felt... he felt that immeasurable unseen ghost clutching at her, roiling about her.

And he knew it would pull her over.

Would pull them all over if it was allowed the time to do so. If given eternity, it would consume everything. It would pull everything over and down if it could. Someone had once said, *Some people just want to watch the galaxy burn*. This force, whatever it was, wanted to crush the galaxy all by itself. In that rescuing-the-medic moment of nearness.... Casper felt its wild and unrestricted power.

"*No*!" he shouted at it.

Except in the dream, later in the desert, asleep in the canyon, his voice sounded slowed down, as if time dripped like molasses. He reached for the young girl going over the rail, wanting to save her and knowing that it was all but impossible. And also... and also wanting to *touch* that force that was pulling at her. Wanting to *know* it.

Wanting... it.

And knowing that he had found the thing that could have made the difference in so many of the other stories that had added up to the sum total of his life.

His parents.

The *Obsidia*.

Martian infantry who had boarded the destroyer he'd been assigned to during the War for Martian Independence. A destroyer that been scuttled to avoid capture. Seven hundred and forty-five lost in the nuclear flare.

So many stories would have ended differently if the power he was now witnessing had been his to use as he saw fit. Had been used for good, and not evil. Had been used to do *the right thing that needed to be done*, never mind questions of good and evil.

He caught the girl's web-belt as time began to return to normal. As she was going over and down. To die and be lost as so many had.

He caught her harness.

Maybe LeRoy's grenade had sent some needle-sharp fragment into the brain of that severed head. Maybe the focused energy, kinetic and explosive, had been too much for... it.

Whatever *it* was.

Maybe there was, even within fantastic powers, only so much one could do with such incredible power. Only so much the mind could handle and process.

Maybe.

But he caught the girl medic, and he held on to her.

And she did not go over.

A Savage marine, held aloft near the amphitheater's ceiling, suddenly fell, a puppet whose strings had been cut. But had he hit the ceiling?

Casper would never know, because so little time remained to the *Moirai*. She was not long for this reality. This plane of existence. All her stories were about to be lost forever.

She had always been doomed. Now her doom was upon her.

"Major's got her, let's boogie!" cried LeRoy, pulling Casper and the medic away from the balcony. They ran for the dark passages and away from this theater of horrors.

THE LESSON OF FEAR

He did not turn back after he entered the open tomb, because he knew he could not. He walked into the tomb of an ancient Spiral King and was enveloped by the darkness.

There are "other" places, his mind whispered. *Places where you can become lost forever. Dangerous places.*

And yet this was the lesson. One of the last lessons the Master would teach.

"Confront your greatest fear you must," the Master had whispered in the moment before the student had stood up from their little fire within the gloomy Hall of Kings. "Then you will become what you will be."

Ten steps into the darkness of the tombs and the blackness felt like a physical thing. Like a smothering cloak. Like a hand about his neck. Gripping and threatening to cut off his air all at once. He coughed and moved forward into the darkness.

In time he came to blocks of stone. Or rather, the blocks of stone formed the walls of the passage. Except they weren't blocks of stone. They were alive, with a strange glowing alien circuitry within them. Like the runes he'd learned to read, except math too, and also some kind of powerful operating system language. Alive within the stone after ten thousand years.

This was the tomb of Xu Zyglax, Eater of Children.

The tomb was still dark, but the glowing red circuitry threw a soft bloody light across the tomb's inner chamber. The walls were alive, in bio-electronic detail, with an obscene recounting of the reign of Xu Zyglax. So many worlds ruined. So many souls consumed. So many lives enslaved.

And directly ahead, sitting in a throne that was more starship command chair, rested the space-suited corpse of the ancient Spiral King. The face plate was dark, tinted against the suns of a thousand worlds. But the suit itself was made like an armor of dead emeralds and obsidian flakes. One gauntleted hand rested on the pommel of a great single-bladed sword, gleaming in its razor-sharp keenness. The gentle curve of its blade reminded the student of other lost weapons from Earth's past. Like the katana. Or the wakizashi. Like that, only somehow large and less delicate.

These are the ceremonial weapons of the Spiral Kings. And not for the first time did the student wonder if these same Sprial Kings were the Ancients who'd left their enigmatic pyramids across the galaxy.

The other hand of the resting corpse gripped the barrel of what had to be an alien's version of a blaster rifle. Except there was what looked like a chainsaw attached to the front. The weapon was made of a black metal, and it looked like the most deadly weapon he'd ever seen. Far more deadly than anything the Legion carried.

Beyond the resting king lay a dark passage.

The Way of the Void, some voice inside his mind whispered.

And the student knew that was the way he must go to complete the lesson. To confront his fear.

He considered taking the blaster. It seemed far too large for human hands, but he wrested it from the dead king's grip and felt along its surfaces for how it might work. After a moment he slung it over his shoulder and back and then reached for the sword. He might not understand how the blaster worked, but the sword... The sword worked like all swords.

As he took it, it came alive with a gleaming red glow that soon turned the burning white of a firy sun. He held it out in front of him, gave the dead king one last look, and set his shoulders as he proceeded past the ancient monarch and into the darkness of the Way of the Void.

Fear stalked him.

Came for him.

But it never made its presence known.

Not even when he came to a place he called the Palace of Dead Worlds, even though that might not be its name. Beyond the Way of the Void it lay, an open expanse, like something one might find on some large and featureless world no one had ever bothered to explore. The silence here was a thing that could be felt and even heard. And in time it became deafening.

And upon that gray and shadowy plain rested great globes that towered above him. They were like dead moons, or dead worlds. This was their resting place.

He held the sword at the ready, sensing the fear circling out beyond the worlds that stretched off in every direction now. It was a twisting thing he could only barely see out of the corner of his eye. Like a serpent. Or a dragon. A Black Dragon. Running and twisting among a thousand dead worlds. Whispering nothing that could be heard in the deafening silence through which the student passed.

"What are you afraid of?" it hissed a thousand times before he finally answered. Before he was finally honest.

He'd given it every answer. And not just answers, but the truth. Or at least, the truth as far as he was concerned.

"What are you afraid of?"

Nothing.

"Nothing?" he shouted.

And the dragon may have laughed, but it never come forward, or close enough to be seen by the light of the bloody sword.

Death.

"Death!"

And still the dragon laughed like the lost echo of a roar and refused to be seen.

Failure.

"Failure!" he tried.

And there was nothing.

He wandered for days and began to be afraid that he had truly found the "other" places of the temple.

"I can go back," he thought to himself, and turned in the charcoal-gray darkness among the frozen worlds.

"Can you?" hissed the dragon, and seemed to laugh when the student realized there was no back to go to. He wasn't even sure if he was walking a straight line.

He stared all about him, feeling the fear begin to close in. Close in more than it ever had.

The dragon would attack now... and knowing that... knowing that was like waiting in a pitch-black room with someone who was swinging a sledgehammer at your head.

"What are you afraid of?" the dragon whispered in his ear.

The student whirled. Blade out. Only to find nothing.

He could sense the dragon and its immense coils looping about him. Soon they would constrict and squeeze the life out of him. Soon...

He began to run. He ran for his life. He lost the blaster. Felt it go clattering off in the darkness behind him. Nothing in the temple, no skill or feat he'd learned, could resist the Black Dragon. It was like trying to punch the galaxy. How? Where did one start?

Even the glowing blade was gone.

And still he ran.

Hearing the dragon coming for him. It roared, and the sound was like the sound of motorcycles echoing off canyons of ruined buildings and rubble.

"The Goths are coming..." he heard his mother say. Long ago. Before they'd murdered her.

28

The desert faded away behind them as they climbed into a tropical forest that grew near the mountains' upper reaches. One moment they'd been threading a high desert plateau, looking for ways up along the rising canyons and draws, and then within the space of a hundred yards they'd crossed a ridgeline and entered a beautiful mist-shrouded valley full of palms, waving grasses, and dense clusters of alien trees. The smell of salt came on sudden breezes rushing through the valleys and between the passes. It reminded Casper of an ocean, and it felt good on his sunburnt skin.

He realized, in a brief moment of clarity, that he was starving to death. The nutrition bars had run out in the desert, and he had learned to eat the two-headed rats Urmo caught. Sometimes they shared one, and other times the creature caught one for each of them. Now he pulled a thick, rind-laden fruit hanging low from a strange palm, and he cut it open. It was bright yellow like a mango and filled with ruby-red seeds. He was too hungry not to eat it, never mind the hallucinogenic qualities of some of the plants on this planet. Starving to death was a whole other trip.

But the strange fruit didn't kill him—not right away, anyway—and in fact, not only was it satisfying, it was deeply refreshing. He ate so many of the low hanging fruits that his mouth started to develop small sores from the high citric content. After this he lay back and waited for either a drug trip, or death. He listened as THK-133 wandered back and forth across the hill, moving through the tall grass that blew from side to side.

Casper drifted once more back into that other waking dream of things from long ago. As though there might be some other ending than the one that had inevitably found them. That had been headed for them all along.

They ran from the carnage and horror unfolding behind them. They ran like the devil was at their heels. Several times they hit dead end passages and had to backtrack, all the while expecting to be suddenly attacked by the unseen pursuers their minds had conjured.

And the more they ran, the more it felt like they were running for their lives. Like something was behind them, chasing them down the corridors, an angry presence at their heels. In memories of that moment Casper could almost hear its low moan just behind them. But he distinctly remembered turning to see what it was that was chasing them... and finding nothing but darkness.

As they raced back toward the rail system, the pristine lab complex that was the Center for Advanced Cognition aboard the ghost ship *Moirai* entered some sort of emergency mode. The brilliant antiseptic lighting became a bloody wash of strobes casting their undulating lighting across now-shadowy rooms. The soft-hued office and administrative sections were bathed in blues, with rapidly pulsing white strobes indicating emergency egress routes.

It was against this backdrop that they met two of the Savage marines, armored just like the marines in the surgery amphitheater. The Savages were guarding an intersection that Casper, LeRoy, and the medic needed to pass through. Glass-walled cubes, behind which research had once been conducted, formed the intersection, and the whole area screamed science and innovation. The two dark figures in heavy armor, helmeted and scanning, vicious automatic weapons at the ready, were at odds with their surroundings.

What became of these people? Casper wondered, not for the first time aboard the *Moirai*. Whoever they'd been, they'd left Earth full of optimism that they would uplift humanity in what they saw as the right way. Yet here, hundreds of years later, they'd clearly gone the opposite direction, devolving into something ancient. Something animal. Something warlike and vicious.

He wondered how much humanity was left in them. Or had they removed it? Cast it off.

Letting go of the vestigial tail for something better, as it were.

LeRoy opened up on them at first sight, intent on blasting his way through to the hangar deck and the *Lex*. A hurricane of rounds smashed into the frosted glass cubes that shaped the office complex intersection, shattering them instantly, or cracking straight through them to race off into the other partitions. Some of the bullets found their mark, but they simply ricocheted off the advanced armor of the Savages, sending misdirected slugs in all directions.

In other words, LeRoy's first sustained burst turned the combat area into an explosion of flying glass.

One trooper pointed while the other fell to one knee, his wicked matte-black automatic weapon opening up in a lethal burst that tore LeRoy to shreds.

Casper pulled the medic behind cover as a hail of gunfire filled the area where they both would've been in the next second. She in turn took off running down a new passage, towing Casper after her. They could hear the armored Savages' boots against the polished deck, giving chase, and then an insane and almost insectile high-pitched electronic comm transmission echoing over ambient.

They're calling in our location, thought Casper desperately as he ran for his life. But maybe it wasn't that. Maybe they were receiving their orders. Except whatever it was wasn't orders in the way we think of them. Giving and receiving. Maybe it was more input. Like turning on an appliance.

He and the medic were too busy running for their lives to care. And from the sound of it, the Savages were closing fast.

At the end of a long, frosted-glass hall, each window reinforced by gleaming chrome bolts, Casper turned, planted both feet, aimed, and fired at their pursuers.

He'd been here before. Dangerously close and firing point blank in the face of certain death.

The shots hit the lead Savage in the chest armor. Dead center. And then bounced off into the ceiling. The man, or once-man, checked his rush, but the other continued past his comrade, raising his battle rifle to engage on the fly.

Registering the ineffectiveness of his own attack, Casper danced away from the spray of gunfire.

The medic had popped two grenades.

"Run!" she screamed, rolling them straight at Casper.

He felt his legs wanting to slow and just give up. He told them to push harder. There were mere seconds to get out of the most lethal radius of the blasts. But explosively accelerated needle sharp fragments traveled; everyone knew that.

Pulling hard, legs and arms pumping, they made it most of the way down the corridor before they heard the explosion behind them. It was like a cross between a bullfrog's croak and audio-electronic feedback gone haywire.

The two explosions tore the deck to shreds.

Casper felt grit and blast pepper his uniform as he skidded to a halt. Instantly there was blood running down his fingers. Something had caught him, but there was no time to see how bad the injury was.

He turned. Both Savages were still coming at them, racing down the hall as though the explosion had been a mere distraction.

They've got some kind of personal defense shield, thought Casper. That's what the high-pitched electronic haywire sound had been. It had activated just before the blasts, protecting the Savages.

He remembers, while climbing into the tropical forest, he remembers how hopeless that feeling was. His energy sidearm hadn't stopped them, nor had LeRoy's automatic gunfire. Even the grenades had done nothing. They were coming for them, and there was nothing that could be done.

In that moment his feet were rooted to the deck. And he knew deep down inside himself that he was probably going to die in the next few seconds. Because... what could one do against that kind of tech?

Back in those days, Casper thinks almost two thousand years later, that tech seemed like sorcery. It may as well have been sorcery. It was as unfathomable then. And unstoppable even now.

His mind thinks about this sorcery as that terrible titanic roar sounds again, except much nearer. *Very* near. And in this heart-stopping, fear-struck moment, Casper feels a kinship with that long-ago Casper who stood frozen as the two Savages closed, guns ready for the final burst. Beyond the valley's edge something is coming this way. Something huge. Something that roars like a prehistoric monster from a lost age.

And it is as clear now as it was then, back on the *Moirai*, that there will be no escape. No savior. No Rechs. This time.

Because he is here out beyond the galaxy's edge. Beyond the perimeter of the known. Lost in the land of the insane and the unknown.

The monster roars and comes forth onto the valley floor, making Casper feel as small as Urmo must feel beside him. Even THK-133, the lethal killing machine, seems stunned at the sheer size of what has come out of the forest ahead of them in this final reckoning. It's as though they have all known what was coming all along, but never really expected it to actually show up.

Just as those Savage marines came for him in what would one day be the prototype for the Legion's iconic armor. The galaxy, the Republic, would never know that this armor had come from the minds of the mad on the *Moirai*, in a place that didn't really exist, aboard a ghost ship of damned souls still doing R&D out in the dark like sorcerers translating ancient tomes and formulas.

Imagine that, Casper tells himself as a giant monster charges across the valley, the ground shaking beneath his feet.

I don't have to, he reminds himself. *I lived it. I was there.*

Another armored Savage came flying through the smashed glass cubicles and slammed into both marines. Suddenly all was chaos as the three figures were carried off in another direction.

In seconds, the one—and this was hard to tell because of their similar armors—but the one who had attacked was up and delivering kicks and throwing punches, even though there was clearly some kind of massive pistol strapped to his thigh.

A hand cannon.

Rechs never called it that, but when he drew and fired, everyone else did, thought Casper. But at that moment his oldest friend didn't know how to actually use much of the armor he'd just requisitioned from an R&D lab, which, he would later tell Casper, had had many far stranger wonders than just this prototype.

Of course, at the time, neither Casper nor the medic knew it was Rechs inside that armor. That it was Rechs who appeared at the very second before they would've both been murdered.

One of the Savages hit Rechs hard enough to send him flying back across the corridor and through what remained of a glass cube partition. That marine then charged at the prone Rechs like a raging bull with nothing but the red cape in sight.

That was when Rechs first drew and fired his legendary weapon. On his back, as a sociopathic post-human rushed him. The hand cannon boomed rapidly on auto-fire, like some battleship of old unloading a full salvo from its main eighteen-inch guns.

Casper watched as the subsonic dumb slugs smashed into the charging marine's chest armor and tore out the back. Three shots echoed bombastically across the science complex, their sonic explosions causing tenuous glass shards to give up their hold and finally fall. The first round took the man dead center, spinning him to the left. The next round struck the man's upper chest, and the third smashed into his helmet. Each concussive explosion demolished the man a little more, pushing him back, and finally onto the floor.

Rechs pushed off the floor with one mailed gauntlet and continued firing, drawing a line of blossoming damage across to the other marine, who'd recovered his own weapon and begun to fire back. Rechs was hit, but the rounds bounced off the armor and into the destruction all around.

Rechs's shots didn't bounce. They blew large, gaping holes in the Savage's head.

How is that possible? Casper wondered in horrified astonishment.

Casper, like all Terran naval officers, had studied to the graduate level in naval gunnery. He knew more about physics than most. There was no way the weapon Rechs was using could explode, recoil, re-aim, and then fire again as rapidly as it was, and with such deadly accuracy. Casper estimated that the weapon was easily firing fifty-caliber ammunition. The explosions were deafening, yet Rechs was firing as though he were aiming some child's first low-power target blaster.

Later they would learn that the armor did all kinds of wonderful things. Its cybernetic targeting assist system was among the least of its features. It was with this armor, even though it was only a pale imitation, that the Legion would become formidable and would one day conquer the galaxy.

Only for the House of Reason to misrule it badly. And that was an understatement, given the dumpster fire it had become by now.

Both marines were down, and Rechs got to his feet.

Reina Benedetti emerged from the ruin where Rechs had begun his charge.

Rechs popped the helmet off the armor with a hiss of escaping oxygen and wiped the sweat from his forehead. "I can't figure out how to communicate externally," he rumbled.

That was when Casper learned who his savior was. His oldest friend. His warrior in shining armor. Not some other Savage who wanted the kill all for himself.

The medic ran over to check Rechs for injuries.

Rechs waved her away. "I'm fine. Nothing's broken."

She checked him anyway, then stood back and swore. "Full-auto CQB. Broken glass firing everywhere. And a blow that sent you flying like you'd just been hit by a truck. And you're completely unscathed." She gave a low and long whistle of admiration and disbelief.

Rechs smiled grimly. "Not saying I didn't feel it, Corporal."

Reina threw herself at Casper, grabbing him and pulling herself into him.

Casper was at a loss. She had been... something special to him. And then he'd seen her participate in the vivisection of a sentient entity. And now...

And now, she was *still* something special to him. He loved her. Always had. Always would. She was his blind spot in the galaxy, and she knew it. But they never spoke about it.

He could feel her tears. Her heaving sobs.

"She was under... some kind of mind control," Rechs explained. "I don't fully understand it, but she came out of it pretty quickly. She's back. She's all good, Cas. It's time to go now."

Casper felt himself embrace Reina in that moment. Fully. Like he'd always wanted to. And in that closeness was all that might have ever been. All that the galaxy could never be.

Even now, all these years later, Casper still feels that moment as some kind of fulcrum on which the fate of the universe might have changed. Might have gone a whole different direction.

"What was all... that?" he asked. And the meaning to everyone was clear.

Except now, as he waits to face the monster coming for him in that high valley, the intent and the meaning are all for him.

Even then, he has asked himself throughout all the years of the long questing to find the power, *even then you wanted it, didn't you? Even then you knew you'd seek it out?*

Even then.

He answered that question once. Long ago. When he first realized the only way to change the way things were was to find a power that bypassed all the petty power systems of the galaxy, all the machinations of her denizens always seeking their own advantage over others for the greater good of all.

Power was only ever the way.

What he had seen had been but a small taste of something outside their ken. Beyond their ability to control and manipulate. A hint that whispered in his mind, even then—*even then*—that there was so much more for the taking. If its source could be found. And once it was, good could be done with it. In the right hands, of course. All the wrongs could be made right. Casper was sure of that.

"Here's the plan," Rechs began. "I need you to get yourself back to the *Lex*. I need you to lift off and get into a firing position. Use the SSMs to nuke the ship. Then get out of the Dead Zone."

There was a long silence in which only the roar of Rechs's hand cannon seemed to still echo in Casper's ears. A memory of white noise that didn't easily fade into the background hum.

Then Rechs added, "If you can."

Because there was still the Dead Zone to deal with. Even if they got off this ship... could they escape whatever the Dead Zone actually was?

No, thought Casper. *Probably not.* Because no one ever had. And there was still the theoretical nightmare possibility, even now, on this lost planet cast out from the galaxy, that they had never actually survived their incursion into its unknown extent in the first place—that all of this was just some two-thousand-year probability simulation the Quantum generated like a byproduct.

But long ago Casper had needed to put that scenario aside… just to remain sane. Because that way lay madness unending.

"What about you?" asked Casper.

"I'm going for the pyramid inside the main hab. Apparently it's some sort of gate."

"It's a door for a creature the *Moirai* made contact with," Reina said breathlessly. "They call him the Dark Wanderer. He'll use it to escape. And that can't happen."

"Why?" asked Casper.

"Because," said Rechs, a man Casper would've told you was the most serious, non-hyperbolic, and blunt-to-the-point-of-deadly person he'd ever met, "it would be the end of everything as we know it."

THE SAD TALE OF THE *MOIRAI*

The ship is a ghost ship. A thing of legend fading into the darkness. And because her time is short, it is time for you to know what very few ever would. The ship's story will never enter the galactic record. All the horrors and madness of her long journey are shortly to be lost. But this is her tale. Or at least, some of it. This is what her ghosts whisper and mumble in their torment. As though crying out all the wrongs done to them. As though seeking some absolution never obtained. This is the story of the ghost ship *Moirai* that was lost in the Dead Zone during the days of pre-Republic exploration.

A grand experiment.

That's what they called it in those last heady days as the world came apart at the seams. Food shortages. Global disaster. War.

The Earth was ruined, and the elites were convinced, as Sartre once wrote, that hell was, indeed, other people. Namely the great unwashed. The masses. The takers. The hordes. The common people, as they were referred to in thought and secret memos. Their fellow men and women who never could quite get around to evolving. Like *they* had.

Those people had elevated the elites, the Brights, to the lofty heights of industry, media, and government. The result was an unlikely coalition, as the Brights needed the Hordes' cheap and easy votes. Needed their cheap and easy labor. Their backs. Their sweat.

The elites resented that dependence. Those poor sad people who led common ordinary lives of desperation, they ruined everything with their mere hungry-mouth handout presence. And in order to maintain their grip on power, the Brights were forced to pander to the Hordes, to support their basic human rights campaigns, to mouth their salt-of-the-earth platitudes. They were forced to live with them.

Well, not *with* them. Ideally, and by long and careful design, a Bright would never encounter an actual living Hordesman in any other than the most purely transactional capacity. But they were forced to live on the same planet. Which was a kind of horror to them, in the end. A horror that could not be borne for one moment longer.

Finally, that would change. It was time to go.

Originally the Rama-class ark ships, designed and built by Krupps-Mitsubishi under a UN grant charter, were financed as survival arks when it looked like World War III was about to break out. Each ship could carry more than one hundred thousand refugees in the event of a global catastrophe. A slick massive media campaign was spat out across the internet, to which most people were constantly glued when they could get the bandwidth to log on, assuring those in dense population centers that in the event of a nuclear exchange there was a plan in place to rescue everyone who could get to the ark ships in low Earth orbit. Which was not an impossible feat given that most airliners were then using scram-jet technology to make the trip from New York to Tokyo in under two hours.

Awaiting the survivors who reached the ships were vast living worlds looking in on themselves. There the survivors would wait out the nuclear holocaust in relative comfort, or so they were assured in hip-hop soundbite twenty-second display ads on powerful social media sites.

But of course, this was all a big lie.

As almost everything had ever been.

Originally, the plan, organized by the Brights, had been to release a series of plagues that would rid the planet of its "excess population." Where mass abortion as a way to a better life had failed, SARS, weaponized Ebola, and Superflu-42 should have done the job in lowering the population density to a level that would allow the elites to live out their best lives. And for a while there these terrible-horrible wonders did brisk business in the wholesale death trade—until things got a little out of hand and AIDS 2.0 made the leap from contact to airborne.

But by that time China and India had gone nuclear on each other, ruining much of the East and Middle East. Europe and North America were fighting over what remained, and it wasn't pretty.

Unless you consider a no-holds barred conventional naval conflict that had poisoned much of the Atlantic with a bonus round expenditure of tactical nuclear ordnance and sunken reactors gone meltdown, pretty.

And both sides still hadn't pulled out the strategic nuclear weapons—the big ones, the ones with yields in the megatons, designed to destroy wide swaths of infrastructure, military or not. Although, as the ark ships lumbered out of orbit, this seemed a done deal within days, if not hours.

But there were hundreds of thousands of survivors in those ships, heading out into the relatively shallow dark of the local solar system lagoon, soon to be traveling into the empty seas between the giant suns.

There could have been many more survivors. If that had ever been the plan, there would have been. But instead, each ship carried far fewer people than it could hold. Rather than the promised one hundred thousand per ship, there were only about ten thousand: perhaps one thousand elites in oversight positions, and nine thousand of their inner circle. The latter were slaves, really, though they might have defined themselves as entourage, personal assistants, crew, and playthings. They didn't know they were slaves. Yet.

Departing a burning, ruined, poisoned home world for the promise of something at least forty and perhaps well over a hundred years away on the other side of the interstellar hauls between the habitable systems, the massive ships approached just this side of light speed. Or, that is, they would. Acceleration to maximum speed took about ten years of constant acceleration. But what did all that matter inside a living, breathing world that was devoted, almost unanimously so, to a worldview that was so wise and prosperous, surely it could never descend into such madness as the world they'd left behind?

In Greek mythology, the Moirai were known also as the Fates. It was they who decided the lengths of lives of both men and gods. It was they who were the final judges, never mind who you thought you were.

The head of the oligarchy of elites who ruled the lighthugger *Moirai* was a former weather newscaster who'd founded his own personal empowerment religion called "I Power" back on Earth. After a career-ending technical mishap during a news report, the huckster had reinvented himself as a man who had sought the counsel of the wise and come away as some sort of mystical savior guru who specialized in pseudoscience TED talks and who felt compelled to uplift humanity from its constant struggle with baseness to a fabled land awash in aromas of hope... one personal empowerment course at a time.

He came to give them a better life, and in turn they signed up for his classes, seminars, websites, health products, and eventually private floating cities, by the millions.

While not initially a member of the power-elite cabal that had long planned to rule Earth alone at a much lower population density, he was eventually accepted into their secret global planning sessions when his wealth and sway became so great that the hidden cabal had no choice but to recognize his place in the world. Plus, they'd been working on a long-term plan to use his popular health products to spread a form of time-release gene-editing cancer that had a mortality rate of 74.8% in the first month.

So as dozens of ark ships, each with its own core group of elites and special utopian philosophy, climbed away from Earth and into the stellar dark, Whip Hubley, former weatherman and now the First Councilor of I Power, ruled the *Moirai* with a genial smile and absolute authoritarianism.

Yes, aboard the lighthugger *Moirai* there were all the usual abuses common to the powerful once they've acquired absolute power.

Sex. Drugs. Murder. Humiliation. Insanity.

But that goes hand in hand with being the victor.

The *Moirai* society went from quasi-religious to full-blown cult within twenty years. Factor in the longevity research the elites had been holding back for themselves on Earth, and the revolutions provided by the constant research aboard the paradise-pleasure ship, and the situation was soon ripe for the insanity of self-proclaimed godhood.

Sixty-five years into the flight, the *Moirai* slowed from light speed and hove into orbit around a small star. But the only world there was an almost dead one that promised a harsh existence. So the Moirai, as Whip and his fellow elites now called themselves, chose to leap starward once more, promising the masses a world beyond their fading memories of Earth. Promising what they had no idea how to actually deliver.

What they found instead was the Dark Wanderer.

They encountered a derelict alien starship, unlike anything known, drifting in the dark wastes between the stars. Later, much later, they would find that it wasn't so much a lost starship as a prison, and its sole prisoner's sentence had been imposed by a civilization far older than any of humanity's outreaching explorers had previously discovered.

Who the Dark Wanderer really was, they would never know. But they marveled at the wonders he provided them. Portions of the derelict ship were cannibalized and remanufactured to give the *Moirai* faster-than-light travel. Hyperspace engines were constructed along the aft portions of the main cylinder, and the *Moirai* leapt away toward its fate. Other marvels were acquired as well, including a superior form of advanced longevity, and innovations in stellar navigation, food production, and cognitive powers.

Yes... cognitive powers.

What had started long ago, back on Earth, in seminars at hotels out by the airports, promising happiness, wealth, prosperity, and success, had become a religion that boasted of the ability to grant not just life after death, but life eternal as a sort of god. The Dark Wanderer ensorceled the feverish minds of the Moirai, taking their cockamamie belief system and riffing it into an ancient power that accessed what some might have once called *superpowers*.

There was, of course, a price to be paid.

There always is.

There came a night when the Dark Wanderer held his ebony blade aloft and sacrificed a screaming and stunned Whip Hubley. The Dark Wanderer offered godhood, and he demanded the worship that was his due. I Power became what the faithful tribes of the *Moirai* now misguidedly called the Quantum, and it promised them an eternity of their own making if they would help the Dark Wanderer on his own personal quest.

That quest was to leave physicality, to shed the real, and to become a superintelligent being who ruled the universe in a place beyond time, space, and reality. This was the true power. Once he obtained it, he would bless his faithful servants with the gifts they deserved.

According to the Dark Wanderer, the Quantum—a place distinct from reality, a place driven by pure intelligence and information—provided access to powers of the mind, or rather information-driven cognition, that could be used to manipulate physical reality. The Dark Wanderer trained those who were able to use this power, and they became his prophets and prophetesses. He enslaved the rest with chains biomechanical, turning them into chimeras that served as slaves and warriors in a state somewhere between eternal torment and drug-induced euphoria.

Long before the advent of the Galactic Republic, after the Exodus, and decades after those who had been left behind on a dying Earth had made their own Great Leap, the *Moirai* was capturing stray explorers and lost colony ships, or arriving at lost planets, wiping out lesser civilizations, and scouring the ancient records and sacred places for clues the Dark Wanderer sought. Clues to a place called the Quantum Palace. Progress was slow, but it was progress that drove them on to other genocides.

In time they picked up whispers and rumors of work being done on quantum consciousness. And that to led to the raid on Al-Baquar Seven—and the capture of Dr. Reina Benedetti. Her work on intelligence preceding physicality contained the path into next-level evolution the Dark Wanderer had long sought.

Based on Dr. Benedetti's work, the Dark Wanderer made his final plans to ascend into a post-physical existence beyond the present reality. To do that, the *Moirai* would have to navigate deep into the Dead Zone, to an area where data became real and information manipulated reality. This had been the focus, a working hypothesis really, of Dr. Benedetti's research, and it was that research which led the *Moirai* to begin navigating the unnavigable.

29

"If he succeeds," said Reina in the most sober of terms, "this Dark Wanderer will effectively become something like—and believe me, I know this sounds crazy—he'll become what we might have once called... a god."

Rechs, Casper, and the medic stared at the doctor. The look in her eyes said, *Yes. That's crazy. But after everything I've experienced on this ghost ship... sure. I believe it. Why not? The galaxy is a weirder place than we ever thought.*

Or some variation of that.

The four of them parted ways, breaking up into two teams. One "team" consisted solely of Rechs, in the commandeered high-tech battle armor forged by the Savages with the help of the Quantum Palace. He would prevent the Dark Wanderer from escaping the ship via the pyramids, which apparently enabled some kind of transportation between worlds. The Dark Wanderer had to be stopped; Reina had made that abundantly clear to Rechs during their journey through the labs of the complex. She'd shown him things. Shown him experiments that never should've been undertaken. Nightmares that never should've existed.

And if there was one man who could stop the Dark Wanderer—if the Dark Wanderer even *could* be stopped—then it was probably Rechs, Casper thought. Or at least his oldest friend would die trying.

The second team, consisting of Casper, Reina, and the medic—the lone survivor, besides Rechs, of the Martian light infantry task force—was to return to the *Lex*... and destroy the *Moirai* with ship-to-ship missiles.

"He has to be stopped," Reina said as they made their way through the sub-levels of the main hab. "If, as I and others have theorized, the universe is a data construct... information at its most basic level, like here in the Dead Zone... then him using that pyramid would be like giving him the ability to rewrite everything on an informational level. I don't know what the Dark Wanderer is exactly—some sort of exile or criminal from a dead race we haven't discovered, or maybe he's even one of the Ancients. But whatever he is, he's evil. He is pure evil. That's why Rechs is going to stop him. If he doesn't... or if we don't nuke the *Moirai*... then he has the potential to take control of everything we know as reality. And I mean *everything*. Seriously, Casper. He would make the Pantheon back on the *Obsidia* look like volunteer charity workers feeding the homeless. With the ability to manipulate reality via cognition alone, he could theoretically reshape the entire universe based on a thought."

They were heading for the cross-cylinder transit that would take them back down the spine of the ship to the aft hangar deck and the *Lex*. If it still existed. If the crew had waited. If they hadn't been overrun by Savages. More of the gibberish graffiti decorated the tube that led toward the other rail lines.

"Whoever's alive aboard this ship is little more than an animal now," Reina sighed in disgust. "This... Dark Wanderer... has bent and twisted their minds until there's very little left of whoever they once were back on Earth."

"What about... what they can do..." Casper said, and it was clear he meant the powers of the prophetesses he'd witnessed. Because... looking back, years later, he would see that Reina, too, in that moment, had been just as intoxicated by their powers as he had been all along.

"Real," said Reina, quickly and earnestly. "They're all real. And there's a part of me that knows...." She hesitated. Only the sound of their footsteps could be heard in the irregularly lit darkness of the corridor they were following. "A part of me knows we should just walk away from this. That it's something humanity was never meant to mess with. That it isn't even an option with regard to the evolutionary process. We're not looking at ourselves ten million years from now. We're looking at monsters coming in from some void in the universe that was sealed off for a reason. Some dark place. Part of me knows that's the truth. But..."

And then she added, as though having won some argument within herself, "I know that now. I should've known it before... I should have. And I didn't."

They reached the cross-rail transit.

The transportation hub was now some kind of ghoulish tribal temple. Candles, actual candles, guttered in the barest of breezes beneath shrines to gods that were chimeras of man's bones and machine's parts. Dim dreams of what could be. Sweet jasmine burned on joss sticks beneath altars dedicated to these hoped-for monsters. And every so often they heard the *clock* and *chock* of bone chimes.

Casper cleared the car with his sidearm out, and the medic, Bones, set to figuring out the controls to get the rail line going. By the ghostly blue light of their devices, Reina seemed older. Tired. Weary.

"How could you have known it would lead to this?" Casper said. He was trying, still trying, to give her some kind of absolution for what she'd unleashed. What he'd seen her do. But was it for her, or for him? He'd never answer that question.

"After the *Obsidia*..." she began, then hesitated.

And in this pause, a terrible history passed over them both once more. Both were suddenly unwilling tourists forced to remember some horrible vacation every time they came across the photos they'd so carefully hidden away. Hoping never to find them ever again. Because, of course, they'd both lived through that terrible vacation in hell. Lived through a long nightmare in which every moment was a never-ending hell in and of itself.

Whenever some religious nut had tried to put the fear in Casper with their talk of eternal damnation, his reply had always been, "Don't talk to me about hell. I've already been there."

Except often, later, in the quiet of his solitary life, he would admit that he was still afraid of going back to hell. Just a taste of it had been enough for him. And the taste itself hinted that yes, true hell might be real enough to consider.

He shuddered in those moments and felt like he was drowning.

"After the *Obsidia*," Reina started again, "I let go of my old research. I floundered for a time. I'll admit that, Cas... I was lost. I was really lost."

Casper swallowed as the car came to life around them. For no reason, he checked his watch, staring at the old Omega Seamaster. As though he were somehow synching with Rechs out there in the darkness of the tunnels of the ghost ship. Rechs, who had most likely gone off to his death. Or maybe he was just trying to find something to hold on to in a galaxy that seemed to be slipping off into dark waters no one had ever bothered to map.

But really, he told himself all those years later in that high mountain valley as the giant monster charged at them, *really you knew it was because she saw the look on your face in the half-light of that rail car.*

The look that said, *Is that why we lost contact after...*

And...

You knew I loved you.

"Can you believe I worked as a bartender on Oberon?" laughed Reina in disgust at herself. "In a club where children come to play day and night and all year long. Boozing and drugging themselves to trick themselves into thinking they're feeling something. I became one of them... if you can believe that. I drank, and danced, and... loved, because..." Her mouth moved, struggling to find the words.

"Because you wanted to live again," whispered Casper. Finding them for her.

She nodded. Her eyes desperate. Desperate for him, and even herself, to understand.

Casper thought about the people she'd... known then. People who hadn't known her back on the *Challenger* and during the rebellion aboard the *Obsidia*. They'd thought of her as just another lost soul like them, seeking temporary company in the warm tropical nights of paradise Oberon. They'd tasted her lips, probably tasted the salt and lime and tequila the pleasure world was famous for.

Casper wished he wasn't Casper. Wished he'd been any one of those strangers who'd had the chance to...

On any one of those tropical nights. Just the once would have kept him.

But they never loved her as you did, the voice whispered. *Like you always did.*

And do, he added in his head, because that seemed right. True still.

The transit car started, and they shot off into the darkness along an upward-curving tube. They were fully aware that a ghost ship run by madmen might have obstacles along the rail, and that any such obstacle could kill them with unforgiving physics. But they had no choice. Staying was not an option any longer.

Reina spoke as though in a trance now, and Casper wondered how long it had been since any of them had slept.

"Eventually I went sane again and picked up my research once more. But this time I wanted to understand the very nature of the universe. I wanted to know if it was random, or..."

She stared at him for a moment. Daring him to ask her to explain herself after what she was about to say. Seeing the disbelief forming in his eyes.

Then she tilted her chin defiantly and told him anyway.

"I wanted to know if intelligence precedes physicality."

Casper eyed her in wonderment. Not totally sure he believed her. Not totally sure he even knew her.

"Do you mean... Intelligent Design?"

She nodded. "There are many reasons why it makes sense. But if I'm honest.... none of those mattered to me, Cas. So trust me, it took a long time for me to be completely honest with myself about why I was looking for what I was looking for."

"And... why were you looking for... that?"

Intelligent Design.

"I wanted justice," she whispered after a long moment.

Casper shook his head. Of all the answers he'd expected to hear, that wasn't one.

"What do you mean?"

She looked away. Looked forward and watched the young female medic driving the rail car into the curving tube and the unknown darkness beyond. Only occasionally did they pass through bare fits of ghostly illumination. And somehow that made the darknesses beyond and in between much worse.

"Those things," said Reina, staring ahead into that uncertain dark. "That were done to us by... them... by the Pantheon... they couldn't just be wiped. Couldn't just be zeroed out on some balance sheet. They couldn't just *get away* with it. Because when you think about it... they did. They got away with it. Like... like..." She struggled to find an example. Then she looked at Casper as if only then remembering who he really was. Because the truth was... she had known him. Had watched him when he was a sleeping slave. Had awakened him.

She had seen inside that tortured mind of his like no other.

A moment passed between the two of them where he knew, *knew* she had been able to love him once. Maybe a long time ago. They might have...

If there hadn't been Rechs.

A man who seemed not to care. Immovable in a constantly shifting galaxy of objects and lives. A prominent rock along a dangerous coastline that sailors used to find safe harbors.

We are all sailors, thought Casper. *Except Rechs. He is the lighthouse we steer our courses by.*

Casper knew that she too had held that other possibility of them in her mind, just as he had. But there was something about that giant, immovable rock. It was a safe place to the frightened children of the galaxy.

"Like the Nazis," she said finally. "Of ancient Germany. You, with all your history, you know about them, right? All your 'before' history acquired in all those books you were always spending your money on. The Nazis who almost burned up the world long before our mothers and fathers succeeded."

Casper nodded. "I know of them," he whispered.

"And if you know, then you know that right up until the moment they died, they were busy stuffing the innocent into ovens as fast as they possibly could. Like it was some game for them. Like they were trying to break some record, never mind the consequences. And do you know *why*?" She practically growled at him through gritted teeth in the humming darkness of the speeding rail car. "Do you?"

Casper said nothing. Because she wasn't looking for a reply, or an answer, or an insight. Or a lesson by some perpetual amateur historian who'd read all the books that purported to have all the answers.

She continued. "Because the Nazis knew there were no consequences for what they were doing. They weren't religious, contrary to misinformation. They believed in nothing but blood and soil. They were the ultimate Darwinian evolutionists' murder machine. They knew it was survival of the fittest and that there were no consequences for the 'winners' except winning the genetic survival lottery."

She looked at him with hard eyes that searched his soul.

"So I went looking for that to be wrong," she said bluntly.

They were coming into a station. To a platform where hopefully they could find a rail car going back down the spine. Back to the *Lex*.

What about Rechs, that other voice asked Casper. *Your oldest friend. He's still out there, and he probably isn't coming back from this one. What about him?*

And yet Casper had seen the look in her eyes. The look that spoke of other worlds than these. Of worlds where it was just him and her, and not Rechs.

"I wanted justice for the Pantheon on the *Obsidia,*" Reina said. "I wanted justice for the Nazis and all the mass murderers who ever thought they were going to get away with burning, shooting, and stabbing their way to the top. I wanted them to *pay,* not just escape into death. And one night, underneath the stars and cruising on narco-tequila, I realized that the only way I was ever getting that was if there was something bigger than all of us. Something... some*one*... let's call it God. Call it power. Call it the Grand Weaver. Whoever it was, I wanted someone who made sure the bad people paid in the end on the other side of this joke we call reality. Because if it's all nothing, then where exactly is the justice for Nazis who get to go on doing what they're doing right up until death? Where are *their* ovens? *Their* torture chambers? Where is their court and who is their judge?"

She stared at him in the shifting light of the passing tunnel. "If there is someone in charge of all this... then that's who'll give us our justice. That's what hell is for, Casper. And I needed to find out if that was possible."

30

It was like a mad bull, that monster that came out of the forest in the mountains where the smell of salt washed down over the ridge in great cool winds. And it was also like a giant gorilla. Like King Kong, who'd once destroyed New York.

Casper knew the story of King Kong. One night around their fire inside their home that had once been an old chain restaurant, Casper's father had told him the story. He'd listened in amazement, and even laughed, as his father made all the noises and even capered like a giant ape climbing up the side of a tall building. Like the skeletal buildings that Casper sometimes saw in the ruins of downtown LA, those that had been spared most of the damage from the nukes that had been used out in the ocean, off shore.

It was only years later, after his parents were...

It was only years later that he found out *King Kong* was just a movie. Not a true story.

Still, every so often, at a certain time of year, he would have the dream of being in a city and being chased by a giant ape. And the city was always alive. With other people running and screaming for their lives.

But now, as that beast, which was easily the size of a small building, tore away the trees and came loping, impossibly loping, lowering its massive horns atop its simian head, it was like that nightmare was made real.

It hit THK-133, literally batting the bot—who'd been firing at the monster with its heavy blaster—off into the nearby woods of the high valley. It was all Casper could do get out of its way, to run for his life as the beast howled and screamed above him, beating its rippling, hairy chest.

He was dimly aware that even tiny Urmo had dodged.

And all this was like the last moments of the *Moirai*, and his desperate attempt to save them all.

As though any man can ever save anyone.

It had taken hours. Hours to make it back up through the outer decks after they reached the ship's spinal rail system. From there it was a straight shot to the hangar deck.

And when they reached the hangar deck they found it surrounded. Savage marines had formed a ring of defensive emplacements near every blast door, control balcony, and maintenance lift leading out onto the sprawling deck where the *Lex* waited.

Casper had gained a look at the situation by maneuvering up along a series of gantries in the upper reaches of the massive complex. From there they were able to see the field.

"Looks bad," said the medic as she stared through a Martian Infantry tactical monocle. "We're not getting through that without taking fire. I give us a less than good chance of not getting hit before we reach the ship."

Reina waited in the shadows below them.

Casper was lying next to the medic, using his SmartEye to study the situation. "Right… but the *Lexington* is still under our control," he reminded her. "Nattersly has most likely activated the auto-turrets and PDCs. Anything moves, those guns will target and engage. See all the corpses near the blast door entrances? Those didn't happen during the initial firefight to take the hangar deck. They've been trying to get close, and have been denied." Rail guns designed to throw up a wall of lead slugs did nasty things, even to the post-human man-machine body.

"But those PDCs will recognize us as targets too," said the medic. "We're going to get killed just as dead as they are."

"Maybe," said Casper. He rolled onto his side and pulled out a small pen-shaped object—a laser designator. Leaning on his elbows, he began to click it on and off.

"What are you doing?" asked the medic. She'd been there through thick and thin, fighting right alongside the rest of the legendary Martian light infantrymen, pulling them out of danger and patching wounds amid hurricanes of lead slugs.

Where others had not survived, she had.

For the first time, Casper looked at her. Really saw her. She wasn't just the team's medic. There had been others. They'd been killed too.

She had brown hair. Pink freckles. Hazel eyes.

"They call you Bones," he said. "What's your real name? Someone changed it in the HUD roster."

She stared through her monocular once more, obviously uncomfortable with the question.

Then: "Medics get assigned a call sign. For some weird reason. Something about work focus and all under battle conditions. But my real name is Laura. Laura Maydoon."

Casper continued to click his laser designator on and off. Aiming it at the flight deck of the *Lex*.

"Well, Laura Maydoon. This is an ancient system of communication called Morse code. And I'm telling the crew to reset the guns to not engage our biometrics. We're not going to die today. We're all going home."

Rechs too? asked that other voice.

He remembered the look of possibility he had seen in Reina's eyes.

"Yes," he whispered. Though it surely seemed a non sequitur to the medic named Maydoon.

A moment later the *Lex*'s engines booted up, growling to life, steadily rising into their high-pitched whine.

"So, the guns wont shoot at us," said the medic. "But the Savages will. How are we going to get through that?"

Casper turned toward her. "By just walking."

"Walking?" she said incredulously.

"Yeah," replied Casper. He got to his knees. "Those PDCs run massive intercept algorithms that crunch physics, angles of intercept, and many other things. That's how they knock out missiles inside the vastness of space at speeds the mind can't comprehend. Not only will those guns not hit us, but as long as the munitions in their magazines hold, they'll prevent anything aimed at us from hitting us either—by intercepting the bullets or knocking out the source."

"You're saying we just walk through a hailstorm of bullets and make the boarding ramp?"

"Theoretically." Casper smiled.

"Theoretically!"

"We designed the system for hostile first contacts. Allows us to not get wiped out if the natives go hostile."

"Have you ever used this system in this scenario before?"

"There is a first time for everything, Corporal Maydoon. Plus... it's the only way through this. Or at least, the only way I can see."

The young girl swallowed hard. And Casper saw the look in her eyes. A look that said she wanted to go on. That today was not a good day to die.

She bit her lip and nodded, knowing she was once more about to do the hard thing the hard way.

"When there's nothing left to do but fight, then fight," she whispered to herself.

"What?" Casper asked.

"I'm in. Let's do this."

Casper looked over to Reina, who had listened to all of this silently, without judgment. She simply nodded.

When all was ready, the crew of the *Lex* signaled back. "They're ready," Casper said. "Thirty seconds and the guns go live. They're also going to pop smoke to give us cover. Reina, take my hand. Corporal Maydoon, just stay on course and follow your HUD to the ship. Got it?"

The girl tried to say something, but whatever it was got caught in her throat. Instead she just raised her glove and tapped her bucket in the affirmative.

They descended on flight of stairs and turned down a short corridor. Casper peered around the corner. A team of Savage marines guarded the exit onto the hangar deck.

And then there was the long walk through flying lead.

Casper tossed a grenade and waited for the explosion. After a count of three, he and Maydoon pivoted from behind cover and sprayed the area with fire while Reina remained pinned to the wall out of sight.

Beyond the dead Savage guards lay the octagonal opening that led onto the massive hangar deck of the sprawling generation ship. And for a brief instant, far down the runway and past the other docking bays, through the opening in the hull, Casper saw the Dead Zone.

And where space was... it wasn't.

Never mind that, he told himself, pushing the madness-inducing images away.

They strode toward the hangar deck. "Remember, walk slowly," he said over the comm. "Don't hurry. The PDCs will have a much better time of protecting us if we move slow and steady and allow them to calculate the intercepts."

Ahead, the mighty *Lex*—mighty in her day, small by the standards of the future—loomed on all four gears, forward flight deck nosed up and forward like some proud bird of prey, her wing engines spread off to the sides. Smoke popped from launchers appearing across the upper hull. The PDC guns went live at the same instant the Savages opened fire on the three survivors of the rescue mission.

The billowing smoke came at them like a rolling tidal wave of blossoming white cotton. The massive PDCs erupted in titanic *BRAAAAAAAAPs* as their processors calculated trajectories and filled the volume in between with clouds of whistling lead slugs, keeping enemy rounds from hitting them.

Casper felt Reina's hand dig into him as her body went rigid. The smoke raced out toward them and swallowed them up, and the sound of bullets colliding with other bullets echoed all around them. The ricochets went off like high-pitched screams as math incalculable by the human mind raced to save their lives and keep them out of harm's way. The roar of the guns made the deck and even the very air shudder; the sound was titanic, monstrous, and accompanied by hurricanes of invisible angry wasps that raced to meet their impossibly fast targets. The hornet swarms of bullets tore the swirling mad maelstrom of smoke to shreds, even as more smoke rushed in to fill the volume recently displaced.

Reina was screaming.

From Maydoon, Casper heard nothing.

"Are you there, Corporal?" he shouted, turning up the gain on his comm. He couldn't see her through the smoke and the blur of flying metal. What if she had panicked and run?

No doubt the *Moirai* was being holed all across the superstructure. It was probably even starting to vent oxygen in distant compartments as loose rounds finally violated the outer hull and raced off into space.

No, not space. What he'd seen beyond the hangar exit.

Don't think about what you saw, he screamed at himself.

"Don't run!" he shouted across the ether at Corporal Maydoon. Not wanting the girl's life to end here. Too many lives had ended today already.

Just not her. Let her make it.

Let me save one, he thought in some part of his mind that had always wanted to save everyone ever since the day he hadn't been able to save his parents from nomadic murderous thugs who couldn't have cared less that the world was trying to get back on its feet. Who'd never birthed pigs. Or grown corn. Or... Or... Or...

He hadn't cried for his parents.

He never had.

The world had been too hard to allow for the luxury of grief.

And now, hundreds of years later, in the middle of a storm of sudden death, he felt the tears come.

I tried to save you, he thought about them. *And I failed.*

He reached a hand out into the smoke for the young medic. Shouting over and over for Corporal Maydoon.

"Take my hand! Don't run!"

I'll save you. I'll save you. I'll save you.

But in no direction could he find the girl.

And then he did.

His hand found her arm. And pulled her close. He felt that ancient glove of the long-forgotten Martian Infantry grab him. He heard the girl's breathing, so rapid it sounded like she was gasping for the last of the air in a rapid decompression.

"I've got you!" he shouted at her.

He still couldn't see her through the smoke.

But he had her.

And he dragged her and Reina through it all. To the boarding ramp. Onto the ship.

To safety.

The *Lex* fired her maneuvering thrusters and cleared the billowing smoke. Already the landing gears were up and the ship was hovering for takeoff.

The PDCs ran dry. The magazines were empty.

The monster had ceased its roar.

The monster had ceased its seemingly unending rushing roar in the high valley beyond the endless desert.

The apelike, bull-like beast had howled at them as though banishing them to some nether realm. As though offended at the presence of the human and the whatever Urmo was.

Because of its reach, speed, and stride, there was nowhere to run. Nowhere to hide. No weapon. Nothing.

Standing beneath its looming presence, beyond the edge of the galaxy on a planet that never should have been... Casper came to the end of himself. As one does when there are no other options left.

The massive beast towered above him and raised fists the size of hammers that never were.

31

Both that nightmare past and the terrible present were colliding inside Casper's mind as he froze beneath the enraged glare of the monster. He was rooted. He couldn't move fast enough to escape. There was no obstacle he could cover behind, nothing he could put between him and the threat.

There was nothing he could do. He'd come all the way across time and the galaxy... to end like this.

As he waited for the inevitable, the little beast next to him shouted uselessly, and defiantly, up at the roaring titan.

"URMO! URMO! URMO!"

It was a small defiance against something bigger than mere sanity could comprehend. It was like watching Rechs battle the inevitable all over again in those last moments of the *Moirai.*

"XO!" shouted Casper once the hatch had sealed. The crew chief and the ship's doctor were swarming Reina, Corporal Maydoon, and Casper. Casper was shouting into his sleeve comm to be heard over the powerful whine of the *Lex*'s maneuvering thrusters. The ship was no doubt pivoting and powering up for a fast departure. "Get us out of here now! Best speed!" he shouted to the flight crew.

And then he was pounding down the tight passages, racing for the flight deck.

When he made it forward, the *Lex* was just clearing the hangar's force field barrier and entering what should have been open space. Instead, they were entering what resembled a nebula of swirling multi-colored gases, electrical storms, and violent gravitation wells made of... made of what Casper's mind chose to call *energy locusts*.

Except this was no nebula. Whereas the gases in a nebula would have formed dense storm fronts, these masses of... whatever they were—the energy locusts... swirled and shifted, interacting with other fronts of different-colored... insects. And behind all this were other layers of insects. And others beyond that. There were layers upon layers of the shifting insect storms stretching off into spatial distances reminiscent of deep space.

"Where are we?" he heard himself asking the flight crew.

The XO appeared at his elbow. "We have no idea, Captain. No stellar signatures. No star fields. Nothing. We may not even be in the reality we know as our own. Your guess is as good as mine, sir."

Casper leaned forward and rested his hands on the backs of the pilots' seats. Staring out through the latticed canopy of the cockpit.

"It's called the Quantum Palace." It was Reina. She was behind them. Her voice was soft, almost hoarse. Like she was in a trance.

Casper turned.

The *Moirai* was beginning to fall away from the departing *Lex*. The ship shuddered and bounced.

"What is that? The Quantum Palace?" he asked her.

She moved forward. Touched his hand.

"Something very ancient. Something we don't fully understand. But... as best I can tell... it's like a computer, and it's not. It can talk to the galaxy. Though there is some processing function we were feeling our way around."

We, thought Casper. He didn't like the answer he heard inside his own head.

"All of that," she said, pointing toward the energy locust swarms shifting, twirling, forming new shapes and fusing with other swarms, "is data. Raw data. Data from long ago, and from even now, I suspect. This was some project of the race we all call the Ancients. They... constructed... a repository for all the knowledge they'd acquired. And even the knowledge of those that came before them. The Dead Zone was the input, if you will, in how data was stored. In other words, we're inside some kind of pocket universe where everything can be rendered down to data. It's an example of what I was trying to prove."

"That intelligence precedes physicality?"

Reina nodded. He watched a bare moment of guilt cross her beautiful green eyes.

"And the other ships that were lost here?"

"Most likely they're still in here. Somewhere. Unable to figure out what's going on. Dying, eventually, once their life support and supplies give out. Or they've found exits that might, we theorize, lead to other galaxies... or even somewhere else in time."

Casper stared at her incredulously.

"Or even other realities. Parallel universes. But that's all just a guess. We only just barely comprehend how this place can even exist. We don't actually know what it *does*. Or how to use it. We were... experimenting."

He straightened. Staring at her. Knowing that what he would say next would change all the possibilities that might ever have been considered of him... and her.

"You were working with them."

His tone was angry. His eyes hard. He pointed his thumb over his shoulder at the massive cylinder of the Rama-class ship known as the *Moirai*.

She nodded. Barely.

Then she lowered her eyes, dropping her head to her chest. When she spoke, he couldn't tell if she was sobbing or just speaking quietly. Or if her voice had simply been scarred and ruined by the smoke and gunfire back on the hangar deck.

"In reviewing some of the survivor accounts from the *Moirai*'s raids against the colonies... our science team got wind of what they were doing. What they were after. The questions they were asking of the few who managed to survive their attacks and interrogations... they led us to certain conclusions. In time we figured out the *Moirai* was making runs into the Dead Zone... and coming out. Incredibly."

She paused.

"Bring us about," Casper ordered. His voice was hard and cruel.

She looked up in surprise. But the look in his eyes demanded she finish the explanation of her betrayal.

"We made contact," she said. "I... made contact. Yes. I offered to work with them."

"Why?" Casper hissed.

"Because they were close to knowing everything that can be known. Don't you understand what that thing *does*,

Cas?" She practically shouted in his face. "This thing we're surrounded by. It makes the intuitive leaps. Because all the data is there, and all it needs to do miracles is crunch that data and fill in the science you're missing to get an answer. Cancer. Space folds. Interdimensional travel. Eternal life. It's all there, Cas. Test, develop, and design, and the Palace can lead you to reproduce a result you can measure, deconstruct, and extrapolate. If I was ever going to find the answer to whether intelligence precedes physicality, this side of death, it was here. And they were the ticket in."

She stared at him as hard as he was staring at her. She wasn't sorry in the least.

"So I did it," she whispered. Her voice was almost gone.

But then she composed herself. She looked away, and came back to him anew. And her look this time was pure poison. There was a defiance there. A challenge to indict her for what she'd done.

"They wanted to know, too," she hissed. "As badly as both you and I want to know right now."

Casper flinched. His head involuntarily went to the side, forcing his dominant eye to watch her warily. As though he were watching some dangerous animal he'd met out in the forest. And when he realized this he leveled his gaze and stared her in the face as he spoke to the crew.

"XO, unlimber the SSMs."

There was a pause during which no one in the flight crew moved.

"Do it. Now!" he growled, watching Reina the whole time.

The flight and weapons crews sprang into action.

"Make our range at max engage!" the XO ordered.

"Thirty seconds," the pilot responded.

"Weps—crack the seals on one and two," said the XO.

The weapons officer to the rear of the flight deck responded that both the ship-to-ship missiles were ready for action. Then he added, "Targeting solution coming through now."

In the silence, Casper watched her face change. It changed from the hard witch who'd done a deal with the devil in the night... to the girl he'd once known. The girl who had loved his best friend. And maybe even him.

"You'll kill him if you fire."

They both knew who she meant.

Casper shook his head and turned away to watch the *Moirai* off the forward quarter.

He reached forward and stabbed a finger at the targeting layout. "Hit her here," he muttered, pointing toward the bow. "One torp. Once it detonates, we're going into the superstructure. Comm and sensors, I need you to scan for Major Rechs's transponder."

"Ready to fire," the weapons officer announced from the rear of the flight deck.

"Ready to fire," confirmed the XO.

"Fire," Casper ordered.

The SSM whooshed forth from its tube, rattling the whole ship as it went. These were the most powerful weapons in the Terran Navy's arsenal, and they would remain so for many generations.

Then Casper was showing the pilot a flight path they would take inside the superstructure of the *Moirai*.

The crew watched as the missile sidewindered out into the energy locust–swarming void, its white-hot engine almost blue, dancing like a star, streaking forward toward the ancient cylinder.

It detonated.

A brief star burned bright inside the storm of data, flooding the shifting sky with sudden light, and then the front of the immense cylinder peeled away, sending debris in every direction.

"Now, now, now!" ordered Casper to the flight crew. "Thrusters to full. This'll be close."

One of the pilots might have been heard remarking that "close" was an understatement of the most extreme category.

The assault frigate closed on the burning bow of the *Moirai* rapidly, the massive ship growing in size to fill the cockpit window, making it seem as though the *Lexington* were diving straight down into the burning, gaping maw of a giant eel.

And then they were in. In the ship, in the ruptured main hab. Sections of the landscape were breaking loose around them in a maelstrom of burning oxygen. The *Lexington* was fighting heavy, gale-force atmospheric turbulence. A strange assortment of debris flew past and tried to escape with the tornado out the ruined bow.

"This is insane," hissed the pilot through gritted teeth.

The *Lex* shifted, engaging her maneuvering thrusters into a howling scream to avoid an actual building that had come loose and was spinning in at them. A moment later what looked like a tractor tumbled toward them and slammed into the forward deflectors, obliterating itself in a spray of parts and displaced energy.

"She'll hold," said the XO as the emergency power diversion warning lights and a harsh bell erupted across the damage control panels. "Rerouting batteries into forward deflectors."

The crazy world inside the massive generational ship was spinning and burning all at once. The *Moirai*'s hull ignited and caught fire, melting away in large sections. The *Lex* raced ahead of the wave of damage spreading from the bow.

"I have the LZ," shouted the co-pilot, peering down into the terrain sensor display. "Locking in flight path now."

Casper turned back to the sensor/comm station. "Anything on Major Rechs?"

There was a long pause in which nothing could be heard beyond the howling burn of the wind screaming along the fuselage of the assault frigate. The ship dropped down toward the bizarre pyramids on the hab's curving plain.

"Got him!" shrieked the sensor operator.

Casper scanned the tactical display. Rechs's signal came up. He was down there in the midst of the pyramids.

Four pyramids, just like on every world they'd ever found.

"And there's someone else down there too."

But Casper was gone from the flight deck, heading back to the cargo area and the boarding ramp.

When he reached the hold, he ordered the crew chief to measure for an ambient oxygen reading.

The chief pulled out his tablet and studied the data the ship's external sensors were feeding him. "It's a massive ship, sir. Even though it's been holed, it's going to take a few more minutes for all the ox to burn up. Five minutes at best. I can get you into an EVA, but that'll take ten, minimum."

"Clear the hold, Chief." And when the chief looked like he was about to protest, Casper cut him off with a sharp, "That's an order."

When he was alone, he raised the cargo door.

The ship was five hundred feet over the nightmare plain now turned apocalyptic dust storm.

His comm chirped with an incoming message. "Captain. Forward hull is collapsing. We got two minutes at best. This thing's coming down all around us."

"Never mind that. Put us down as close as you can get to the major."

The *Lex* circled the pyramids, dropping in low. Beyond the open cargo door, deadly debris shot past like twirling phantoms in a tornado.

But the *Lex's* pilot was good, and he angled the cargo door and crabbed the frigate in to bring it as close to Rechs as possible.

Rechs was holding on for dear life, gripping the edge of a pyramid with one gloved hand. With the other he was firing at a tall creature dressed in shrouded rags.

The Dark Wanderer.

The wind howled and shrieked in wails and whistling screams, threatening to rip Rechs from his precarious hold, threatening to rip the air straight out of Casper's lungs. The oxygen was thin and getting thinner.

Rechs was still twenty meters out.

"Captain," came the pilot over comm. "We can hold this position steady, but we can't get closer."

The engines howled and whined. The ship danced at the behest of the storm-current's buffets.

Out across the uncrossable void, Rechs turned his head and shook it in the negative. The message was clear. Leave him. Now.

"This is the captain," Casper said over the comm. "Take us upwind. I'm attaching the cargo line to my gear. Give me about thirty yards of slack and try to get me close to him."

He didn't bother to listen to their protestations. Instead he busied himself with the cargo line and a series of D-clips.

A moment later the *Lex*'s engines strained and howled to pull the ship sideways and up, away from Rechs. And Casper stepped out into the void of the howling storm.

He felt a sickening moment of floating and then being jerked violently downward. Except he was going sideways across the debris-littered hull-scape that now seemed to be in list rotation. Overhead and far down the spine, the hull was burning up like a metal sky on fire. Great sections of it were shorn loose by explosions that ripped through the superstructure.

Casper had just enough time to wonder whether the line would hold before what little oxygen was in him was knocked completely out as the line jerked taut. Stars swam across his vision and he blacked out, briefly, dangling helplessly in the blast of the rushing oxygen escaping to be burnt up.

He wasn't far from Rechs. But he was far enough away that he would never reach him. There would be no leaps in this gale-force storm. No handholds that could remain in these tornadoes. For Rechs to even reach out to him, he would have to loosen his hold on the pyramid. And then...

Darkness.

32

The monster in the high valley beyond the endless desert roared like some immense giant demon from unknown nether hells. Its maw dropped open, revealing impossibly long fangs. Powerful simian arms reached out toward Casper.

Casper fell backward onto the ground, helpless beneath the titan.

Seeing only Urmo standing in front of him.

Thinking... *It'll run him down and not even know it as it comes for me.*

Because coming for him it was.

The ground shook.

And the lost world all around disappeared.

When Casper came to, he was still at the end of the line in the windstorm, being thrown about by the violent winds rushing toward the distant bow. But Rechs had a hold of him. Was holding on to Casper's gear, his heavy armor attempting to drag the gear off and away into the swirling storm.

"Reel us in!" Casper gasped in the thin oxygen. Hoping his comm would pick up. Hoping they were watching the external cams.

And that was when he looked toward the largest pyramid. Some object the size of a naval gun had just whipped past them. They were being winched back into the bright and clean cargo hold as the air burned up and disappeared all around them, and that massive object had gone by, almost hitting them straight on. Almost carrying them off into the unfolding destruction of the ship.

They would've been lost forever.

That would've been the end of them.

And the end of everything that would come.

But the object missed, and merely drew Casper's attention to the main pyramid. It was just like all the enigmatic and impenetrable pyramids every explorer had found on all the other worlds. Sealed. Impervious to investigation. Guarding all the secrets of what everyone called the Ancients in lieu of any real and actual knowledge of who and what they'd once been. Its angular surfaces never surrendering to the slightest inspection, cut, damage, or penetration of any kind.

Except *this* pyramid was open along its facing side. And within, looking back at him, was... a blank space in the universe. Not just space, as in outer space. Not just emptiness, as in nothing. But a blank space in the known. A place one could see even though the mind wouldn't allow it to.

And walking into it was a tall being, cloaked in a shroud and limping. Head down, arms out, as though wading through the sea.

It was an impossible thing in the middle of a hurricane. Inside a ship venting oxygen and coming apart at the seams. Physics, gravity, mass, energy, motion, and all the other laws that defined the undefinable were being broken right in front of his eyes.

And he would often wonder, in the spare moments of the long journey to know what this power was, whether, maybe, he'd simply been hallucinating from the lack of oxygen.

Maybe.

The Dark Wanderer disappeared into the blank space in the side of the pyramid.

Gone.

And then Casper passed out again. The oxygen was all gone now.

The savage monster stopped dead in its tracks, looming above Casper. Mid charge. It halted as suddenly as if it had hit an invisible wall. Dirt and debris flew out at them as its terrible claws dug into the dirt of that lost world.

Casper opened his eyes.

He had closed them expecting only death. Expecting nothing—or perhaps the answers to all things.

And instead he had found himself here. At the end of himself.

Finally.

In the high valley on the lost planet. Beyond the desert.

And Urmo standing between him and the terrible titan that was about to end his existence.

There was nothing to be done now. Nothing but to die.

The valley was silent. The monster had stopped its roar.

He heard a distant, small hum. Almost like a monastic buzz.

And as he scrambled to his feet, he saw that the triangular head of the towering beast had begun to sway above them. Its alizarin eyes were distant and far away. Its massive shoulders slumped, and then they too began to sway from side to side. The hum increased, buzzing in Casper's ears.

And when he looked down he saw little Urmo, eyes closed, one hand out, with two little furry fingers pointing at the giant killer above their heads. Pointing as though he were reaching out to touch the thing's heart.

The look on Urmo's face might have been described as beatific. Transcendent. Peaceful. As though this little thing knew all the things that needed knowing. The good and the bad of the universe. And it was comfortable with that knowledge, knowing that all things can be made right.

The beast groaned and fell over onto its side, causing a small earthquake. Its heaving chest neither rose nor fell. It was clear that it had just suddenly, and instantly, died.

Casper, mouth agape, looked down at Urmo.

Urmo's eyes fluttered open. The delightful little creature that had once been there, constantly obsessed with the minutiae of two-headed rats, various rocks, and miscellaneous pieces of Casper's gear, was gone. In its place was a new Urmo. A tired Urmo. A knowing Urmo, who looked deep inside Casper.

The creature nodded at him once, slowly, with sad, mournful eyes. He nodded at Casper with a look that said, *All that you know... is gone now.*

And what came next was...

THE LESSON OF BECOMING THE THING YOU FEAR STARTS WITH TRYING TO CHANGE THE THINGS YOU NEVER COULD

Deep within the Temple of Morghul, the student is running in a darkness that strangles. Like running from a dragon that cannot be defeated. Because some things cannot be defeated by mere mortals. Some things can only be feared. Some things one must simply run for their lives from.

This is the end of the Lesson of Fear, and now begins the next lesson. The final lesson before all things learned can truly be understood. This is the last lesson. The lesson where you confront yourself, thinking you are confronting your worst fear.

The void swallows the student, and even in the swallowing there is a way through. Even though the dragon, a Black Dragon, is just at his heels and he has lost all his weapons, including his most powerful one.

Which is reason.

Space, reality, whatever you want to call it here within the strange temple, opens up before him into a void. And yes there are stars. Stars within the temple. Stars within the void.

It is full of stars.

Whatever it is exactly.

For an insane moment, that giddy kind of insanity that seems to be the very opposite of reason, he feels like a constellation. The frightened student running from the dragon feels like all this is part of some particular arrangement of the stars. The Black Dragon. Himself. Surely on all the worlds that consist of a galaxy, there must be some only-for-that-planet alignment where such a constellation might be drawn and mythicized by observers on the surface of an alien world.

"Tell me the story of the frightened student, Papa," some child might say while pointing

into the night sky. Pointing at the broken glass up there we call stars.

Tell me why he was afraid. Tell me why he runs.

Tell me, Papa. Tell me the frightened man's story.

Well, my child, the wise one might begin. Long ago he was just a child such as you. Living in the ruins of a ruined world. His parents were murdered by savage ones who took, plundered, and murdered because there were always such. Murdered by strangers who called the endless road home. Murdered by hard and wild savages who'd gone almost animal, become less than what they once were, in order to survive. Even if that meant someone else must die. They took, and in the taking they slaughtered. And one day they slaughtered the frightened child's parents while he was away from their farm.

Why, Papa? Why would they do such a terrible thing?

Who can say? Who can say why the galaxy is so hard and cruel on the innocent and why such wild people are allowed to ruin the simple lives of others? Who can say?

And what became of him? What became of the frightened child, Papa?

He fled. Fled his home. Fled his memories. Fled so deeply within his mind, walling off the fear of the dragons such savage ones are who had come and slain his parents. He fled the Black Dragon whose name was Goth. Of the Goths. Whose home was the endless road called the stars. He fled so completely that in time even he forgot he was running, though he lived a long time and crossed the galaxy from one end to its other.

And does he run, Papa? Does he always run from the dragon called Goth?

He does, child... until one day he doesn't.

And then the student was falling. And if all that has happened before in the strange and bizarre tale wasn't insane enough... then this part is the part that makes no sense to the rational mind. Because that's where we've come to. To the part that makes no sense, particularly if you're not insane.

The void became real and opened out into reality folding in on nothingness.

And a moment after that the student was vomited back out into reality, into spacetime, once more. Into some "other" place. Some "other" when. Whether it was real, or just a different reality, or something other, was not known.

When he came to he was halfway up the pyramid at Giza. Egypt. The dark sprawl of Cairo in the distance, lightless save for the cook fires. And it could have been any time in the hundreds and even thousands of years that existed before electricity. But the ruined flying wing Airbus Luxliner that lay in the sand, half buried, told the student who'd once been a child of the post-apocalypse, that he'd arrived in the years after the Exodus, that this was some time he knew from his own past.

Much of the Middle East had gone up in nuclear fire during those last years before the Brights had boarded their ships and hauled themselves up and away from Earth as if out of sheer embarrassment for the state of their civilization. He'd arrived in the years after that. And most likely before the discovery of the hyperdrive.

When the lawless really ruled the world, and only small groups tried to hold the world together, tried to put out the fires by restarting civilization through farming and research. When the savage bands fanned the flames by burning down and looting the little that was left in the wake of the global destruction the Brights had fled.

The ruined flying wing scramjet was proof of that. Some desperate pilot, avionics lost due to high-altitude EMP, had dead-sticked it into the sands between the ancient monuments and the burning city Cairo.

He'd seen such sights before, in and around Los Angeles, and all along the other places of Earth where he'd spent but a small part of his long existence. He'd seen wreckage that would be salvaged for little more than metal, to house the survivors who would most likely spend the rest of their lives living near the wreck where they'd only been accidentally stranded by the happenstance of someone needing to annihilate someone else on that particular day at the end of the world.

The pyramids of Earth were like the pyramids of the Ancients. Just like the pyramids they'd found on all the worlds hyperspeed had sent them to. That long-ago memory of the giant ship, an arc ship, the *Moirai*, on fire and burning down all around him surfaced like some ancient leviathan within the seas of his memories. And the memory showed him a dark figure, a wanderer of the stars, entering the un-enterable pyramid while the *Lexington* raced to get beyond the *Moirai*'s destruction. He remembered seeing the face of the pyramid on the curving plain of the main hab, folding in brick by brick... like a gateway to other places opening into the galaxy.

Like a gateway into the void.

And the Way of the Void was like a path between all the "other" places.

In time the student stumbled down the stony face of the ancient Eygptian pyramid, bloody and cut, making the soft still warm sands below. When he passed the wreck of the flying winged airliner he could tell, by the pale moonlight, that it had long ago been abandoned. But not so long ago, as the remains of looted suitcases still lay strung out along the shifting sands like the flotsam of some wrecked ship. And nearby were the bones of those who had not survived the crash, or the looting that came after.

In Cairo no one paid attention to his strange rags. Strange rags from the future. Rags ruined by a jungle, and a desert, and the many years in the temple. In a future still yet to come.

In Cairo, after the world was ruined, everyone is in rags. New clothing hadn't been manufactured in two years. Or ten years.

"Eleven years since they left," he was told by a street merchant in a crowded alley that passed for the bazaar. A bazaar that sold clean water. Cans of food not rotted or ruined by radiation. And of course weapons.

The toothless man nodded at him and offered to sell him some water that hadn't passed the purifications tests. At a discount, of course.

Eleven years after the Exodus is the Now of When.

Which meant that the pyramids that were like gates in the Way of the Void had brought him back in time. Back to Earth, before the whole mess began. Which was a strange statement to make, seeing exactly the mess Earth was in.

So, asked that other voice inside him. *What "mess" do you mean exactly?*

The mess of the Savages?

The mess the Galactic Republic will become?

The mess of your wasted life seeking a power that intoxicated you long ago?

But the student was thinking about none of those things. He was thinking about his parents.

He didn't nail down an exact date, though he asked many refugees and people who swore their smartphones still worked, he didn't know if they were still alive until he managed to force his way onto the UN air base beyond Cairo. For a moment, being back on Earth, it was easy to think that nothing, none of it, not even the hyperdrive, had ever happened. Or rather, would ever happen. But when he dominated the will of the gate guards, and the officer checking papers at the refugee entrance, he knew it had all happened. Especially the temple, where the Master had trained him to do such things as dominate the wills of the weak with a simple trick of forced persuasion.

The Lesson of Will, it had been called.

"I'll need to pass."

"Of course you will," said the UN refugee officer.

"I'll need a new set of maximum clearance travel papers and a QR code for travel... direct to LA."

"You'll need travel and QR codes direct for the Los Angeles Reclamation Zone," mumbled the officer, unaware he was even saying such things. Knowing only that it was his desire to make such things happen as soon as possible.

"And after I'm gone," the student leaned close and whispered in the feeble-minded man's ear, "you'll forget you ever saw me. You'll forget everything about me."

"I will forget everything about you."

Twelve hours later he was on a military flight across the Atlantic. It wasn't direct to Los Angeles, but if the date was right he still had time. Time to reach LA. Time to stop his parents from being murdered. Time enough to change everything that would ever happen.

His parents would live. He'd nuke every Savage ship, especially the *Moirai*, on sight. He knew these future events would happen, because he'd lived through them already—he knew where the Savages would set up their secret bases during the war. He would know their every move. And he wouldn't let the Republic get away from him this time. He would stop all its foolishness. Prevent it from navel-gazing itself to death.

For a moment, lying in the cargo net seat wearing a UN uniform, he tried to run through the implications of what would happen if he changed the past. If he rescued his parents from their fate, and somehow rescued himself from his own.

What other things would he change?

And what would happen if he did?

Don't ask such things, he told himself when his mind almost came unraveled as it considered the sheer volume of possibilities. Just do it. Do it because you've been offered the chance to do it. And because you've seen the future and it's not so great. And if there's a chance to change things on your own, then maybe you don't need the powers of the Temple of Morghul, maybe you just need a do-over.

Maybe there's another way.

PART THREE

THE LAST CASUALTY OF KNOWLEDGE... IS EVERYTHING YOU ONCE WERE

33

Casper found himself stumbling away from that high valley where the dead monster now lay among the tall grass. He'd gone forward to stare at the dead beast, his own chest heaving, fear coursing through him like a rushing river, to stand in awe of the dead behemoth. But when he'd turned back to look at the little creature called Urmo, the tiny beast that had saved him from being stomped to death or rent into a million pieces... Urmo was gone.

Instead there was only the whiskbroom sound of the tall grass and the distant flutter and hush of the salty breeze through the high forest that surrounded the clearing.

He climbed up onto a ridge, from which he could see down onto the desert plateau he'd crossed in the days and weeks before. It seemed such a vast and wide thing he wondered how he'd ever done it. How they'd ever done it.

Everything, the entire world on which he'd left the galaxy to reach, was smothered in a deep quiet.

He was suddenly afraid. Afraid not that there might be more of these same monsters in the forest all around, but afraid of the one called Urmo. The tiny creature he'd found in that jungle of his own insanity, now lost beyond the desert he stared down into. A creature who'd followed him across those seemingly endless sands, all the time unconsidered beyond being a minor nuisance. The same creature that had brought down the most fearsome alien—no, monster. Little Urmo had brought it down with those same powers Casper had witnessed all those years ago aboard the doomed *Moirai*. Powers he'd searched the galaxy for.

Just like the prophetesses.

Just like the Dark Wanderer.

After the *Moirai* disintegrated in a mass of flaming oxygen and exploding hull plating bursting away in every direction, the *Lex* had shot free of the Quantum Palace, the old Dead Zone marked on the stellar charts, and just barely at that. Reina had secreted a navigational program that allowed them to exit—though any deeper inside the pocket universe and they would've been lost forever, or so Reina had grimly reminded them as the assault frigate spooled up and leapt free of the final blast wave of the massive ghost ship *Moirai*'s apocalyptic last moments. They escaped... and it ruined each of them—Casper, Reina, and Rechs—forever. They had witnessed the powers... something beyond the known and even hoped-for technological wildest miracles of the future. They'd witnessed something... "other."

Power.

Powers.

Powers he'd sought for years, scouring the depth and breadth of the galaxy. His journey leading here. Here on this forgotten and forsaken planet.

And now he was suddenly afraid again. Just as he'd been, really, in the dark depths of the *Moirai*. Running from the Savages and the prophetesses of that damned vessel. He was so afraid that he forgot all about THK-133, who'd been batted aside by the monster like a mere toy.

Now Casper was running. Running from the desert below. Running into the dense forest that clustered along the ridgeline. Running and trying to ignore the whispers filling his mind.

He just ran, crashing through the feathery forest that was anything but. Being caught at. Torn at by jagged vines. Pushing through dense stands of thorn and creeping bush, and breaking out onto a trail that wound its way up along the jagged rocky outcroppings and steep draws, drawing him ever upward. He ran, ignoring what these trails meant. Instead running for his life in an almost mad and mindless state. Because all of this was an old fear. A fear from his childhood, what little there had been of it. And the whispers that kept whispering in every bush and tree and through his mind whispered the sound of someone being choked.

And the sound it made... was *Gothhhhh*.

Fear had taken hold of him, and there was no reason in this, even though his mind screamed at him that this, what the little creature wielded, was precisely what he had come looking for all along. This was the end of the quest. He had found the answer to all the problems he'd never been able to solve. What partnership, diplomacy, and war had never been able to address, he'd fix with raw power. Not because he was mad. Or power-hungry. But because he wanted to save them all in the way he'd never been able to save his parents.

His whole life had been that of a viewer watching a disaster unfolding. Yes, he'd tried to save what could be saved. But what had he really saved, in the final tally? The galaxy was on the edge of ruin. Some force from the Outer Dark beyond the galaxy was headed this way, if Reina's last transmission was to be believed. All of it, all of everything they'd fought for and built, was spinning apart.

And now, he'd finally found the power to fix everything. This was the end of his quest.

Except it was really the beginning.

That would become clear soon enough. And more so in the long and hard years to come.

He followed the trail that led through the jagged little hills. It was little more than a grassy track that wound alongside the steep inclines of the upper reaches of the tiny mountain range, and soon he found a narrow pass that let out onto the other side. The breeze, which had been shaking the trees back and forth in gusty breaths, now turned into a gale as air from the other side of the range was forced into the small tube of the pass and rushed to shoot out the other side. And in it he smelled an ocean, and iron, and rust, and stone, and tropical flowers, and even the scent of a thousand tallow candles scented with something exotic like sandalwood, all guttering and adding their scents to the wind.

He smelled time.

A lot of time.

He had to lower his head to cross the pass to get to the other side, and what he saw stunned him more than anything he'd ever seen in his very long life. What he saw took the breath from his lungs and changed everything he ever thought he understood. And now he knew, as old as he was, that he'd come to this planet as a mere child. The universe was now a much bigger place than he'd ever imagined.

34

Casper saw the Temple of Morghul.

It was massive in its entirety, though it was really made up of hundreds, if not thousands of ancient structures. Large and small towers stood alongside small pyramids and oblong ziggurats. Sprawling, crumbling-columned pavilions stood before enigmatic structures that could have been anything from necropolises to libraries. But the rough shape of the entire place was circular, with concentric rings of roads and fat walls tapering near their tops, guarding all the rings from inner to outer.

Through one section of this massive complex, a tropical river had washed away the buildings and structures in its path, even battering down the mighty walls that circled the inner districts of the place. The river originated from the terminus of a waterfall beyond the city, falling off some higher peaks closer to the mist-shrouded coast beyond. Casper could see it from here, its fall seeming slow and luxuriant as multicolored hues shimmered forth from the chaos at the end of its descent. The falling water and drifting river were the only things that moved.

In the center of the temple complex rose a circular tower that was more a squat funnel than tall defense. It was open at the top, roofless, and it reminded Casper of some kind of hunter-gatherer village oven more than a tower. Except that its sides were innately carved, and it was at least ten stories tall. It looked like the kind of place where ceremonies and sacrifice were carried out day and night. As though some perpetual dark smoke should be drifting up from its open mouth into the sky at all times.

This had to be the Temple of Morghul. And in time he would find this to be true. Much to his sometimes regret in the hard years to come. But this fantastic find of a vast temple complex that held the power he'd crossed beyond the galaxy for... this was not what stunned him. What stunned him and left his mouth agape lay beyond. Out in the turquoise and translucent aquamarine shallows of an ocean that washed up along the temple's outer coastal walls.

It was the ships that stunned him.

The graveyard of starships. That was what left his mind reeling.

Hundreds of interstellar craft the likes of which he'd never seen in his two thousand years of spaceflight. And in among only some of these were ones that seemed known to him.

There have been others, he thought as he looked out at the wreckages above and below the water. *Others, even from your own galaxy, that made it here. Seeking what you sought.*

Had they found it?

Would he find Reina's ship here? Would he find her?

There were massive behemoths of ships out there in the ocean shallows. Ships far bigger than the Rama-class generational ships of ancient Earth. One of these ships in particular was shaped like a mighty crescent that must've spanned sixty or eighty kilometers. One wing of that crescent lay submerged beneath the ocean waves, out in the depths. Towers had collapsed all along the top of the crescent, though there were still many standing along the upper line of the massive hull. No ship like that had ever been built within the Galactic Republic.

In the shadow of this massive ship were other ships like globes, and some ships shaped like starfish. And in all of these he could see missing hull plating, or some collapsed drive system. Or even ancient glass, still reflecting the dying red dwarf's light, reflecting amid the wreckage. He could spend lifetimes wandering their abandoned decks.

These are ships from other galaxies.

And there were so many others, too. Ships that seemed to defy practical ship design as the best of the Republic understood it. Ships that seemed fragile in their interconnected rings linked by a spindly central spine. All of these resting for eons in the gentle surf that rolled in slowly from beyond the breakers and the reefs. Schools of multicolored fish swam in and among the ruined hulls and collapsing drive systems, and lone predator fish, large enough to be whales, moved in lazy patterns in the bays created by the clusters of ruined metal, idly hunting their prey.

Casper spotted an ancient scout vessel of pre-Republic make. An Ardent class from the old scout service. Diamond shaped and turned rusty with age, she lay along the beach with her hatches popped.

Those ships were in service nine hundred years ago, he remembered in amazement.

And...

Others came looking too.

And...

Where are they?

Reina?

He followed the trail down along the grassy, tropical flower-laden slopes above the temple. In time he picked up a small road that wound down through the outer districts, passing forlorn stone buildings, all of them adorned with Medusa-like faces carved in stone, tongues lolling, eyes wide with some kind of communicated knowing. The buildings seemed more ancient than anything he'd ever known. As he passed by one such structure, with a tall roof like the hull of a boat, he decided to ascend a short flight of low crumbling steps in order to peer into the darkness within.

The building was empty.

And still.

Outside, he'd heard the slough and response of the distant surf down along the outer coastal walls. But here, within the shadowy building, he heard nothing.

As his eyes grew accustomed to the darkness, he spotted a round hole in the floor. The absence of light that came from it was deeper than the gloom of the empty chamber. Cautiously, hearing only the sound of his beaten boots against ancient flagstones, he approached. The hole was a pit, and there was no bottom to it—not that he could see. He kicked a small pebble over the lip, and heard nothing. No reply from the unseen bottom. And that, too, disturbed him, just as the knowledge that Urmo was... something more than he'd guessed. Something like the Dark Wanderer. Except—in some way he knew this, without knowing why—maybe even something worse.

He left the empty ancient stone building, and felt glad to be back out in the high tropical sunshine. Smelling the distant and somehow melancholy flowers of the hills that surrounded this place, and the closer scent of the vines that clutched at every structure.

It took him hours to make it down into the bowl of the temple complex. He watched the ominous tower at its center, squat and ever rising, as he threaded the ruined districts and found gaps in the cyclopean stone walls that guarded the inner rings. At times he thought this place might once have been inhabited by giants. At other times, doors and openings seemed normal-sized, or even too small.

In the afternoon the red star began to sink into the ocean, turning the beached whale skeletons of the alien extra-galactic starships into dark and shadowy silhouettes, like the skeletons of damned men hung at the crossroads for crimes they never should have committed. Night fell, and both moons rose over the silent temple city where no one seemed to live anymore. He gazed up at them as he passed down a wide street lined with monolithic open porticoes that led into massive edifices. These structures reminded him of the most august of government buildings the hubris of the House of Reason had ever dared to construct in their own honor. Or perhaps temples to forgotten dark gods that were really demons.

At the end of what must have once been a triumphal way lay the final high wall that guarded the innermost ring. Beyond it rose the massive tower like some fat idol watching over the silent districts of this ancient and lost place. He knew he would go there. Knew he must. Knew that when he did he would find the tower was nothing more than high walls. That within its circumference he would find something terrible and open to the stars. Like something he'd read about in some lost fantasy epic from long ago. A place where mortals angered the Immortal with obscene rites meant to make them gods among men.

Turn back, tried some quiet and fading voice for almost the last time.

"I've come too far," he whispered to the starless night as he gathered grass and dead wood that had clustered against one of the decrepit old buildings. Probably blown here by eons of typhoons that crossed this planet, much like the tiny planet had been blown here, out beyond the galaxy, circling a dying red star.

I've come to far too turn back, he told the night as a wind came up from off the ocean, bringing with it the smell of dead starships long overdue from the dark.

At midnight he saw the Master. He was as surprised as he ever could have been. The Master came close to the small and pathetic fire shifting in the night winds off the ocean. The Master was holding his own guttering torch, and within his mind Casper heard the final offer. The final call.

The summons to seek power.

I thought it was the end, he thought before he surrendered. *But it's just the beginning. Just as it was always meant to be.*

Casper rose. In his left hand was the head of THK-133. Beaten, battered, somehow perpetually smiling in its machine way. He could hear its droll yet taunting butler's commentary. Still, even, inside his mind. Had the bot been destroyed in the crash? Had he carried it all this way because he'd lost his mind and needed something to talk to?

He set the head of the machine down next to the fire. How much was real? he wondered. How much had actually happened?

And...

What happened that I'll never know? Never remember...?

He smiled wanly at the processing unit of the bot, the head of his only friend, and thought, *Let some other stranger find it and wonder who he was. Maybe it will be the final straw, in its own enigmatic way, that turns them back from what I'm about to do.*

But then he thought of his own wrecked ship out in the jungles. And all the ruined ships along the coast beyond the walls that guarded this place. *How could you turn back*, he thought, *when you'd been headed here all along?*

The Master led him beyond the last wall, and into the tower of the temple.

THE LAST LESSON IS THE LESSON OF BECOMING THE THING YOU FEAR

Part One

The man who was once Casper came too late to save his parents from the past. The old military transport had broken down over Texas, and they'd had to make an emergency landing on the freeway alongside a UN refugee camp. Three days later the military supply train headed for the LA Reclamation Zone had lumbered into Union Station beneath the crumbling ruins of downtown.

He was away from the platform at almost a dead run, shaking off the familiar smell of burnt smoke and overwhelming dust that had been his childhood. Because, after all, he was actually back in his childhood. Two blocks from the station he flung himself into an abandoned building, gutted and looted. He shrugged out of the UN uniform he'd been using as a cover to travel with. He'd acquired other clothes. Rougher clothes. He was going out beyond the downtown perimeter, into the farming districts of Midtown and Beverly Hills and the West Side.

Familiar names he'd made himself forget nearly two thousand years ago.

As he pulled on the faded jeans and laced up the combat boots he'd stolen from within the refugee camp, he felt giddy. All the old names. Midtown. Beverly Hills... the West Side. All places from his childhood. He'd played in those places.

He pushed away the date.

The date said he was late. But that had been two thousand years ago, and he'd been a child. Maybe he'd had it wrong. So he strapped on the pistol belt and the 1911 he'd taken, though he asked himself... did he need such weapons now?

He'd learned so much in the temple.

A temple he'd pursued across almost his entire lifetime. Which was the length of many lifetimes. But the weapon comforted him on some level. He'd always worn a sidearm. A blaster. As the captain of a UN assault frigate. As a legionnaire. Even as an admiral in the Republic Navy. And all the other many things he'd ever been. He'd always had a weapon.

He pulled on the faded green trench coat. It was spring. And he remembered spring in Los Angeles being cool. Biting winds and sudden rainstorms that swept across the dust-covered ruins of an ancient city that probably never recovered from the death of civilization.

Had it?

There were things about Earth that he'd forgotten and would never remember. One thing especially. But that wasn't important.

And then he ran. Ran for all he was worth. Getting through the flimsy barriers that protected downtown and out into the wild and deserted streets north of the reclamation zone. It wasn't far to La Brea Boulevard. To his family's farm. To where it had happened.

Later, when he found their fresh graves, he would tell himself, yell at himself really, that he should have asked someone in downtown. They would have known. Known that raiders had come in and killed a few settlers in the days and weeks before. That was always the big news back then.

Which ones?

The Sullivans and a few other families, they would say. Would have said. He couldn't remember those other names now, though he knew them then. He did remember a blond-haired little girl who'd been his friend. Her family had lived in movie theater a few blocks away.

It had happened three days ago. His parents had been murdered three days before he arrived at what remained of the farm.

Their bodies were buried in the dead landscaping of a burned-out gas station a block away from the house. Their house. The house he'd grown up in two thousand years ago. The markers he'd made them were still there, though the other families had helped bury them. All of them coming from their own reclamation farms in the blocks they'd been allocated.

Someone had even come by and shot the marker that lay over his father. Blowing his first name away and making a new word out of what was left of "Sullivan, Justin." Sheriff of La Brea. Some old score finally settled in the bare days after the funeral he could only just remember.

And this was a strange thought he had while standing over their graves. He knew where he was. He being the child who'd been salvage-wagoned off into the reclamation zone, to the orphanage there. And he being the very long-lived man, here and standing over their graves.

Had he perhaps passed himself, his now-self, as a child, back in the zone? Had child-he seen some man running like the devil was at his heels? Racing to beat a clock that had been struck long ago?

"It's all... some cruel joke," he muttered in the afternoon light of the quiet street.

The temple was ever that way. It was full of cruel jokes that somehow taught you a lesson you needed. If you survived.

And he knew that the temple could violate the laws of time and space to teach such lessons. That there were ways to use it to do such things as travel to places "other." To give you the feeling that in other realties they, his parents, had not died. That they'd been there at his graduation from NASA. Giving him an Omega Seamaster watch as a present, when the real gift had been the pride in their eyes and voices. They were alive somewhere, just not this reality.

The temple was cruel in its lessons that way. As though everything in the universe was connected to the temple via some insane hyperloop that never really quite took you where you wanted to go, but instead dropped you off in some nightmare station along the line that only served to remind you that you'd never really make it back. And that the hour was getting late indeed.

It was a cruel joke that had sent him here, all the way here, all the way back in time, only to arrive just a little too late to do anything about what had...

... what had made him become...

... who he would become.

The child he was, from that moment, that very moment when he heard the distant gunfire back at the farm, that child who came running, had always been afraid, ever since that moment. That moment when he'd known, by the echo of the distant and sudden reports, that everything had changed forever. But instead of surrendering to the fear, or running away from it, he'd fought it. That child had fought... even though he'd run away. Even though he'd always and ever been afraid, he had fought anything that was like the looters who'd slain his parents.

He'd fought as if trying to make right what he'd been unable to as a child. He'd fought death on alien worlds and collapsing starships. Fought tyrants that wanted to turn the galaxy and its citizens into playthings for their own personal amusement and pleasure. Fought monsters who just wanted to watch it all burn down. He'd fought everyone—instead of fighting the monsters who'd started it all. The monsters he would always be afraid of in the night when he felt like he was smothering.

Gothhhhhs.

He'd always hoped the fighting of other monsters would banish the fear of the first monsters who had taken everything away. Destroyed everything that had been built. Murdered the child he'd once been without ever touching him.

But it never did. They were always back there, in the shadow forests of his memory.

And as if on cue, his blood froze at the sudden eruption of sound he heard out across the dead city. Sound traveled for miles in this city that had been blow to smithereens by massive weapons. The sound was distant, and building up into a full-throated roar—like the roar of monsters he'd one day stand before in high and distant valleys. Or the roar he'd one day hear across dark jungles as he ran for his life in the moonlight.

It was the sound of a motorcycle winding up along some distant road. Speeding off into the night. It was the sound he heard when he found his dying mother. His father's body out in the yard.

Goths.

The word was like ice in his veins. And even though he was two thousand years old, it made him feel small and frightened once again. Powerless as he stood over his mother, dying inside the house. His father already dead.

It froze him because he'd heard that sound, the sound of their motorcycles fading into the distance, when he'd reached their dead bodies.

As if they'd only just left.

You've always been afraid of monsters because you've always been afraid of them.

The man who was once Casper had once more come too late to save his parents from the past.

Casper.

He hadn't heard his own name in years. Centuries. In the temple he was merely the student. And there was only the Master. And the dead who had tried and failed to learn the ways of what was being taught.

And before the temple... he was many men. With many names.

Casper.

Who was that anymore?

The frightened child of the dead in the graves before him? But he'd become so much more than that. Not just in his two thousand years before he left the galaxy, but in the unmeasurable time within the temple. Days? Years? Decades? In the temple, time has no meaning, and that's why the story can be told all at once and alongside all the other parts that need to be explained.

He had no idea. And long ago he'd stopped thinking of himself as Casper Sullivan or any of the many other aliases he'd once used to try and save the Republic from itself. By any means save one.

That had been the agreement. Between Rechs, Reina, and Casper. They would never seek the power they'd seen inside the Quantum Palace. They, the only three survivors of the horrors on the ghost ship *Moirai*.

And the girl.

The girl, the lone surviving medic from among the Martian light infantry who had set out to rescue Reina from inside the *Moirai*. She had survived, too.

Take my hand, Corporal Maydoon! I'll save you.

They, the triumvirate of Rechs, Reina, and Casper, had kept an eye on her, because that was what they'd sworn to do. To watch and wait.

For whom? And what?

For the Dark Wanderer.

That was one answer.

And for someone to try and become him.

That was the other.

They would watch for anyone who would ever try to use that terrible power they'd witnessed. Because as Reina said... with just a thought, one could rewrite the rules of the universe. Among other things. Theoretically. Imagine the terrible possibilities the mind of a psychopath might dream up...

In time the girl, who was once the medic everyone called Bones, died an old woman. She hadn't been a slave on the *Obsidia*, and so she had lived a normal life, of normal length, with a husband and children, and good health, and, hopefully, her share of happiness. She died peacefully at a good old age. Long ago. And they, the triumvirate, committed themselves to their watch once more.

They would watch the entire galaxy. Reina would watch the sciences; she would stop any development in a direction that might lead toward the paths the Savages had been wandering down. Rechs would watch the power struggles; he would see who might be putting themselves in front of the others a little too effortlessly. And then they would be smitten. Hence the Legion.

And Casper... Casper would beat, cajole, and manipulate from behind the scenes. In a galaxy full of aliens, connected by the gossamer of hyperspace, he would form a government that might work together to keep an eye out for the Dark Wanderer. That might respond when the time came.

But the Savages, who even then were beginning to come into communication with one another, were taking worlds of their own in which to grow their nightmare societies. The galaxy-wide conflict that would be known as the Savage Wars was coming. And that too was the reason for the Legion. And the Republic and its mighty navy.

Standing over the graves of his parents, he thought: *You did all that because of fear.*

Fear that the Savages, the barbarians, the Dark Wanderers of the universe would come in from the fringes of reality... like some no-name biker gang that called itself the Goths. Come in and ruin the fragile jewel of your civilization. Your family. Your galaxy.

It is them you've always been afraid of. And it was easier to sail off into the dark cosmos and fight Savages, monsters, and even the Dark Wanderer... than to confront the real monsters who made you who you are. Set you on this course. Of them you will always be afraid. Until one day you aren't.

Then... as the Master had often said, *Know you will.*

So move, he told himself. Knowing now what the lesson was. He would confront his fear. His deepest fear. He hadn't been brought back to save them. He'd been brought back to be set free. To *know*.

Except his feet did not move. He remained rooted before the tragedy of his parents. He'd never come back to visit their graves. Never ever. Not in all that time in the orphanage. Not on leave from NASA. Or in the UN Navy. He would never come back here to the place where they were buried.

He stared around at the silent intersection of ancient buildings. Buildings his father had mined and farmed for salvage. He tried to see them. Tried to see his parents and himself as they'd once been. Tried to see the ghosts of who they once were moving about, as though all the bad things that had happened never did. And never would.

But he couldn't.

So move.

He waited one moment longer. Just hoping. Hoping to feel some echo of all that he once was before the day, three days prior, that had set him on his course like some starship that cannot be dissuaded from light speed and its final destination.

Finally he turned, and set out to murder the ones who'd made him.

THE LAST LESSON IS THE LESSON OF BECOMING THE THING YOU FEAR

Part Two

In the night he made a bar called Spider Mike's. West of the downtown rubble sites being cleared by the teams working out of the zone, east of the falling moon. He entered looking like any other scavenger/salvager that was so common in those days. He'd smelled the chargrilled meat of the place in the barest of night breezes in the junkyards he'd crossed to get here.

A gang of desperate dirty children had come with pipes and studded nail boards to take what little he had. He had sensed their menace and hidden himself from their starving minds.

He'd known of this place, of Spider Mike's, as a child. But he'd never been here. Other farmer men who worked with his father on the big salvage jobs said it was a good place to go for a drink. They brewed their own liquor and beer, though there were rumors that they used mutie meat for their burgers. Stuff that might not even be cattle, and couldn't be graded for sale inside the reclamation zone.

But he was hungry, and he couldn't remember when he'd last eaten.

In the temple, eating wasn't always guaranteed. One got used to not eating more than eating.

He approached the claptrap honky-tonk, its oldies blaring out across the still night of the surrounding junkyards. Distant gunshots punctuated the night. Bikes and rides were out in the yard in no orderly fashion. Some singer was singing over the static-filled PA system about guitars and Cadillacs, but the student paid it no mind as he pushed the mesh screen door open and made for the neon-adorned bar where crazy-shaped bottles of liquor glowed from the candles set behind them. The bartender was covered in dirty tattoos, and half her face had been horribly burned years ago. She showed a lot of skin and her nicely shaped body to distract from the injury that had never healed. In the moment Casper stood before her, he read her entire life story in her face, and sensed her mind with his.

A thing he'd learned to do in the temple.

She was just another girl on the day it all went down.

A hard life. Years lost in drugs and skin trade just to survive. Finally she'd learned to fight and trade, and she'd clawed her way into this position. Spider Mike's main lady. Within her mind he could sense a predatory animal that would just as soon knife him as she would pleasure him, depending on which seemed to yield the most profit to her.

Behind her lay the backlit bottles, and behind those was a dirty cracked mirror that ran the length of the bar. In its reflections he could see all the other people who hadn't died long ago, drinking to forget all those who had. People left behind by the Savages who were only then starting to become the horror show they would turn into. People who had just barely survived the end of civilization. And people who would inherit the galaxy in just a few short years, once the schematics for the hyperdrive were put on open-source servers. Except they didn't know that just yet.

The scarred beauty who was the bartender appraised him, leaned forward, and asked, "Whatcha want?" with a hunger in her eyes that verged on the sociopathic. She'd once been a bank teller. Back on that last day before the end of all things.

In the dirty dark mirror that was cracked, Casper saw who *he* had become.

He'd always been slight. Now he was rippling with bulky muscles from the rigors of the temple. His iron-gray hair was all gone. His skin was tight and drawn over his gleaming skull. Skin that was tanned and lined by the brutal red sun of that lost planet. Drawn tight by the salt-laden wind of the sea. He looked like a brute and a bruiser. Not the dashing naval officer he'd once been.

But his blue eyes remained the same. If even more so. They stared back at him like gems. Gems burning with fire.

"Two burgers. Two beers," he said. His voice was rich and sonorous. Though he'd seldom used it for conversation in all the years at the temple. It was the chanting during the focused meditation that had strengthened it, grown it, grounded it to a deep baritone. Even when he whispered, his voice struck the listener with a heavy presence that could not be ignored. Or denied.

She made a face that might have been a smirk, then turned away to head for the kitchen.

He remained still, not moving, as he stared back at himself in the mirror. Smelling the meat begin to grill. Letting the rowdy boasts and machine-gun chatter of the broken and ruined lives all around him fade into the background noise of the galaxy.

He'd never abided by their pact. The pact made by Rechs, Reina, and himself. He'd thought he had. But really he'd been looking for it all along, though even he hadn't known it.

At first he'd justified his quiet inquiries in a thousand different libraries on a hundred old worlds as doing intel. Finding out who, or what, this Dark Wanderer actually was. Surely there were ancient myths and legends that had made their stamp on the story of the galaxy. That's all. *Just seeing who we're up against*, he would've told Rechs or Reina if they'd confronted him. But he'd never shared any of his findings with Rechs or Reina.

His findings were for him.

He remembered the old scout who had found the Temple of Morghul out beyond the galaxy's edge, but couldn't remember exactly where, or how he'd found it. Or how he'd gotten away. Could the Master have allowed that old man to escape? Sent him back, to draw forth someone who was worthy, someone who would seek and one day find the lost planet?

Then there were the accounts of ancient heroes with fantastic powers from before the age of hyperdrive. He investigated these unexplained phenomena that were so often easily explained... unless they weren't. And therein lay the few and far between jackpots he waited patiently for. He tracked down anything that smacked of the "supernatural" or "miracles." Tricks, like those the Dark Wanderer had used to bend the twisted minds of the Savages to his will. To his purposes.

He, too, could do a "miracle"—right here, right now, in this bar. With what he'd learned in the temple, he could move things with his mind. Break a neck. Send the old rotten furniture flying into the boom box on the shelf, where someone with a heavy voice was singing about a ring of fire, and falling down, down, down into it. He could turn out the lights and knock the building down. He could make them think they were in a storm.

He could do all that and they'd probably worship him in the end.

Because to him, to whom he had become, they were just savages now with their mewling little existence, shooting each other down for a few meager scraps of all that once was.

Or was it he who was the Savage now? Just like the elites who'd left and become post-human. Doing "miracles" with their strange tech. Seeming like gods to the hyperspeed travelers who finally went looking for them after half the galaxy had been staked and claimed.

Was he the Savage now?

He'd been looking in all the cracks and crannies of the universe. Finding things that never should have been found. Watching the Republic turn into a beast that would destroy everything, through the sheer self-indulgent folly of the privileged few he'd never been able to defeat. They were like cockroaches. Every time he stamped out one, ten more scurried for the darkness.

He'd tried to save the Republic from itself. With war, assassination, intrigue. But in the end he'd realized what so many in the past had also come to know. If the cockroaches could weaken the system for their own gain, they'd do it in a heartbeat.

It was a broken system. Because the people were broken.

The Legion had seemed like an answer to everything. It had defeated the Savages in what was the most brutal war of all times; surely it could handle whatever the "other" side of the galaxy decided to throw at civilization. But the monster of government... that was a different problem. It was intent on all the power with none of the sharing. And the Legion couldn't stop it. Even during the Savage Wars, even during those glory days of brave and capable legionnaires, the cracks had begun to show. The Legion was crumbling, ever so slightly, beneath the oppressive weight of the perpetual do-gooders who didn't actually do any good for anyone beyond themselves. And once the Savage Wars ended, the balance of power shifted—fast. The Republic no longer felt it needed the Legion, and it wasted no time taking steps to reduce its power. To control it.

Casper could see what would happen next as clearly as if it lay before him. The cracks were beginning to appear. So thin you could barely detect them, but in time, the Legion would be, at best, a useless praetorian guard protecting the House of Reason from the greedy masses. They could even become as bad as the House of Reason itself, if they chose to.

The war would end, but the rot had set in. That was all too clear.

And you created the Republic. And Rechs created the Legion. All in an attempt to save the galaxy from whatever the Dark Wanderer was. And in the end, neither of you could save the Republic from itself, much less the unknown threats waiting on the other side of the curtain of reality.

And Reina....

Missing. Gone dark. Maybe even dead. One last transmission telling Casper she'd been up to everything he'd been up to. She'd seen the writing on the wall, had known the stakes, had taken the same chances.

And she'd never returned.

The scarred bartender set down a chipped plate with two burgers. She added a lascivious wink, giving the student a generous view of her goods while pulling two mismatched brown beer bottles from a cooler beneath the bar.

Casper regarded her for a long moment before taking up the first burger and biting into it like some hungry monster surfacing from the deeps of time. Its juice ran down onto his scarred and calloused hand. He chewed once, twice, tasting garlic and even... mayonnaise. Then he swallowed.

He closed his eyes.

He felt whatever he'd become fade away for a moment. He felt some lost connection of what he'd once been signaling to him from out across the distance of a dark and storm-tossed ocean on a rainy night. Like some passing ship in the stellar dark reminding him he had once been these people around him.

He finished that burger. Popped one of the beers and drank it down in one cold gulp. He emitted a gusty "ahhhhh" and belched. Then he finished the second burger and downed the last beer. He left the bar, selected a ride in the parking lot, and slid behind the wheel of the ancient armored muscle car adorned with impact damage and bullet holes. It was black.

He sensed the trap that had been laid upon it, and within his mind he reached out and disabled the gel-ignite canisters beneath the fuel tanks. He forced the vehicle to rumble to life without a key, and a moment later he was headed north with the night, leaving the dead city behind.

In time he picked up their trail. At an armored gas station beyond the Sepulveda Pass. Out in the valley, which he remembered as a child to be a wild place akin to an old frontier filled with wild stories of survival, as told by travelers who stopped by to visit with his father. A grizzled oldster gave him the information he sought. He didn't have to be coaxed, persuaded, or dominated. Merely asked.

"Them boys ain't what they seem," said the oldster, speaking of the bikers knows as the Goths. "I know wild when I see it. I know'd crazy too. Was friends with it on occasion. They'd act the part, shore 'nuff. But they somethin' more."

Casper felt the cold sweat on his back. One hand shook ever so slightly, and he stared at it until it stopped. None of them possessed what he wielded. None of them knew what he knew. So... why so afraid?

Yes, whispered that other voice. *Why so afraid,* boy?

For Casper, who had just given the man all the cash he could find in the old armored muscle car to top off the tanks, the fear started under the hot white blaze of the station outpost's neon lights. Out beyond the ramshackle salvage walls as the gentle gloaming of the night was coming on. Flights of dark crows, grown bold and numerous off the scavenging of bodies left by the war, crossed the deep blue sky turning to purple hush, like tiny flapping shadows in the night. Cawing and crowing to one another.

Right then the student's fear began.

He felt it take hold of him like a cold iron hand whose grip would never relent. There was no after, no release in that fear-struck moment of forever. After all, these were the Goths he'd fled from, knowingly and unknowingly, for all these years. He controlled his breath, because it was all he could do, and in time he got hold of his mind. Taking the reins of rationality in hand once more. He screwed in the cap on the gas tank and thanked the oldster. Moments later he blew out of there in a screech of tired grit that sent the dust of destruction blooming into the night once more.

The Goths made their camps up along the "one-oh-one," the oldster had said, east of the ruins of a place the old man called "San Barbara." If he would find them, he would find them there.

Before dawn he came upon one of their patrols. He spotted them on the highway ahead, wound up and making for the coast. Out to sea the sun was throwing its light over the tops of the mountains and turning the ocean all gold and blue at once. He mashed the accelerator hard and came up on them faster than they suspected. He tried to run the rearmost bikers down, and he got two of them, but the rest scattered, one dropping his bike and kissing the pavement in a long slide. He was doing well over a hundred.

He dropped through the gears, hit the brakes, and heard the tires squeal as he threw the car around at the top of the rise.

They were on him in an instant.

With a wave of his hand he swept one biker skyward, bike and all. But three passed, one firing and another hitting him in the throat with a small hard chain. It knocked the air from him, and he was down on his knees, struggling to breathe. It felt like he'd been hit in the throat with a baseball bat.

Two bikers circled him now, hitting him with their chains. The third, off his bike at the side of the road, was trying to reload a pistol.

He was blacking out, and the fear had hold of him. He tried to use what he'd learned within the temple, but none of it would come, and all he heard was the sound of himself choking. It sounded like *Gothhhh* in his ears.

If he was going to die... he thought to himself... then he didn't have time to be afraid. Not anymore. Not now. Not of these monsters.

He got hold of their chains with his mind and sent them flailing around the bikers' own necks. Both bikes dropped as each man struggled with the hard iron coil about his own neck.

The student clenched his fist. Those chains would never budge. Now he stood, straightened, and made for the man reloading the pistol. The man chambered a round, raised the weapon—and felt it fly from his fingers. A moment later the student had his own iron grip around the man's dirty throat. He raised him off the ground with one arm. The man gagged.

"Where are the rest of you?"

The man shook his head, fear in his bulging eyes.

"Tell me now!"

The man gagged and sputtered. "Road... north of Santa Barbara. East... Totems lead the way."

The student broke the biker's neck and tossed the man aside.

He drove through the rest of what remained of the night.

Just after dawn he pulled off into the cracked parking lot of an old hotel that looked out over the sea. He lay back, drained and tired, feeling his body shake softly. In time he would grow strong. The more he used what he'd learned, the more... powerful, but that was the wrong word, the Master had used another... something more similar, but not quite, to "knowing"... he would become. He slept through the day, and when night came on he continued on up the highway toward the ruins of the old seaside village.

Toward the road that led to the lair of the Goths.

THE LAST LESSON IS THE LESSON OF BECOMING THE THING YOU FEAR

Part Three

Beyond the silent and fire-gutted ruins of Santa Barbara he found an ancient road headed east into the coastal mountains. The road wound and climbed the heights, and he passed strange totems, illuminated by the muscle car's one working headlight. The totems, clearly meant to warn him away, were made up of the remains of men and birds, crows, crucified and made into almost artistic chimeras. Like those he'd found long ago on the *Moirai*. Except... that hadn't happened yet.

He sensed them before he came upon them. Sensed their menace for everything. Their rage to survive. Their fear of nothing.

Just as he'd learned to within the temple.

"Height nor depth has not the power," the Master had taught. *"Neither on a side it is. You determine how great it can be used. Which side it will serve."*

The Master's powers were great. Except it wasn't... powers. It was just... *a* power. And it wasn't even that. It was... something else.

He had some of it. In time, he would acquire more. If he survived. Perhaps he would even have as much as the Master. But for now he had... some. And with that he would have to face the final lesson.

He sensed the Goths on the road ahead, so he slowed, knowing they had heard the gutter-growl of the ancient muscle car's rumble. He pulled off the road, well below the zenith of the forested hill, and stopped the car in the dirt.

"Become what you are afraid of. Afraid you will not be anymore."

The Master had paused. There had been some pauses within the temple that seemed to last for years. He, the student, had waited for the lesson to drop. For the pearl to be revealed. Waited for the next clue to come.

"Knowledgeable of the Crux you will be then."

The Crux, he'd thought when he first heard it. After all these years, *that* was what the power was. Yet the hearing of it didn't stun him like he'd been stunned by the ships in the graveyard of the ocean beyond the temple. It was as if the word had always been there, right in front of his face. Which was what the Crux really was. At the center of all things.

As if sensing this, the Master smiled a cruel smile.

"The center of all things is the Crux. Not a power... but the ability to use power that is in everything. At the center... lies the Crux. Knowing... is power."

And now he understood. More and more since he'd been taught what it actually was. It wasn't a power. It was the ability to convince powers to act on the user's behalf.

"Ancient orders used the Crux, long ago in the mists of time. Powerful they were," continued the Master. "Ruled the galaxy. Brought destruction and chaos, claiming different. Bah! Nothing they knew of the hidden nature of the Crux. The Crux only is. Either good or evil, light or dark, is what you decide to become. The Crux is neither. With the Crux, nothing else is needed. Understand ... know you will then."

And to know... knowing... was the real power. Knowing was the Crux.

Casper undid the pistol belt that had once comforted him and placed it on the warm hood of the ancient muscle car. If this was the last test, then he would use only what he had learned. The Crux... would be enough.

For what?

For revenge?

No.

For power?

No.

To save the galaxy?

No. Not even that now.

Then what? Answer, Casper! some dying child screamed, reminding him for the last time that his name from long ago had once been Casper. Casper Sullivan.

"Sull-" (bullet hole) "-us-" (bullet hole). Just like the grave marker he had carved himself. Placed over his father's grave. Except someone had shot at it in the three days between eleven-year-old him burying it in the hard dirt above his father's corpse, and two-thousand-year old him showing up just a little late for revenge but right on time for the final lesson.

Sull-us

Sullivan, Justin

That's how he'd marked the grave. All those years ago. No time, no date, no cause.

And when he found it he found... Sull-us. A reminder that to him... with power... what good is good?

The bullets had smashed away the "ivan," the "J," and the "tin."

Death had revealed *Sullus.*

He walked up the road. Pushing away all the thoughts that tried to come for him.

This is the test, he screamed at himself as he neared the sentries.

Rechs had warned him once, "Go looking for it ... and I'll be waiting for you out along the edge if you come back. I may forget many things if I live a long time, Cas, but I'll never forget that."

His best friend, Rechs. The meaning had been clear. Rechs would kill Casper if he ever went looking. Even then when, finally, toward what they both knew was the coming collapse of the corrupt Republic, when neither of them saw a way to save the galaxy from itself, when Casper told Rechs all he knew. Or rather suspected. That the powers the Dark Wanderer wielded could be found out beyond galaxy's edge on a lost planet only rumors named. Casper had hoped that Rechs would come with him. Seeing that since they had not forged a coherent galaxy, or a military machine to respond to whatever the Dark Wanderer was... that *becoming* him was the only option left.

Together they would have found some way to set the galaxy aright with the strange powers the prophetesses and the Dark Wanderer had used. They wouldn't fall into corruption. And if they did, they would destroy themselves first. It had taken Casper years to work up the courage to approach then-General Tyrus Rechs, the T-Rex of the Legion, with a mere hint of his foolhardy scheme. And he'd only finally done it when everything seemed so hopeless and lost. So corrupt and dire. When finding the Temple of Morghul had seemed like the only hope to save them all.

He hadn't even told Rechs what Reina had found. Or what she'd disappeared to do. Because Rechs would have made the same promise to Reina he made to Casper.

I'll be waiting for you out along the edge.

In his imagination, he'd seen Rechs grudgingly agreeing to the plan. Laconically realizing how much sense this plan to find the lost planet and the Temple of Morghul made. This was in Casper's imagination, of course. He'd imagined a different outcome.

But Rechs, ever Rechs, had simply held course and told Casper what the consequences would be if any one of them violated the pact they'd made after the *Moirai*. The pact they'd held as they struggled to build a fighting force, and a political entity, that could defeat the Savages... and the Dark Wanderer. One day.

"It's out beyond the edge, Tyrus. We can go there. Together," Casper had pleaded.

There had been a pause in which the emotionless Rechs stared into him like he was making some kind of promise to himself. Some chivalric vow that needed occasional reminding.

And then his oldest and best friend spoke. Slow and steady. As constant as an ancient star that would stay lit until the heat death of the universe. This had been just before the last battle they'd fight in together. The defeat at Telos, when the Savage battle cruisers overwhelmed the Republican armada.

"Go looking for it... and I'll be waiting for you out along the edge."

Then... Casper disappeared. Knowing Rechs would never come with him. Knowing he'd have to confront him when he returned. Knowing that one of them would finally die.

In the darkness he approached the handful of sentries guarding the hideout. They were clustered in a dirt parking lot that had once been a turnout at the top of the hill that rose above the old dead seaside village of Santa Barbara. Out beyond this, on the other side of the rise to the east, lay a wide spreading valley of oaks and long pastures, made silvery by the ghostly moonlight.

He could hear their wild tribal acid rock music in the woods farther up the hill. Densely clustered oaks surrounded their hideout and tents. But he could sense them all up there, reveling in the debauchery they'd chosen for the end of the world.

"Lookee what we got he—" began the first sentry before the student choked off the man's air with a mere gesture. He flung that dirty, leather-clad man into the side of a nearby dusty vehicle. Even now, using the Crux, knowing that it was not a power, but a knowing of how to use a power that clung to the center of everything, he could feel his facility with it increase. Given time... he would become more powerful than even the Dark Wanderer.

The others drew their weapons quickly. Ancient slug throwers like the Savages had out there in the dark in the stars above, drifting through space in their spinning cities. The student had nothing but contempt for them and their feeble weapons. His fury sent them all flying before they could fire. Scattered across the chalky dirt and slammed into the motorcycles they used. They were broken in a sudden stunning instant.

Now the student spent a few moments killing them quietly. Driving rocks into their skulls. Rocks that lifted off the ground of their own accord and sped forward into unprotected skulls faster than speeding bullets. Blood spray and gore soaked the chalky dust of the lonely place.

One managed to get his fingers around a pistol he kept inside a boot. He brought it to bear quickly, like a rattlesnake. And as if time were slowed, the student sensed all this even before it happened.

Was this the one that had shot his father? Raped his mother? The fear came at him, calling "Goth" over and over at the little child he'd once been. He hesitated, and was too slow with using the Crux to cave in the man's head, or crush his windpipe with a thought, before the man applied just enough pressure to ignite the round inside the weapon.

The bullet leapt out at him, reminding the student that he knew the Crux of all things.

The student held up his hand and stopped the slug from hitting him. Then he leapt forward, dark and furious rage suddenly taking over. He leapt from a standstill toward the biker who was about to die, farther than a human being could leap in just the blink of an eye. He landed just to the side of the pistol from which the man was about to squeeze off another round, and he pushed the hand that gripped the pistol up under the savage man's chin just an instant before the biker pulled the trigger. The weapon exploded with a terrific bang, tearing up through the man's chin and mouth and coming out the top of his skull in a small volcano of brain matter.

The report resounded through the still night.

All of them, all of the men at the student's feet, were dead now.

Up the hill their music was still playing inside their camp. But the noise of the revelers had died at the sound of the gun.

Good, thought the student. *Let them be afraid now.*

He went to them. Climbing up along the shadowy wooded path in the pale moonlight. They tried to ambush him with gunfire and knives, but he crushed their skulls and broke their bones with mere gestures. They fell like they'd been hit by ocean waves turned to steel.

With each kill he grew more and more enraged. The raw power surged through him. He felt stronger with each blow. Each death. Knowing a little bit more how far he could go with each manipulation of this fantastic thing known as the Crux that lay at the center of all things. Even as held a shaven-headed man aloft, the man screaming and cursing, waving the machete he'd been about to cleave the student's skull with, the student wondered at all the possibilities of the Crux beyond even this night.

Was the Crux the quintessence of life whose existence so many philosophers had theorized so long ago?

He slaughtered them. And then he slaughtered their women and children knowing this was just an appetizer for all that was to come. The fear was afraid of *him* now. It circled about the slaughter, waiting and biding its time, hoping for a chance to strike out at him, to strike him down.

He listened as their minds screamed out in raw terror and fear. Read their paralyzed emotions. Even saw glimpses of them at other times before this. They'd been part of a government agency once. Paramilitary of some type. After the collapse, they'd organized and preyed on others just to survive. They'd lost themselves, as all such men do.

They'd preyed on his family.

And others.

But there was one among them. Weaving in and out of the shadows of their camp, staying clear of the slaughter. And this one was different. This one was not afraid. This one wanted him to be afraid. He was their leader. MacRaven was the name that appeared in the student's mind as he faded into the shadows, searching the last memories of the dead and the dying everywhere about the camp.

This was the one he'd come for.

The one he'd been afraid of all along.

This one was their Crux. At the center of everything. The Black Dragon of this moment.

"Come out, come out, come out and play... little boy," howled the madman he could sense among the stolen booty of their lair. Christmas lights hung in the trees of the wide oaks that covered their camp. "Come out, come out, come out and die... little boy," crooned their leader as though he knew who exactly had come for them.

The student came to himself. He was sweating... not from fear, but from sudden hunger and weakness. He'd lost track in the killing, gotten carried away. But now, meditating in the darkness out of sight, listening to the killer run and scurry all around him, he felt suddenly weak and tired.

He tried to meditate.

He remembered the ice he'd lived in for years.

The cavern of his blindness where he'd learned to truly see.

Remembered all the lessons and so many more throughout all the years uncounted in the temple's depths.

The Crux was great... but the vessel is not, he thought to himself.

He felt the killer coming for him as though somehow the madman sensed his weakness now. The man was coming at him with a massive sword. Like something from an old movie about barbarians and wizards. He could sense this.

The student stepped from the shadows and saw the Dark Wanderer. Tall and looming, over eight feet tall. Carrying the sword and coming for him. Just as he'd seen him all those years ago on the *Moirai*. And the fear of this "other" being was the same as his fear of the Goths who'd plagued his childhood nightmares until he'd forced himself to forget them just to survive.

"Stupid mortal!" laughed the Dark Wanderer from within his flowing shrouds. "I've come for you at the last!"

The Dark Wanderer swept the gleaming sword in a wide arc. The student had just enough time to leap away. But not far away. The Dark Wanderer pivoted, dark shrouds twirling in the firelight, and raised the giant sword over his head to bring it down on the student with another strike.

A final strike.

The student tried to use the Crux... willing the sword to fly away or to stay where it was... but the power of the Dark Wanderer was great. Greater, because the Dark Wanderer had so much of it. Had had so much since so long ago. Since the beginning of time. Or so it felt like. To the student, what he felt in the picosecond that stretched almost infinitely out between them, was a battle of wills using merely the Crux.

The sword slammed down into the dirt as the student shifted away, leaping on top of salvaged vehicle that had become someone's home. The student sensed the vehicle and ripped parts from it with the Crux, sending them to flying at the Dark Wanderer.

Objects scattered away of their own volition as they came close to the tall and dark being from the other side of this reality. In that moment the student saw that the face of the thing was a void. A gaping void that only wanted to destroy and was never satisfied.

This nightmare thing was the Goth. This was the very essence of the word *Goth* to the student as he leapt away yet one more time, this time to avoid an ancient engine the Dark Wanderer had torn away from some hanging chains and sent careening toward the student with the invisible power it wielded.

A raider. A destroyer. A taker.

Goth.

There is no knowledge in this thing. It seeks only destruction, his mind reasoned. Connecting the Crux with the Knowing the Master had been trying to teach all along. Only now did the student realize the wisdom. The lesson. It all fell into place as the ancient greasy engine flew past him, missing by only inches. Destroying some ramshackle wall of the compound like a loose thunderbolt.

"With the Crux, needed nothing else is. Understand... then you will know."

It wasn't power. The Crux wasn't power. It wasn't the raw power that failed the galaxy every time. The Crux was the thing that convinced the power to do what needed to be done.

Now the Dark Wanderer stood beneath the Christmas lights, gleaming sword held aloft in imminent victory. The small ramshackle salvage hideout littered with bodies was catching fire as runaway flames spread from a cookpit.

The student ran, not away, but to the side, hurling himself over the flying tornado of debris the junkyard was becoming. Not waiting to not be where the Dark Wanderer was sending flaming debris at him.

One of the vehicles lifted up with titanic groan of rusty springs and immense weight. It was an ancient five-ton truck, outfitted with machine guns and spikes. Sand and debris rained down from it and scattered off into the whirlwind as the Dark Wanderer effortlessly caused the war vehicle to rise into the air of its own accord.

He won't even need to be close, thought the student as he circled out and away in leaping somersaults from one platform to the next. Staying out of reach of the immense and dark being from the void. *He'll crush me if he even gets it in the vicinity.*

"With the Crux, nothing else is needed."

And in that moment, the student learned. Learned all the lessons as they came together as one at the center of all things. The most important lesson was the last.

It wasn't power. It was *knowing* that touched all things.

The student stopped. He cleared his mind as the storm tried to tear him away. Just as he had in all those other terrible lessons where he'd died a thousand times or frozen for a thousand years. Those things, the physical, meant nothing. Knowing was the only way out.

The only way, in fact, through.

He reached out and felt the massive and near-limitless power of the Dark Being from some other when who'd come to destroy the galaxy. He sifted through the madness of the thing and found the key that unlocked the door.

Was this what Reina had gone off to find, and in her own way to beat?

The last message from her said that she'd found another way. A way other than what they'd witnessed on the *Moirai*.

"But you can't," he'd told her. "Remember the pact."

Remember Rechs.

Beware of Rechs.

That was what he was really saying. Because in a galaxy of shifting values... Rechs remained constant. Even Reina wasn't exempt from his vow.

"We have to," she'd pleaded.

"Why? Why do we have to destroy ourselves? Do we think we'll be the ones to beat a thing no one else has beaten? Isn't that what every junkie gambler thinks on their way to losing yet another paycheck? Or a drunk on their way to the drink? Or a drug addict handling the injector? This time... things will be different?"

"We made contact, Cas," she whispered softly across the ether that connected them for the very last time ever. "There's a galaxy full of them out there. And they're trying to get in. We have to be ready when they come. We have to fight them with their own weapons. We have to..."

"Who?" he asked.

But he knew.

The Dark Wanderer.

Somewhere out there, beyond the dark between the galaxies, across the incalculable gulfs that made even hyperspace seem slow... were more of *them*.

"No," he said, and didn't really mean it. Because hadn't he been looking for it all along? Hadn't he needed a reason to find the lost planet and the Temple of Morghul? Here was the reason. She was practically giving it to him on a silver platter. She was practically giving *herself* to him... finally.

"There is another way..." she said.

And it was everything he could do to close the contact. Finger shaking. Thinking at the time that he would be able to convince her to reason at some other time.

Except she disappeared after that. And not even the entirety of the Repub Navy, or all the intelligence services, or even Rechs himself, would ever find her. It was as if she simply vanished from the galaxy.

Except you *found her,* he remembered as the Dark Wanderer fought with all its screeching power to toss the vehicle down on top of him.

Yes, he remembered. *I blocked that out in the temple. But I found her there.*

Once, she too had been a student. Long before he'd arrived. After she'd disappeared. The temple was littered with the skeletons of those who had failed some lesson. He'd never found her bones... but he knew she lay among them. Done to death by some lesson that couldn't be passed. Failed where he had succeeded. He'd known that, found it while meditating on failure in a dark and forgotten place lost in the temple deeps.

Or maybe, that fading child's voice of his from long ago whispered, maybe that other way, the one Reina had found, was on another planet, lost like this one.

No, he grunted, and he fought to wrest control of the hovering multi-ton vehicle from the creature looming above.

No, he told himself again. Maybe somewhere in that graveyard of ships beyond the temple, out in the waters of the ocean, shimmering beneath the waves, you'll find a small light freighter and the skeleton of a girl you once knew long ago.

A girl you once loved.

The student felt the Crux at the center of the massive vehicle being lifted overhead. With his mind he reached out and took hold of it, wrenched it away from the being that opposed him. Ice water flooded his soul as he made mental contact with the thing's mind. And in that instant he was suddenly aware of just how hungry the thing was. And... how weak the Dark Wanderer really was also. Yes, it had near limitless power. But there was no *knowing* in it. Regarding the Crux... it was little more than an animal.

It was like a simple dumb battery. All power. No intelligence.

The Dark Wanderer, for all its searching, had no idea what the Crux really was. That was what the student found inside the ancient thing's mind. Beyond the millennia of torment and pain and images of some fantastic civilization that had spanned the galaxy long ago, ruling from star towers, the thing had no idea what the Crux was.

It just had power.

The student, fighting the power of the creature, shifted the massive weight of the hovering wheeled vehicle over the Dark Wanderer's head. He pulled the gleaming sword from the creature's claws.

Its shroud seemed to reach out for the weapon as it strode toward the student, crosssing the distance between them.

Holding the sword now, the student forced himself to dig deep and overpower the Dark Wanderer, overcome its hold on the vehicle. But it would not relent. It would never relent. This battle would only go so far before the sheer, unknowing power of the creature wore him out.

So he let go.

He let go and raced forward before the creature known as the Dark Wanderer realized what was happening. Instead it remained intent on not letting the vehicle crush it. And in that instant the student drove the gleaming sword straight through the being, cutting it in half as he raced past and out from under the hovering vehicle. A moment after that the vehicle surrendered to gravity and smashed down on the Dark Wanderer.

He was back inside the temple. Inside the central tower that was like a wide oven open to the dark night sky above.

The Master was there. Just as he had been from the start. Legs and arms folded in meditation.

"Finished you are now."

The student who was no longer a student fell to the ground. He was breathing heavily. Spent beyond anything he'd ever known.

He heard the tiny creature approach him. The creature he'd followed for so long. Once, long ago, it had followed him through the jungles and across the desert.

"What is your name now?" asked the Master.

"What were you afraid of?" asked Urmo.

The man who had once been Casper Sullivan got to one knee. He saw the galaxy aflame. Saw the inevitable ruin of the Republic. Saw the vain death of the Legion he'd helped form. Saw none of it able to stand against the things Reina had warned him, and him alone, of. Saw the images from the probe they'd sent into another galaxy. The Lesser Magellanic Cloud.

Saw things that were demons. Their madness. Their enigmatic structures that dwarfed Dyson spheres and spoke of torture and imprisonment.

"I was afraid of the Goths, Master," he whispered. "But they are dead now."

"What will your name be?" asked the Master.

What was it? What had it been when he'd been a child? A captain? A legionnaire?

He tried to remember. But it didn't matter now. He wasn't that person anymore. Those persons.

He heard the sound of himself whispering long ago, and just a few minutes ago. Standing over the graves of... whoever he'd once been.

"Sullus," he whispered.

The little Master chuckled as the flames began to rise at the center of the temple. His voice was a low papery rasp now. And it was old. As old as the galaxy since it first began to spin. Inside the temple those flames leapt to life inside the large bowl that was probably last alight eons ago with sacrifice and carnage in bloody delight. Above, over the rim of the tower, the stars of his galaxy formed.

"Then arise, Goth Sullus. The time of your destiny... is now."

35

The Present

All of that was a long time ago.

Since then he had returned to the galaxy. Forged a rebellion. Then a fleet. A Legion of his own. And finally... an empire.

And yes, he and Rechs had finally met out there on the edge of the galaxy. But Rechs's memory had faded. For centuries his mind had stayed sharp, sharper even than Casper's, but something had happened to him after the Savage Wars. Perhaps he'd needed those wars, that cause. Needed it to remember who he was. *Why* he was. Needed a cause, a purpose. Like Casper had. And Reina.

Casper had searched his friend's mind when again they met. He was still as tough and determined as ever. Living steel. But he had no idea why he was still just waiting out there. His best friend was like a watchdog that had forgotten what it was watching for. He saw himself as a bounty hunter now, hunted by the Legion he'd built.

But that was another story.

And the defeat of Tyrus Rechs had been no story at all.

Goth Sullus had merely broken the man's neck with a flick of his wrist, bending the powers of the Crux to do his bidding. To do what needed doing. He'd felt no strange tinge of friendship or melancholy as he stripped the iconic Mark I armor of the *Moirai* off the body of his dead friend. He'd even searched for the feeling, daring it to hide somewhere within him.

And hadn't killing Rechs been a kind of mercy after all? What the galaxy had failed time and time again to give his friend was an honorable death in combat. Goth Sullus had provided that final of all gifts. Later, as the night winds came up on the backwater desert world, he'd burned what remained of his oldest of friends with a pyre Goth Sullus had made himself.

And from that moment forward, there was no one to stop him from destroying the Republic and installing an empire to do what the feeble-minded demagogues of the House of Reason had never had the guts to do. Rule by benevolent dictatorship. Do what was the best thing to be done and ignore the mewling of the kittens and whining sheep of the galaxy.

Except now, at this crucial moment after the great victory of Tarrago, when the empire he'd forged was just beginning to rise, his own generals, a cabal of power-hungry men just like any he'd find within the House of Reason, sensed their moment of taking. Of looting. Of destroying what was his. He was wounded. Badly wounded from the Battle on the Tarrago moon. The armor was being re-forged several decks away. They knew he was powerful. And they knew he was weak at this moment. So they'd sent their assassins, in the form of his own troops.

If one is to have power, then one must gamble. It was almost a thing he could feel as he reached out to touch their shadowy images... the image of them letting the dice fly. Like bikers on the road. And howling Savages in the outer dark. They were takers who took.

So it would be now.

Two companies of shock troopers comprising ex-legionnaires, two HK-SK mechs in case he dared try to escape via his personal shuttle on his private hangar deck, and beyond the ship... he could sense fighter support. Willing to attack the ship just to get him.

"Pathetic," he heard himself murmur as he hobbled to seal the blast door to this deck. His personal guard was gone. So they'd thrown in too, he realized with disgust and contempt.

Well, he thought to himself, they really have no idea what they're dealing with.

He'd just reached the upper platform that guarded the entrance to his inner sanctum aboard the battleship *Imperator* when behind him, the blast door irised open from all four corners. Instantly the dark legionnaires he called his shock troopers were shooting en masse at him from the corridor beyond. Red-hot blaster fire filled the wide passage. The shock troopers were positioned behind cover all down the corridor, their dark armor gleaming like greased lightning as they fired and shifted positions to get closer to him.

He absorbed the first shot that would have hit him. Channeled the Crux into a temporary deflector field that lasted but the instant it took the bolt to almost hit him. Then he swept his hand across his body, throwing a field that redirected any nearby blaster bolts away from him as he scrambled, as best as his wounded body would allow, back into his private sanctum.

If he'd had Rechs's Mark I armor, he wouldn't have needed to use his powers to defend himself. That ancient armor still defied the best engineers in the galaxy in its ability to protect the wearer. But then again, none of those engineers had access to the Quantum Library.

Never mind that, he told himself as the darkness of his private deck swallowed him into its gray and blue shadows.

Already the shock troopers were swarming forward into his chambers. "Idiots," he swore under his breath as he sent a wave of energy at one of the troopers who'd come too far forward too fast. The man was thrown back against a bulkhead in an instant and knocked unconscious. Never mind the broken back.

I'm using too much of the too little I have, thought Sullus as he sensed how much access to the Crux was at his disposal. How much of it he could reach out and touch. Control. Shift. Bend to his will beyond the screaming pain of his wounded frame.

He didn't chastise the assassins for coming for him. He'd known all along that such a moment must come in the march toward total domination of the galaxy. That the wolves he'd formed would have to try the pack leader to know that he was indeed... their leader. And if he was to remain the pack leader, then he had to face this test. Now.

With his body working as best it could despite his wounds, he pulled himself deeper into the lower columns of power control bulkheads that supported his meditation chamber above. He could sense them coming into the shadowy darkness, sweeping the gloom and scanning for him.

Sullus stopped and pinned himself behind a power column. Out of sight he could feel the warm hum of the powerful processors at his back. Display lights and readouts spoke softly in the quiet of this hidden place. He closed his eyes and focused as he tried to build up more of the Crux for his next engagement. He could only think to give ground and make them pay with each step.

But there was only so much ground to give.

There was at least one company coming for him here. Now. Where was the other company of shock trooper assassins? He could try to reach out and sense their location, but even that little trick would cost him the precious energy he needed to defend himself in the right now of this desperate moment.

The line of highly disciplined combat veterans that were his shock troopers coming for him were just a few power columns away. He stilled the beat of his own heart. Their sensors could detect that if they'd switched over to that imaging mode. For a moment, a long moment, his heart stopped. His blood ceased to move. He was as still as a corpse.

In his mind he floated in an immense pool of darkness. Around him, ancient leviathans as old as time swam in the shadows deeps.

A shock trooper appeared next to him on the other side of a nearby power column. But he was looking in the wrong direction as he swept past the column, searching for the target.

Sullus opened slitted eyes.

"There he is," he whispered to the feeble-minded soldier.

The man shot his nearest squad mate with a blaster bolt. Suddenly blaster fire was everywhere.

Sullus threw his heart into overdrive and moved fast, very fast, watching as blaster fire came at him from all directions, but to him it was as though all of it, each individual shot, was moving through some incredibly dense liquid. He could hear the chatter of their voices inside their comm. The frantic calls about where they thought he was. The last groans and yelps of those upon whom he dealt sudden deadly blows of energy as he evaded their targeting. Getting as close as he could, he hammered the troopers with intense bursts of the Crux at close range. The cost to him was less this way. The damage to his attackers was great.

When he'd cleared the nearest troopers, he grabbed one with the invisible hand that was the Crux and smashed the man into the low ceiling. Then he sent a broad wave of power against an entire squad that had targeted him for concentrated fire as the man he'd smashed into the ceiling fell back to the deck. The shock troopers went sprawling, and Goth Sullus hobbled away into the forest of power columns, now sending surges of wild and unrestricted power into the conduits all around. Within moments the entire deck was alive with the blue fire of released electrical explosions that fried the surviving shock troopers of that company in snapping explosions that cooked them inside their high-tech armor.

One down, he thought, and he hobbled up the dais to his personal meditation chamber within the innermost sanctum. Before him, the wide impervisteel-laced window that looked out on the galaxy waited. Stars like tiny bits of shattered crystal shimmered out there in the deep distances. And it was his, even if they didn't know it yet. It was his.

He could sense more now. In the heights above his meditation chamber. His once loyal personal guard had flipped, and now they were merely waiting for the order to shoot him down, should he appear.

Who was giving the orders? wondered Sullus.

And...

I'm weak. Better to admit that than not.

And then his personal guard was firing at him from the dark heights three stories above the central deck. Their aim was perfect. Because of course they'd been the best of the Legion. Handpicked to defend him. It took almost all the Crux he had left to deflect their fire as he stumbled into his sleeping quarters and away from the central meditation dais.

I need a weapon, he thought, and for the first time wondered if they might not get away with this today. Didn't they realize he'd come all this way to save them from...?

Didn't *he* realize that perhaps this might be his last day?

A hot blaster shot hit him in the thigh, and he leapt forward through a blast door that he closed with his mind behind him.

This bought him only a moment.

A last moment that felt like all the last moments he'd ever faced.

Already the other squad of Dark Legionnaires who'd turned assassin were flooding the central chamber. They'd either cut through the blast doors or used a bridge override to force them open in order to get to him. He had but a moment now.

Focus, he yelled at himself inside his mind.

It's not about power. It never was. It's about *knowing*.

Except that his mind was having a hard time focusing with the intense and searing pain from the blaster shot that had nailed him in the thigh. And with the awareness that all his plans, all his efforts, were about to be wasted by yet another group of power-hungry tyrants trying to take for themselves what he had built.

He screamed and got to his feet. He was sweating in rivulets. His breath came in short gasps as he tried to control the pain and focus his mind in order to access the powers of the Crux.

They'd taken the House of Reason from him and turned it into their personal clubhouse to line their own pockets with wealth and power. It had never been intended for that. Just like the once-powerful legion of Tyrus Rechs had been intended to protect the weak from the strong. To save the galaxy from tyrants. Instead it had become a tyrant in its own way.

He remembered fighting the Dark Wanderer. Passing the final test of the Master. Being fully initiated into what was called the Crux in the days that followed. There had been no defeating that monster… and yet he had. Even though the Crux had been much greater in that Dark Being from the "other," beyond the reality of this present galaxy.

He had killed the thing with a weapon. Not the Crux.

A sword.

The blast doors irised open just a bit.

He could see the shiny black boots and leg armor of the dark legionnaires waiting to get to him. Some of them fired a few shots that skipped off the deck around him.

The torch.

The gift from the black giant who'd captured an entire starship on his own. The torch the man had given him out of loyalty and respect when they'd awarded the loyal shock trooper a medal for his actions. These men trying to kill him were not representative of all those legionnaires, pilots, and service people who'd rallied to him to fight the injustice of the House of Reason and the Galactic Republic. These who were trying to kill him were just the chaff. Weeding themselves out.

He fought off a wave of nausea and pain and stood erect and tall. Now they would face him in full.

Goth Sullus closed his eyes and took a deep breath as he sensed the blast doors finally heaving themselves open. Then he reached out, pulled the torch he'd left on the pedestal into his grip, and activated it.

The twisting fiery blade sprang up from its central housing like a shining beacon in the darkness of the galaxy.

When the dark legionnaires saw what they were facing... they stopped.

These were men who'd fought at Tarrago. And for the Legion when they'd served the Galactic Republic in a hundred conflicts across the galaxy. Often against overwhelming odds.

They were brave.

They were deadly.

They'd never faced anything like what they saw when the blast door opened.

Goth Sullus began to strike them down with the burning torch in his hand. He dodged in and among them, hitting the first few with savage slashes that melted armor and separated men from their limbs and weapons.

The man in the dark robe slashed and smashed in a whirlwind fury of burning blows from his fiery brand. Aimed blaster fire fled from him in harmless directions as he slew them en masse, only occasionally pausing to issue some gesture that sent a man skyward, or into a comrade.

The captain in charge of the assault saw only one final option as the men under his command were cut down.

"Wyvern Six, this is Assault Leader!" he practically shouted into his comm as he cowered behind a pillar. "Strike our position now!"

Two tri-fighters, loyal to the cabal, were on station and ready to actually hit the private decks of the emperor with concentrated blaster fire. The deck would be instantly holed and exposed to the vacuum of space, because the *Imperator* wasn't at battle stations and the deflectors weren't up. The deck would vent, and the shock troopers, those that weren't being sliced into burning pieces by the whirling dervish the emperor had become, would survive the vacuum because of their armor's zero-oxygen capabilities.

They would survive. But the emperor would not.

"Stand by, Assault Leader," replied the tri-fighter pilot. "Inbound for strike. Weapons hot. Secure for rapid decompression."

The assault leader in charge of the shock troopers cast a quick glance out the emperor's massive meditation viewing port as he shouted for the men to secure themselves. He could see the two deadly fighters turning for approach to target in tight strike formation. Side by side they'd smash straight through the hull with concentrated fire, probably killing a good many of his men in the process.

But this was the only way.

Goth Sullus laid waste to the troopers, who now realized the folly of their blaster fire and tried to rush him. The three that remained flew at him, and in an instant Goth Sullus pivoted and swept the burning torch across their midsections, slicing all three in half.

And then he sensed the hostile intent, the menace, of the approaching fighter pilots.

He had only seconds before they fired.

Focus, he heard the Master say.

So many times.

Focus.

He flicked off the torch.

"With the Crux, nothing else is needed."

He drew everything he had left, all of it, into his open palm. He closed his eyes and felt, saw, both pilots leaning forward to target their fire. The hum and scream of their fighters echoing like a drowning ghost throughout their tiny cockpits. The targeting and intercept data scrolling across their HUDs.

He closed his fist.

The two fighters smashed into one another and exploded. The sound of their sudden demise and released energy penetrated the massive hull of the battleship.

"With the Crux, nothing else is needed."

Officers and loyal shock troopers were swarming his deck now. They'd come for him. Come to rescue their emperor. The traitors were being shot down even as they tried to surrender.

"With the Crux, nothing else is needed."

Casper.

Reina.

Rechs.

The Republic.

The once-mighty Legion and its formidable legionnaires who were like the heroes of old. They would've fought the Devil himself in their day.

Gone.

Even whoever he'd once been. All of it... all of it was gone now for the emperor.

With the Crux... nothing else is needed.

And finally, one last thought, as order was restored and the traitors shot down without mercy or indecision. One final thought before the last of all that he once was slipped off and away like a half-remembered dream told by another on a distant planet. Maybe it was a confession. Or an absolution. Or the truth.

It was just a whisper. So low it might have even been a thought.

What I have done, I have done.

THE END

ABOUT THE AUTHORS

Jason Anspach and Nick Cole are a pair of west coast authors teaming up to write their science fiction dream series, Galaxy's Edge.

Jason Anspach is a best-selling author living in Puyallup, Washington with his wife and their own legionnaire squad of seven (not a typo) children. Raised in a military family (Go Army!), he spent his formative years around Joint Base Lewis-McChord and is active in several pro-veteran charities. Jason enjoys hiking and camping throughout the beautiful Pacific Northwest. He remains undefeated at arm wrestling against his entire family.

Nick Cole is a Dragon Award winning author best known for *The Old Man and the Wasteland, CTRL ALT Revolt!,*and the Wyrd Saga. After serving in the United States Army, Nick moved to Hollywood to pursue a career in acting and writing. He resides with his wife, a professional opera singer, south of Los Angeles, California.

GE BOOKS

(CT) CONTRACTS & TERMINATIONS

(OC) ORDER OF THE CENTURION

1ST ERA BOOKS

THE FALL OF EARTH

01 THE BEST OF US

02 MOTHER DEATH

2ND ERA BOOKS

SAVAGE WARS

01 SAVAGE WARS

02 GODS & LEGIONNAIRES

03 THE HUNDRED

3RD ERA BOOKS

RISE OF THE REPUBLIC

01 DARK OPERATOR

02 REBELLION

03 NO FAIL

04 TIN MAN

OC ORDER OF THE CENTURION

CT REQUIEM FOR MEDUSA

CT CHASING THE DRAGON

CT MADAME GUILLOTINE

Explore over 30+ Galaxy's Edge books and counting from the minds of Jason Anspach, Nick Cole, Doc Spears, Jonathan Yanez, Karen Traviss, and more.

4TH ERA BOOKS

LAST BATTLE OF THE REPUBLIC

OC **STRYKER'S WAR**

OC **IRON WOLVES**

01 LEGIONNAIRE

02 GALACTIC OUTLAWS

03 KILL TEAM

OC **THROUGH THE NETHER**

04 ATTACK OF SHADOWS

OC **THE RESERVIST**

05 SWORD OF THE LEGION

06 PRISONERS OF DARKNESS

07 TURNING POINT

08 MESSAGE FOR THE DEAD

09 RETRIBUTION

5TH ERA BOOKS

REBIRTH OF THE LEGION

01 TAKEOVER

02 COMING SOON

HISTORY OF THE GALAXY

1ST ERA BOOKS

THE FALL OF EARTH

01 THE BEST OF US

02 MOTHER DEATH

1ST ERA SUMMARY

The West has been devastated by epidemics, bio-terrorism, war, and famine. Asia has shut its borders to keep the threats at bay, and some with power and influence have already abandoned Earth. Now an escape route a century in the making – the Nomad mission – finally offers hope to a small town and a secret research centre hidden in a rural American backwater. Shrouded in lies and concealed even from the research centre's staff, Nomad is about to fulfil its long-dead founder's vision of preserving the best of humanity to forge a new future.

2ND ERA BOOKS

SAVAGE WARS

01 SAVAGE WARS

02 GODS & LEGIONNAIRES

03 THE HUNDRED

2ND ERA SUMMARY

They were the Savages. Raiders from our distant past. Elites who left Earth to create tailor-made utopias aboard the massive lighthuggers that crawled through the darkness between the stars. But the people they left behind on a dying planet didn't perish in the dystopian nightmare the Savages had themselves created: they thrived, discovering faster-than-light technology and using it to colonize the galaxy ahead of the Savages, forming fantastic new civilizations that surpassed the wildest dreams of Old Earth.

HISTORY OF THE GALAXY

3RD ERA BOOKS

RISE OF THE REPUBLIC

01 DARK OPERATOR

02 REBELLION

03 NO FAIL

04 TIN MAN

OC ORDER OF THE CENTURION

CT REQUIEM FOR MEDUSA

CT CHASING THE DRAGON

CT MADAME GUILLOTINE

3RD ERA SUMMARY

The Savage Wars are over but the struggle for power continues. Backed by the might of the Legion, the Republic seeks to establish a dominion of peace and prosperity amid a galaxy still reeling from over a millennia of war. Brushfire conflicts erupt across the edge as vicious warlords and craven demagogues seek to carve out their own kingdoms in the vacuum left by the defeated Savages. But the greatest threat to peace may be those in the House of Reason and Republic Senate seeking to reshape the galaxy in their own image.

4TH ERA BOOKS

LAST BATTLE OF THE REPUBLIC

OC	STRYKER'S WAR
OC	IRON WOLVES
01	LEGIONNAIRE
02	GALACTIC OUTLAWS
03	KILL TEAM
OC	THROUGH THE NETHER
04	ATTACK OF SHADOWS
OC	THE RESERVIST
05	SWORD OF THE LEGION
06	PRISONERS OF DARKNESS
07	TURNING POINT
08	MESSAGE FOR THE DEAD
09	RETRIBUTION

4TH ERA SUMMARY

As the Legion fights wars on several fronts, the Republic that dispatches them to the edge of the galaxy also actively seeks to undermine them as political ambitions prove more important than lives. Tired and jaded legionnaires suffer the consequences of government appointed officers and their ruinous leadership. The fighting is never enough and soon a rebellion breaks out among the Mid-Core planets, consuming more souls and treasure. A far greater threat to the Republic hegemony comes from the shadowy edges of the galaxy as a man determined to become an emperor emerges from a long and secretive absence. It will take the sacrifice of the Legion to maintain freedom in a galaxy gone mad.

HISTORY OF THE GALAXY

5TH ERA BOOKS

REBIRTH OF THE LEGION

01 TAKEOVER

02 COMING SOON

5TH ERA SUMMARY

An empire defeated and with it the rot of corruption scoured from the Republic. Fighting a revolution to restore the order promised at the founding of the Republic was the easy part. Now the newly rebuilt Legion must deal with factions no less treacherous than the House of Reason while preparing itself for war against a foe no one could have imagined.

HONOR ROLL

We would like to give our most sincere thanks and recognition to those who supported the creation of *Galaxy's Edge: Imperator* by supporting us at GalaxysEdge.us.

Janet Anderson
Robert Anspach
Sean Averill
Russell Barker
Steven Beaulieu
Steven Bergh
WJ Blood
Christopher Boore
Aaron Brooks
Marion Buehring
Alex Collins-Gauweiler
Robert Cosler
Andrew Craig
Peter Davies
Nathan Davis
Karol Doliński
Mark Franceschini
Kyle Gannon
Michael Gardner
John Giorgi
Gordon Green
Michael Greenhill
Joshua Hayes
Jason Henderson
Bernard Howell
Wendy Jacobson
James Jeffers
Kenny Johnson
Mathijs Kooij
Byl Kravetz
Clay Lambert
Grant Lambert
Preston Leigh
Richard Long
Kyle Macarthur
Richard Maier
Pawel Martin
Tao Mason
Simon Mayeski
Joshua McMaster

Jim Mern
Alex Morstadt
Daniel Mullen
Eric Pastorek
Jeremiah Popp
Chris Pourteau
Walt Robillard
Andrew Schmidt
Glenn Shotton
Daniel Smith
Joel Stacey
Maggie Stewart-Grant
Kevin G. Summers
Ernest Sumner
Beverly Tierney
Scott Tucker
Eric Turnbull
John Tuttle
Alex Umstead
Christopher Valin
Nathan Zoss

Made in the USA
Las Vegas, NV
29 November 2024